Twins

Shari Shattuck

This book is for everyone who cares—nurses, doctors, social workers, first-responders, foster parents, teachers, and caring individuals who help whenever they can without looking away. The world is brighter and more hopeful because of you.

Thank you.

There are so many people to thank with any book, but I cannot send this story out into the world without a short list. My husband, of course, who supports me in everything, thank you Joseph P. Stachura. My sweet cousin, Amanda Lize, I'm so grateful for your help with a cover concept in the midst of a tsunami of difficulties. Gary Sweeney for the actual cover design and his many pieces of advice about all things technical, you made it look easy. Susan Waterman for the endless hours of copy-editing, thanks for all the coffee! And a huge shout out to my favorite editor Nita Taulib for her invaluable notes and insights, you're the best.

Table of Contents

Prologue.

For the very first time, they could not hear each other's heartbeats. The boy slipped from his mother, arriving with thin but hearty fledgling wails that filled the delivery room. After a quick check by the waiting pediatrician, he was wrapped in a blanket and handed over to his father. As Andy took his son in his arms, everything he knew to be true changed. The boy objected loudly to the intrusive glare and the cold, unfamiliar space around him, and no amount of comforting or swaddling quieted him. In a few moments, the second baby, a girl, entered the world. This child, unlike her brother, was silent.

Her mouth drawn into a tight line, Dr. Ely, the pediatrician, took the baby from the obstetrician, quickly cleared the nose and mouth then checked the heart and lungs, finding them strong and steady. She moved to the baby's eyes, which were wide and staring up into the bright light of the examining table. That wasn't right. The doctor flashed her penlight into the iris. There was no response, no dilation of the wide pupil. She tried again.

Meanwhile the boy, now in his mother's arms, continued to cry.

The obstetrician checked the placentas as they were expelled while Dr. Ely finished her examination of the girl, handing her to the nurse to be swaddled. Then the pediatrician came to lean over the mother, who tore adoring eyes away from the boy in her arms.

"Dory?" the doctor spoke softly. "I don't believe the girl is in any danger, but I think we may have a problem. Her pupils aren't reacting to light."

"What?" Andy cut in. "What's wrong?" Standing over the examination table where the baby girl lay quietly, he placed one hand over his daughter's fragile, blanket-wrapped chest.

"I don't want to alarm either of you. But we need to do some tests…" The boy child's crying was increasing in volume as his lungs cleared and grew stronger, "…we need to find out what's going on. I want you to know that everything else seems fine. Strong heartbeat, clear lungs, everything looks good."

Tears of panic drenched Dory's eyes, and she pulled the infant on her chest closer, rocking him gently, but still he bawled. "Will she be all right?" Dory asked. Her husband crossed the delivery room in two strides and encircled her in protective arms.

Dr. Ely fought to keep her increasing urgency from her voice. "I think she'll be fine, but there may be some vision issues, and sometimes—but not necessarily—that can mean other complications as well. We won't know until we get a chance to examine her more fully. We'll take her for tests. She needs to be looked at by a pediatric optometrist." Even as she spoke, the nurse laid the baby girl in a rolling bassinette and started purposefully toward the door.

"No! Don't take her," Dory said firmly. She pleaded with her husband, "Andy, please. We need to hold her first."

"Dory, honey," he told her, "if Dr. Ely thinks it's best."

"Just for a moment, then I won't argue," Dory said. Her exhausted face, drained and sweaty, was set. Maternal instinct, fired by the hormones of birth, surged in her. The baby needed her family first, and Dory knew it in her bones. "Give her to me." Her husband squeezed her hand and nodded. "Please," he said to the doctor, "I think it's important that we hold her before you take her away, and when you do, I'll go with her."

With only a second's hesitation, the doctor nodded to the nurse, who picked up the pink bundle and brought her to Dory.

When Andy made a move to take the fussing boy, Dory tightened her grip on her firstborn and shook her head as she held out her other arm for her daughter. Dory took the baby gently, staring intently into the dark, almost pupil-less eyes, eyes that registered nothing. Instinctively, Dory pulled the child against the bare skin of her neck, where she could smell her mother, and the baby nestled there. The boy's reedy protests continued without pause. Shifting her two children carefully, Dory cradled the two swaddled babies head to toe on her chest, the girl just above the boy, one head nestled in the crook of each of her arms. "Andy," she said, "they need to touch. They've never been alone."

Andy reached down and gently released one of each of the babies' arms from their blankets on the sides that touched. The arms flailed, uncontrolled, and then found each other, and petite fingers gripped each other tightly.

The boy went quiet, his eyes opened.

Dory smiled at them both. "She'll be fine," she said with conviction. "See how she's calmed him down already? She has strength to spare."

Andy leaned over his new family and encircled them all in his arms. "She's got a hold of him and she's not letting go." His laugh ended in a hard swallow. "She's the brave one."

Through tears that twisted her voice, Dory said, "She *is* brave. Strong. I think we should call her Temerity." She looked up at her husband.

Andy cleared his throat, and then he whispered, "Temerity, yes, that's perfect. Welcome brave little one." He kissed the top of her pink cap, then brushed at his eyes with the palm of one hand, overwhelmed. Vertigo struck Andy as he watched his new family. As though he'd been hurled headlong from a precipice, he fell in wind-rushing, elated love with both his children. "And what about her brother?" he asked Dory, pushing a strand of hair from her face. "What shall we call him?"

Dory thought for a moment, gazing down into the tiny face as grayish blue eyes regarded her. "Justice," she said. "We'll call him Justice, because he's the perfect balance to her. Because they are equal, and he will know it and defend it." Without realizing she was doing it, Dory set her teeth with determination.

"Temerity and Justice," the father said each name, leaning down to kiss the soft crowns of their heads as he spoke their names together for the first time.

Urgency outweighed Dr. Ely's regret and she stepped in again. "I'm sorry, but I have to take the girl, it's important that we get her assessed as quickly as possible."

Both parents turned faces fractured by pain to the doctor. "I understand," Dory said, an uncontrolled sob racking her body with a violent spasm. "Okay." She trembled and pressed her lips to the baby girl's perfect head as she lifted it from her breast, which ached from the loss, and handed over the child. It felt as though a part of her own body were being ripped from her. The fingers of the infants were still clasped tightly and the nurse tried to separate them. The twins resisted until only two tiny forefingers were linked together and the nurse had to gently pry them apart. Dory clutched her boy to her, but the moment the physical connection between the babies was broken, he let out a wail, waving one tiny fist in the empty air. As his sister, his constant companion for nine months, was placed in the bassinette, he began to scream in earnest, hearty, wrenching cries.

"Shh-shh-shh," Dory shushed him, the sound shuddering as it caught in her throat. "Shhh, I know, it isn't fair. She'll be back, you have a lifetime together. Don't be afraid."

As the bassinette was rolled toward the door, the baby girl finally began to cry, matching her brother's tempo, pausing to draw breath just as he did. The twins' wails rose and fell, matching and keeping pace, a duet calling out for each other with one voice.

1

The big shaggy dog sniffed and whined at the door. Then, as the key jangled in the lock, he danced to one side and barked an unexpectedly high-pitched "woof," while his tail wagged so vigorously it generated a breeze that fluttered the rain slicker hanging from the coat hooks next to the door.

The huge metal fire door opened into the spacious loft and Temerity Bauer came in, folding her white, red-tipped cane as she entered. "Hush it, Runt," she said. Her straight black hair swung forward as she leaned down and found his moving head. She rubbed behind the ears vigorously, and the dog leaned into the rapture of it, almost knocking the slim twenty-nine-year-old off balance. "All right, that's enough. Justice?" she called out. "Justice? Are you home?" The blind woman straightened up, stepped around the dog, and started confidently toward the open kitchen area.

In three steps, her foot caught on something that shouldn't have been there and she flew forward, thrusting out her hands instinctively to catch herself. She hit the hardwood floor, breaking the fall with her palms, and rolled to one side, cursing, while Runt offered assistance by sticking his wet nose in her face and sniffing loudly. Flat on her back, she checked over her hands and fingers, rolling her wrists to feel for any injury. Other than her smarting palms, there seemed to be no damage. Her relief was brief, quickly replaced by a flood of anger. Sitting up, she felt for the offending object and found a small suitcase that had been left in the middle of the floor.

"Justice!" she shouted at the top of her lungs. She heard the door to the hallway open and then the sound of rapid footsteps, too light to be her twin's.

"Oh, hi, Amanda," Temerity greeted her brother's girlfriend. "Just a shot in the dark, but...I'm guessing you guys are going away for the weekend," Temerity said dryly.

The steps faltered. "Temerity, what are you doing on the...oh my God! I'm so sorry! What an idiot I am, I thought we were going right back out again." Amanda was kneeling at Temerity's side by the time she had finished exclaiming. "Are you all right?"

"Fine," Temerity waved her aside. "No permanent damage done. But my half-wit brother should have told you."

"He has told me, a hundred times. It's completely my fault," Amanda insisted, hooking one arm under Temerity's and helping her up.

"Somehow I doubt that. Where is he?"

"In the shower," Amanda told her. "He wanted to clean up before we left. "Wait a minute, let me see your hands."

Temerity held out her hands to the young doctor, who took them in her own and turned them over. The tickle of long, curly hair brushing her forearms made Temerity want to giggle as Amanda leaned close to examine her fingers, and the vague, antiseptic hospital smell mixed with lilac perfume, unique to her twin's girlfriend, teased at her nostrils. Amanda said, "You've got a small abrasion here," she ran a soft finger pad along the outside of Temerity's right pinkie. "Let's get that cleaned up and I'll put a bandage on it."

Temerity, a violinist with the city's small orchestra, did not object to the ministrations. Even a minor scratch could interfere with her playing, and an infection could keep her from playing at all. The two women made their way to the kitchen where Amanda held the finger under warm running water, cleaning it with gauze and antibacterial ointment from the kit under the sink and applying a small band aid.

Footsteps in the hallway across the big room made Temerity turn her head toward her brother.

"You shrieked for me?" he called out, and as his steady strides came closer, Temerity picked up the fresh creaminess of coconut-scented shampoo.

"Yes. I was just curious."

"About?"

"Well, I thought obstacle course day was Tuesday, and today is Friday. No doubt the element of surprise was all part of the tactical exercise. Didn't you want to put some low-hanging barbed wire around so I could practice belly crawling, and maybe a pit with pointed sticks in it?"

"My fault!" Amanda called out to him. "I left my suitcase in the entrance, I thought we were going right back out, and you told me Tem wasn't here when I came in."

Temerity smiled at the use of her abbreviated name. Justice had been the only one who ever called her that, but since his girlfriend had adopted the moniker from Justice, she had accepted it without complaint. It didn't hurt that Temerity had liked Amanda ever since she'd been in pre-med with Justice. Though Justice had ultimately shifted out of medicine to finish with a Ph. D. in anthropology and could neither set a bone nor diagnose a virus, he *was* still a doctor, as he liked to remind his sister every chance he got.

A tortured sigh came from him now. "Tem, I'm sorry, but you've tripped over Runt and Mouse enough times to know that you still have to be careful."

"I do? Wow, I guess it true what they say, you learn something new everyday. You know what else I learned?"

"What?" he asked, like he didn't really want to know.

"I do not *bounce*."

Justice glanced at Amanda and Temerity could hear the smile in his voice when he responded. "True. Well, except that one time when they delivered the new sofa."

"Will you never let that go?" Temerity crossed her arms and glared sourly in his direction.

"What happened with the sofa?" Amanda asked.

Temerity opened her mouth to shut it down, but Justice was already off and running. If she could have seen his gray eyes, she would have been annoyed to find them dancing with amusement. "So, we had this new sofa delivered, and the delivery guys set it down so that it was blocking the hallway while we rearranged the big rug. Temerity comes running down the hallway like an Olympic gymnast headed for the vault, hits the back of that sofa, flips all the way over, I'm talking three-sixty, sticks the landing with her butt on the sofa springs, and gets launched back into the air onto the rug, which was thankfully still rolled up." His face was screwed up with the effort of not laughing, but he lost the battle as the mental instant-replay sent him into fits of laughter. "You…were… butt bounced!" he wheezed.

Amanda said, "Justice, that's not funny!"

"It was *hysterical*!" Justice insisted. "Funniest thing I've ever seen, except of course, for some of my sister's outfits."

Temerity stood with her hands on her hips and cocked her head to one side, tilting her face up slightly to point it directly at her three-inches-taller brother. "Please say you're leaving soon."

"Yes, yes. We'll be out in a few minutes. Patience is its own reward," Justice teased his sister. "I think that's from the Bible."

Temerity smiled sweetly. "So is fratricide," she said.

"What are you doing this weekend?" her brother asked.

"Working. I have to learn a new piece before rehearsal Sunday. Have you seen Ellen?"

"Barely, she got home from work, slept a few hours and then ran out before noon. Said she was going somewhere with Rupert and wouldn't be back until late."

Temerity's reaction was bittersweet. "Oh right, the revival film festival is this week." It pleased her that their roommate Ellen, an extreme introvert, had discovered an activity she could enjoy, though it was one that excluded Temerity for the most part. Sitting quietly in the dark and watching classic movies was the one social outing Ellen had learned to brave and even enjoy. It was a huge step for the reclusive young woman, whose early life had damaged her to the point that before she'd met the twins, she'd lived an invisible life.

And who could blame her? Ellen, an almost three-hundred-pound, five-foot-four loner, had barely survived a horrific childhood. When she was five years old, Ellen's mother had maliciously burned her face on an electric cook top unit and left the wound to fester untreated. When the painful, infected wound had finally sealed itself, the scar tissue had twisted half her face cruelly, dragging down one eyebrow and warping her mouth and cheek. Not long after that, Ellen's mother ran away, taking only her crack pipe and a half-empty vodka bottle, leaving her small daughter to starve in a halfway house. A series of foster and group homes followed, where Ellen became adept at hiding herself from abuse and ridicule. Because no one wanted to look at her, it was easier than she had thought it would be. She got so good at avoiding notice that she could go for days unseen and forgotten in a closet or a crawl space; her only comforts were stolen books and an excess of snack foods. Finally released by the state at seventeen, she had set out to find a job that demanded no human interaction and landed on the nighttime cleaning crew of a local Costco, where she snuck in and out to avoid human interaction, content to be ignored and anonymous to the other employees and the rest of the world.

The two had first met when Temerity had literally fallen into Ellen's lap on a bus. Ellen had been so surprised to be "seen" and so intrigued by the blind woman's obvious courage that she had followed Temerity when she got off at her stop, only to rescue her from would-be muggers. Over the next few months, Temerity, to whom the concept of judging someone for their looks was as absurd as it was impossible, had discovered how Ellen helped people who never even knew or cared that she existed, and the two had become best friends and partners in the crime of interfering in lives that needed help. After all, Temerity had said, who would suspect the two of them of meddling? One of them was blind and the other invisible.

Temerity smiled at the memory of their early adventures and felt pride in how far Ellen had come, though the memory of almost losing Ellen was a distinct fissure in those happy peaks. In a grand effort to protect a co-worker from assault, Ellen had taken a bullet in the arm and torn open the scarred part of her face as she fell. The surgeons, friends of Amanda touched by Ellen's act of sacrifice, had worked hard to reconstruct Ellen's face, and the result was a distinct improvement from the twisted scarring she had lived with all her life. But even with the lessening of her frightening appearance, the small act of attending a movie in public was a huge landmark for the woman who had lived her whole life in physical and emotional isolation. Much to Temerity's dismay, a little bubble of resentment rose in her chest at the thought of being excluded from Ellen's newfound interest and relationship with Rupert, one of Temerity's fellow orchestra members. She reminded herself that, after all, she had introduced them and hoped for this very outcome. She tsk-tsked herself for being so petty when Ellen had tried to include her.

"I could tell you what's happening, like we do at home," Ellen had insisted.

"No," Temerity had told her, "I don't think that would be fair to everyone else. Film buffs are *serious* about quiet in the theatre." Then she had shrugged. "Don't blame them." So Ellen and Rupert had gone together, sneaking in after everyone else was seated and leaving before the lights turned back on, and Temerity stayed home and felt left out.

Temerity sighed and told her brother, "It's probably best. I've got to have my part down cold before the group rehearsals start. Not being able to read the music and play simultaneously, I've got some extra homework."

Justice made a sympathetic noise. Then trying to keep it casual, he asked, "Are you seeing Hugo?" but his sister read the subterfuge in his voice.

"Don't know, don't really care," she said.

"Yeah, right." Justice reached out and punched Temerity's arm lightly. She slapped his hand with well-timed accuracy. "Ouch!" he said. "Well, will you at least ask him to help with walking Runt when Seth doesn't come, even if you're *not* interested in him?" He made a face at Amanda.

"Don't think I didn't see that!" Temerity wagged a finger with disconcerting accuracy in his face.

"What?" Justice asked with profoundly fake innocence.

"Sorry, buddy," Amanda laughed to Justice, "she knows you too well."

Temerity sat down in front of her computer and selected news items for it to read her as she waited for the couple to gather all their things and say their goodbyes.

"Go on!" she insisted as they both asked her for the third time if she needed anything. "Go have sex, drink wine, wear lacy underwear, and say silly gooey things to each other."

"Boxers don't come in lace," Justice fired back. "Though I do have a lovely mesh jock—"

"Stop!" Temerity commanded. "Don't want to know."

"Are you sure...?" Amanda began.

"That my brother owns a mesh thong?" Temerity cut her off. "Sadly, yes. Some horrors cannot be hidden on laundry day." Amanda laughed, and Temerity ordered, "Get out!" while pointing imperiously toward the door. Her brother caught her hand and squeezed it in his. They interlaced their forefingers, the way they always had, then he kissed her hair and let go.

"Bye, don't do anything I wouldn't do," he chided.

"Like that narrows it down." Temerity shook her head. "Now beat it!"

When the door closed behind them, Temerity stood where she was, feeling the ripples of stillness expand away from her and then settle into a broad, flat emptiness. She could sense the feeble March sun through the huge warehouse windows that lined the entire back wall of the once-industrial loft. She turned her face up to the bashful warmth and felt the emptiness press down around her. With a sigh, she slipped into a lower place, weighed down by leaden sinkers hooked in her chest. She lowered herself to the floor and then slumped onto her back and lay spread-eagle with her arms out beside her. She felt so depleted that she imagined just seeping into the wood grain like a stain. As often as she'd reminded herself that Justice must leave, reminded herself that he must move on, that the healthiest thing for them both would be independent lives, the conscious mental efforts to acclimate herself to the impending event had done little to mollify her sense of impending doom. Her fear of that inevitable separation remained as unyielding as the oak planks digging painfully into her shoulder blades, no matter how hard she tried. And she *had* tried—encouraged him, urged him, chided him—to do exactly that, but now, this weekend, she sensed, would be the snapping point of the cord that bound them.

And it scared her to death.

For a long while she thought of nothing, sunk into the grayness of forced solitude without stimulus. After a while, she felt something compressing the soft tissue of her stomach, something heavy, but soft and padding in a steady rhythm. At the same time, a rumbling sound infused her chest with the reassurance of company. She was not alone.

Raising one hand, she stroked the gnarly-eared head of Ellen's cat, Mouse. "Hey buddy," she whispered, and got an answer. "Rrraww," he said, and then bit her hand.

"I'm going to interpret that as... 'get off your ass and feed me,'" Temerity said, lurching upright with an effort. "And don't worry," she added to the substantial feline, "I get the message. That's enough of that self-pity crap. Things change, get over it." She went into the kitchen, used one hand to trail along the edge of the counter until she came to the corner, then leaned down to open the cabinet where the cat food was kept and took out a scoop. She explored with one foot until she heard the plastic bowl scoot across the tiles. As she leaned down to spill the food into the bowl, she scratched Mouse's scruffy head once more and said, "If you catch me being pathetic, bite me again."

The only reply was the satisfied crunching of tasty, bacon-flavored bits.

2

Justice pulled the suitcases out of the trunk of the BMW and checked the zippered pocket for the umpteenth time. He carried the bags into the little cabin, breathing in the pine-scented air and letting it cleanse the city smut from him. He paused to kiss Amanda who was in the tiny kitchen putting away the groceries they'd brought. She shivered.

"I know. It's cold in here. Do you want me to go ahead and start a fire or would you rather walk down to the lake first?"

"Lake please," Amanda said, turning to look out at it through the small window over the sink. "The sun is almost down."

She turned back to her task and Justice allowed himself a moment to admire her physically.

She was tall and slim, her body was athletic more than curvy. She had full, wavy hair that seemed intent on escaping any type of restraint she imposed on it. Now it was up in a thick ponytail, but a few renegade tresses fell against her slender neck, an imperfection that Justice found irresistible. He carried the suitcases through to the bedroom, which was freezing, and put them on the bed. After checking to make sure that

Amanda was still in the kitchen, he pulled a small, black velvet box from a side-zippered pocket and slipped it into his pocket. He liberated a bottle of champagne from between his rolled-up T-shirts and, holding it down by his side, took it into the kitchen and snuck it into the fridge.

"What's that?" Amanda asked, and he turned to face her with a guilty grin.

"Oh, just a little something for later, if we warm up enough to drink something chilled," Justice joked.

"It might chill faster if you leave it out." Amanda smiled at him and Justice felt his heart thrum.

"You ready?" he asked.

She closed the cabinet door where she'd deposited the cereal and coffee and glanced at the single bag left on the floor. "Let me just get this cleared away… "

Justice laughed. "We'll get it later. Temerity isn't here, and we can actually walk *around* things." Even as he said it, he felt a little pang as a memory rushed back at him.

When he and Temerity were seven, they had gone to their neighbor Ray's house to play. The boy had built an elaborate racetrack for matchbook cars, a sprawling course that covered half of the rec room, and Justice, who always had to be careful about leaving anything on the floor because of his sister, was entranced. In two minutes, Justice had dropped to his stomach and had the controls for one of the cars in his hand. He and Ray began racing the cars through loops and around curves, pushing them so fast that they sometimes flew off the track and had to be retrieved from across the room.

Temerity sat near her brother patiently, her head tilted slightly as she listened to their game, though Justice had all but forgotten her until she tapped his back. She leaned down and whispered, "I have to go to the bathroom."

Justice looked up at Ray, "Where's the bathroom?"

"Down the hall, first door on the right," Ray answered, never taking his eyes off his car as he maneuvered it through an s-turn.

Glancing over his shoulder to get the layout of the finished basement, Justice told his sister, "The hallway door is right behind you, turn right, first door on your right." He knew that he should help her in an unknown space, but he was caught up in the speed and the game. "You can do it," he told her when she hesitated. "There's nothing on the floor." He felt her stand, but the carpet muffled her tentative steps as she moved toward the back wall, her cane tapping experimentally in front of her, snagging repeatedly on the shag carpet.

"Last lap!" shouted Ray, and with whoops of challenge both boys redoubled their efforts, watching the tiny cars streak along the track.

From behind him, Justice heard a bump and then a muffled cry. He sat up and, still holding the control, spun on his butt to see what had happened.

His sister stood there, one hand pressed to her temple as blood dripped from between her fingers. To the right of the doorway, which Temerity had found with the stick extended low in front of her, was a glass shelf that ended flush with the doorjamb. Unaware of the protruding obstacle at eye level, she had walked right into it.

"Tem!" Justice cried out, throwing the toy control aside and rushing to her. "What did you do?" He pulled her hand away and saw a neat slice, less than an inch from her right eye. "Now we have to go home!"

In the cabin, Justice winced as the guilt inserted a cold wire into his gut and twisted. He could not remember that day without a jab of shame that he had blamed her for walking into a shelf she could neither see nor feel with her stick. It had been his fault, his responsibility, and he had let her down.

But he couldn't always do everything. His parents had reminded him of that all his life. Yes, she needed extra attention, but she had to learn to do things for herself. It was hard to watch the mistakes, the accidents, the people who gawked at his beautiful sister with unfounded pity. In the cabin, Justice shivered.

"You okay?" Amanda asked, moving in to put her arms around his waist under his jacket, resting her head against the strength of his chest.

"Yeah, I'm fine. I'm better than okay. I just, you know, still feel badly leaving Mole home alone. Habit."

Amanda grimaced. "I know, but she spends lots of time on her own, and Ellen is there," she said, but Justice knew that Amanda too felt a sense of responsibility to his sister, and guilt for drawing him away from her. "And she gets to work and walks around everywhere." She shook her head, "I really don't know how she does it. She's amazing."

"So are you," Justice said tenderly, and leaned down to kiss her. "Come on, let's go down and watch the sunset." As they turned toward the door, he felt the box in his pocket and thought, *Maybe it's too soon.*

They went carefully down the steep hill path and out onto the dock. The water was high this time of year and it lapped at the few boats tied up to the floating dock. They sat down with their backs against a metal bench locker, which stored oars and lifejackets, and nestled together.

"Finally," Justice said into the top of Amanda's head. "I get you all to myself. No on-call at the hospital. No pesky sister."

"Speaking of your sister," Amanda said, and sat forward a bit. Their intimate moment was being ceded to what Justice assumed would be a serious discussion and he resented it. "We need talk about how our relationship will affect her."

"I know," Justice said with a sigh. "Listen, Tem and I have both always known that we wouldn't live together all our lives. She's one of the most independent people I know. I think I have more of an issue with her being on her own than she does. She's fine with it!"

Amanda turned, and the warm glow of the sunset hit the side of her face and haloed her hair, turning the medium blonde to gold.

The combination of gilded light and Amanda's spirited compassion was stunning, and Justice knew that he would never forget that image of beloved beauty. "Justice, this is an unusual situation, and we can't ignore it. I want to be with you, and no matter what, Temerity is going to be a part of our equation."

Justice let his eyes drift across the sunlit water near the dock and fall into the deeper blue reflection of the mountains on the far side. "I can't be there for her all the time," he whispered, "I can't take care of her, I need us to have our own life."

Amanda threw her head back and laughed. "Temerity would kick your ass if she heard you say that. I do not, for one second, believe that she wants you to 'take care of her.' But family is part of the package in any relationship, especially since you've asked me to move in with you, but I'm not sure that me moving into the loft is such a great idea. Look what happened today!" Amanda shook her head and made a face. "God, I could have really hurt her! And what if she'd broken a hand or finger." She dropped her face in her own graceful fingers and moaned.

"I'm sure Temerity wouldn't mind you living with us, you're there most of the time anyway. I just don't think it's fair to you." Justice said, "Look, I'm used to it. There's never been a moment in my life when I didn't consider Temerity and her blindness in every decision, it's just a part of life for me. But for you it's different, you don't have to take on this responsibility." His voice trailed off, and he watched her uncertainly.

Amanda lifted her face until he had the sense that she was peering over a fence and directly into his deep gray eyes. "Your sister," she said very clearly, "is a part of you, and I love you. Hell, truth be told, I'm pretty damn impressed by her. It feels weird to be talking about her as though she's disabled. She's more capable and braver than just about anyone else I know. Your relationship is a huge part of you both, you think I don't know that? That's one of things that makes me love you more, in fact." She positively glowed at him and his heart almost lifted up out of his chest. "So, I don't want to waste a second moaning that anything is not fair. It's what it is, and Temerity will be in our lives, and partly our 'responsibility' if you want to put it that way, just like she'll always worry about and take care of you." She reached out and laid one chilly hand on the side of his face, leaning in toward him. "Could be a lot worse. She could be a crack addict, or…"

"Don't say it!" Justice begged, pretending to block his ears.

"…a *politician*."

"Noooo!" Justice wailed, the sound echoing over the lake. He raised his hands to the sky and cried, "Take me instead!" Then he joined in her laughter and accepted her mouth on his. It was warm, and their lips lingered for the pressure, for the softness, for the connection. When they pulled away, he stood up and took her hand. "Come here," he said.

He pulled her up and they moved to the edge of the dock with the great, indigo-blue lake stretched beyond and below them, while on the far shore fir trees sloped up the hillsides in textured greens and hinted shadows that deepened even as they watched. Justice turned to face Amanda and felt absolute confidence in this moment, in her face, in their future. He went down on one knee and pulled the small box from his jacket pocket.

Amanda gasped as he snapped it open and looked up at her. "Amanda Bendon, will you marry me, and put up with me and my crazy family?"

Slowly, Amanda came down on her knees and faced him, putting her hands around his so that the box nestled in two pairs of hands like a shining promise in a protected nest. The wind from the lake blew tendrils of renegade curls across her face like a veil, but her eyes shone through in the last of the warm, magic light. "Justice Bauer, I love you, *and* I love your crazy family. Yes. I will marry you." She burst into tears, he slipped the ring onto her finger, and they kissed until the cold and the coming darkness drove them back to the cabin and the crackling comfort of a wood fire.

3

Nightfall meant nothing to Temerity, but she could feel the moist, chilly air that twilight sent wafting into the loft. Just as she was closing the windows the door buzzer sounded and she answered it with, "Hi, Seth!"

"Hi, Temerity. Runt ready for his walk?" he asked, the hairline fractures in his voice betraying the impending shift from boy to young man.

"I'll meet you on the stairs." Temerity called for the dog, which was already galloping out from the hallway at the sound of the door buzzer, and retrieved his leash from the hooks by the door. Panting in delighted anticipation, Runt danced and shook himself as Temerity fought to find the loop on the collar of the moving target. The leash finally secured, she opened the door, leaving it ajar behind her and went down two flights to meet Seth halfway.

"Hi, buddy!" The boy greeted the dog, which went into ecstasies verging on convulsion at the sight and smell of the young man who came to walk him three times a week.

Temerity felt a bittersweet pang at the sound of the thirteen-year-old's deepening voice, with the occasional squeak, but of course she said nothing about how she would miss the child he had been or her pride in the man he would become. "How you doing, Seth?"

"Great!" he replied, and she could hear that his words were slightly muted by the sound of sloppy dog kisses. "A little damp now. Ew, Runt, stop it."

Laughing, Temerity handed over the leash and asked, "Do you want to stay for dinner?"

"Can't. Homework, and Thelma says I have to be home for dinner, otherwise she doesn't get to see me before she goes to work."

"And she's right. How're the moms?" Seth had been adopted a few months before by a childless couple after being rescued by Temerity and her friend Ellen from an abusive uncle and life on the street. Since then life had not just improved for the intelligent young man, it had begun in earnest, and he was thriving.

"They're good. Beth is letting me help out at the clinic. Runt, stop pulling!"

Runt was whimpering with excitement. "You'd better get going," Temerity told him. "You going to the dog run?"

"Yeah, he likes it. I brought a ball."

"Does he chase it?" Temerity asked, surprised.

"Sure, then he barks at it. He just doesn't bring it back. Maybe he's just a slow learner," Seth said dryly.

"Good luck with *that*," Temerity told him. "He's not the brightest mammal."

"He's a good boy though, aren't you, buddy?" Seth said, and Temerity smiled at the sound of vigorous scratching, accompanied by the thump, thump of the large shaggy tail.

"Okay, see you in about thirty minutes?" Temerity asked.

"Yep!" The pair tromped down the last two flights of stairs, having a dog-to-boy conversation as they went, and Temerity went back up. When she reached the fourth-floor landing, she paused to listen, but all was still and silent in the stairwell. Telling herself that it didn't matter and she wasn't disappointed, she went through the big door, closing it behind her.

She brought out her violin and some large sheets of braille music, which she set up on a music stand. For the next twenty minutes, she ran her fingers over the musical score and then practiced it repeatedly until the first movement of the symphony was roughly familiar, though it would take several more sessions to commit the nuances fully to memory.

Because she couldn't watch the conductor, Temerity had a seeing helper for dress rehearsals and concerts. The young man or woman, usually a student from the music academy, would sit right next to her and cue her with pressure on her thigh to indicate direction from the conductor. Small squeezes gave her the countdown to "begin." A quick tapping meant "increase the pace," solid pressure meant "softly," and so on. At regular rehearsals the conductor gave verbal cues, making it much easier.

She was just putting the instrument away after wiping it down when she heard a thump on her door. "Coming!" she called out.

Wondering how Seth had gotten in without her buzzing the street door for him, Temerity swung the heavy metal fire door wide and instantly knew it wasn't Seth. The smell was wrong, and there was no odor or panting of a mutt-but-mostly-giant-Schnauzer dog.

But the smell that filled her nostrils was not completely unfamiliar, or unwelcome. It was a combination of soap and pepper, clean and masculine. Temerity felt her pulse quicken.

"Are you missing someone?" asked her downstairs neighbor, Hugo. His question was followed by an annoyed "meow" from mid-air, or more accurately, she guessed, from the six-foot-four man's arms.

"Mouse!" Temerity reprimanded. "You little boogerhead. Did you sneak out?"

"And into my loft and flopped himself down on the sofa as though he owned it."

"Yeah, that's how he adopted Ellen, too. Hi, Hugo," Temerity said, "Come on in." She turned away as she felt the flush of blood on her cheeks. She remembered being told that there were two emotional reactions Caucasian humans couldn't hide, a blanche and a blush. From the hot sensation in her cheeks, she could well believe it. It amused Temerity to think that people came in different colors, which she thought of as temperatures. She wondered at the insanity of judging people by their pigment, when their words and behavior said infinitely more about them.

She heard a thump as the pudgy cat jumped the last couple of feet to the floor, and a simulated groan from Hugo as he straightened up. "Uh," he complained, "my back. That cat must weigh twenty pounds."

"I think it was sixteen at last check up," Temerity said. "Which neither he nor the vet enjoyed very much. You want some tea, or…a glass of wine?"

"Anything with stimulants, I'm working tonight," he told her, with a yawn rounding the words.

Temerity said, "I'll throw some amphetamines in a mug, I think I have some packets left from Tami's."

A rolling chuckle filled the immediate space, vibrating the still air and lifting the mood. "So, Justice said that Ellen is working at Tami's now," Hugo said, then he added quietly, "Good for her."

"Right?" Temerity agreed with enthusiasm. "She found out she loves baking, and she actually went and *asked* if she could apprentice. I'm so proud. It's perfect for her. She still works nights, only has to talk to a couple of people—which is two more than usual for her, as you know—and, most importantly, she brings me home lots of free pastries and bread."

"Good to know you have your priorities in order," Hugo nodded, with his usual droll amusement.

His footsteps trailed Temerity to the kitchen area, where she filled the electric kettle and turned it on, found two mugs, then began to search through the teas by reading the braille tape stuck to the side of each package. There were at least fifteen flavors.

"Do you need help?" Hugo asked.

"No, I got it," she bristled at the phrasing of the question. Temerity had been so militantly independent for so long, so worried that offers of help equaled pity, that she automatically, and routinely, refused offers of assistance. Less routine was being flustered by the presence of this man who sounded and smelled so good, so much so that she pulled out a box without checking to see what was on top of it, and was rewarded with an avalanche of boxed teas and tins, which she fumbled to catch by feel even as she ducked.

"You know," Hugo said with measured calm, "I read somewhere that teamwork can expedite a task." He hadn't moved from the stool on the other side of the counter.

"No, no, I'm fine, no problem." Temerity was awkwardly balancing the few packages she'd snatched on their way down in a jumbled pile in her arms. Before she could shift them onto the counter, one of the flimsy paper boxes collapsed from the pressure and a hundred individually-wrapped tea bags spilled onto and around her feet. Hugo said nothing.

"Okay, fine." Temerity said in a small voice. "Help."

Hugo came around the counter and took the boxes from her hands and then stooped to pick up the ones on the floor, lining them up on the counter so that Temerity could replace them on the shelves. "Ooh, Darjeeling. Can I have this one?" His voice was coming from near her knees where he was gathering the packets into a pile.

"Dealer's choice," Temerity said. As she moved her hands through the air in between them as though sweeping leaves from the surface of a pool to locate the proffered box, her fingers brushed the top of his head and she felt the waves of his hair sweep back with the touch. She tightened her lips to hide her pleasure at the sensuous rush—and found the box.

"It's awfully quiet in here. Oh yeah, where's Runt?" Hugo asked, rising and stuffing the errant tea packets back into the appropriate box.

"On a walk with Seth." She frowned and felt her watch. "He should have been back ten minutes ago.

"I wouldn't worry too much," Hugo told her. "Dog walking seems pretty innocuous for a kid who survived hell on his own."

Temerity experienced a curious combination of pride and sorrow, a mixture she often experienced when thinking about her young friend. "True that," she agreed.

Roughly six months earlier, right about the same time Hugo moved into the building, Ellen had discovered that the sickly 12-year-old Seth was living in the unheated basement of their building, and she recruited Justice and Temerity to rectify his situation. The pianist was loft-sitting for his cousins who were out of the country for a year and now that year was half gone. Temerity wondered where he would go when that year was up, and for some reason the idea of Hugo leaving made her short of breath. Over the last months, Hugo had become a friend, coming up and working on new pieces of music with Temerity, usually pieces he had written. Temerity thought his compositions were very good. As a musician, she respected him; as a woman, well, she wasn't sure. Though he made it clear from the beginning that he would like to know her better, he hadn't pressed. The result was a pleasant, but uncertain, stall.

The phone rang five minutes later and Temerity buzzed Seth in, then opened the door for boy and dog.

They stomped noisily onto the landing and into the apartment. Runt barked loudly at Hugo, causing Seth to stop in the doorway.

"It's okay, it's just Hugo," Temerity told the boy, who had good reason from his past to fear strangers, especially male ones. Even after all these months of being loved and protected by his two moms, he kept his distance from men in general. "Seth, you remember our neighbor, Hugo," she told the boy to settle him. "He's a musician like me."

"Oh, that's cool," Seth mumbled and came warily into the room, keeping space between him and the relative stranger. "I gotta' get going. I'm late."

"Okay, tell the ladies I said 'hi' and be careful walking home," Temerity warned, though she felt the irony of telling a kid who had *lived* on the street to be careful walking on it.

"Nice to see you again, Seth," said Hugo in his smooth, easy way.

Seth made some garbled reply and shut the door behind him as he went out. Runt ran to the door and scratched at it, whining until his almost-favorite human's footsteps faded away before trotting dejectedly to the rug and collapsing on it with a life-is-barely-worth-living-without-your-boy sigh.

Alone with Hugo. Temerity felt the blush rise again, and tried a distraction. "Where are you playing tonight?"

"The Piano Bar, mostly jazz. You know, you could come sit in sometimes. We could play one of the new pieces or just jam."

"I don't jam," Temerity objected.

"Why not?"

"I'm a structured classical musician. I don't think Mozart would approve."

"Well I'm not going to tell him," Temerity could almost hear the shrug. She laughed and sipped her own tea, cooled now.

"I don't buy that anyway," Hugo said. "When we play together, you always add in touches that I didn't write, you just do it. What do you think jazz is?"

"Random notes. Music on drugs."

Hugo snorted a laugh. "Then why don't you just come and enjoy a contact high? You can be my guest."

"Mmmm, clubbing," Temerity pretended to consider. "Tell you what, when Justice gets back in town, I'll make him bring me one night."

"Do you need a chaperone?" Hugo said. And though he'd said it lightly, Temerity could sense the suggestion in it.

"It's a good idea for me to take someone with eyes the first time I go anywhere completely new, in lieu of a guide dog," she said, pretending to have missed the innuendo, an avoidance tactic she'd employed since Hugo had first asked her out and she'd pretended it was nothing more than a friendly invitation.

"Well, if you're accepting applications for a seeing-eye guide, I have my own service vest and come with an excellent pedigree. Thanks for the caffeine," he said, and she heard him set his empty cup down on the counter. "I'd better get going, the dog and pony show can't start without me."

"Who's the pony?"

"My sound guy Steve," Hugo said, without missing a beat. He stood. "Okay, I'll see you around."

"Hard to miss me."

He went out. In the rippling solitude that remained in his wake, Temerity was suddenly overwhelmed by the sensation that her childhood friend Aaron was standing near her. With a sharp intake of breath, she reached out to touch empty air and then smiled sadly at the hopeless gesture. Aaron's absence was a constant underlying stream of grief that flowed from her past and occasionally bubbled up and soaked her in melancholy. Yet, in spite of the familiar, steady sadness, it confused her to sense his presence so lucidly that it caused her a sharp stab of sorrow after all these years. A dull ache, an empty feeling, the loss of a friend—these things were old companions, so why now?

And then it came to her. She was feeling lonely and deserted. Left behind. Left out, again. Depression was not a luxury she tolerated in herself. She had always fought it off diligently, but she was conscious now of the rumblings of battle in her distant self. She leaned over the counter until her cheek was against the cool granite. "What is wrong with me?" she asked herself.

But as her open eyes stared unseeing into permanent shadows, she had to work hard at pretending that she didn't already have a pretty good idea.

Justice awoke and felt the warmth of Amanda's body against his. Without opening his eyes he sensed the world around him. Birdsong filtered into the room with the early light, a constant conversation of warnings and appeal. *Not so different from us humans,* Justice thought. His face was nestled into the back of Amanda's neck, and he realized that he had put it there to keep warm in the unheated cabin. He pulled her closer against him and stroked the almost frictionless skin of her inner arm under the thick comforters.

"Mmmm. Morning," Amanda purred in her deeper, not fully awake voice.

Justice lifted his head and opened his eyes to look out the window just past her. It was sunny outside, and he knew from experience that the only way to warm up would be to brew something hot and stand in that sunshine until they'd absorbed enough of both. "I'll make coffee," he said, kissing the back of her neck and squeezing her once.

She made a noise of objection as he slid from the covers, allowing the frigid air to intrude into the toasty cocoon of the bed. Justice put on his sheepskin slippers and his down coat, and went to the bathroom, where he brushed his teeth with water so cold it hurt, but it was warm enough to splash on his face by the time he was done rinsing. Then he shuffled into the kitchen and plugged in the electric coffee pot.

It was an old one, the kind that percolates. It could have been replaced with a newer drip version, but this coffee maker had been here as long as Justice could remember, and somehow the coffee just tasted so much better after waiting through the reassuring, constant gurgles. The fresh, filtered spring water helped, of course.

When it was ready, he heated dollops of milk in ceramic mugs, filled them with the scorching coffee, and carried them through to Amanda, holding one out close under her nose. She sniffed the curling white steam rising from it and sat up. "Ah," she said, "The elixir of life."

Justice took a sip of his own scalding brew and studied her. She was even more beautiful with her hair mussed all around her and the imprint of the pillowcase on her high cheek. "You look different," he said, cocking his head to regard her.

Amanda immediately reached up to try to calm her wild hair. "I do?" she asked self-consciously.

Nodding, Justice sipped his coffee, slurping deliberately. "Yeah. Last night you looked like my girlfriend."

"Whom do I look like now?" Her eyes had caught his mischievous intent, and they glinted it back at him.

"Like my fiancé," he said, and leaned down to kiss her. She kissed him back and then raised her left hand into a ray of sunlight from the window, letting the light glint off the faceted blue sapphire set in gold.

Her face filled with wonder. "I can't believe your mother parted with this. It's so beautiful, and it belonged to her mom?"

"My dad's mom actually, who gave it to him for my mom, and then on their tenth anniversary, he replaced it with a yellow sapphire they bought on a trip to India."

"I don't blame her, that's a gorgeous piece," she said, and then added with a faux sniff, "though no where near as good as this one!" She admired it for a moment, glowing, and then shifted her high beams to him. "So, your parents knew about this?"

"Well, I could have kept it secret, but then I would have had to steal the ring, and I didn't think that would be a very nice 'welcome to the family.'"

"But Temerity doesn't know?"

"No. I wanted to surprise her," he said, but that wasn't quite true. To change the subject, Justice jumped up. "All right, get up, time for a morning dip in the lake. Get your suit on."

"Are you *insane?*" Amanda looked terrified.

"But not committed," Justice told her, hovering one finger in front of his face. "This time of year the lake is basically barely melted ice water, and *I'm* sure not getting in it!"

She threw a pillow at him.

They sat on the porch in the warming sun, the same porch that Justice had played on as a child, making piles of found treasure with Temerity, pine cones and smooth stones and oddly shaped sticks, and later leading her through the woods nearby as she experienced the wilderness differently, but just as fully, as he. There was nowhere that Justice could turn without seeing some joy or challenge he had shared with his sister. He had thought then, or no, that wasn't right, he hadn't thought, he had just *assumed*, that since they had always been together, that they always would be.

"What are you thinking about?" Amanda asked, as a blue jay landed on the railing and chittered loudly at them, demanding food.

He sighed. "The mole."

"You really are worried about telling her, aren't you?" she asked gently.

"I know, I know, I shouldn't be. But, except for college, while she was still at home with mom and dad, we've never lived apart."

Amanda lifted her face to meet a chilly breeze rolling up the hill from the lake. "You know what I think?" she asked.

"Not really."

"I think that you're the one I should be worried about."

"I'm much more fragile than Tem, it's true," Justice said, nodding sagely, and then he became serious. "But there's a side of Tem that most people never see, she's more vulnerable than she pretends."

"Aren't we all?" Amanda sighed. She waited for a moment, and when he didn't follow that up, she said, "Tell me something."

"What?"

"A story about you and Temerity from when you were kids together."

Justice knew that the invitation was a sincere offer of intimacy. "Okay, uh…" He thought about it. "She had a friend when she was little. A boy named Aaron, they went to school together, he was blind too, and he had…other problems."

"Mental, emotional or physical?" Amanda asked in her doctor voice.

"Oh, physical, definitely physical, he was a great kid. When they were together, it was the first time I really got left on my own. Honestly, it was a bit weird for me, but I don't think I noticed that at first. They had known each other since they were seven or so, but this is when we were about ten." Justice sipped his coffee, found it stone cold, which happened fast at this high altitude, and set it down on the peeling green paint of the decking. "We all went on this special zoo outing together, you know, for the blind kids. I got to do a lot of that, being a twin, and I have to say, sometimes the perks were pretty cool. Anyway, we went into this big room where there were lots of cages and glass aquariums, all holding some kind of animal that the kids could touch. The first one they brought out was an armadillo." He smiled at the memory of the tiny armored ball. "They got him out and the keeper carried him around, letting each kid feel him. As you might expect, they were all pretty tentative."

Justice shifted in his chair, pulling his jacket closer around him as the wind picked up the chill from the patches of snow left on the ground and tossed it playfully at them. "So, each kid sort of cautiously ran a finger over his back, and maybe patted it, but when they came to Temerity, she reached out with both hands and took it, she pulled it right into her arms and hugged it, rocking it and cooing like it was a newborn."

Amanda laughed, delighted. "Perfect, that's so her."

"It is," Justice agreed. "And then she turned to Aaron and said, "Here's our baby." He laughed. "I completely expected him to be embarrassed, I mean, not many ten- year-old boys react well to playing house, or husband, or whatever. In fact, I'm sorry to say, I made some smart-ass comment."

"So, *you* were being a ten-year-old boy."

"Exactly," Justice confirmed, not without chagrin. "But Aaron didn't care. He put one arm around Tem and the other on the animal, then he said, 'What shall we name him?' It was so, completely natural for them, like they were already married and always would be, and they both knew it."

"He sounds sweet," Amanda said. "Where is he now?"

Justice gazed up at one of the huge Douglas firs and said softly, "He died, about a year or so after that. I told you he had some other physical problems, he was just…sickly."

"Oh, how awful. That must have been hard on Temerity," Amanda half-whispered, her eyes filling with tears.

"You have no idea," Justice said. "They had, I don't know, some kind of special bond, and the funny thing is…" he trailed off, considering what it was that he wanted to say, he knew it was there, but he'd never admitted this before, not even to himself. "The funny thing is," he picked up, "I was jealous of him." The words felt sharp coming out, as though they might tear his throat, but he went on, "Even after he died." Justice felt a hot tear leak from his eye and chill instantly in the mountain air.

38

He was halfway there, and with a huge effort, he forced himself to expose the rest of his pain, to her, to himself. Very quietly, he said, "At first, I was glad when he died. I think that's the worst thing I've ever done."

They sat quietly, only the wind rustling the pine needles spoke. Then Amanda put down her cup, stood up and came to wrap her arms around Justice from behind. "You have nothing to be ashamed of," she whispered to him, "You love her very much, and it must have been confusing, at that age, to know that one day, you would have to share that love."

Justice sobbed once, deep and quick, and then sucked it back in and nodded, his throat too tight to speak.

Temerity was sipping coffee at eight a.m. when she heard the key turn in the lock. Runt raised his head from his paws and bolted to the door, claws scrabbling wildly for purchase on the smooth floor.

The door opened to Temerity and Justice's roommate. Ellen Homes was a rounded, compact woman. At twenty-five, she was a few years younger than the twins. She wore her straight brown hair up in a twist, which—with the addition of a hair net—was required for her work at the bakery. This was new for Ellen, who had always worn her hair down, concealing as much of herself as possible. Now, the pulled-back hair revealed a fine networking of scars around a patch of skin on the left side of her face that was a different color and texture than the rest of her skin, a surface-only repair of her abused childhood. Ellen was not tall, about five feet, four inches to Temerity's five-eight, but she was considerably heavier.

"Morning. How was work?" Temerity called out when the door had closed and she could hear her friend hanging her coat on the pegs.

"Good," Ellen responded. She was a woman of few words, none if she had her way.

"Did you bring me anything?" Temerity asked, feeling, not unpleasantly, like a kid.

There was the rasp of a duffle bag zipper, and the rustle of paper, then Ellen's careful, almost apologetic gait as she crossed the room and placed the bag in front of Temerity on the counter. Temerity felt for it, found it warm, and opened the top, releasing the scents of strawberry and chocolate.

"Mmm. Muffins?" Temerity asked.

"Croissants," Ellen said, and Temerity was amused to hear a slight French pronunciation she'd no doubt picked up from the other bakers. In spite of insisting she didn't, Ellen had a rather good ear, which was not surprising because in place of talking and participating, like most people, she'd listened—and watched—through most of her life. "Where's Justice?" Usually, Justice made breakfast on Saturday mornings.

"He and Amanda went up to the family cabin, the one on Pine Lake. Did you forget, I told you?" Temerity reminded her.

"Oh," said Ellen.

Temerity got up and, without asking, poured a cup of coffee for Ellen, adding a large helping of cream and then a teaspoon of honey. Ellen hesitated when Temerity held it out to her. She didn't usually drink coffee when she got home from work as it was her bedtime, but she took it with a soft "thanks," wondering what was up. She sat down at the counter and waited.

Her friend was obviously distracted, Ellen could see that, but having very little experience with human interactions, it was still difficult for Ellen to identify and process other people's emotions, or even her own. Usually so full of energy and enthusiasm, Temerity's brow was drawn, and she listlessly fingered the pile of linen napkins in the holder, fretting and flipping. Finally, Ellen asked, "What's up?"

"I think this is it, the big one," Temerity said.

Ellen looked around, everything seemed normal, and the earth did not move. "The big what?" Ellen asked.

The blind girl sighed, "I think he's going to ask her to marry him." Temerity couldn't see Ellen's reaction, but the creak of the stool as she shifted suddenly and the quick draw of breath told her it had happened.

"And…that's good, right?" Ellen asked.

"Of course, it's good!" Temerity said with forced determination. "Hurrah! Three cheers for the new queen!"

Ellen was somewhat confused. As far as she knew, Temerity both liked and admired Amanda. In fact, she had been relentless for the last few months in her insistence that Justice get more serious about the young doctor before she got away, so why the forced joviality? But before she could ask for clarity, Temerity changed tacks, "So, what's up for today? I know you need to sleep, but there's a street fair on Grand, and I thought we might make an appearance."

The truth, of course, was that Temerity was feeling the need for some company, and now that Ellen was spending more time with Rupert, and Justice had paired off with Amanda, she was spending most of her time alone.

"Okay," Ellen agreed. "I'm not that sleepy this morning." She did not add that it was because she was anxious about something she needed to tell Temerity.

"You want to go now?" Temerity asked, her hope raising her voice as well as her spirits.

"Sure…uh…can I eat something first?"

Temerity clutched the bag to her chest. "That depends. Did you want the strawberry or the chocolate?"

"I had both already, a couple of hours ago. I'm going to make a sandwich."

"Well I'm not," said Temerity, taking one of the flakey pastries from the bag and inhaling the fruity, buttery, warmth. "I'm having this!"

And she sank her teeth into it. "Yummy," she said with her mouth full. Then, unable to stop all the flakes from spraying as she spoke, she managed to say, "Have I told you how happy I am that you are working at Tami's now? Love the benefits!" She took another bite.

At the fridge, Ellen cleared her throat and tried to find some courage. "I…uh…have to make a decision," she told her friend.

Temerity stopped chewing for a second, then swallowed and asked, "About what?"

"My boss Ricco says that…" Ellen blushed, a Caucasian reaction that Temerity would have seen if she could see, "…he says that I'm pretty good with cakes, you know, decorating and…stuff."

"I'll bet you are!" Temerity encouraged. "I mean, I can't see them, and trying to feel frosting is a bit messy, but I know that they *taste* heavenly!"

"He said I could actually take over the wedding cakes if I get the right training. He thinks I should go to this, uh, pastry course school thing."

Temerity felt a slight shiver. She set down the croissant and wrapped her hands around her mug to ward it off, but the chill wasn't from the outside. "Oh?" she asked, "Here, in the city?"

"Well, no, I mean it's not far, like, two hours away, but that's the thing, and I…I just don't think I can do it. I mean, go away and stay in a dorm and you know, stuff."

"I see." Inside Temerity's refrigerated reaction a pilot light went on, and then the burners caught and began to spread warmth as the truth dawned and thawed her out. She wanted what was best for Ellen, even if it meant separation. This was her friend, this was *Ellen*, who had not been able to show herself to anyone when Temerity had first met her, and now, she was considering school with other people and a future for herself. It was brave, it was…"Amazing," Temerity said with genuine enthusiasm. "Yes! Ellen, you should do this. I'm sure you can get a private room, wherever it is, and, well, you'd be wonderful! Would you take other classes?"

"No!" Exclaimed Ellen. "No, I would just learn cooking stuff, mostly baking and decorating."

"And how long would this be?"

Ellen dropped her head. She'd never had friends before Temerity and Justice and the thought of moving away from them was intermingled with fears of being forgotten, of no longer mattering to them. She licked her lips and said, "Six weeks."

Temerity laughed, a full, gut laugh, real and energizing. Ellen felt balminess flood her chest, she loved Temerity's laugh best. Then her friend put on a serious face and asked with mock-sternness, "And what does Rupert think of all this?"

Ellen blushed again—she couldn't help it when she thought of him. It still made her dizzy to try to reconcile her opinion of herself with the fact that a grown man, a talented, kind, intelligent, grown man, was interested in *her*. But she couldn't deny she liked it. "He says that I should do it, and that, uh, he'd come and visit me, if I baked him something special."

The laugh came again. "As if he needed an excuse. A likely ploy. I think this is wonderful, Ellen, and you should definitely do it! Six weeks isn't long at all. Okay, make that sandwich and then we'll hit the fair. I'm getting dressed."

Temerity crossed the big room, avoiding the furniture and doorjambs with practiced ease. Runt's claws clicked along behind her, rendering his location a non-mystery. She went through the door to the hallway, trailing one finger along the wall, passing the narrow opening to the stairs leading up to Ellen's little bedroom, and continued on down to her own room on the left. She went through her drawers, feeling for two socks of the same thickness, then she chose jeans, and then a turtleneck and a sweater from the "blue" drawer. She ran a brush through her long dark hair and put on some lip balm and moisturizer in defense against the brisk breeze outside. She took her phone off the charger and slipped it into her back pocket, put on her watch, and returned to the main living area.

She paused at the door and listened. Ellen was coming down from her room behind her. She turned, "Should we take Runt?"

"Has he been out?" Ellen asked.

"Yeah, I took him out this morning, but only to the alley. He's just too rambunctious for me first thing."

"Then we'll take him," Ellen decided.

"And speaking of getting out," Temerity said, as they went to the door and found their coats and Runt's leash, "Mouse took a little stroll down to the second floor and claimed a strange sofa. Hugo brought him back up."

While Temerity locked up, Ellen watched for a reaction to Hugo's visit from her friend, and saw none. She took a firm hold on Runt's lead. He was unpredictable, he might take off chasing a bus, or run in terror from a squirrel, and it was best to be ready. Ellen glanced curiously at Hugo's door as they passed it on the way down the stairs, but she was unwilling to question Temerity who, for some reason she still could not fathom, was being resistant to the handsome man's attentions. Hugo seemed so perfect for Temerity. He was a pianist and composer, he was soft-spoken and smart, and he was very laid back, which left enough space for Temerity's exuberance and energy. Though it was perfectly clear to everyone else that Hugo felt romantically inclined, Temerity had kept up the pretense of ignorance. Ellen found this curious, as Temerity, blind though she was, noticed more than most people.

The two unlikely companions walked the few short blocks briskly, and as they drew near the noise and hubbub of human congregation, they had distinctly different reactions. Ellen withdrew, caving forward and watching the ground go by, avoiding any kind of eye or physical contact. Temerity folded her stick, put one hand on her friend's shoulder, and lifted her head, eager for the sounds and energy of the lively community.

Without warning, shrill obscenities broke out a few feet away. Ellen automatically shifted in front of Temerity, and watched the drama unfold with fascination, absorbing details to be diligently recorded in her journal. A twenty-something man was holding his phone above his head while a woman clawed at his arm, trying to reach it. "Give me that you…" she unleashed a stream of creative profanity. "That's her, isn't it?" she shrieked. "You cheating…" the vocabulary ceased to be anything that could be found in a dictionary.

The man responded in kind, calling the woman a number of names. A police officer approached and tried to separate them. The woman took the opportunity to physically attack the man, a move that ended with her wrists in restraints.

Temerity sighed. "Why do people stay together if they don't trust each other?" she asked. "In fact, why do they even get with someone who would speak to them like that? It's insane."

Ellen watched the woman crumble into angry, helpless sobs, and the man's pained face as he tried to explain to the cop that she was just overreacting, as the woman screamed "Liar!" through a voice choked with betrayal. The only thing Ellen could tell for sure, was that the man was afraid now, and she was pretty sure that what he feared was losing the very woman he'd just treated so badly.

Ellen had a shelf of notebooks filled with observations of people doing things that would never make them happy, and she had only recently begun to wonder *why*, instead of just noting down the episodes. And she did see them as episodes, theater in real time. "Maybe they need that drama," she suggested shyly to Temerity. "Sometimes it seems like that's what people want, so…they make it happen."

"Well, you're on the money there!" Temerity agreed. "But I'll pass, thank you! I choose sanity." She snickered a bit, but it sounded less like amusement and more like sadness to Ellen.

"So…" Ellen thought about how to phrase her question, not just so that Temerity wouldn't be offended, but also because she really didn't know, "...so, you think if you have a relationship with someone, you should never fight?"

Temerity's brows went up in surprise. "No! I just think you should always fight fair and try to never say or do things you can't take back. Like, let's say, cheating on them! She'll never trust him again. Game over."

Ellen filed that as they continued on. She remembered being told that someone had cheated on Temerity, and wondered if her friend was really talking about herself.

They passed several street musicians, something Temerity couldn't do without contributing money to the open instrument case, hat, or basket, and then they went through a plethora of food smells: barbeque and cheese, popcorn and sweet fried bread. Then came the jewelry and the crafts. With Ellen's help, Temerity examined a few ceramic bowls, eventually purchasing a large, gracefully shaped one for her mom Dory, who loved ceramics.

"What color is it?" she asked Ellen.

"Green."

"Just green? Good green or yucky green?" Temerity plied.

"Uh...green like the trees in spring. It sort of makes you happy to look at it, I guess."

"I call that a good green!" Temerity decided. "Whatever green is," she added ruefully.

But even the purchase of a gift, something that usually brought Temerity great pleasure, didn't do much to cheer her up. Her self-pity was morphing into self-incrimination and she was angry with herself—this was ridiculous. She needed to get over this crap. Justice was happy, and that's all that should matter to her. She mentally kicked herself for being so selfish.

They had gone a bit further, with Ellen naming each vendor as they passed it, when Ellen suddenly stopped.

"What is it?" Temerity asked.

"It's a guy, with a small table and two chairs, but I'm not sure what he's selling," Ellen whispered.

"Is he a psychic?" Temerity asked.

"No. I don't think so. Wait, there's a sign." Ellen read the sign aloud to Temerity.

For the first time since Justice had kissed her head the day before, the clue that had sent her spiraling, Temerity perked up. "That's awesome, actually," she said. "Is anyone there?"

Ellen yawned and tried to suppress it. "No, he's just sitting there watching everyone, smiling."

"Oh, that's kind of sad." Temerity could well imagine it. Ellen yawned again, more audibly this time. Temerity knew it was way past her bedtime. "Okay, you need to get home and get some sleep."

"I don't want to make you leave, I'll be all right."

"So will I." Temerity followed Ellen's arm down to her hand and squeezed it.

"If you'll take Runt and the package home for me, I think I'll walk back through the park and maybe get some soup at Figaro's. It's so nice out, I don't want to go in yet."

"Are you sure?" Ellen asked, though she knew it was useless.

"Have stick, will travel," Temerity said, and gave Ellen a little push. "Go on. I'll see you later?"

"I'm going back to the film festival this afternoon, 'Casablanca' is playing, and Rupert says it's one of his favorites. You want to go?"

Temerity smiled. "Maybe, but I might need to practice. I'll let you know later. Bye, sleep well!"

Ellen took the package from Temerity and turned to go. Then walked a few paces, paused to look back, getting her arm yanked by Runt, who was eager to get closer to a sausage vendor. Temerity was still standing where she'd left her. Ellen assumed she was listening and getting her bearings. She often did that before she made a move, it was her equivalent of looking around. With a flush of affection for her brave friend, Ellen turned for home.

Temerity stood until she was quite certain that Ellen would be gone, and then she faced to her immediate right.

"Excuse me!" she said, hoping the volume she had chosen was appropriate. "Are you available?" she asked.

"Absolutely. Sit down, young lady. Here, let me get the chair for you."

The sound of a chair scraping on the sidewalk informed Temerity as the silver-haired man with the pleasant face that she would never see but somehow knew he had, laid a gentle hand on her arm and steered her into the folding chair.

Then he retuned to his own chair and sat regarding her with open, patient interest over his sign, which read, "FREE EMPATHY."

6

Justice stirred in his sleep. Somewhere in his subconscious, the smell of wood smoke rekindled a memory, and the drowsy recall blended with the unfathomable reasoning of the human brain, until the dream became clear.

He was younger, a teenager, and he was standing in the hallway of a home he did not recognize, but knew to be his own. He had to get to his father, who was up those stairs, but every time he tried to move forward, they moved farther away. He labored on, calling out for Temerity, who was standing beside him with her arms crossed, completely calm. "We have to go!" Justice called to her, but Temerity did not move.

The smell of smoke grew stronger, and a there was a burning in the back of his throat. In the dream, he thought, "I can smell and feel." That was wrong.

Justice sat up in bed, waking Amanda with the suddenness. What should have been a lingering smell of a dying wood fire was choking, thickening smoke illuminated by streaks of moonlight through the window.

"What's going on? Why is it so smoky?" Amanda asked, reaching for her jacket.

"I don't know." Justice snatched up his coat and ran toward the living room, switching on lights as he went. The soft lamps of the living room illuminated only gray, swirling smoke, and beyond it, at the far side of the room, Justice could hear a strange roaring sound, the whoosh of a speeding train in a tight tunnel. As he moved to investigate, crouching low to avoid the worst of the smoke, he could see through the window to the left of the big stone fireplace a miniature fireworks display of falling sparks.

"The chimney's on fire!" Justice called out. But Amanda was already headed to the kitchen for the extinguisher she'd seen under the sink. Justice put a forearm over his nose and mouth to filter some of the acrid smell and grabbed the extinguisher near the woodbin. But even as he pulled the ring, Amanda flew past him, dropped to her back on the hearth and released a spray of foam up into the chimney.

"The roof!" she called to him. "You have to get up on the roof and make sure the wood shingles don't catch. Hurry!"

Every fiber in Justice's body was straining to hold him back. The smell and the sound were bringing back the horror of the worst night of his life, but he did not question Amanda's directive. In seconds, he was out in the freezing, but mercifully clear air on the back deck. Ignoring the stairs, he set down the red canister, leapt off the deck, and dragged a ladder out from below it. Glancing up, he could see a flurry of red embers spewing from the stone chimney, and black smoke was obscuring the pines above him. Shaking with fear and regret, Justice braced the ladder, grabbed the extinguisher and went up, climbing carefully onto the steep shingle roof, slick with moss. On all fours, he scrambled to the chimney and saw flames.

He unleashed a spray of foam and the flames died with a blast of acrid smoke. He waited, then moved in until he could point the nozzle of the extinguisher straight down into the opening and sprayed again, then stood shivering, the fear sweat drying on his body. Below him, Amanda came onto the deck, coughing. In the yellow light from the porch, he could see her look up at him, but she was coughing too hard to speak. Instead, she gave him a thumbs up, then looked around, before descending the porch steps to the ground. She disappeared around the side of the house and returned with the hose, with which she immediately began to spray down the wooden decking, where embers had landed and flickered orange, before dragging the hose up the ladder and handing it over to Justice to give the roof a thorough drenching.

In ten more minutes it was over. Justice came cautiously down the ladder and they circled the cabin, watching for any signs of the fire relighting or embers they might have missed.

"Should I call the fire department?" Amanda asked.

Justice turned to gaze at her in awe. "I think you *are* the fire department, damn, that was amazing!"

"I was a cadet," she said with a grin. "Ever since kindergarten, I wanted to be a firefighter, and then I got so fascinated by the medical aspect of it, I decided to become a doctor."

"Is there no end to your hidden talents?" Justice drew her close to him, and pressed his face into her hair, inhaling the strong charcoal smell. He shuddered again.

"Are you okay?" Amanda asked, her voice muffled by his flannel shirt.

"Honestly, no. But I think we can wait until tomorrow to get somebody out to make sure things are safe. I'll bet that chimney hasn't been cleaned for twenty years. Wow, that happened fast, huh? I guess we'll stay up for a bit to make sure it's okay."

"I'm not going to back to sleep anytime soon," Amanda agreed. "My adrenaline has decided that I need to stay up and vibrate." She rubbed the small of his back in a tight circle, trying to calm them both. "How about you?"

Justice nodded, and they opened all the doors and windows to encourage the smoke to exit. Amanda went into the tiny kitchen and returned with two small juice glasses, each with a generous shot of amber liquid, and a blanket.

"Here, take your medicine," she told him, handing him the brandy. She sat down on the porch steps and invited him to join her, wrapped in the heavy wool.

They didn't speak for a few minutes, just watched the moon shadows of the pine needles on the rocky ground. After a prolonged pause, Amanda asked again, "You okay?"

"Oh, Jesus, no," Justice slugged back a large gulp of the liquor, and rubbed his face hard with his other hand.

Amanda waited. She knew the horror that this incident must certainly dredge up for Justice, and she also knew that he had to be the one to talk about it.

"I never, ever wanted to face that again. I mean, this turned out okay, but…" Justice stopped, his voice cracking a little, "…that brought up some ugly feelings."

"Your dad," she said simply, aching for him. "You've never told me about that, I mean, I know it was a hotel fire, I know that it was in Mexico when you were on a family vacation, but that's all you've told me. You don't have to, if you don't want to."

But Justice knew he would have to tell her, have to relive the horrible night himself, not just this one more time, but over and over again. Somehow, the moonlight, cold, and isolation of this place distanced him enough from the tropical atmosphere of that other incident so that he could detach, just enough, to tell the story.

"Okay. So, yes, we were in Mexico, but it wasn't a hotel, more like a rental, you know, small houses on the beach, that sort of thing. Temerity loved the ocean, so my parents had picked out a little house right on the water. There were those old- fashioned Christmas lights strung all over it, you know the old kind, with the bigger bulbs."

She nodded, and ran her hand back and forth a few inches just above his knee, calming him, reassuring him that she was there, that she would not leave or let go. She would catch him if he fell.

"I was sleeping on the porch, I loved the sound of the waves. Temerity was in a small bedroom upstairs, near the back, and my parents were in a bedroom on the ground floor.

"I woke up, I'll never know why, and I saw what I thought was a bonfire on the beach, but I realized that it was actually a reflection in the half-open window of the back of the house that had caught fire. Someone had decorated the outside of the house with driftwood, and the lights had torched some of it like the kindling it was. I jumped up and started yelling. I ran into the house, meaning to go get Temerity, but my parents were coming out of the bedroom and Dad grabbed me and told me I had to stay with my mom. She dragged me outside and then ran to the rental office to get help, my dad…" Justice cleared his throat, and then went on, "…he went up those stairs. I could hear Temerity calling for us. Each of us by name. She was trapped down the hallway, and of course, she couldn't see where the danger was, or how to get out. I went back in, but by then the smoke was so thick I couldn't see my hand in front of my face. I crawled across the floor until I got to the stairs and started up. About halfway up, I could see Dad was standing at the top, there were flames behind him, I screamed at him to come back, but he turned and looked down at me. I'll never forget the look on his face. It was—" Justice choked off and took a sip of the brandy to brace himself. "It was the last time, I saw his face, like…like that." Justice drew a ragged breath and found Amanda's hand. He squeezed hard.

"He saw me, and said, 'Justice, don't come up here! Go outside below the window, I need your help!'" Justice gulped. "So, I went back out, and ran around until I was under Temerity's window, standing in the sand. I heard her screaming for me, and I was trying to get her attention, trying to find a way to climb up, to do something, anything." He tightened his grip on Amanda's fingers so strongly that she grimaced, but did not let go. "In a minute, I heard a crash, and then, Temerity screaming for Dad. Justice's throat had gone completely dry, and he ran his tongue over his lips. "The window was open, and the next thing I knew, I heard scrabbling, and my Dad's voice, all weak and strained saying, 'Catch her!' and Tem came tumbling out the window. She came feet first, and I was able to grab one of her arms and break the fall, but the soft sand did most of the work. Then I looked back up, all I could see was the silhouette of my dad, and then the room sort of exploded behind him. He climbed onto the window ledge and jumped.

"It was like a comet, a streak of hot light, and then he was lying there in the sand, not moving, not making any sound. I ran over and pushed sand all over him, his head and his arms, putting out the rest of the flames, but I could see the blisters and the...."

Justice couldn't say any more, he stared out, unseeing, into the forest.

Amanda waited, but he did not need to say more. She had met his father, who had lost his face and most of his hands to that fire. Though he had lived, and prospered, he did so with no semblance of his younger, unscarred self. As a doctor, she knew the months of recovery he had endured, the skin grafts, the danger of infections, the unbearable pain of sloughing dead, charred flesh. She shuddered, and pressed Justice's cheek to hers.

"He was very brave," she said. "And so were you."

"No, I let him go back in alone. I let him down."

"That's complete bullshit!" Amanda shocked herself with the force of her reaction. "You did the right thing," she went on sternly, surprised by the anger that filled her. "You would have only been scarred or dead yourself, and no father could endure that. You did what he wanted and needed you to do. One day, when we have children, you will understand that." Amanda did not quite understand herself where her rage and certainty came from, but she knew that she would not tolerate Justice condemning himself for a cruel act of fate in which he had behaved the best he could. "Do you hear me?" she demanded. "You have to forgive yourself!"

She pulled away and was disarmed to find him looking at her, a quavering smile of rescue playing at his lips. She smiled back. "One day," she said, "I'll tell you all the things that I'm sorry for, we all have them, you know."

Their emotions spent, they lay back together on the cold, wooden planks of the deck, the woolen blanket wrapped around them, and stared up into the sky while the waves of adrenaline broke and dissolved into foam. They stayed there, feeling the flow of a powerful past ebb away.

Then they talked about how beautiful the moon was.

7

Temerity sat up suddenly in bed, a cold sweat sending a creeping sensation over her whole body. She sniffed at the air, but did not smell the smoke she had imagined so vividly in her dream. With a moan of relief, she reached down to pet Runt, who was snoring softly next to her bed. He did not raise his head, but his tail thumped on the carpeted floor. She felt for her watch on the dresser and read the time with her fingers, 5:47 a.m. She thought she might as well get up. That particular nightmare wouldn't let her sleep again tonight anyway.

Pulling on a sweater robe, Temerity went to the kitchen and filled the electric kettle for tea, hoping to still the throbbing of her heart in her throat. It had been a long time since she'd had that particular dream, part memory, part unresolved paranoia.

She needed reassurance, but it was too early to call. Her father would be up at seven, and she'd call then, just to hear his voice, and be comforted. She crossed to one of the big windows and cracked it open, then stood with the clean air, as yet unsullied by the coming morning traffic, blustering on her face. She could smell rain in the light wind, and she inhaled, letting the sensation of moisture and movement fill her body. Temerity loved the rain. It was nature's music and poetry, if only you listened. To her rain wasn't, as it seemed to be to so many of her friends, background noise, but tempo and harmonies, highs and lows that moved and altered and illustrated the world around her.

For a moment, she stood reveling in the mystery of it all, while the moonlight she couldn't see shone down on her, creating a silver shadow on the floor crisscrossed with the framed panes of the factory-sized windows.

Without warning or reason, the thought of her friend Aaron returned, engulfing her in sadness, and she wondered why she was feeling his presence so distinctly. She thought of him often, occasionally with a few tears, though the pain had lost its devastating force as the years had gone by. That was natural, they had been so close, but these last two occurrences were so strong, visceral. It felt almost as if….Temerity reached one hand out the window into the cold, almost believing she would feel his hand touch hers, but only the mist met her fingertips. With a sigh, she let her arm drop.

This wouldn't do. She had to move, to do something. She decided to take a walk, she'd just go down to the park or maybe she'd walk the few blocks to Tami's and pay a surprise visit to Ellen.

She dressed and was headed down the stairs when she heard a door on the landing below open. She stopped, holding her breath to listen. Usually more of a night person herself, she was curious what kind of maniac started their day this early.

She heard the sound of someone moving about, exhaling forcibly, a few gripes and groans, and she guessed they were stretching, preparing for some form of exercise. There was a muted thump as someone rested something heavy on the hollow metal railing, possibly a foot.

"Ow," she heard Hugo grumble.

Temerity leaned over the railing and said, "Calf strings a little tight?"

There was a grunt and a swoosh of nylon fabric before Hugo answered, his voice echoing softly up the stairwell. "You know, for a blind chick, you are remarkably accurate. Yes, I've been promising myself I'd get up and run for the last three months now, and my legs are voting against, in fact, they've formed a coalition to veto this new policy."

"Well, you're in luck," Temerity started down toward him, "because as a career diplomat, I'd like to broker a compromise."

"Bring it," Hugo said, and swung his arms in big circles while he waited for her to reach him.

She paused two steps above the second-floor landing. "Okay, here it is. Instead of running right off, you walk for a few blocks, get a snack at Tami's, we'll call it fuel, and then jog as long as the sugar rush lasts."

"You're good," Hugo said, impressed. "Let me confer with my ministers of exercise. All in favor? The Ayes have it. Let's go."

With that wonderful sensation you sometimes get when you feel like you are the only people awake in the world, they stepped out into the alley and headed for the avenue at the corner.

"So how did you spend your Sunday?" Hugo asked.

"Oh, I went to the street fair and made a new friend."

There was a small sniff, and then Hugo asked, "Just picked them out of the crowd?"

Temerity said, "Well, it was a little more complex than that, I mean, he *was* advertising."

"For a friend?" Hugo asked, amused. He looked down at Temerity and liked the way her nose had turned a soft pink in the cold and first gray light of day.

"No, actually he was advertising to *be* one. So, naturally, I signed him up."

"Naturally," Hugo agreed. "Were there any special skills required?"

Temerity cocked her head, thinking. "Yes, actually. I had to talk to him."

"What did you say?" Hugo asked softly.

Temerity didn't answer. Instead she fell into a paced stride beside this energetically serene man, and thought about how much to tell, and considered how it would hurt if he didn't get it. And that made her feel like a coward. With a sharp lift of her head, she said, "I told him all about how screwed up I've been feeling about my brother wanting to have a life of his own. I know, it's not fair, but then, it's not fair, if you know what I mean."

Hugo considered this, then to Temerity's surprise, instead of offering judgment or minimizing her concern, he said, "And what did this new friend say?"

She laughed, "He said I was human, and that it was okay to forgive myself. Actually, it helped a lot."

"And what did you say about you having *your* own life, separate from Justice?"

Temerity stopped as suddenly as if she'd run into a wall. "Wow," she said, "That's a different perspective."

"You definitely have that," Hugo said, and she could hear him smiling, even from a few feet ahead of her. "Come on, we're almost at Tami's."

The bakery didn't open until six, which was still fifteen minutes away, so they crept down the side alley and found a window that had been left cracked open. Hugo looked in and Temerity asked, "Do you see Ellen?"

He leaned forward and craned to see around the large kitchen. "Yeah, she's filling muffin pans."

"Can you get her attention?" Temerity asked.

"She...uh, doesn't seem to like it when I look right at her."

With a little snort, Temerity said, "Yep, leave it me to pick a best friend who avoids eye contact."

"Maybe it was the other way around," Hugo mused.

"Okay, I'll do it. She felt for the crack in the window and then put her mouth right up to it. "Ellen?" she called softly, not wanting to frighten her friend. There was a cessation of movement, and then Ellen's voice came from just inside.

"Temerity? What are you doing here? Is everything okay?" She sounded anxious.

"Why shouldn't I be here?" Temerity pouted.

"It's not even light yet," Ellen pointed out.

"Yeah, like that matters to me. You got anything we can get an advance purchase on?"

"Cheese Danish just came out of the oven," Ellen said. "Meet me at the back door."

Hugo led Temerity down the alley and around the corner where they found the door propped open, then he watched from behind the grated security door as Ellen found the tray, wrapped two pastries and bagged them. "Here," she said, handing them over.

"Hi, Ellen," Hugo said gently. Ellen jumped a bit, but adjusted and forced herself to meet his eyes as she replied. "Hi, uh…Hugo," but she couldn't hold the honest gaze, so she pretended to swipe flour from her apron as an excuse to look away.

"Okay, see you later, thanks!" Temerity told her. "I have to go in to the concert hall around noon, I'm meeting the new pianist. He's supposed to be a real difficult character. Brilliant musician, and knows it."

Behind her, Hugo muttered, "Don't you just *hate* that?" and Temerity laughed.

Ellen said goodbye to both of them, which was somewhat new to her, and went back to work. The other two returned to their walk, munching the Danish as they went.

"She seemed somewhat suspicious," Hugo said.

"Ellen?" Temerity frowned. "Of what?"

"Us, I think. You know, being together at dawn and what that might imply."

To avoid that conversational thread, Temerity pulled a bite-sized piece from the flakey pastry and put it in her mouth. Then she said, "She's going away."

This surprised Hugo. He had noted how devoted Ellen was to the twins, especially Temerity, and vice-versa. "Where is she going?"

"To school, for six weeks. I'm really proud of her." In spite of this happy declaration, Temerity sounded drained and sad. "You know what you can count on in this world?" she asked him.

"Death and taxes?" he tried.

"Well…yeah, and?"

"Losing your keys?"

She laughed, then said, "And *change*, always change."

Hugo slowed to a stop and popped the last bite of his cheese Danish into his mouth, chewed happily, and then watched the steam from his breath, made warmer by the oven-hot pastry, dissipate in front of him. "Is that scary?" he asked, without betraying a point of view one way or the other.

Temerity turned to the sound of his voice, tilting her head up to answer. "No," she said definitively. "It's just that sometimes I would like the world to stay where it is for a little longer. Silly of me, I know."

Hugo noticed a flake of the pastry on her chin. "I'm just going to do this," he warned, and reaching out, he brushed it away with a soft forefinger. "And anyway," he said, pleased by the color that rose to her cheeks, "Maybe things will get better instead of worse, you don't know. Things change, yes, but how we react to it makes all the difference. I mean, I think. So what cha' gonna' do? Resist or embrace?"

Temerity swayed slightly, rocking from side to side as they stood at the edge of the park, the smell of damp, early spring grass and half-veiled buds bursting into fragile splendor wafted enticingly toward them. Then a smile started on one side of her mouth and crawled across to hike up the other. "Bring it," she said, then she threw her arms out and took a huge gulp of air and exhaled. The whiteness of her expelled breath hung over her for a second and then disappeared. She called out, "I embrace change!"

"Good," Hugo said. "Temerity, will you please go out on a date with me?"

She jerked slightly, then corrected and stood still. "Why?" she asked softly.

"Because…I'm so good looking?" Hugo suggested.

"Are you?" Temerity couldn't help being amused.

"Devastatingly. At least, that's my story and I'm sticking to it while I have this window of opportunity. Okay, how about because I own an '09 Mustang?"

"No, not *why would I want to go out with you?* That part I get. I mean, why in God's name, would you want to go out with someone who is blind?" Temerity hadn't meant to let it get this far, to let her troubles surface, but she was in now and she couldn't stop herself. Even she could hear the frustration in her voice as she asked, "You understand that a relationship with me would be limiting, right?"

Hugo puffed up his cheeks and looked up at the lightening sky, still gray, but with the hint of promised blue. He said, "Did you ever even stop to consider that I might be superficial and shallow? Maybe I just want to have casual sex, I mean, come on, give me *some* credit!"

He turned to look down at her and saw the shocked expression on her face, then those wonderful dark eyes crinkled at the edges and Temerity began to laugh, bubbling little giggles at first, but the mirth seized her whole body and she shook with laughter until she had to wipe spittle from the corner of her mouth and gasp for breath until she was recovered.

"Well," she said, "in *that* case, I'm free on Tuesday."

8

It was a glorious day. The sun sparkled on the tiny ripples of the deep blue lake, and Justice and Amanda decided that this early in the season, when none of the other cabins on the tract had even been opened for the summer, it would be safe to hike nearby while they left all the windows and doors open to air out the cabin. So they pulled all the cushions and anything that was movable out of the living room and onto the porch to air, while they took a short trip to the tiny store at Lakeshore Resort and asked about someone to clean the chimney. As luck, and the high demand for just such work in this area, would have it, the owner's son was in the business. They made an appointment to have him come up late in the afternoon, bought sandwiches, and hiked back along the lake.

As they puffed up the short, steep path to the cabin, not yet acclimated to the altitude, they heard a crash.

It didn't sound like a branch falling, or boulder displaced by the melting snow, it sounded like…

"Oh my God, someone's in the cabin," Justice hissed, and pulled Amanda back behind the large rock formation that was just off the path.

They peered around the mossy granite and listened intently. From inside, they could hear someone heavy moving around, occasionally smashing something.

"Do you think someone's robbing the place—or vandalizing it?" Amanda asked.

"I don't know. You go back and use the phone at Lakeshore to call the sheriff, I'll see if I can sneak up to the window and take a look."

"Sheriff? What is this, Dodge City?" Amanda demanded. She glanced up at the rocks and then found a good foothold and climbed to the top. There, she crouched low and shouted, "Hey! Who's in there?"

Her only answer was another crash. Justice shook his head. "Okay, I'm going to have a look." He called up to her, "Stay here!" and started for the house. He went around the kitchen side and pulled himself up by the windowsill to peek in. Then he let himself drop, came hurriedly back, and climbed up next to Amanda.

"Bear. It's a bear," he said. "Big bear, really big. He found the cereal, and everything else we left in the kitchen. And since he doesn't know how to open doors, he went *through* them. Tore them off of the cabinets *and* the refrigerator."

"What do we do?" Amanda asked, wide eyed.

Justice frowned. "Well, we could ask him politely to clean up and go, or we could try to scare him off, though the idea of a pissed-off black bear doesn't really appeal, or..." he held up one finger as though this were the idea that counted, "...we can wait until he's finished and is damn well ready to leave."

"I'm going with...C, we wait," Amanda nodded. "I guess we shouldn't have left the doors open."

"Judging from the new accessibility of the Fridgidaire, I don't really think it would have mattered."

At this moment, a small bundle of brown fur appeared on the porch, quickly joined by a black one. The two cubs sat heavily in the sun and scratched lazily at different parts of their bodies. One of them had brought out a loaf of bread. The cubs clawed at the plastic until they ripped it off and nosed at the brown slices. But they didn't seem to be interested in eating them.

"I think our papa bear is a mama bear. And she has twins!" Amanda said in delight.

"Funny how much trouble twins can be," Justice muttered.

One of the cubs looked sharply up at the sound of their voices. His small eyes seemed unable to focus on them, but his nostrils were twitching furiously as he raised his nose in the air, and then, very slowly, he started toward them.

"Oh boy," Justice said as the cub began to bleat, a plaintive cry for mother.

And she came, filling the doorway where she paused, sniffing at her cubs to reassure herself that they were safe, and then, she too caught the scent of humans. Justice and Amanda watched from their perch, lying flat on their stomachs now, but their smell was as good as a spotlight to the woodland creature and the huge mama bear began to lumber toward the base of the rocks, then she put both forepaws on the rock, so that she was standing up, stretching at her full height to investigate. Her nose was less than three feet from them.

And then she began to climb.

"No!" shouted Justice, pointing a finger at her. "Bad bear!"

The bear paused, confused, and sniffed again.

Over his head, a sandwich sailed through the air and landed on the ground behind the bear. She turned and went to investigate.

"You're not supposed to feed them!" Justice whispered.

Amanda snickered. "I don't think you're supposed to reprimand them like kindergarteners, either. Anyway, they've already raided the cupboard."

They settled in and happily observed the furry wildlife for half an hour. After that time, mama got to her feet, shifted her weight back and forth twice, and then huffed to her cubs. She started back into the forest, the cubs climbing over sticks and sniffing at patches of snow as they followed behind her in spurts and strolls.

Justice went into the cabin first, with Amanda right behind him. The living room wasn't too bad; a chair had been knocked over and one cushion had been eviscerated, but the kitchen was a sight. The refrigerator was canted wildly against the stove, its door torn partway from the hinges, hanging askew. Two of the kitchen cabinet doors were in pieces tossed across the floor, and several others had long scratch marks in them. Part of the sink draining board, a solid, two-inch-thick piece of pine, had been torn away. The floor was covered with flour, boxes, cartons, broken eggshells, and smashed glass. A plastic mayonnaise jar had been torn open and licked clean.

Amanda stepped out from behind Justice and gaped at the mess. "I guess I know what we'll be doing this afternoon," she said.

"Me too," Justice told her. Without another word he picked her up in his arms, carried her to the bedroom, slammed and locked the heavy door behind them, and tossed her on the bed.

9

The cab dropped Temerity off at the artist's entrance to the Music Hall. She collected her violin case and bag, paid the driver, and climbed out. She took a second to listen to the way the traffic bounced off the solid walls in front of her, By moving slowly forward and turning her head left to right, she was able to discern where the break in solid wall meant the top of the stairs leading down to the basement and dressing rooms.

"Hi, Temerity!" an almost breathless man's voice called from a few paces behind her, and Temerity turned.

"Hey, Rupert!" she answered. "You and Ellen taking a break from the silver screen?"

She heard him wheezing slightly as he crossed to her. Rupert was a large man, and a brilliant cellist. He was the only person she knew who was almost as introverted as Ellen, though for very different reasons. Rupert and Ellen had met when he had come to rehearse at the loft, and it tickled Temerity's heart to think that the two most solitary people she knew had become friends. She hoped they would eventually find their way to being more.

The cello case thunked against Rupert's leg as he shifted it to his left hand and offered his right arm to Temerity by touching her elbow. "Walk you in?" he asked. She folded her stick and took his arm gratefully. Temerity thought again how ironic it was that the most prominent smell of this substantial human was baby powder. It suited his almost fetal social innocence. "Hey," she said brightly as they started down the cement stairs, "Ellen told me about the cooking school. I think it's great!!"

The arm twitched a bit in hers, and Temerity realized it was thoughtless of her not to consider that he might be upset by Ellen's going away. It had depressed her somewhat, after all, so perhaps she'd taken too much of a liberty with this deeply private man by being so casual in her approval.

"I'm happy for her. She's actually a really good baker already," Rupert said. Both his surprise and pride were evident in the words and Temerity felt relieved.

"Well you should know," Temerity hummed her agreement, "You got her started!" Rupert was an excellent baker himself and he had taught Ellen most of what she knew before she started at Tami's. The very first thing they made was cinnamon rolls, a treat that had been Ellen's favorite before she'd come to live at the loft, though Temerity hadn't understood why until much later when, after a great deal of coaxing, Ellen had told Temerity a few details of her horrific past. Ellen's mother, she explained, had deserted her at five years old, leaving her to starve in a derelict tenement. Ellen waited for two days, hungry and alone in the filthy room, until the gnawing emptiness in her tummy surpassed the fear of strangers enough that when she had heard someone on the stairs Ellen cracked open the door and whispered to the drunken man, "I'm hungry." He had winced, repelled by the sight of her distorted face, grunted, begrudgingly fished a package of mini-market cinnamon rolls from his plastic bag, and threw them to her before going on his way. That act, and the fact that he had called the police, had saved her life.

As much as Temerity wanted more detailed information about the state of Rupert and Ellen's relationship, she understood that questioning either of her shy friends could easily backfire into silence, or worse, debilitating self-consciousness that would cause a rift or even a mutual retreat. So she just said, "Ellen told me you might visit her?"

"I will, if she goes. Apparently they have tasting days, you know, where they can invite friends in to try things. And I've always wanted to see the college's modern art collection."

"Do you think Ellen will go to a museum with you?" Temerity was honestly curious. It had been a huge step for her friend to go to the movies, and there she could remain mostly hidden in the dark. Well-lit public venues were alien planets to Ellen.

Perpetually winded by his excess weight and sedentary lifestyle, Rupert huffed a bit as they reached the bottom of the long staircase and started toward the artist dressing rooms. He whispered, as though someone else was around, "I'm trying to work her up to coming to a performance," he confided.

"Rupert, my man," Temerity said as they reached the area known to music center insiders as the catacombs, "if you can do that, you'll be my hero." She thought for a minute and then added, "Again."

Because Rupert had been a hero before. This shy, seemingly timid, cello player had stepped up to save Seth when the option was sending Seth back to an uncle who routinely sold the twelve-year-old for sex. Rupert pretended to be a 'client' to lure Seth's uncle to the loft where he could be recorded and arrested. And Ellen, invisible Ellen, had been amazing, absolutely amazing. It was Ellen who first discovered the boy living in the crawl space of the building and recruited Temerity and Justice to help the child. It was Ellen who had understood the boy's preference for life on the street to the alternative, and Ellen who had convinced Seth to trust their help. In spite of their crippling timidity, neither Rupert nor Ellen had hesitated to put themselves in jeopardy to protect the boy. The fact that these two extreme introverts had exhibited

70

more courage and sacrifice than anyone else Temerity had ever known only made their actions all the more remarkable.

Now she said, "Seth is alive and thriving because of you. I'll never forget what you did."

True to his humble self, Rupert deflected the compliment by saying, "It's Thelma and Beth who saved Seth, they're the ones who adopted him." Temerity respected his reluctance to discuss himself and they navigated the subterranean corridors in silence.

The area below the theatre was massive. This lower level stretched beneath the seating, the stage, and backstage area. There were hallways leading to dressing rooms and a warehouse-sized open area for storage. Here, lighting, extra seating, props, curtains, flats for building sets, and a thousand other things were kept. They were organized in a grid pattern, each section taking up a fifteen-foot square of floor space that was crisscrossed with open safety corridors, which enabled items as large as scenic backdrops or as small as light bulbs to be accessed from all sides. About half of these cubes were gated off with chain link and locked, but many of them were little more than carefully stacked props, set pieces, and flats stored on huge rolling carts. Temerity always loved the feel of this place. The lingering vibrations of a thousand performances lived here. She loved to think of it; each opera character, and the performers who played them, each instrument with the work and talent of its musician, each part brought to life by actors, their collective energy lingered here. This place was redolent with the retention of creative magic.

They had passed the storage areas and entered the hallway to the dressing rooms when Rupert drew Temerity to a stop. "Hold on," he whispered.

Temerity cocked an ear and brought her awareness back to the space immediately around her. A ways down the hall, she could hear the muttered fluctuations of voices in conflict. Rupert was clearly uncomfortable with happening on a confrontation in progress. He came to a stop.

"What's going on?" Temerity asked him.

"It's Regan and that husband of hers," he said. "The one who's not supposed to be here."

"Simon?" Temerity creased her brow. "I thought Regan divorced Simon."

"That was the plan, but didn't you hear?" Rupert asked in a whisper, "He's refused to give her a divorce, claiming it's against his religion. She's having to jump through legal hoops, and from the looks of it, I don't think he's cooperating."

That was obvious from the heated timber of the exchange. Suddenly, Rupert jerked as the retort of a slap reverberated sharply.

At the sound, both Rupert and Temerity shouted, "Hey!" and started forward again, Temerity beating him there by several paces, "What's going on here?" she demanded. "Regan, are you all right?"

Confronted by two angry defenders, Simon started for the exit. Unable to move out of his way in the narrow hallway, Temerity was shoved hard in her shoulder, spinning her around and slamming her up against the wall. Her senses were filled with a harsh, sharp smell, something like acetone, but she couldn't quite identify it.

"No!" Rupert's voice was tremulous, but determined. Simon's footsteps stopped abruptly.

"Let him go, Rupert," Temerity insisted, terrified that her gentle friend would be hurt. She heard shuffling as Rupert moved aside and the other man broke into a run.

"I'm sorry, I'm so sorry," Regan, a petite, dark-haired beauty who played the flute in the orchestra repeated as she hurried to Temerity. "Are you all right? Oh my god, that *bastard*!"

"Oh, I'll live," Temerity said, rubbing her shoulder with her free hand. "But what's going on? What *was* that?"

"That was my ex...actually, unfortunately, *still* my husband, Simon."

"But you have a restraining order!" Temerity exclaimed, remembering an ugly scene a few months ago outside the concert hall that had ended in threats and a police report.

"Yes, but he doesn't care."

"What was he doing here?" Rupert asked.

"Trying to scare me, and succeeding."

Temerity could hear the trembling in Regan's voice and she reached out to put a hand on her friend's shoulder. "Should you call the police?" Temerity asked steadily, trying to calm the terrified woman.

"I have, twice before, they just talk to him, and he promises to leave me alone. They claim there isn't much they can do, and they always insinuate that it's my fault or that I'm making too big a deal of it. It's like I get run through the ringer and he just gloats about upsetting me. Simon wins, I lose. It sucks." Regan's voice shook with impotent fury.

"But he just hit you!" Temerity exclaimed, gritting her teeth in anger. "He can't do that!"

"But he did, and he could do worse, and he knows I know it. Even if they arrest him, he would only get maybe probation and he'd be that much more intent on making me pay for it."

Temerity felt the rage of her gender that had been building for millennia. Shaking, she turned to Rupert who was still standing behind her. "Rupert, I think we should call security and make sure that son of a…" she reined herself in, "…that Simon, doesn't get back in—at the very least. Then we'll go from there," she added grimly.

"Good idea," said Rupert. "I'll call from the green room phone. Are you all right, Regan? Do you want me to get you some ice? Your cheek is pretty red."

"I'll be fine," she said, sniffling. "At least he didn't use his fist this time." She laughed shortly, and then she burst into tears. Temerity raised her arms to encircle the smaller woman, while Rupert seamlessly liberated her violin case from her hand so that she could do so.

"Shhh. You'll be okay," Temerity said to Regan, rocking slightly as the woman cried against her chest. "Come on, let's go sit down and we'll get you some herbal tea." She patted Regan's back. "Tea helps everything," she attempted to lighten the heavy atmosphere with a joke.

With Rupert's assistance, Temerity walked the distraught woman to the green room, the only place in the cement-shrouded catacombs with wifi and therefore any cell phone reception, and got her settled on a sofa. A few of the other musicians were there, putting their belongings in lockers or chatting before rehearsal. All of them came to offer sympathy and concern. One of them, a huge bald man who played percussion, Terrance, pushed through to Regan, wrapping her in his massive arms as though she were a child in his protective custody.

"We got you, girl," he rumbled, "You're okay now."

Terrance exuded a sense of security that calmed Regan considerably, and she had settled down a good bit by the time Temerity handed her the cup of chamomile tea. Meanwhile, Rupert called the security desk, then reported to the rest of them, "They're sending someone down. They want to know if you have a picture of Simon."

Regan sniffed and blew her nose on a tissue Temerity had produced. "Uh...on my phone, I think."

"That's good," Terrance said. "We can send it to the security office and they can print it out. Now we should call the police."

Regan made a little noise of confusion. "I just don't know. The last time he violated the restraining order they put him in jail overnight, and I came out the next morning to find all my tires slashed. I couldn't prove it was him. So...I just don't know," she hiccuped, and tried to take deep breaths. "Even when I had bruises, before, when I was still with him, the judge just gave him some community service and let him walk out."

Terrance rested his cheek against the top of Regan's head and pulled her tighter up against him. "What is *wrong* with these men?" he spat, the shiny dome of his head glinting in the fluorescent light. He was genuinely, almost irrationally, infuriated, Temerity could tell from his voice, though he kept it contained, no doubt for Regan's sake.

"I really think you should report this, Regan," Temerity encouraged. "No one can help you if they don't know the facts, and since he actually struck you, I think the police should have this on record."

For a moment, the young flutist didn't speak, and then she said in a voice so soft it was almost a mew, "He said if I did he would kill my dog."

"Oh boy," Temerity sighed. "Well, it's up to you. In the meantime, why don't you tell us what's going on so we can help?"

Another hiccup and Regan blew her nose again. Then, after an encouraging, buck-up shake from Terrance, she said, "He won't sign the divorce papers. He says that I'm his wife in God's eyes and no effing piece of paper is going to change that. He thinks…" her words caught in her throat, "…he thinks he *owns* me. Oh my God." She shifted forward as she put her face in her hands. "How did I let this happen?"

Terrance growled, then in his deep bassoon of a voice he said, with absolute certainty, "You didn't 'let anything happen,' Regan. Simon made this happen, and only Simon. This kind of abuse can happen to anyone. Strong, even powerful women have been blindsided by this kind of toxic masculinity bullshit."

"This is not your fault!" Temerity confirmed vehemently, reaching out to rub Regan's back.

Terrance asked more gently, "Does he drink?"

Regan snorted without amusement, "He used to," she said. "And then….he just…changed. After we got married, he got involved with this really extreme Christian church. I went with him once, and they did things like speak in tongues and 'battle with the devil.' It was alarming to say the least and I tried to get him to see the insanity of it. That just made him angry, and he told me that I should stay at home and 'serve him' as God intended for women to do. It's beyond scary, that cult mentality. I would never have thought someone as logical and scientific as Simon would fall for that kind of superstition, but then, I don't think he's completely…sane. At first I thought he would come to his senses, but something was wrong with him. I still think it's a chemical imbalance and he needs help. I thought I could help him, but after he came home a few nights and…abused me, I knew I had to get away. When I told him he needed professional help, he flew into a rage and I barely got out. I really thought he would kill me. That's when I left him, left the state, and moved here to get away from him," she shrugged hopelessly, "but he followed me."

"Is there anyone else you can stay with?" Temerity asked.

Regan shifted deeper into Terrance's protective embrace and said weakly, "I don't know anyone outside the orchestra yet, I've only lived here for six months. And anyway, what good would that do? He knows he can find me here and he knows when. There's no way to keep him out of the audience or off the street outside."

Terrance cleared his throat and said, "You can stay with me. I have a guest room just sitting there empty. It's a big apartment and I live alone."

"It's nice," Temerity added encouragingly. "I've been there for parties. As I remember, it's not easy to get in without an invitation and a security code."

"It's a very secure building," Terrance explained. "You can park underneath and come up without having to worry."

"I couldn't impose on you!" Regan exclaimed.

"Sweetie," said Terrance, shifting so that he could look straight down into Regan's face, "I had an alcoholic, abusive father who beat the crap out of my mother until he drank himself to death, and she was so deep in denial that even years later she still won't admit he was anything but a saint. At his funeral I swore to never let that happen to a friend. You can stay as long as you need to." Temerity was touched, Terrance was known as something of a loner and a tough guy, but his voice, as he made his offer, was pure concern, he was sincere. And since he described himself as "militantly gay," the possibility of ulterior motives was at a minimum.

Regan laughed nervously. "But...my dog."

"Is it a small, yappy dog?" Terrance asked.

"No, she's a medium-sized mutt. She's very quiet."

As if he'd planned for this eventual outcome, Temerity heard the jingle of keys on a ring. "I was hoping you'd say that," Terrance told Regan, "but even if it *was* a small yappy dog, you'd be welcome. I'll write down the address and all the security codes for you when we finish today. But I do have one requirement," he said, and Temerity could hear the joke coming.

But Regan was so wired for drama that she asked fearfully, "What?"

"No Fox news or reality TV," Terrance said. "They make my brain bleed."

Regan laughed her relief. "I think we'll get along just fine. It won't be for long, I promise, just a few nights."

The security guard appeared at the door, and after Temerity suggested to him, quite forcibly, that someone might want to actually watch the entrances, since it was their job to see that random people couldn't wander in off the street, she sat quietly while Regan showed them the picture of Simon.

"He's pretty distinctive looking," the guard said. "Shouldn't be too hard to spot, we'll post his picture to all of security and at the stage door entrance."

Regan insisted she was fine to go to rehearsal, and the three musicians went upstairs, though Regan stayed close to Terrance. News of the argument had traveled among the orchestra members faster than an E flat, and when Anton, the conductor, strode onto the stage and the musicians instantly came to respectful attention, instead of going to the podium, as he usually did, he made a beeline to Regan.

"My darling lady, are you all right?" he asked with his almost indiscernible European accent.

"I'll be fine, thank you, sir," Regan answered, and Temerity could tell she didn't know what else to say.

"I would prefer," Anton said, raising his voice, "if the gentlemen will make sure that the ladies do not go out alone. Please see that they are escorted to their cars or bus stop. This is not just for now, but for always. Yes?" There was a murmur of enthusiastic agreement. "Very well, we rehearse," he said, and went briskly to the front.

Temerity let Rupert walk her to her chair, which was near his. She placed her braille music on the stand, unpacked her violin, lifted her bow to the strings and tuned up, following the note played by the pianist. She would use the music to follow the symphony when she wasn't playing, though she had already learned the pieces by heart.

There were three sharp clicks of the baton on the conductor's music stand, and then, his quiet voice perfectly audible in the magnificent acoustics of the auditorium, Anton said. "And, one, two, and ....begin."

Music filled the air around them, drenching their senses and demanding all their focus, making them, for a few precious hours, unite into something so beautiful that they could forget all the troubles in the world.

10

When they left the concert hall, it was dark, and Temerity stepped out into the chilly air and shivered. Rupert was close behind her, and he offered to drive her home.

"Thanks, but not tonight," Temerity said. "I'm going to take the bus. I want to make a stop on the way."

"Okay, I'll wait with you," Rupert said. Temerity heard his stomach grumble and she laughed.

"I'll be fine," she told him. From the shifting and sniffling around her, she could tell there were several other people at the bus stop. One of them blew their nose in the cold air, honking loudly. Someone else sneezed. "See? I definitely won't wait alone. I've got a dozen fellow citizens and a few trillion airborne germs to keep me company. I'm safe, except of course from viral illness, but I'll risk it. You go on. It's a straight shot to my stop."

"Well, okay then," Rupert sounded reluctant. "I'm supposed to meet Ellen before she goes to work at ten."

"Oh," Temerity remarked, trying to keep a frisson of disappointment that her friend would once again not be home from her voice. Instead she smiled and said, "Then you'd better get going!"

Rupert patted her shoulder awkwardly, then shuffled away toward the parking lot, and Temerity settled in to wait, canting an ear to listen to the traffic. She asked a man to her left, "Can you tell me when the number twelve comes?"

"That would be now," the man answered without inflection, and sure enough, seconds later, she detected the whoosh of the large vehicle as its airbrakes hissed to a stop at the curb.

Listening carefully for the shuffling of people around her, Temerity fell into the line boarding the bus. She had just found the handrail and was stepping up onto the rubber-stamped step when she stopped, her nostrils flaring.

There it was—that smell, like a petrol station mixed with human sweat smell. With a flush of fear, she turned her head briskly from side to side, but the smell had faded away and she heard people shifting impatiently in the chilly air behind her.

She decided that one of her fellow passengers, who hadn't showered for a few weeks, combined with the bus exhaust, had recreated the alarming scent. Shaking her head at her unnecessary alarm, she boarded and took one of the handicapped seats. She didn't usually, but the bus was crowded and it was easier than accidentally sitting on someone.

Four stops went by, and then Temerity stood and pulled the cord. When the next corner came, she asked the driver if this was Grant.

"Yes, Ma'am," replied a cheerful voice. Temerity thanked the woman and stepped off onto the street. She unfolded her accordion stick, calculated which way was west, and started out. Halfway down the block, she moved to the shop side of the sidewalk and paused.

There, just ahead of her, she heard the bells of a door chime, and started toward them. She was feeling for the opening when she heard a gentle voice she recognized say, "Allow me," followed by the sweep of the door being opened. "There's a small step up, be careful," but Temerity had already navigated over the threshold with the use of her cane. Once inside the pleasantly warm and stuffy cafe, she turned back, "Thank you," she said.

"Anytime."

"Wait," Temerity said, placing the voice, "You're the guy who was offering free empathy the other day at the street fair, aren't you? I talked to you."

"Yes, you did."

Temerity searched her memory. "Geoff," she said. "Is that right?"

"And you are Temerity. Nice to run into you again."

"You must really like this place. You recommended it and now here you are. Are you eating here?" Temerity asked him.

"No, I work here," he said. "In fact, I own it. Let me get you a table." He brushed her arm with his and she took it, letting him lead her to a small booth. He was about her height, she could tell from her shoulder against his, with well-toned arms that she could feel through his sweater, which had a thick, ribbed design, and she decided Geoff was a man who liked to be comfortable as she slipped into the padded booth.

"I won't ask if you want to see a menu," Geoff said, teasing. "What are you in the mood for?"

"Oh, comfort food," Temerity told him. "You said that's the specialty here."

"Macaroni and cheese, pot roast, or chicken and dumplings?" Geoff reeled off.

Temerity laughed and searched in her bag for a braille novel. She always carried something to read. "Do you have tomato soup and grilled cheese?"

"If you count roasted tomato bisque and gruyere-arugula melt on homemade rosemary loaf, then yes."

"I count roasted tomato bisque with…all the rest, among the things I would most like to eat right now," Temerity confirmed. "And Geoff? Thank you so much for listening to me the other day, it really helped a lot."

"Sometimes, that's all we really need," he said, and she could hear his authentic kindness as the welcome pool of healing refreshment it was in a frantic world.

Footsteps approached behind him, and a harried voice told the restaurant owner, "Geoff, there's a homele—uh, a…man out back who is asking if we have any left-over food, and he won't go away. He's insisting he knows you, I'm sorry." The server sounded put out. Temerity could tell it was a server from the clink of ice in glasses they were carrying.

Geoff said, "This is America, of course we have extra food. I throw away more perfectly good food than people eat at this restaurant. It's the law. I'll be right there." He leaned down to Temerity and asked as though sharing a conspiracy, "How did your situation turn out? Any developments?"

"It's ongoing," Temerity confided. "I'm a work in progress."

Geoff sighed. "Aren't we all?"

In spite of the happy exchange, Temerity frowned. "Well, we're supposed to be." She felt a light, sympathetic touch on her arm, and then the kind giver of free empathy was gone, no doubt to give food to someone who seldom saw a meal that hadn't been discarded as trash by someone else. Temerity thought to herself, *Some people aren't a work in progress, some people are done. They just arrive that way.* Geoff was one of those, she could tell.

She had known one other. Aaron. He had been finished too. Her friend had always been different than the other kids. It was as though he had known why he was on this planet, and he was going to make the most of it. Temerity opened her book to the page she'd marked with a ribbon, but let it sit under her idle fingers without reading.

She'd met Aaron when she'd started at the Braille school. She had been afraid of the new sounds and smells, and after her mom, Dory, had walked her around the classroom, letting Temerity touch everything and acclimate herself, she prepared to leave.

"Don't go, Mommy," Temerity remembered saying. She could perfectly recall the terror. "Why can't Justice come with me? I don't have any friends here."

Dory's sweet breath had tickled Temerity's face as she leaned down to whisper to her daughter. "Temerity, my darling, you know that Justice has to go to his own school, but he'll be home this afternoon."

Then a voice had piped up, "I'll play with you."

And that had been it. Aaron, a slight boy with a high, reedy voice, had taken her hand, and led her to sit on the floor next to him, explaining how the day would go as they went. He barely let go of her hand for that whole first day. He talked to her and explained about things, made jokes, and was so brave that it was a half hour later before Temerity even realized that her mother was gone, and she had been too busily occupied to notice.

The classroom was an open affair, designed especially for children who were legally blind. For some, that meant thick glasses, glimpses of light and shadow, blurry forms even, but many of these children weren't only visually challenged, they had multiple problems, as Temerity learned that first day.

They had just listened to a story that featured the letter "E", Temerity recalled as she sat in Geoff's restaurant, and the teacher had passed around a board with the raised shape of an "E" and the braille dots that represented it.

Aaron took Temerity's hand and guided her fingers over the board, singing softly, "eeeee." Temerity was repeating the sound, and giggling when she felt a small, clutching hand feeling for the board, which was suddenly torn away from her.

"Lena, we don't snatch things," the teacher said calmly, but this had been answered with an almost animal-like howl. "Lena? It's okay," the teacher was crossing toward them. Temerity assumed that she tried to take the board from the girl, because the next thing that happened was a scuffle. Temerity was kicked as the girl went into a raging tantrum, squealing in high-pitched shrieks and hurling herself around on the floor.

"Lena, stop it! You need to try to get control of yourself." The teacher's voice was raised, adding to the hysteria level in the room.

Temerity recoiled from the frightening activity, and Aaron pulled her further away, then released her hand. "Stay here," he whispered. So she did, listening to the uncontrolled screams, then from the floor she heard Aaron call cajolingly to the distraught girl, "Lena, I'm here. Be still or you'll bang your head again. It's okay, just try to calm down. I know it's hard, but you can do it." The screams continued, but reduced in volume and intensity. "You can do it," Aaron repeated encouragingly. "Come on, we'll have snack soon, and it's sugar cookies today. You like that, you always like that. You can have my cookie, okay?"

Temerity got onto her hands and knees and crept forward carefully, drawn to the calm voice that somehow enveloped the panic on the carpet. She felt forward until she found an ankle, a slim, girl's ankle in a thin sock. She patted it and said, "It's okay, Lena, we'll stay with you. You'll be okay." She moved in more and discovered that Aaron had lain down on the carpet next to the disturbed girl and was holding her. Temerity sat cross-legged in front of them and began to sing her favorite song. "Winnie the Pooh...Bear, Winnie the Pooh...Bear, silly little..." all the while rocking back and forth to the tempo of the simple tune.

With effort, and great, gasping breaths, Lena calmed down, and Temerity could hear the sound of thumb sucking.

When it was quiet, the teacher had said, "Thank you, Aaron, thank you, Temerity, and thank you, Lena, for trying so hard. Are you better now?"

Shari Shattuck

"Your soup and sandwich," the server's voice on Temerity's immediate left interrupted the memory, and she jumped slightly, then leaned back as she heard the satisfying thunk of a heavy ceramic bowl on the tablecloth. It smelled delicious. "Do you need anything else?"

"Some water would be nice," Temerity answered, but she was thinking that what she would really like was a sugar cookie.

11

When Temerity hung up her coat next to loft's front door, she felt Justice's heavy jacket on the next hook.

"How was the cabin?" she called out.

"Flammable," her brother answered from the sofa, where he was reading.

A noticeable hitch in her step told Justice that he'd startled his sister and he hastened to reassure her. "Just a chimney fire, we got it out and had it swept and cleaned the next day. No structural damage."

"I wondered," Temerity said, coming to sit in the armchair near him. "Was this in the early a.m. last night?"

"How did you…" Justice began, but he didn't finish. "You knew?" He shook his head with a little laugh.

"Not exactly. Let's say I dreamed of smoke and woke up with a strong urge to call Dad and make sure he was okay."

They both sat quietly for a moment. It surprised neither of them that she had felt his distress. It had happened so often that they found nothing remarkable about it.

"Did you happen to dream about any large omnivores?" Justice joked.

"No," Temerity said, her brow creasing. "Don't tell me bears started the fire." She clucked disapprovingly. "Fur balls shouldn't play with matches."

Justice laughed. "They didn't start it, but when we opened the windows to air it out, they decided to see what was in the fridge and the cupboards. I have a guy from Lakeshore stopping by to rehang the cabinet doors and drop off a new fridge."

"Yikes," Temerity exclaimed, laughing. "I guess the bowl of porridge on the counter was too hot."

"No, that one was just right. The counter, of course, faired less well. He's installing a new one of those too." Justice cleared his throat to give his even more exciting news, but lost his nerve and countered with, "How was your weekend?"

"Oh," Temerity told him, "Pretty quiet actually, for me anyway. We had a little adventure of our own at the concert hall. You remember Regan?"

"The pretty Asian lady?"

Temerity scowled at the physical description she could not share, and its limitations. "Try again."

"The flutist?"

"Yes, her. Her estranged husband— who apparently received instructions from God about how to navigate his relationship, mistranslated the directions, drove headlong into a brick wall of male dominance mortared with religious indoctrination and the impact smacked what little sanity he had out of him—came by to harass her, and Rupert and I interrupted things, but not before he slapped her."

Justice swore and dropped his head in frustration. "What is *wrong* with people?" he bemoaned, echoing Terrance, though he didn't know it. "And by that, I mean men in particular, and religious oligarchies in specific." His hands formed into fists of frustration. "Who told them their beliefs give them the right to harm anyone?"

"Well, quite a few people, judging by how often it happens." Temerity thought of how many women lived in fear around the world because there was no one to stand up for them, not even their supposed God, and that inherited anger churned in her DNA again.

"She okay?" Justice asked with genuine concern.

"Yeah, Terrance invited her to stay with him until she gets some stuff straightened out—that was really cool of him."

"Terrance? Big, bald, tattooed, gay Terrance?" When Temerity affirmed the big and gay part of this description, as the bald and tattooed part was beyond her ken, Justice said, "He seems an unlikely feminist."

"It's funny how you can never guess where help will come from," Temerity agreed.

They both knew they were skirting a major headline, but they were also both reluctant to be the one to bring up the potentially life-altering news.

"So," Temerity steeled herself, "how did Amanda like the cabin?"

"She loved it; she was a real trouper about all the excitement. Way braver than me as it turns out. With the fire *and* the bears."

"Aw," Temerity teased him, "are we feeling a little emasculated?"

Justice thought of their afternoon after the bear invasion. "I wouldn't say *that*." He laughed. "In fact, as far as feeling masculine goes—"

"Okay, okay, no need to expound, thank you." Another pause, Temerity thought her gut might jump out and throttle her if she had to endure any more suspense. "Yep, Amanda sounds like an all-around keeper," she prompted. He did not speak. "Justice," she snapped impatiently, and stomped one foot.

"I asked her to marry me, and she said 'yes,'" came out in an uncertain rush.

Temerity felt the shiver of insecurity go through her, but instead of vexing her, it checked her with its density. Her nerves lay down, drained and accepting, into electrified goo. A strange panic was filling her, but a thick and viscous panic, as though she were drowning in dirty motor oil and had no will to resist. She stood up, walked a few feet away and turned back to face her brother.

"Tem?" Justice asked. "Are you going to tell me how you feel about that?"

Temerity threw her head back, raised both hands in the air and shouted, "Hallelujah!" She put two fingers in her mouth and whistled. "About frigg'n time! I better start planning the engagement party! Do you want to invite just close friends or everyone you know? Does Amanda like brie or should I stick with cheddar and gouda? Of course, Ellen and Rupert will have to make a cake."

Justice was thrown. "Tem, come sit down," he said, a little unnerved by her reaction.

All the energy seemed to seep out of his sister on her return to her chair. He scooted down the sofa until he could take her hand. When he did, he linked their forefingers and held on tight. "You know, this doesn't mean anything has to change."

Temerity laughed, and then wiped away a tear, furious with herself for the emotion that was escaping, sentiments she didn't even understand. "Don't be stupid," she snapped. "Of course it changes things, that's the whole idea, otherwise, why get married and give up half your closet space."

"We want you to know that there will always be a place for you in our home, Amanda was really adamant about that."

"How very generous of her," Temerity said, unable to stop her voice from sounding petulant. She shook herself, resisting the powerful urge to slap her own face. "Listen, I really *am* happy for you. I don't know what—" she shook her trembling free hand in front of her face to illustrate her reaction, "—*this* is. But it'll pass, it's just going to be… different, I know that, I've always known that. I'm fine with it."

Justice squeezed a little tighter and rocked their locked fingers in a slow arc, back and forth, back and forth, like a cradle. "It's funny, but I always thought you'd be the first one to get married, you know, run off with some musician or something."

"I think you mean…or some *one*." Temerity said wryly. "Not really much chance of that though. I'm not exactly anyone's first choice for a life partner."

A suspicion started in Justice. "Why would you say that?" he asked.

A short, humorless laugh came from Temerity. She pulled her hand from him and rubbed her face briskly in an attempt to pull herself up out of her funk. "Well, let's review," she said, and assumed a sitcom mom voice. "Honey, can you help Junior with his homework? I would, but I can't read his book. Come to think of it, have you seen Junior? Cause I fucking lost him!" The last phrase exploded from her.

Justice was so startled by the blast of anger and Temerity's use of the curse word, something she only did in extreme stress, that he recoiled slightly. "Tem, that's just not true."

"Really?" she said bitterly. "How irresponsible would I have to be to bring a life into this world and then not be able to keep it safe? Do you think I should get married and have a kid so I won't be lonely? I call that the height of selfishness."

Justice did not speak. He knew that it wasn't for him to claim to understand her frustration. No one could who didn't share her circumstances.

Temerity stood again. "I'm sorry," she said abruptly. "Speaking of being selfish! Here you are giving me this amazing news and all I can do is overreact and make it all about me."

"Don't be sorry. That I won't accept," Justice told her flatly. "We've been a team our whole lives, hell, before we were born even, so this is a big change. And," he found his own voice breaking as he went on, "if you think this isn't emotional for me too, then you're dead wrong." He leaned forward and tried to stifle his own irrational anger.

For two long beats they both remained stock still as the emotions they shared swirled between them and the emotions they didn't share walled them off like protective shields. Then Temerity came and sat down next to him again.

"I really *am* happy for you," she whispered, tears streaming down over a crooked smile. "I really am happy for you both."

Justice leaned toward her until their foreheads were touching, wishing, as he had always wished, that he could make things easier for his twin, that he could show her all the colors and brilliance of the visible world, that if it had to be one of them with this challenge it just wasn't fair that it was his sister and not himself. He gulped and said, "I wish I could change..." his throat tightened, and he swallowed hard.

Temerity understood, and she cut him off. "And you wishing it was you instead of me has made all the difference for me. I was always okay being the blind one instead of you, and that's because...*I had you*. It's strange to say, but we shared this." She let the suggestion of the end of that connection linger.

He smiled. "We've been through some stuff, that's for sure. And this is just more stuff, there will always be more stuff, good *and* bad. It's not like stuff stops happening or being hard to deal with just because we grow up, or get married, or have families, or whatever. We'll still have us."

"Plus one," Temerity said.

"Us plus one," Justice agreed.

"We three, we happy three."

"So," he stood up and laid his hand, palm up, on her shoulder, tapping twice with his knuckles, his way of offering his hand, "wanna' congratulate your future sister in law?"

Temerity exhaled hard and took the hand, allowing him to pull her to her feet. "Okay," she said, "but is that fair? I should probably tell her to run while she still can."

Justice laughed out loud and hugged her quickly. "I wish you wouldn't," he said. "She can run really fast."

12

Outside their home in the woodsy suburbs, Justice kissed his mom Dory, and gave his father Andy a hug.

"Congratulations!" Andy said. One hand, missing two fingers, held his son's head against his shoulder as he embraced him. "You couldn't have done better."

Justice pulled back and looked into his father's face, once so handsome, now scarred and ravaged by fire, and saw only the love and pride in the gray eyes that were so like his own.

"Thanks, Dad," he said warmly. Next to them, Dory was congratulating Amanda. "Welcome to the family, officially!" she said, wrapping her in a hug. "So, have we talked about dates yet?" Dory, a very elegant woman on whom the eve of sixty looked like a beautiful place to be, took the bottle of wine from the younger woman and they started into the house.

"Let us catch our breath," Justice called laughingly. "We got engaged, prevented a forest fire, and played host to Goldi-Bear and her twin cubs. Isn't that enough for one weekend?"

Laughing, Dory waved his objections away and continued pelting Amanda with questions. "Will your mom be coming in from Ohio? I so hope she'll be able to help you plan the wedding. By the way, any thoughts on how big a wedding you want or where you'd like to have it? You know, the Arboretum is lovely, and Andy and I are on the board there, so you *might* have an 'in.'" Dory winked at Amanda, whose smile twitched nervously.

"Oh, what a good idea. I mean, we haven't even thought about locations or dates yet, just got through the proposal part, no specifics on the books at this point." Amanda threw a nervous glance toward Justice. He shrugged helplessly.

"And speaking of the ring…" Andy released his son and reached out one damaged hand to take Amanda's perfect one, examining the antique ring on her finger. "Stunning. It suits you perfectly. My mother will be very happy."

"We're going to visit her when I get a weekend off," Amanda told them.

"She'll love that," Dory said warmly.

The four of them moved into the house and went through to the open kitchen and den area. The entire back of the house was windows, giving the effect of having gone out into the forest rather than into the interior of a house. Without even realizing it, Amanda took in the greens, the sway of the pine needles, the bright spring buds, and the overcrowded, angry tensions of the city melted away. She exhaled audibly. Dory smiled at her. "Yes, we call this the breathing room."

Andy went to the counter to open the wine. He read the label. "Montepulciano d'Abruzzo. Nice. Your sister told me there was a chimney fire at the cabin?"

"Oh yeah," Justice nodded, suppressing a small shiver of revulsion at the ugly wad of old memories the incident had churned up. He switched gears quickly, saying cheerfully, "But Amanda—revealing her secret past as a fire department cadet—went into incident commander mode, and we got it out before any damage was done." He grinned, then his face tightened and he added, "It *was* scary though."

"I'll bet." Andy looked at his son and Justice knew that his father too was thinking of the multitude of scars that night long ago had left on both of them.

"Temerity dreamed about it, and it woke her up," Amanda said incredulously.

"I know," said Andy, as the cork slid from the bottle with a satisfying, vacuum pop. "She called me right when I was getting up, just to check on me."

Amanda looked from one of her future in-laws to the other. They smiled calmly at each other. "Don't you find that extraordinary?" she asked.

Apparently neither Andy nor Dory found it at all out of the ordinary. "She's done that her whole life," Dory said. "And Justice too, they're just, you know, *connected*. We didn't move them to their own rooms until they were eight, and every night for a month they would both wake up and cry at the same time. Andy and I would go from room to room like a situation comedy. I've done extensive research on the phenomenon and it's fairly common for twins to have an exceptional level of empathy, even at a distance. Statistics show it's usually most pronounced in identical twins, more than current science can explain. Still." She shrugged.

"And they would be *particularly* sensitive to sharing that kind of trauma," Andy contributed without naming it.

Amanda nodded. Then she turned to Justice whose eyes were fixed, unfocused, on the counter, trailing one finger along the grain of the wood with his mouth tightly pursed. "Honey?" she asked softly. "Are you okay?" Dory watched her son and felt a pang of frustration.

He looked up and assumed a quick smile, but before he could respond to his fiancé, Andy called out, "Amanda, I've been saving something for this occasion. I want to show you."

"What is it?" Justice asked suspiciously.

"You'll see, *after* Amanda."

"Well, I'm intrigued." Amanda got up, squeezed Justice's hand, and then followed Andy to his office, off the big den.

Dory watched her son for a moment, letting him process his thoughts, and then she sat down next to him, setting a glass of the famously violet-tinted wine down in front of him. He blinked at it as though surprised to find it there.

"The fire must have brought up a lot of old feelings," she said gently. Then she laughed a little. "Big weekend for you!"

Justice looked at his mom, and then, without warning, the panic he'd been containing surged up. He said, "I just can't…. I'll never be able to forgive myself for what happened to Dad, and this minor fire really brought it all rushing back. I mean, Dad is amazing, he's handled his disfigurement with acceptance that I've never even seen in anyone else. He's…well, he's *Dad*," he laughed, though his sadness was evident.

Dory felt the old pain rise in her as well. Empathy not for her husband's pain, but her son's. So many times she had tried to alleviate his pain, to lessen his guilt, but it had never stuck. As a psychiatrist it disturbed her, as a mother it wounded her. She tapped her fingers thoughtfully on the counter and then she said, "Do you remember afterwards? When your father was in the hospital back here?"

Justice shuddered. "How could I forget? It was the worst time of my life."

"It was his, too," she whispered. "You were only eleven, so we didn't tell you everything, but your father *wasn't* always all right with what the future would hold for him. In fact, he wasn't sure he could go on at all." Justice reeled back a bit, making the wine in his glass slosh, and his mom went on quickly. "I'm not telling you this because you were in any way responsible. You were not. You did what your father asked you to do, and that's the only reason you were spared. The floor exploded behind him when he got to Temerity at the window. You would have been on that floor and you would have been killed." Dory paused to shake away her own worst nightmare, and the jagged pain passed on through, but she felt the emotional scarring tighten and ache.

"But the fact that you lived, that you and Temerity were unharmed, those were the reasons that he *did* go on, that he suffered all that pain of recovery. It gave him the courage to face the world again, even without a face." She waited for her son to look up at her and then she smiled at him. "Of course, I still think he's the handsomest man in the world. To me, he is." The statement was so simple, and so true, that Justice felt a kind of proud elation tingle through his chest.

"I know mom, you're the bravest woman I've ever known."

"No," Dory shook her head firmly. "No, not me." She blew out her cheeks and glanced toward the doorway through which Andy and Amanda had disappeared as the sound of laughter floated out of it. She turned back and her voice dropped to a whisper, not to hide her words, but because she was afraid of what they were. She was about to disillusion her son, but it was time. "I was terrified," she said. "I didn't know if I could face life with your father, the way he looked—" she broke off and tried to shake the image of his bloated, red, oozing wounds, the yellow puss in the gauze that had to be changed every few hours, the smell of the rotted, cooked flesh peeling away—she made a growling noise to steady herself. "I *wasn't* brave then, I wasn't strong. I was barely able to hang in there with a kind of detached numbness. And then, I brought you and your sister to the hospital to visit your father. Knowing how hard it would be for you, but also knowing that this was a reality for you too, something you both would have to deal with and live through."

Justice nodded, a sudden smell reoccurring to him, the smell of antiseptic and charred meat. His stomach lurched and twisted. He set down the wine.

"I know," Dory took his hand. "It was horrible, and the hardest thing I have ever done. Walking you two down that hallway..." a tear came ran down her face, she wiped it away. "I almost turned back. I seriously considered leaving and never coming back. I'm not proud of that, but there it is." She shrugged, disappointment in herself showing the lines in her face. "But Temerity just pulled me right along, and then we went into the room. Andy was barely visible through all the bandages, and he was heavily sedated, but his eyes were open and he started to cry when he saw you both, and he turned away, trying to hide himself." Dory took the hit of the visual memory and went on. "He was ashamed, terrified that he would frighten you."

Justice said, "I remember," though it almost killed him to do it. "I was so afraid, I couldn't even accept that this was my dad." He exhaled hard, trying to rid himself of the shame. It didn't work. It never had.

She leaned in toward him and spoke very clearly. "And that was completely expected, and very appropriate. You were brave to go in at all. Of course, you didn't want to see your father's pain and vulnerability. You are *human*. Sorry," she shrugged a little laugh. Then Dory straightened her spine, a look of wonder replaced the sadness and she asked, "Do you remember what Temerity did?"

Justice thought hard. His memories of that day were almost completely shrouded by his own veil of regret and inadequacy, his cowardice. "No, not really," he confessed.

"She let go of my hand and went right up to him. We'd all been told not to touch his upper body, so she felt her way down the bed and put a hand on his leg. Then she said cheerfully. "Hi, Daddy!" Dory wiped away another tear, but this time her eyes were shining. "She stood right there and told him how much she loved him, and that he needed to try really hard to get better soon because she wanted him to come home and help her with a science project they had started together, and she went on and on about how they would finish it."

Justice looked up hopefully, hardly daring to believe that might have been some good to come out of that dark day.

"And your father kept crying, he was not thinking clearly because of the morphine, and he mumbled that he would look like a monster. And do you know what Temerity said?"

Justice shook his head. He had blocked out as much as he could.

"She said, 'Silly Daddy, that doesn't matter to me!' And then, she sat down on the end of the bed, and told him jokes, trying to make him laugh."

"I do remember that," Justice said as it came back to him. "I remember being so…useless."

Dory's brow creased as she considered that. "Not useless," she suggested, "helpless maybe, but you were not useless. Your love and your presence helped bring your father back to life."

"But it was mostly Temerity," Justice said gloomily. "She's always been the stronger one. I know that."

"Oh pish," Dory said with a wave of one graceful hand. "You both have different strengths, and you know it. I appreciate that you have a great deal of residual trauma from that experience, there is no way any us could have escaped unscathed, but I won't allow that kind of self-criticism. Sorry again, but I'm your mom, and I can't have you talking that way about my son."

Her son laughed. "Gee thanks, Ma," Justice joked. "Still protecting me from bullies."

"You're welcome. You've always been your own worst bully, by the way. And if you remember, after your father came home and was recuperating, Temerity would sit near him while he watched TV or worked, and she would run her fingers over his scars. She told him she liked it *better*. It was more interesting, she said, texture suited her. I honestly believe that it was her unique point of view that taught us all that the way he looked didn't matter, she reminded us that he was the same person inside. It gave him the courage to *be* the same person, and to see himself that way."

From the office behind them, there was a shriek of laughter, and then Amanda came to the doorway and called out, "Justice, your dad is showing me this video of you when you were eight and you're talking about the girl you're going to marry. It's hysterical! Come on, you've got to see this!" She turned back in, "Rewind it to the part where he starts talking," she said to Andy.

Justice sulked a bit, but he got to his feet. "It's always fun to be the butt of a joke." He looked at his mom. "Come on, we might as well get this over with." As they walked across the big room, Justice put his arm around his mom, pulled her close, and pressed his cheek to the top of her head. "Thanks, mom," he whispered.

"Niente," she said. "Niente, mon amore."

"No," he said. "It's not nothing, it's everything."

They went into the room. Andy was rewinding the tape. Justice sat down next to Amanda feeling slightly nervous. From the image racing backwards, he thought he'd seen this video before but not for years.

Then his father hit play, and there was an eight-year-old Justice. He was sitting on a garden bench. His dark hair was a mess, the white suit he was wearing was crumpled, his tie askew, and his legs, hanging from the edge of the bench, were in constant motion as he slung them back and forth restlessly.

Off camera, they heard the voice of a younger Andy, an Andy whose vocal cords had not been yet been damaged by smoke and heat. "So, what did you think of the wedding?" young Andy asked his son.

The boy on the screen made an impatient face and sang out, "Bo-ring."

"You didn't think it was sweet?"

"Eww. No, they were kissing and gross stuff."

"Don't you like girls?"

Justice reddened, "Dad!"

"I'm just asking," Andy's voice said, and the camera tilted slightly as he made an adjustment. "Don't you think you'll ever get married?"

"No way! Not unless she was really cool."

"Like cool in what way?"

Young Justice twitched and yanked at the tie, making it more crooked. He looked over his shoulder and then back at the camera. "Like, uh, an astronaut, or maybe a deep-sea explorer, because you know, if she's a *girl*, then she better have a space ship or a submarine!" The boy grinned at his cleverness, his legs kicking madly, one and then the other swinging like alternating pendulums.

Amanda was laughing so hard she was gasping for breath. And then, the camera pulled back to show a beautiful dark-haired girl sitting near him. Her black eyes were unfocused, but flashing anger. Her arms were crossed and she was scowling.

"What about you Temerity? Will you ever get married?"

"You know I am!" she said. "I'm going to marry Aaron, as soon as we're grown up. And we're going to live up at the cabin."

"What do you think about what Justice said?" her father prompted with a lurking laugh in the question.

"I think he's stupid. He's just saying that because Carrie Mitchell told him he had cooties, and he probably does."

Justice was glaring at his sister. "You're not going to marry Aaron," he said.

"Why not?" she demanded.

"Because you're both blind, dummy."

A quiet fell over the office. Amanda glanced at Justice, whose face had gone gray.

On the screen, Andy's voice said, "Justice, Temerity and Aaron can be and do whatever they want to do and be. You know that, right?"

The boy Justice looked sorry, he mumbled, "Sorry," and stared at his hands. Temerity scooted over toward her brother. She searched for and found his hand. "It's okay," she told him, linking her forefinger with his, "I won't leave you. Don't worry, you can come and live with us."

The image on the tape jump cut to a party scene, people in garish nineties colors, dancing in a tent.

Justice stood up and walked out of the room, through the house, and out into the woods.

13

It was late when Temerity got home from rehearsal. She knew from the stillness in the loft as soon as she opened the door that Ellen had left for work and Justice and Amanda weren't back from lunch with her parents yet, and she was surprised to feel relieved.

She put her violin and bag away, then poured herself a glass of wine. Outside the wind was whipping up, and the smell of rain had pervaded even inside the house. Temerity went to crack open a window and stood listening to the wind swoop between the buildings and the mumble of thunder. The electricity in the air made her hair follicles tingle, and she rubbed the forearm of the hand holding the wine glass to settle them. Lightning storms always made her restless, but in truth, she reveled in the excitement.

Suddenly, a loud crack of thunder ripped the stillness, followed by a rolling rumble, the strike so forceful that Temerity involuntarily emitted a small cry, more from the thrill than fear. Her heart was racing as she laughed at herself. She backed away from the window humming a childish tune to calm herself, an old habit, and the rain began to fall.

She moved into the kitchen, thinking to reheat some soup, but when she removed it from the fridge, placed it in the microwave, and pushed the right button, nothing happened. She tried again. No sound, no beep, no hum of twirling tray and microwaves at work. Nothing. She noticed it oddly quiet, no electrical hums at all, only the patter of the rain.

There was a knock at the door.

Temerity jumped slightly, then laughed at herself again and started toward it, waiting until she was close enough to be heard through its thickness before calling out, "Who is it?"

"Hugo. Are you okay?"

Temerity frowned, but her heart thumped for a different reason, and as she opened the door, she asked, "Why wouldn't I be?"

"Because the power's out?" he said with exactly the same inflection. There was a pause during which Temerity tilted her head and waited for it, and then he said, "Oh."

"Aaaand…he gets it. Well that explains why the microwave wasn't working," she said. "Come on in."

"Sure…uh…"

Temerity had already started back toward the kitchen, but she did not hear him following, so she turned back. "Are *you* okay?"

I don't suppose you have a…candle or…" she heard him shift uncomfortably.

"I don't really use a lot of candles," she said, confused. "Oh, it's dark. I get it." She came back to him, and took his arm. "How did you get up here?"

"There are emergency lights in the stairwell. I should have thought to bring a flashlight up with me, or at least my phone."

Temerity drew him inside, and as she closed the door behind them, she said in a mock horror voice, "Welcome to my world. Muh hahahahaha!"

He followed her clumsily over to the counter, where he ran into one of the stools. "Wow!" he exclaimed, but before Temerity could ask what had impressed him, she knew. A crash of thunder spilled through the room. "I love lightning," he said.

Temerity moved toward the window. "I've heard it's quite beautiful," she said quietly. She reached the sill of the open window and put her hands on it, feeling the wetness in the wind as it rushed in on her and whipped her hair back. Drawing in its sharp, delicious scent, she turned her head up, and waited.

In a few seconds, another rumble, lower and more distant, but still powerful, rolled over her. She swayed toward the sound, then righted and found her back against Hugo, who had come right up behind her.

"It is beautiful," he said, one of his large, strong, pianist's hands resting on her shoulder. "It's magnificent."

Temerity initially tensed at the touch, but the warmth from his body reassured her, and she let herself lean into him, almost imperceptibly. "It wouldn't make any sense to ask you what it looks like, but—"

"It looks like the thunder sounds," he said, "only faster." His voice was timbered with a rumble of its own.

She nodded, turning toward him without backing away. Now she could smell the warm pine soap smell of him mingled into the scent of coming rain. She said, "That's exactly how I imagined it."

They stood together for a moment, their bodies touching, but only lightly, and then, when another huge roll of thunder struck them, she heard Hugo's voice, much closer to her face than he was tall. He said, "I'm going to kiss you now."

"Uhm," her heart fluttered, as much with fear as with anticipation. "I guess that's okay."

"Yeah," he said, "I wasn't asking."

His first kiss took her breath away, not because it was powerful or eager or filled with lust, but because it was the opposite of that, soft, almost whispering soft, a brush of his warm lips on her cooler ones that was tender and strong and left her wanting more. Then he pulled back and gently turned her around to face the bracing wind again, wrapping his arms around her shoulders so that she felt invigorated, yet protected.

It was lovely, and it lasted for four straight seconds.

"Hellooooo!" Came Justice's call from the doorway as it opened. "Anybody home? Tem?"

Temerity took a step sideways, away from Hugo and felt a warm flush over her cheeks before she remembered that the lights were out and that meant that they were blind too. The thought made her smile.

"Over here! Hugo came up to see if I was okay. He was worried about me, what with the lights out and me being lost in the dark and what not."

"Fine," said Hugo petulantly, "Make fun of the seeing guy."

Justice was laughing. "Uh…Hugo. I don't believe you've met Temerity. Next time the lights go out? Call her to help *you!*"

"I'll remember that," Hugo said, his voice a low, contented purr. And Temerity thought, *So will I.*

She heard her brother rummaging in drawers and then the strike of a match. "There we go," Justice said. "We'll just shed a little light for us mere mortals without see-in-the-dark super powers."

Temerity knew that Hugo was still standing very close to her. And she realized that Justice had noticed it too when he asked. "I'm sorry, did I interrupt something?"

"No," Hugo answered smoothly, relieving Temerity of the onus, which was good because she couldn't think of anything to say. "We were just enjoying the thunder and lightning."

"Oh," Justice said. "Well don't let me stop you. I'm going in to read, I've got some reports to catch up on before work tomorrow. I do love being a doctor—"

"Of anthropology," Temerity intoned, as she always did to remind him that he had dropped out of medical school to pursue a career in the study of human behavior.

Shari Shattuck

"—but it does involve a good bit of homework, doing studies for the Institute. Enjoy yourselves." Though his tone would have sounded casual to anyone else, Temerity could hear the innuendo in it, with clarity.

"Where's Amanda?" Temerity asked as she started back for the kitchen.

"Dropped her off at the hospital, she has a 24-hour ER shift."

"How did it go?" she nattered on, avoiding the moment when she and Hugo would be alone again. She just didn't know if she wanted to be, or maybe it was that she didn't know if she could stop herself from wanting to be, and for some reason that left her feeling like jelly that hadn't set.

"Great, Except..." Justice seemed unsure of what to say, "...well, we'll talk about it another time. Goodnight, Hugo, thanks for checking on Mole."

"Mole was fine. Full disclosure, I was the one who was scared."

"Well, you came to the right place," Justice said with cheer. "I'm was the only kid in elementary school whose sister wasn't afraid of the dark and it came in very useful for a few exceptional Halloween pranks. I'll leave you the candle, I can use the flashlight on my phone."

"It's okay," Hugo said, moving. "I was just leaving. I've got a student coming at 8 a.m. tomorrow."

"An ungodly hour."

"As an atheist, all my hours are ungodly. Or rather, they are all divine," Hugo said, and started to the door.

"Hugo?" Temerity called out. And she heard both of the men stop and wait for her to speak; Hugo from politeness, Justice—curiosity.

"Yeah?"

"So...uh...tomorrow night? We have plans?" Temerity asked, her throat so tight she was conscious of the air passing over her vocal cords.

"Not yet, but I'll make some," Hugo told her, his level voice full of curves and corners, unseen things ahead. "Seven o'clock?"

"Sure. Good night."

The heavy loft door swung open and then closed. There was a moment of silence. Temerity waited—at first she thought Justice might actually let it go—and then she heard his sing-song taunt. "Temerity's got a boyfriend."

"Oh, shut up. But yes, I have a date. Are you happy?" she retorted.

"Actually, yes," he told her. "Dad played that old video for Amanda from Sue and Abed's wedding when we were eight. Remember?"

Temerity tried, but nothing came to mind, videos weren't really her forte. "Not really."

"The one where I say I'll only marry an astronaut or a submarine commander."

She smiled now. "Yes, I remember that. Amanda must have thought it was hysterical! I wish I had been there."

"It reminded me of something." He came across the room until he was a few feet away. "You were sure you wanted to get married then. You said you were going to marry Aaron."

Temerity took a punch in the gut. She remembered that now. It didn't matter how long it had been since Aaron had died—leaving her to adventure on along without his courage and certainty—it still stung. "I was eight," she laughed it off. "I thought I would."

"Well, it reminded me how jealous I was of him. And I guess, I want to say, I know you're dealing with feelings about me leaving you for Amanda, even though we both know it's not the same thing, but I don't want you to worry about resenting Amanda, it'll pass, we both know that."

"I'm not worried!" she told him. "And I don't resent her, I like her. Sure, I'm beating myself up a little for my irrational reactions, but how else am I going to learn? Now it's your turn, and don't *you* worry, I know you're not deserting me, or abandoning me. Like it or not, you'll be stuck with me for a sister 'til one of us croaks." She snapped her fingers to show that it was a done deal, and walked around him toward the hall door. But when she got there she turned back and said more gently, "Good night."

"Love you," Justice said.

Temerity went down the hall into her bedroom and sat on the end of the bed. She was drained, but oddly vibrant. She listened to the now distant sound of thunder as the storm moved on. As storms always do.

She got up from the bed and went to her closet, and using her hands, she began to search the shelves, feeling among her sweaters, until she found what she was looking for.

She carried it back to her bed, and curled up around it. The slow drip of raindrops on her sill beat a tattoo of memory and loss.

Very softly, Temerity rocked back and forth with the small stuffed bear clasped to her chest, and then, very quietly, she began to sing.

Winnie-the-Pooh, Pooh Bear, Winnie the Pooh…silly willy nilly ol' bear.

14

It was just after dawn when Ellen, making her way home from her night shift at the bakery, spotted a now-familiar pair of figures at the edge of the park. Seth, who less than a year ago had been living on these streets, was taking Runt on his morning walk a couple of blocks from the loft. As was her long and hard-to-break habit, Ellen easily folded into the shadows for a moment to observe the young man.

It was this lifelong habit of remaining unseen that had brought Seth to Ellen's attention almost a year ago, huddled cold and homeless in the crawlspace of the loft, while thousands of other people hurried past the grate he used to climb in and out without noticing or caring what suffering hid just beyond it. It had been Ellen, who watched the young man pulling food from dumpsters, seen him sicken and weaken, then alerted Temerity and Justice to his presence. Together they devised a plan to meet him and get him medical attention, which was how Beth, a doctor at the free clinic, had first met the boy who would steal her heart and become her son months later, but it was Ellen alone who had initially found a way to earn his trust so he would not run away again. Somehow she dredged up the strength to share a fraction of her own past pain with the boy so that a fragile bridge of connection was built. It was that rickety, swaying link that eventually led to Seth's new life with two strong and loving moms and an extended support group who watched over him. For Ellen, watching and observing the details of life around her was old hat, but stepping in and exposing herself to help others was still new, and terrifying. Temerity told Ellen that she was brave, but Ellen would never believe it, she just knew what it was to be alone and desperate. All she had done, Ellen thought, was let Seth know that she trusted the twins, and because she had, he could. What happened after, how she had used her own body to protect Seth from his violent uncle, she neither considered important nor thought exceptional. It had just happened without thinking. Temerity and Justice and Seth's moms, Beth and Thelma, thanked Ellen for her courage. Which, Ellen knew, was just silly—the only hard thing she had done was expose herself to another human being—compared to that, a moment of physical danger was incidental.

Now Seth was standing in the partial shelter of a long-unused loading dock recessed in the side of one of the commercial buildings that lined one side of the park. He was talking to what appeared to be a pile of dirty blankets as he rummaged in his backpack; the dog sat patiently at his side, watching the boy's every move with eager enthusiasm. Ellen guessed there would be food involved. As she watched, Seth pulled out two pieces of fruit and a wrapped sandwich from the bag and passed them over. The hand that reached to take them was dirty, the fingers twisted and gnarled into a single hook. Ellen wasn't much of a medical analyst, but she had heard and read that arthritis could do that to some people. It looked excruciating.

Starting forward unobtrusively on the far side of the street, Ellen came level with Seth and peered into the darkened inset of the loading door. Sitting in the corner of the space on a few filthy cushions, and wrapped in a moving blanket, was an old woman. She was smiling gratefully up at Seth, revealing a set of imperfect teeth.

Ellen could make out what Seth was saying from there. "There you are, Miss Fay. You gonna' go to the shelter tonight? It'll be cold, I hear."

"Oh, I don't know," the woman answered, her voice, though roughened by exposure, sounded younger than Ellen expected. She studied the woman more closely, finding that she was not quite as old as her weathered, dirty face at first appeared. She was saying to Seth, "I don't like that place, it's noisy and crowded. I'll be fine out here, and this is a much better view." She swept a claw-like hand through the cold air in front of her, beyond which lay the park, mist blanketing the ground, and last night's rain clinging to the budding branches. In the hazy morning light, it was an ethereal symphony of silver. "And I don't mind the cold so much anymore. You get used to it. How are things at school? Getting any better?"

Seth shrugged, but looked down at his feet. "It's okay, I mean, I'm kind of making friends, but you know, and…I'm new, and my family is…"

"Different," the old woman finished gently. "Kids can be mean about that kind of thing. You know why?"

Seth raised his face to look at her. She said, "It's because they are afraid. They live in a hostile world and they think if they stand out, they'll be picked off. So they try to blend into the crowd, like prairie dogs or wildebeest. If they stay in a pack, and ridicule anyone who doesn't look and behave the same way, they feel safer. It's the nature of humans to form packs, except for the evolved ones, anyway."

The boy nodded, a serious look of consideration on his face. "That's true."

"Choose your friends for their courage, but forgive the ones who have none. What they say is not about you," Fay said sagely, which did not surprise Ellen, whose lifetime of observation had taught her that just because someone was on the street, it didn't mean they weren't smart and sober. "It's about them," Fay continued. "It always is." She sniffed and wiped her nose with a rag. "How's the school work coming?"

"Thelma and Beth are helping me catch up. I was behind, but they got me this tutor. I told them you could teach me, but they said it had to be someone who was 'bonded' so I'd get the credit. Whatever that means."

The older woman chuckled. "It means that the government stamped them on the forehead, '*Approved*!'" she laughed. Then suddenly she spun to her left and shouted. "You don't know that!" There was a short pause, during which Ellen tried to see who was being spoken to, but there was only Seth, who appeared completely unfazed by this outburst. Fay shook her head. "Don't listen to Trey, he doesn't know if pi is a mathematical constant or a dessert."

"Neither do I," Seth admitted.

"I'll explain it to you later," Fay said, sniffing at the banana Seth had given her. "At least *you're* willing to learn." She turned again, and said with exhausted patience, "It doesn't help to put your fingers in your ears, Trey, and I don't care what they say. All their whispering and judging. I *can* teach, I always could and I still can!"

"I need to go, Fay, I have to drop Runt off and get to school," Seth said, preparing to leave.

But Fay was hearing only the unseen presence, and it seemed to be upsetting her. "Not true!" she shrilled. "It's your fault anyway. You're the one who showed up and wouldn't be quiet. *You* scared the kids. I am not crazy!" Increasingly distressed, Fay began to sway, rocking her body from side to side, and holding on to Seth's gifts as though they might be snatched away from her.

"It's okay, Fay. Trey doesn't mean to make you feel bad, he just can't help it. You're the best teacher I ever had," Seth told her. "You have a nice day, okay?"

The old woman turned mistrusting eyes on him, but at the sight of his youthful smile, coherence returned to her eyes and she relaxed. "I will, you go on now, learn everything you can."

"Okay, you want me to call your daughter and let her know where you are? You know Linda worries about you."

"No," Fay drew back. "Linda wants to make me go back to that hospital. They tied me down there. Straps," she whispered fearfully. She began to rock again.

"I'm sorry," Seth told her. "But you know they were trying to help, right?"

Fay's eyes had grown large. She whispered, "They wanted to steal my thoughts. They tried to keep me there, but I know the rules. They can't make me stay unless I hurt somebody, and I never, ever, *ever* did."

"I know," Seth comforted. "I'll see you later, Fay. You take care, okay?"

Fay was nodding and muttering now, placing the three offerings in a row in front of her, first in one order or shape and then another.

With a lingering look of concern, Seth turned away. Ellen started walking again and pretended to just spot him as she came level.

"Ellen, Hi!" Seth called out. "You coming home from work?"

"Yes," she told him, truthfully enough. "Can I walk with you?"

They proceeded without conversation. Both of them had experienced so many unspeakable things that an understanding silence was more companionable than words. When they came to the alley, Ellen asked quietly, "Is that woman your friend?"

Ellen had lived in the shadows of society for so long that the homeless, the forgotten, and the ignored were part of her everyday reality. It was impossible to forget about people who lived on her doorstep and were unwanted and avoided like she had been. As invisible as Ellen had been up until now, she had never been able to make others disappear.

"Fay?" Seth looked up, surprised. "Yep. I met her when I was living in the basement. She helped me out a lot. She used to teach me math, she was a teacher before…she got confused. She even hid me one time when my uncle came looking for me." He grimaced at the memory.

"Does she not have any family?" Ellen was remembering the mention of a daughter.

"Yeah," Seth said. "A daughter, her name is Linda. I met her when she came to try to get Fay to go home with her, but Fay won't go. She doesn't trust Linda." He sighed. "Linda gave me her number in case something happens to Fay. But Fay doesn't trust anybody, she has this imaginary voice that talks to her all the time and makes her think weird. It must be really awful." His young face twisted under his blond bangs, "I mean, to hear voices that aren't there and be afraid all the time, of stuff that isn't even real."

Ellen agreed. "The real stuff is scary enough, especially for people on the street." She waited, and when no response came, she said, "Not that I have to tell you that."

"Oh," Seth tried for unconcerned, "It's not always so bad. I mean, it's hard, but lots of people try to help each other, like Fay helped me, even though they've got nothing. Fay has a friend named Dan who sleeps in the park and goes around and checks on everybody there, even though he's sick." His voice tightened as he observed, "Did you notice that people who have the most walk past and do nothing? And then some people who have nothing try to help everyone." Ellen made no comment though she new exactly what he mean. After all she had witnessed it thousands of times. "Sometimes when I'd look at them, those rich people," Seth said, "I'd think maybe *really* they have less, because they don't care, if you know what I mean. I'm not explaining it so good. That's why I try to share what I have now that I'm lucky."

Guilty warmth spread over Ellen's ample chest. She had been so busy surviving on her own for such a long time, unwanted in foster families and ridiculed in group homes, that it was only recently she'd even become aware that it was important to do for others. Limited things,

things that didn't draw too much attention, but…things. Temerity called it *being of service to others.*

Ellen opened the street door with her key, still on the keychain with the tiny violin Temerity had given her, and they went up the four flights of stairs to the loft.

"Who wants an omelet?" Justice called out as Ellen, Seth, and Runt came in.

"I do!" Seth said. "Man, I'm hungry. Runt wanted to run most of the way."

"Then, Dude," Justice told him, "you earned it."

Ellen nodded her request to Justice and set down her stuff. She watched Seth as he went and sat at the counter with Runt glued to his side. The big dog sat on his haunches, his large head resting on the boy's thigh, and Seth stroked the dog's ears absent-mindedly.

Temerity came out of the hall door.

"Whew!" she said, waving one hand in front of her crinkled-up nose. "Wet dog. Hi Seth, morning Ellen."

"Morning," they chorused, Seth's greeting considerably louder than Ellen's shy reply. Runt barked, not to be left out.

"Guess what day it is?" Justice told his sister.

"Cleaning day, I know, I know. I call the kitchen and bathrooms."

"Done," Justice told her. "And we have to replace some light bulbs." He looked up, way up, at the high, beamed ceiling of the once-industrial space.

"That's on you," Temerity said. "Seeing how I don't use light."

Seth looked up too. "Are you afraid of heights, Temerity?" he asked, watching her curiously. The question was completely without guile.

Temerity laughed. "Nope! I'm one of those people who can look down from any height and be completely unmoved. Now falling? That's scary."

Justice slipped a fat, cheesy omelet with spinach and mushrooms onto a plate and put it in front of Seth. "Eat up, or you'll be late for school."

Seth looked up at the kitchen clock. "It's cool," he said. "I've got forty-five minutes, and it's not far. I don't have to go home, got my stuff with me."

"Do you have your lunch?" Ellen asked, catching Justice's eye and giving a little shake of her head. He picked up on it, frowned, and paused to wait for Seth's answer.

Seth looked down at the huge, healthy breakfast and said. "I've got lots to eat. More than most people."

"Well that doesn't mean you shouldn't take something in case you're hungry later. I'll make you a quick sandwich," Justice said, opening the fridge and looking in. "Roast beef okay?"

The boy's eye's lit up, and he nodded with his mouth full. "Okay then," Justice said. "And, Tem, grab a bag of chips out of the cabinet, will you? You want an apple?"

"I have a…uh…." Ellen watched Seth remember that he had given his away. "Sure," he finished.

Seth wolfed down his omelet and two slices of whole grain toast with jam before Ellen's had barely started hers. Runt followed him to the door, whining his plea for the boy to stay, but Seth rubbed his back and went out.

Temerity turned her face toward Ellen. "What was that about?"

So Ellen told them. "He gave his lunch away to a woman on the street. He said she helped him when he was living in the basement."

Justice shook his head. "What a kid," he said, beaming with pride.

"Her name is Fay, and she has a, uh, imaginary friend."

"Meaning…she hears voices?" Temerity asked with pathos in the words. "She's crazy?"

But Ellen had lived around so many "crazy" people in her urban life that she accepted all kinds of humans as normal. In fact, in all her years of watching and recording what she called "life's little Polaroids," she had found that the crazy people often behaved more sanely than those driven by society's conventions. Though she wouldn't have been able to explain why coherently, it was hard to miss if you paid attention.

"She seemed pretty smart, actually," Ellen said.

"Many schizophrenics are," Justice said.

Ellen was surprised, but Justice knew a lot of things and he was usually right. "I'd say the voices come and go, is what it looked like."

"Wait," Temerity was thinking. "Does she mostly live down by the park, at this end?"

"That's where I've seen her," Ellen confirmed.

"Oh, I've heard her," Temerity exclaimed. "I wondered who she was talking to."

Justice turned to his sister. "Sounds like she could be a borderline case. Someone whom the right medication could really help."

Ellen finished the story, "Seth said Fay has a daughter who wants to help her, and he offered to call her and talk to her. But Fay is afraid of the hospital, she said they tied her down." She left out that Fay had added they wanted to steal her thoughts. It wasn't fair.

Temerity shivered. "Oh, how horrible. Restraints. I can't imagine trying to make someone suffering from irrational paranoia feel safer or saner by strapping them into a bed." The memory of her childhood friend Aaron holding little Lilly that first day of school so that she wouldn't bang her head while she was having a tantrum flashed back. "I know they think it's for their protection, but holy heaven, it would drive me insane if I wasn't already!"

"I think she used to be a teacher. Seth said she taught him math while he was homeless."

"It's beyond understanding how our society discards people with mental disabilities." Justice sighed deeply and shook his head. "I know sometimes people don't want help, or don't trust it, and there's very little we can do about that. You can't *make* people take help they don't trust.

So frustrating, I wish there were more we could do. I'll try to drop off a blanket and some food for her, at least. I'd like to thank her for helping Seth."

Ellen looked at Temerity, and saw from the tilt of her friend's head and the glint in her dark eyes that the wheels were turning. With a tiny smile, Ellen tucked into her breakfast-slash-dinner knowing that if it were in any way possible, this one unfortunate woman would be receiving more help than just a meal and a blanket from the resourceful twins.

Miss Fay was on the list.

15

They had been cleaning for an hour or so when Temerity said casually, "Didn't I hear Amanda say that they sometimes run drug trials for mental patients at the hospital?"

Justice stopped mopping and leaned on the handle to look at her. "Why?" he asked with suspicion. "You interested for yourself?"

"Just curious," she said, and returned to running a dust rag over the shelves, feeling carefully ahead for the objects set on them, mostly books.

Her brother frowned at her. "Tem, I know it's really sad when people need help, like Seth's friend, and the very thing they are suffering from keeps them from getting that help. We don't know this Fay or her story. For all we know, she's perfectly aware that help is out there and chooses not to get it."

"But that's the point, Justice!" Temerity exclaimed. "Like you said, it's the symptoms themselves that are preventing her from getting help. She is probably experiencing irrational fear of treatment that could be alleviated with the proper medication!"

"And what should we do about that?" Justice asked her.

"It wouldn't hurt to find out her story," Temerity said.

"Tem," Justice cautioned. "We don't know anything about this woman."

"We know she helped Seth. If his uncle had found him, he would have gone back to…that life."

Justice couldn't argue that, and the truth of it left him feeling like someone was running a cheese grater down the back of his neck. He returned to mopping but kept a thoughtful eye on his twin. What could it hurt? He knew that Temerity would feel better if she could focus on somebody else right now, so, although he usually discouraged her propensity for getting involved in problems that didn't belong to her, he did not come right out and say so this time. Careful to show only lukewarm interest, he asked, "Did Seth say that he knew where this lady, uh, Fay's daughter, lives?"

Her head snapped around, but a triumphant smile danced on Temerity's lips. "No, but he said he has her phone number."

"Fine, I'll ask him if we can go talk to her. But don't do anything before then!"

Tossing the rag into the bucket on her arm, Temerity carried it to the kitchen, careful not to slip on the wet floor. "I'm hungry," she said, "We've been doing this for four hours. Let's go get lunch."

Justice glanced at the oven clock and then shrugged. "I could order something in."

"No, I want to take you to this cool, new place I found. It's a few blocks away." She told him about Geoff's restaurant and described the food. She did not explain how she had first met Geoff distributing empathy gratis at the street fair.

"Oh," Justice said, "I noticed that place, it looks homey."

"I think that's the idea. I'll go clean up. We can take Runt, he can sit outside."

"Is there a place to put him where we can keep an eye on him?"

Temerity stopped halfway across the room and put one finger to her lips as if thinking really hard. "I didn't see any."

"So fifty-fifty chance. Meet you back here in five."

Runt was delighted to be out midday, an unusual treat for him. He feinted and pulled against his leash to the accompaniment of Justice's constant intoning to calm down and be good. This collection of sounds from his human, experienced in the fullness of delight, meant that something was going right for Runt, so he kept it up.

"Maybe we'd better take Runt for a run before we tie him up on the sidewalk." Justice suggested. Tem agreed, so they detoured to the dog park, where they could let him off the leash to run like a crazy dog for ten minutes. When he finally returned to collapse at their feet, Justice laughed. "That ought to do it. Come on, buddy," and he refastened his leash and turned to leave the way they had come.

"Let's go out the other way," Temerity said, pulling his arm to indicate the far side of the enclosed area. "We can walk by the pond."

Justice squinted his eyes at his sister, but he didn't object. Though he took a firmer hold on the leash when they passed the lazy ducks standing on one leg in the weak sunshine, the dog was too worn out to do more than waffle at them.

As they approached the row of apartments and industrial buildings that lined that end of the park, Temerity kept one ear cocked. Justice watched her, amused that she thought she was being subtle. Still, it wasn't long before they heard the stream of a one-sided conversation.

"Trey, you're a little liar, you know that?" a woman's voice was saying. Temerity slowed, and then changed direction slightly toward the sound. "You keep that up and you won't have any friends. Oh, just see if I don't!"

"Is that Fay, you think?" Temerity whispered when they drew level.

Justice studied the woman's face, creased with dirt. With a start, he realized she was only maybe forty-five. And there was something almost familiar about her, though the crazy hair and the mud-smeared clothes did not match up to any of the flash cards in his memory. She was sitting on a bench in the sun, a few belongings in bags beside her. There was a half-eaten sandwich, the remains of Seth's lunch he guessed, lying on wax paper next to her. In her gnarled hand was a formidable-looking book.

"Go on, just go then!" The woman shouted at the air. "And good riddance!" There was a short pause and then, as she turned back to her tome, she added, "Trey, wait! Don't wander too far off, you know you hate to be alone when it starts to get dark."

Before he could stop her, Temerity let go of Justice's arm and stepped up. "Fay?" she called out.

Justice watched Fay's face snap around, but she looked less suspicious than curious. "Who wants to know?"

"My name is Temerity, a friend of Seth's. He told me you helped him when he was living in the basement of our building."

"Temerity?" Fay laughed, almost a cackle. "A likely name. Are your parents hippies?"

"Kind of," Temerity said. "They're psychiatrists."

There was a nervous shuffling. "Psychiatrists. I don't care for them much, but at least they're well educated."

"Years of it!" Temerity moved forward carefully. "This is my brother Justice."

Before Justice could say "hello" there was a second loud laugh from Fay. "Another one!" she guffawed. "Ooh, that's a good one. *Justice.* I quite like that."

"I'm so pleased you find my name amusing," Justice said. "Anything for a laugh. Hello."

"Hello, Justice. Wait a minute." The woman rocked forward on the bench and stared first at the brother and then the sister. "I remember that crazy name. Justice. I know you," she pointed her fingers, locked together in a curl, at Justice, "I think I had you in a class I substituted for at Franklin Middle, teacher was out with a severe case of pregnancy for a couple of weeks, but you were a little snot-nose then."

"I still carry Kleenex," Justice said solemnly.

Another laugh came from Fay, and Temerity said, "Wait, what?"

"And I remember you too," Justice said. "You're Ms. Woods. You taught algebra, you used songs. I still remember that."

"And you," Fay said, turning to Temerity. "You're the blind one who walks around all the time, you have that friend who is nice and fat like me, not a twig like you two."

Temerity opened her mouth to say that neither fat nor twig were very nice ways to describe someone, though of course it didn't matter to her, but feeling the restraining pressure of Justice's hand on her arm, she amended her statement. "That's my friend Ellen, she's full-figured, true."

"You need to have some flesh on you for winter. I don't know how you scrawny people endure it."

"Everyone has a cross to bear," Justice said, "Ours is a high metabolism. So, you doing okay today?"

Fay answered sharply, "Why wouldn't I be?"

"Oh, because it sounded like someone was giving you a hard time. I think you called him Trey? I don't remember him in middle school. Was he around then?"

Fay pursed her lips, thrusting them out in a pout and drawing them back in again several times before she answered. "No." She stared at Justice. "He showed up. Uninvited, I might add," she shouted over her shoulder to where, presumably, Trey had been banished, "He's not so bad for company." But one side of her face twitched convulsively as she said it. "Won't shut up for five minutes. Sometimes when I need to think. It's hard to listen when someone is always talking. Always telling me it's my fault. Everything is my fault." Her hands twitched.

"Does he ever leave you alone?" Temerity asked.

There was a long sigh from the bench. "Not any more," Fay said.

"Well, we're going to lunch. You want us to bring you something, Fay?" Justice asked, as though speaking to an office mate.

"Nope, I'm good. Got a feast right here," Fay patted the sandwich.

"Maybe we could—" Temerity began, but Justice cut her off with, "—stop by later! Great idea. We'll see you, Fay." He began to pull Temerity away.

"Hold it," Fay said sharply, and they both paused. "I know that dog. Why do you have Seth's dog?"

"Seth walks him for us. His name is Runt."

Justice watched the woman's face slip from suspicion to something resembling pleasure. "These names," she muttered, shaking her head. Then she picked up a crust of the sandwich and tossed it with her bowed hand, it arced through the air and Runt snatched it with a slobbery snap. "So it is," she said, and returned to her book.

Justice pulled Temerity along and when they were out of earshot he said, "I think that was enough for today."

"How come you get to decide?" she asked sourly.

"Because I'm a doctor."

"Of *anthropology*," Temerity snorted.

"True enough," he agreed easily. "And let's remember that, though I can't prescribe drugs, I am an expert in human behavior. The first thing we need to do is get her evaluated. First, let's ask Amanda about the drug trial and how it works. If Fay could just pick up the drug, not have to spend time at the hospital, she might be more willing to try it. But the whole point of a drug 'trial' is to monitor the results."

"You think Seth could get her to go?" Temerity asked.

"More likely than us. I think we need to get Trey in on this."

"Don't be a jerk."

Justice stopped and squeezed her hand. "For once, I'm not. I'm being serious. I need to do some research, but it looks like what she's dealing with is a fully-formed delusion. A constant companion she's created. He's as real to her as you are to me."

"And that means?" Temerity prompted.

"She trusts him, or she trusts his constancy anyway."

"Well, she certainly listens to him," Temerity agreed.

"Exactly."

16

The restaurant was crowded with faces and happy chatter. There was a long row of picture windows, outside of which was a small seating area made comfortable in the cool weather with overhead heaters. The siblings took a table outside, tying Runt's leash to the outside of a low wrought iron railing that separated the seating area from the sidewalk.

The oblivious server offered a menu to Temerity, but Justice told her they only needed one. Clearly befuddled, the server blinked twice, and her eyes shifted from him to Temerity with cartoon timing while the menu hovered in her hand. Temerity told her if they had the menu on tape, she'd be glad to hear it. "Or you could do a dramatic reading. You are an actress, right?"

"How did you know?" The young woman's blue eyes, heavy with false eyelashes, were wide with delight, and Justice knew that for an amusing second the server thought his sister had seen her in something.

"Oh, just a guess, good luck with that!" Temerity said cheerfully. The server thanked her and went away.

"So, what's good?" Justice asked as he suppressed a smile and perused the menu.

"I've only tried one thing. What kind of soup do they have today? The tomato bisque was amazing."

Justice read her the soups and specials off the board. Then he went quickly through the menu, skipping over the few items he knew she didn't care for.

"Chicken pot pie and curried carrot soup," Temerity said, as soon as he'd finished. Justice decided on the mushroom pasta special, and they were both putting cream in their tea when Geoff arrived with a dish of water and a milk bone for Runt.

"Nice to see you again," he said to Temerity. "Hey buddy," he patted Runt's head as he fed him the treat.

"Oh, hi Geoff!" Temerity turned his direction. "This is my brother, Justice. Justice, this is Geoff, he's the owner."

The two men shook hands, both of them sizing each other up in a friendly way.

"You're busy today," Temerity commented.

"For which, I am very grateful," the silver-haired, fifty-something Geoff answered with a smile. Justice watched him. He was used to his gregarious sister being on speaking terms with people in shops and restaurants, but he could see that there was something a little different here. A kind of understanding, almost… fondness. He watched for signs of romantic interest, but he didn't see any.

"How do you guys know each other?" Justice asked.

"New friends," Temerity said. "We met at the street fair, and we…uh…had a great talk. He told me about the restaurant and I came in the other day. Killer tomato bisque, by the way, Geoff."

"Thank you. The secret is finding ripe tomatoes. We roast them on big pans with whole cloves of garlic and sprigs of rosemary, drizzled in olive oil."

Justice let the menu drop to the table. "That settles it. I'm having that, and the pasta special."

Geoff laughed. "I'll send over your server. I have to get back to the office, our bookkeeper turned out to be bad at accounting, or good at light embezzling, depending on your point of view. So, I'm having to audit the last six months personally until I can find someone I can trust."

"Sounds labor intensive," Justice commiserated.

"And not particularly interesting, or entertaining," Geoff said with a sigh. "Well, enjoy your meal. Great to see you both." Geoff made his way back toward the door, pausing to speak to other tables on the way.

Justice studied his sister, who was sitting with her eyes half-closed as she listened to the chatter and clink of cutlery around her. "So you and Geoff just 'struck up a conversation?'" he asked.

"Yes, and you can drop that suggestive tone, it's not like he offered me candy and lured me into the back of a panel van. He was one of the vendors."

"Oh, you mean the restaurant has a booth?"

"Not exactly," Temerity said. "He wasn't actually selling anything."

Justice frowned. "A vendor with nothing to sell?"

"Nope. He was giving it away."

That made more sense. "Oh, promoting the restaurant, you mean. Good idea actually."

"No," Temerity was enjoying toying with him. "He didn't actually mention the restaurant until the end of the conversation. Which, to be fair, was not so much of a conversation as a monologue. Mostly, I talked and he was encouraging. It was very helpful to get a few things off my chest."

"So, he's what? An amateur therapist?"

"Mmm, no. More like a professional listener."

"Isn't that the same thing?"

Temerity laughed. Her dad had often told them that a good therapist let the patient talk out their own problems, he just listened and nudged them along in the right direction. Of course, he was being modest. Andy was an exceptionally good psychiatrist. "If you must know, he was giving out free empathy, to anyone who needed to vent. Personally, I think that if he decided to charge, he could make a good living off it."

"I can see how such a service would be in great demand." Justice took a cautious sip of the steaming tea, which smelled faintly of orange and cardamom. "I think it's why hairdressers get such good tips. So, what did you talk about?"

"That's between me and my empathy dealer." Temerity answered lightly, but he could see her reluctance to tell him, so he let it go.

" What's up for your date tonight?" he asked instead.

Temerity colored and crossed her arms over her chest. "Well, it's more like a friend thing, you know."

"Mmm, mmm." Justice hummed knowingly. "Does Hugo know that?"

"It's none of your business anyway," Temerity told him sharply.

Justice softened. "Sorry, Tem, I know. Hugo seems cool, though." He played with his knife and spoon, lining them up parallel. "He certainly has been persistent."

"And you think that's a good thing?" his sister asked.

"Well, it's better than—" Justice realized what he was about to say and switched quickly to, "—not."

But Temerity had spent her whole life reading her brother's voice. Her mouth tightened and she said quietly, "You were going to say it was better than Dennis."

"Dennis was a dick," Justice said with feeling. "I'm just sorry I didn't punch his lights out."

"Oh, that's very manly," Temerity retorted. Her tone was playful, but her lips had flat-lined.

Justice had wanted to talk to his sister about this for a long time. At first, after he had caught Dennis actually making out with another girl at a party when Temerity, his date, was in the other room, he thought it would be enough to expose Dennis and get him out of his sister's life, trusting that her natural buoyancy would help her snap back. But in the following months, he had seen the residual effects of that betrayal. Being cheated on was hard enough for anyone, but Temerity had taken it as a humiliation and turned it into a relationship roadblock. She hadn't given another guy a honest chance since then. Still, he wondered if there wasn't more to it than just feeling reluctant to open herself up to someone new.

"You know," he began, "just because one guy was a total dick doesn't mean we're all like that."

"You better not be," Temerity said. "Amanda and I will have to kill you. Fratricide is a very ancient and respected religious tradition, you know."

"Yes, you mentioned that before. I'm familiar with Christian mythology, thank you."

"You're welcome."

"But you're an atheist. Tem, listen. It's been well over a year since you dated anyone. It makes me mad to think that you let that weak asshole make you afraid," Justice said before he thought it out.

Temerity jerked as though she'd been slapped. "I am not afraid," she said through clenched teeth.

"Okay, okay, I'm sorry. I didn't mean that. But, I don't know what to think."

Temerity relaxed a little, reaching out to touch the table and familiarize herself with the placement of her cup and silverware. "It's okay. I just haven't met anybody I'm interested in. It's…well, it's not the same for me."

"I know," Justice said, almost on top of her statement. "Everything is a little different for you, but Tem, everything is a little different for everyone. You want to know something I never told you?"

"*Is* there something you never told me?" Temerity feigned surprise.

"Just the one thing, smart ass." He shifted his chair to straighten it, and said, "It took me six months to get up the nerve to ask Amanda out."

"So, you were afraid of her," Temerity taunted.

"No! I mean, well, yeah, kind of. Afraid she'd turn me down, let's put it that way."

In spite of her efforts to hold on to a façade of indifference, Temerity couldn't keep real curiosity out of her voice when she asked, "So what made you finally do it?"

Justice drew in a deep breath through his nostrils and exhaled it the same way. "The way she scrunched up her face when she thought no one was looking at her. One day, at the library, I was watching her, and her hair was all crazy and she was chewing on a pencil, scowling at some massive medical textbook, and I couldn't take it anymore. I knew if I didn't go and talk to her, I'd always regret it."

Temerity tilted her head. "I don't know how Hugo looks, scowling or otherwise."

"I know," her brother said. "But you have always been able to find out how people truly *are*. You choose friends for their real worth. Honestly, I've always envied you for that."

"You do the same thing!" Temerity insisted.

"With friends yes, and girlfriends eventually, thank God. But to be honest, a pretty face can be misleading. You remember Cathy? That girl I dated last year?" He grimaced.

"Oh yeah, one of the beautifuls."

"The beautiful bitch. She was horrible to people, including me, and I put up with it for a month before I came to my senses. I wouldn't have done that if she weren't so attractive."

"I did wonder about that. It was a mystery to me what you saw in that selfish shrew. I'm not so easily distracted. Lucky me," Temerity drawled.

"In a way, yes," Justice said. "You are a good judge of people and you know it. It's okay if it takes a little longer to decide. That's just smart."

"So chalk up my romantic dry spell to keen intelligence."

They were interrupted by the delivery of their soups. After the server had hovered for a moment, clearly intrigued by her unusual patron, she realized she'd forgotten the breadbasket and hurried off to retrieve it. Justice asked, "Tem, is that all it is? Are you afraid someone new, maybe Hugo, will cheat on you?"

"No," Temerity said. "I'll admit I'm not eager to be publicly ridiculed like that again, not fun, but it's more than that. Let's not talk about it."

"Let's do."

"Jus, please. Okay fine. I've come to the conclusion that I'm not meant to be in a relationship. I'm not saying that because I'm sorry for myself. You know that. I'm saying it because, I mean, what kind of relationship could I have that didn't condemn someone to having to take care of me?"

"So, you think of yourself as a life sentence?"

Temerity huffed, trying to find the words to explain this private feeling for which she had little shared vocabulary. "No. But…think about it. For instance, can you imagine me having a family?"

"Well, honestly no. But that's because you're my little sister, not because you're blind."

"I'm five minutes younger than you, and how the hell would I be able to care for a baby?"

"Tem, that's silly. Lot's of people with disses have families." Long ago, the two of them had shortened the insulting term, *disabilities* to *disses*.

"Don't tell me I'm silly. That's insulting. And I know they do. Good for them. Now let's eat, I've got rehearsal in an hour."

Justice let it drop, but he couldn't help feeling that the remarkable woman sitting across from him, who he had never known to be afraid of anything, was hiding something. Or perhaps she was hiding *from* something.

17

Temerity had afternoon rehearsal, which was good because spending it stressing about her impending evening with Hugo would have been exhausting. As soon as she arrived at the music hall, she went in search of Regan.

"Temerity, hi!" she heard the shorter woman say from a few feet away as she approached the door to the rehearsal hall. "I'm so sorry about all that trouble the other day. Thanks again for being so great."

"No problem," Temerity said, reaching out a hand and waiting until Regan clasped it. "Any further adventures?"

Regan laughed, and Temerity was relieved to hear that she sounded so much calmer, and her laugh genuine. "Nothing from Simon the psycho ex, but staying with Terrance is an adventure. That man can cook!"

"I know," Temerity told her. "I've been to a party at his house. My date sucked fish balls but the crab cakes were divine!"

"Why did your date suck?" Regan asked, politely omitting the elaboration.

"What I should have said was that he sucked face with someone else. Justice caught him, it wasn't a pretty scene, but it was a big one." She sobered a little. "But seriously, you haven't heard from Simon? That's good, right? Do you think maybe he'll leave you alone this time?"

Regan puffed out a breath and said, "I hope so. I've almost got the paperwork done to dissolve the marriage, but he still has to be served, and I have no idea where he lives."

Temerity said grimly. "I'm not sure if that's a good thing or a bad thing."

They shared a nervous laugh. "So Terrance wants to have a, what did he call it? Oh, a *soiree* after the concert on Sunday, can you come?"

"Sounds like fun," Temerity said. "Can I bring my brother if he gets a night off from his fiancé?"

"Bring them both if you like, Terrance said I can invite anyone I want. Big change from my last roommate," she added wryly. "Simon used to freak out if I went to lunch with a girlfriend."

"That *may* have been a red flag," Temerity suggested gently.

"A red flag with flashing neon letters spelling out 'run away!'" Regan agreed, going one better with a shiver in her voice. "God, I just want this all to be over."

Temerity squeezed Regan's hand. "It will pass. Sooner or later, he'll move on."

"In the meantime," Regan said, "I'm living in international gourmet heaven!"

"Score!" Temerity called out, her voice echoing down the hallway.

"Who scored?" Asked a deep voice from a foot above Temerity.

"Oh, hi Terrance," Temerity said, "Regan was telling me about your soiree on Sunday. Is it okay if I bring Justice?"

"*Please* do," Terrance said with a licentious growl, and Temerity smiled. She knew her brother was attractive to both women and men, and she teased him about it often. It didn't bother Justice in the least that men hit on him, he merely pointed out that while it was always nice to be admired, sometimes one chose to be admired from a few feet away.

Temerity said, "By the way, Justice got engaged."

Regan said, "Oh, congratulations! You'll have a sister-in-law. I hope you like her."

"I do," Temerity said, wondering why she still felt that jagged twinge in her chest and hating herself for it.

"Whew," Regan said, "that's lucky. I've got to grab my flute from my locker, see you guys in there!"

Temerity had started to turn toward the doorway when Terrance put a hand on her arm to detain her. "So, he's engaged. Good for Justice," he said. And then he leaned closer and asked softly, "And how do *you* feel about that?"

Temerity considered, then turned her face up toward him and said, "Great…and… if I'm completely honest, irrationally terrified."

She could almost feel the wind of his nodding head. "I hear you. It's weird to bring somebody new into the family. When my brother got married, I kept thinking it was just surreal, having this interloper at our family gatherings, but I got used to them as a matched set. You two are closer than most sibs. Is she moving in or is he moving out?"

Temerity shrugged, but she felt a cold blush numb her face. "Don't know, I wouldn't think he would stay. Not much fun being newlyweds if your sister is tripping over you in her underwear."

"Well," a strong hand landed on the back of her neck and massaged for a moment, "If you want to talk, I'm around. Is she a doctor too, by the way?"

"Of medicine!" Temerity twisted a bit so that Terrance's strong fingers would knead a particular knot. "Oh, yeah baby," she said, "Right there. That's the spot."

Terrance, who had been friends with the twins for three years, laughed. "That means every one of your immediate family went to at least eight years of college, and has letters after their name. Impressive."

"It's not as impressive as you think once you've been around them trying to get the lumps out of the gravy at Christmas."

Terrance laughed. "Uh oh, there's the Maestro, we'd better go in."

Rupert was already in his chair tuning up his cello and he whispered a greeting to Temerity as she sat and pulled out her violin. They worked on the new piece first, Anton calling out subtle directions and changes to various musicians, as though he could hear each instrument playing a solo. After the first hour, they all stood for a ten-minute break. Leaving her violin in its case, Temerity unfolded her stick and started for the restrooms in the hall.

But they were locked. Joanne, the French horn player, called out, "Plumbing trouble. Sign says to use the public bathrooms upstairs." Her heels clicked off down the hallway.

When the elevator doors slid open to the lobby, Temerity could feel the tone of the carpeted space as a muted softness compared to the harsher surfaces in the catacombs below. She stepped out and detected the high-pitched whine of a vacuum on the far side of the vast room with the sweeping staircase. She turned left and went on, following the curve of the lobby's wall as it arced behind the audience seating. She found the restroom door, checked the braille on the sign, just to be double sure it was the ladies', and went in.

It had been cleaned recently and the sharp scent of pine disinfectant made her nose wrinkle. She heard no one else in the large restroom. Choosing the nearest stall, she went in and leaned her stick against the corner. The lobby door swung open again, and she assumed it was one of the other orchestra members. She finished up and retrieved her stick, then went out to wash her hands.

As she crossed the tiled floor, she swept the stick left and right, a second-nature movement that confirmed nothing stood in her path. She had taken a few confident steps when her right ankle struck against something and she pitched forward, throwing her hands out in confusion, Temerity was vaguely aware of a change in scent to something stronger than detergent, something closer to diesel exhaust, and then her head hit the counter.

"Ow!" she exclaimed, using both her hands to cover the sharp pain on her forehead and letting her stick clatter to the floor. The room was still silent except for the hum of climate control for a moment and then the door opened and shut again. The air rushing in from the lobby carried a stronger whiff of that harsh fuel scent.

"Hello?" Temerity called. "Is anyone here?"

But there was no answer except for the whoosh of the door swinging shut.

Temerity found the paper towel dispenser and soaked one in cold water, then pressed it to her aching head. Feeling the spot gingerly with her fingers, she detected tenderness, but no rising bump. She explored the area where she had tripped and found nothing, then left the restroom cautiously, staying against the wall instead of crossing the middle of the floor.

The lobby was still when she went out. The vacuum cleaner had stopped and Temerity stood still for a minute listening for signs of anyone else. She heard shuffling on the carpeted floor behind her and spun around.

"Temerity, are you okay? You look startled." It was Regan.

"I'm fine," Temerity said. "I just tripped over my own feet in the restroom, I guess, smacked my head. How does it look?"

She felt Regan's hands on her shoulders as the smaller woman stood on tiptoe to examine her injury. "A little red, but it looks okay. Do you want some ice?"

"No, I'll be fine," Temerity remembered the particular smell, the restroom door opening, and asked, "Regan, is there anyone else in the lobby?"

"Uh, no, I mean, one of the cleaners is on the upper level. And there's a maintenance guy working on something. They have a panel off the wall."

"Do you know them?" Temerity asked.

"Don't think so, no wait, I do know the cleaner, I've seen him before. The other guy, no. He's all the way at the far side of the balcony level with his back to us. I don't think one of ours, probably a repair guy. Why?" The lobby was huge, the second level taking up about a third of the floor space of the main level.

"Oh, just curious. You know, sometimes I need a friend to fill in the blanks."

Regan laughed. "Well, if you wait a minute, I'll walk back down with you." She went into the restroom. Temerity debated whether or not to share her fears with her friend, and decided not to burden her. It was so nice to hear her happy.

Further down along the wall, Temerity heard the elevator open and the easy chatter of two of her fellow orchestra members as they headed toward the restrooms. Emboldened, Temerity made her way across the open floor until she came to the wide staircase. Pausing to get her bearings, she went up, her walking shoes almost silent on the carpet.

At the top, she stopped, turning her head to listen. She could make out the jangle of a cleaning cart being rolled away from her on the far side of the mezzanine level. The smell of brass polish and that lingering scent of burning dust from the now-quiet vacuum pervaded the air. Closer at hand, the sound of a tool being used on machinery sounded with a rachet-like repetition. She started in that general direction.

"Excuse me?" Temerity called.

There was no answer, but she could tell from the cessation of movement that the person had heard her.

"I'm sorry to bother you, but did you happen to see someone come out of the ladies' room a couple of minutes ago?"

A muttered deep voice, lightly accented, said, "I don't see nobody."

"Oh, well, thanks anyways." She smiled, and turned to go, but as she moved away from the railing, the strong scent of brass cleanser faded and she smelled something else. *Fuel.* Putting one hand on the railing of the stairway and taking a firm grip, Temerity spoke again. "I don't know if we've met, I'm Temerity."

"Raul," the gruff voice replied.

"Nice to meet you, Raul. Have you worked here long?"

"No. Sorry, I have to work now." Temerity listened to the clink of tools being replaced in a metal box and waited as the rattle receded as he walked away before she descended the grand stairwell, following its sweeping curve until it opened onto the wide expanse of floor. Normally, she loved this room and sense of grandness it gave her, but today, its very volume left her feeling exposed and very small.

18

Hugo knocked at seven o'clock. Temerity felt her nerves register a small seismic tremor, but she shook her head and hands to get some of the tension off of her, much like a dog sheds pond water after a muddy swim, and went to open it.

"Hi," Hugo said. "Ready?" Runt sniffed at his legs and wagged his tail. Hugo bent down to pet him.

"Do I look ready?" Temerity asked, not altogether as a joke.

"You look great. How about me? I was worried I was wearing too much makeup."

Temerity laughed and said, "I'm sure you look divine. Or maybe you look like Divine." Temerity had no idea what the actress had looked like, and when she got no answer, she wondered if she'd misunderstood the reference or Hugo had no idea who she was talking about. "Wasn't she a famous drag queen?"

"She was. She died, but I think she went on to become the Patron Saint of cross-dressers and glitter-infused beauty products."

"That's fascinating," Temerity told him, "Would she have been canonized by the church of latter-day interior designers?"

"Special dispensation by the Bishop Fabulous." Hugo was smiling. Temerity could hear it.

"Have we got time for a glass of wine before we...do whatever it is we're doing?"

"We are going to a show," he told her. "It starts at eight, so we could do wine, or if you're hungry I was thinking we could grab a falafel at this great stand on the way, and then we'll get dinner afterwards—the show's only about an hour long."

Temerity could feel her face redden, and she turned away to grab her coat. A show, she thought with a falling sensation. She just hoped it was a musical one. She'd been dragged to plays by seeing-dates or well-meaning friends, and it always ended up being uncomfortable, more for them than for Temerity, who pretended not to be bored. Unlike movies, explanatory whispers were not an option in live theater.

"I vote for falafel," she said, cheerfully covering her disappointment.

They went down to the street. Temerity kept her stick folded and held Hugo's arm. He was a comfortable height for her, about three inches taller, and when they started down the street, she matched his longer stride with easy effort.

"How was rehearsal?" Hugo asked her.

Temerity opened her mouth to say "fine" but didn't get it out. Instead she rubbed her fingers over the sore spot on her forehead and decided to get Hugo's opinion of the event. "Strange, actually. My friend Regan has this scary husband who won't give her a divorce, and the other day he got into the building somehow and confronted her. He actually hit her."

Temerity felt the curve of the muscles in Hugo's arm tense suddenly. "Uncool," he said in a low, angry voice.

"Right? So anyway, Regan went to stay with another musician, a friend of ours named Terrance, so she's safe. But a weird thing did happen today." She told him about tripping in the restroom, about the door opening and closing though no one answered when she called out, and she had been sure she was alone when she was putting water on her head. "The funny thing is," Temerity told him, "that I thought I recognized Regan's husband Simon from the scent in the room, something like gasoline. But when I went back out to the lobby, the only hint of that scent was from a maintenance guy all the way at the other end of the mezzanine level, and he was in the middle of a mechanical repair with a power tool when I got to him and he said his name was Raul. Obviously, someone who works in maintenance could smell like gasoline, they do use blowers and generators, and this Raul had a different voice from Regan's Simon, deeper, and with an accent. Maybe I'm just being paranoid. It wouldn't be the first time I've tripped over my own feet."

They strode along for a few more paces, turned a corner onto a quieter, tree-lined street, Temerity could tell from the rustle of leaves overhead and the occasional softness of those that had fallen on the sidewalk. Hugo asked, "So you can recognize pretty much anyone?"

"If I know them, yes, usually from their scent. There are lots of ways that I can tell who someone is. Everyone has their own smell, sometimes that gets confused if they wear a different cologne, ate a lot of garlic, or didn't shower." She wrinkled her nose. "I'm not sure how visually recognizing something works, but I can 'see' voices. They are all distinct. I mean, as long as I don't know them too well, like Justice, and they don't use a fake one. Oh, and people's walks and breathing patterns are very different too. When I first met Ellen, she had these shoes with a loose sole, so they made a flipping sound, and she shuffles, drags her right foot more than her left. People with allergies are easy."

"How do I sound?" Hugo asked, sounding amused at the moment.

She thought about it. "Like you have a strong foundation, that's your steady breath, but flexible too, that's your underlying humor and the way you bounce on your toes sometimes when you stand still. You sound…" Temerity searched for the word. She wanted to say 'easy' but she was too embarrassed by the sexual connotation. "Comfortable," she chose instead.

"I sound like a *recliner*?" Hugo asked.

Temerity laughed. "Yes! You sound laid back and upholstered in something tasteful."

"Well, as long as there's a pocket for the remote. Oh, here we are," Hugo pulled up. Temerity knew they were in Theatre Square. She could hear the dancing fountain and the chatter of happy people at the outdoor bar. Her heart bobbed again, sinking and surfacing, a play. Oh well. Maybe it was a musical, or Shakespeare, or Pinter. With some playwrights, the language and rhythm were so beautiful it was almost as good as reading or listening to music.

They went in, Temerity sensing the temperature and sound change as they entered the small lobby. An usher showed them to their seats and Temerity cocked her head, listening to the small crowd shedding coats, rustling programs, and settling in. Then a magnified voice said. "Ladies and gentlemen, welcome to the broadcast of *A Murder at Midnight*. We'll be on the air in about five minutes, so I would like to introduce you to the cast."

Temerity turned toward Hugo and asked with delight, "A radio show?"

"Love 'em," he said. "I have a collection of old recordings. I especially love the mysteries. I bought a little second-hand keyboard when I was ten so I could make all the sound effects. I used to produce shows with my brother. It's how I got interested in music."

"Were your shows any good?" Temerity asked.

"They were terrible. Lots of monsters attacking school buses and Nazi spies pretending to be English teachers. Fortunately, this is on a different level."

"Is this a regular thing?" Temerity asked hopefully.

"About once a month. There's a company of actors who rotate parts, but they bring in names sometimes." He fell quiet as the announcer introduced the cast, which did in fact include a fairly well-known film actress.

Then there was applause and then the announcer said, "Quiet please. And we are live in five, four, three…" two and one remained unspoken, and then the sound of organ music and wind as the announcer said, "Welcome to *Murder at Midnight*. We take you now to the Smithfield Inn in Vermont on a blustery January night."

As Temerity sat, charmed by the voices and the mystery, she found herself falling more and more into this other world, until she was clutching the velvet of the theatre seat with both hands, and when a shot rang out, she actually grabbed Hugo's arm in alarm. He covered her hand, and then took it into his. From that point, Temerity's attention was divided between the story and the warmth of his touch, which was distracting in a good way. Hugo's hands were strong, as any pianist's would be, but they felt graceful as well, long-fingered, and steady as he stroked his thumb across the top of her hand. She couldn't stop herself from wondering how that touch would feel on her body, smooth and capable, and she shifted in her seat, reminding herself that this was only a trial date. In spite of her trepidation, Temerity found herself leaning a bit more into his shoulder, breathing in his subtle but spicy scent of black pepper and pine needles.

Back out on the street, Hugo, who still had her hand, asked, "What did you think?"

"It was wonderful!" she enthused. "It was like we were right in the room! I've heard radio programs before, of course, but being there somehow made it more…"

"…like you're there, I know. I wondered how it would be for you. You can understand why people used to pay to go to these performances, even though the actors are just standing in front of a microphone. So, what do you want to eat?" He wrapped her hand under his arm and pulled her closer as they circumnavigated a noisy group of teenagers in front of a coffee shop.

Temerity didn't answer. She could feel the cool mist of fog on her face and the snuggling heat of Hugo's body against her arm, and she was enjoying it too much for it to end. She wanted to walk for a while, still feeling the thrill of the adventure they'd shared and the sensation of walking in the city with someone who was looking out for her, so that her senses were free to roam and discover.

"How about The Den?" Hugo suggested. "It's new."

"Oh, I love that place, I know the owner, Geoff, and it's far enough to enjoy a nice walk. Can we go via the park?"

"Is there a better way?" he asked, and Temerity knew that he didn't mean better as in faster or straighter, which it wasn't, he meant better as in more pleasant to the senses. She felt the click of their common preference slotting into place and smiled.

They were near the duck pond when Temerity heard a woman's pleading voice. "Mom, please come in tonight. It's cold out here. I promise you, I won't take you anywhere else, no one but Joey and I will be there. Please, mom." She sounded earnest, but exhausted, there was the sense that these words had been said so many times and gotten the same reaction so often, that it was madness for her to expect a different one.

"Wait," Temerity whispered to Hugo. "What do you see?"

Hugo looked over to the bench where a woman, obviously homeless, lay sprawled on some cardboard. Near her was a younger woman in an inexpensive down jacket. She was the one who had been pleading. She shifted her feet, stomping at the cold ground, which would be covered in silver frost by morning, and dug her hands further into her coat pockets.

Hugo positioned himself and Temerity as though they were looking out over the lake, in which the lights from the far shore danced a mambo on the rapid beat of waves produced by the fountain in the center.

In a quiet voice he said, "Two women, the older one of them looks set for the night on a bench, and the younger one isn't happy about that. I think she might be the other woman's daughter."

Temerity made an unhappy sound. "Can you imagine? How horrible to have someone in your family lose it enough to choose the street."

"Can't she just have her committed? Or, I don't know, something?" Hugo asked with pathos.

"Apparently not," Temerity told him. "Unless Fay hurts herself or someone else, there's nothing her family, or anyone, can do, apparently. Not without a lot of money anyway. We're talking about state laws here, I think. That's Fay, by the way, she used to be a teacher, and her daughter Linda, whom I haven't met yet."

Hugo looked at his date's scheming face with his eyebrows raised, but Temerity missed it.

Fay was talking. "I'm not going back to that horrible place, Linda. You lied to me before, and you're trying to trick me now."

"Mom, I'm not. I swear. I just want you to sleep in a warm bed, and have a bath and a good meal. You don't have to be afraid."

"The hell I don't," snapped Fay. "Trey told me how you've been plotting to have me put away. They want to make me eat electricity in that place! It burns."

Hugo watched as the younger woman pulled her hands from her pockets and buried her face in them. "Mom, please," she moaned, close to breaking. "You know Trey doesn't exist, he's just a delusion."

Fay came up off the bench. "How dare you! He warned me you would say that. He's the only one who stays with me."

"Mom, I have a kid, I can't stay with you out here. You know that. Please. I have to get home, I had to leave Joey alone. Please come with me."

Hugo could see pain and frustration streaking the woman Linda's face. He whispered his impressions to Temerity, who set her mouth in a grim, thoughtful pout and waited patiently.

"I'm not going! Shut up, Trey, I already told her!" Fay shouted over her shoulder.

"Mom…" Linda trailed off, her shoulders slumping despondently. "I have to go. I'm leaving food and some money for you." She gestured to a small bag on the end of the bench.

"Is it drugged?" Fay snapped.

"No mom, it isn't drugged." That seemed to be the final push, the blow that knocked both the breath and the strength from Linda, who backed up a step in defeat and said flatly, "I'm going now. Please be careful. I'll come tomorrow."

She started away, while Fay continued to mutter angrily even as she snatched up the brown paper sack her daughter had left her, and Hugo asked Temerity, "What now?"

One side of Temerity's mouth curled up in a wicked smile. "Now, we have an adventure. If you're up for it."

Hugo sniffed a bit, and she felt his body straighten up. "If that's a challenge all I have to say is 'What do we do?'"

Temerity snickered. "Talk about the blind leading the blind. We follow Linda and check out where she lives, and then maybe, if we can think of a way, we help her with her mom."

"So, we're going to spy on people's private pain and interfere with their lives, uninvited?"

Temerity realized how bad it sounded. "Well, yeah," she shrugged. "But we're also going to involve an innocent kid and a hallucination. So…what do you say?" She held her breath.

"Sweet," said Hugo.

19

Justice sat at the desk in his room, several psychology journals surrounding his computer, each of them marked with post-its covered in his own notes. He scanned the computer screen, checking that his list of resource materials was complete before powering down. He sat still, listening to the lingering hum of the electronics as it closed files, saved information, and finally fell silent.

He didn't move, feeling the swirl of energy winding down in his body for the night as well. For a long beat he sat, not thinking, but feeling the tension that consistently twanged at his shoulders when he thought of Temerity and the contentment that lolled, fat and happy, in his chest when he saw Amanda's picture, in front of the lake, on his laptop. Why, he thought, can't I let this worry go? Then he laughed. It was so human to worry, to stress, to create drama and stories where there might be none. As a student—in fact a doctor—of human behavior, he knew this was part of the psychological curriculum of life, but that knowledge did not give him a hall pass to avoid the lessons. Finally, he slapped his thighs to spur himself to movement and stood to stretch. He had heard the door open and close around ten, and he knew it was Ellen leaving for work. His sister was on her date with Hugo.

Justice liked Hugo, as much as he knew of him anyway. The two men were matched in height, though Hugo was slightly thinner, and more lithe. A big change from the short, compact figure of that failed boyfriend Dennis.

Justice remembered meeting Dennis when the guy first came to pick up Temerity for dinner. He was an outgoing, charming, decent-looking guy, who had been introduced to Temerity by a friend. It bothered Justice that Dennis looked at his sister like a fat cat spotting a field mouse, but he said all the right things, was attentive and thoughtful of Temerity, and she seemed so flattered and pleased that Justice held his tongue. After a few dates, still uneasy, Justice had tried to mention his concerns, but Temerity snapped that he didn't know Dennis at all, and so Justice kept his opinions to himself. But he had not been able to shake the suspicion that Dennis was presenting a handsome, friendly veneer, like a painted movie set with a false back, and it was impossible to know what was lurking backstage.

The two had seen a lot of each other for a couple of months, and Justice had found himself fighting annoyance when Dennis started appearing in boxer shorts for coffee in the morning. Dennis always accepted meals, but he never cooked or cleaned up, or even brought food over. Though he was outwardly considerate of Temerity, attitude, in Justice's opinion, was more one of a doting pet owner than that of a respectful boyfriend.

Then one night, Temerity had gone with Dennis to a party at Terrance's place. Justice went on his own and didn't arrive until later.

The place was crowded when he arrived. Two of the musicians had commandeered the piano and were playing show tunes, and rounds of drinks had increased the volume of the chatter and laughter in the room to an expressive din. Terrance, a martini glass in one hand, kissed

Justice on both cheeks and got him a beer, then hurried back to the kitchen.

Justice stood, sipping the beer and scanning the room. He knew quite a few of the people there, but he was still an outsider among his sister's work associates. He spotted Temerity on a sofa, legs curled up under her, a champagne glass in one hand, enjoying a lively conversation with two of her friends. He maneuvered his way across the living room and touched her shoulder with a tap of two fingers, his habit for identifying himself to her in a crowd. "Hi," he said.

"Oh, hi Justice!" Temerity's cheeks were flushed from the alcohol and the heat in the room. She introduced him to her friends and they returned to debating the intricacies of music composition. After a few minutes, Justice was completely lost. Mumbling that he would mingle, he got up and wandered down the hallway to a den, where a small group of party guests, none of whom he knew, was smoking a joint. He went in and sat down but refused the drug as it was passed. "No thanks," he said with a smile, "I'm sticking with beer and antihistamines tonight. Just getting over a cold."

One of the women, an attractive blonde wearing too much makeup, coughed as she inhaled and tried to hold the smoke in her lungs. Justice laughed and made some comment he couldn't remember now. He did remember that he had been sitting at an angle to the door, so that Dennis did not see Justice when he appeared in the doorway. Dennis locked eyes with the pretty blonde, who gave him a look so suggestive that it was clearly an invitation. Dennis's consenting smile sent a frozen shard into Justice's spine. Dennis gestured with his head, subtly, that the girl should follow him, and moved on down the hall.

The blonde went, straightening her blouse and running her hands over her tight pants as she went. Justice, his heart thumping now, stood and followed a few paces behind. He was just in time to see one of the bedroom doors open, and Dennis's arm reach out and pull the blonde in. His face burning and his chest pounding, Justice approached the door, which had been left open a crack, and pushed it. The room was dark, but the light from the hallway offered just enough illumination for Justice to see what he had hoped he wouldn't.

Dennis had the woman against the wall, her legs were up around his waist and their faces were mashed together. Without even thinking, Justice flicked on the light and spoke. "Oh, hi Dennis, I think you forgot you already have a date." His whole body was tense, as though a force was driving him forward, and he felt his hands form into fists and his biceps tighten as Dennis pulled away, dropping the girl awkwardly. She slipped sideways down the wall, her garish pink lipstick smeared across both their faces.

"Justice," Dennis fumbled, wiping his mouth with the back of his sleeve and producing a stupid grin. "I didn't know you were coming. Uh…"

Justice took a step toward him, and the girl on the floor said, "Hey!" in an insulted way, but both men ignored her. Justice took one more step forward and he could see a flash of fear in Dennis's eyes. The tendons of his neck tensed unconsciously as he began to draw his shoulder back, readying for the swing.

"Hey, man," Dennis sputtered, putting both hand up, palms out in front of himself, "this isn't what it looks like, she's an old friend."

"I don't care," Justice said and took another step.

"Are you going to hit me?" Dennis asked, his voice rising in an incredulous squeak. The girl on the floor scurried out of the room.

Justice held his right fist hard against his thigh and forced himself to take a deep breath. "No," he said at last.

"Well chill out, dude," Dennis said, "It was just a moment, you know. And it's not like your sister and I are exclusive or anything."

"Really?" Justice said with bite. "Does *she* know that?"

"Well, sure. I mean, I don't want to hurt her feelings or…"

"Me neither," Justice said. "Let's go tell her, so she won't feel left out.

"Come on, man," Dennis whined, and then tried a smarmy smile. "You know how it is, old girlfriend, a few drinks, moment of weakness, give me a break."

"I would love to," Justice said. His hand lashed out and Dennis shied protectively away, but Justice caught hold of the back of his collar and marched him out into the living room, lifting him so that his feet were barely touching the ground. When the struggling pair appeared, everyone turned to gape. The conversation fell to a tense murmur.

Justice kept moving until he was right in front of his sister and her friends. "Hey, Tem," he said, "Dennis has something he wants to clear up with you."

Temerity, who had reacted to the change of mood in the room with alarm, seemed to relax a little. "What?" she said, and laughed.

She laughed. It broke Justice's heart to remember it. He had forced Dennis to tell Temerity that he'd been making out with someone else in the next room, and Temerity, shocked and humiliated, had wordlessly gathered her things, unfolded her stick, refused help from her friends, and headed to the door. Justice followed her, but when he caught up to her in the hall and took her arm, she shook him off.

"Was that really necessary?" she said, spinning on him with a vehement growl.

"I think so," he said, still full of indignant righteousness.

"You couldn't have told me later, somewhere private?" she shouted. "Instead of in front of fifty of my friends?"

"Tem, it's not *my* fault the guy is a dick."

"Thank you so much for pointing that out to me," she said. Terrance came out of the apartment into the hallway, reclosing the door on the eager audience behind him.

"You guys okay?" Terrance asked, his deep, rumbling voice echoing in the hallway.

"Terrance, can you get me a cab?" Temerity pleaded, tears beginning to spill from her eyes.

"I'll take you home," Justice had said.

"No, you won't," Temerity said firmly. "I don't want to be with you right now."

Justice had been so filled with confusion and rage at the unfairness of the situation that he opened his mouth to argue, but Terrance's strong hand landed on his shoulder and he shook his head in warning. "I'll get you a cab, Temerity. Do you want me to come with you?"

"No, thank you, I just want to be alone." Temerity turned her back on her brother.

And that was it. Justice still didn't really understand why, but from that day, he had somehow felt responsible that Dennis, and men like Dennis, were such dicks. And he had been reticent to rekindle the uncomfortable scene with explanations or discussion.

He washed his face and brushed his teeth to expunge the bad taste the memory left in his mouth and when he came out of the bathroom, he saw the light on under his sister's door. That was unusual. He moved toward it cautiously, listening, but he heard nothing. "Tem?" he called, and then knocked, no answer.

He pushed the door open meaning to switch off the light but something on her bed, a toy, arrested his attention. Leaning his back against the doorjamb he considered the relic for a moment and then moved into the room, drawn by an unexpected rush of melancholy.

Leaning down, he picked up the thread-worn, stuffed bear and regarded it. Two black button eyes, dulled now by time and scratched with years of love, looked blindly back at him.

"Hey, Winnie," Justice said, and he was hurtled backwards in time.

Temerity's best friend Aaron had died just short of his thirteenth birthday from complications with his heart and liver, which had always been weak. Justice had been terrified to go to the funeral, but he stuck close to his sister, who sat, frozen with loss, and stared at nothing. When it came time to go to the casket, their parents had gently helped them both up and into the line of mourners waiting to say a final goodbye before the coffin was closed.

Justice remembered being glad that day for the first time that Temerity couldn't see. She couldn't see the wasted exhaustion on Aaron's parents' faces. She couldn't see the small coffin, dark blue with silver handles, she couldn't see Aaron inside of it, dressed, unnaturally, in a suit, his face pale, lifeless, nothing but a shell.

As they came up, Temerity put her hand on the coffin, then reached inside and felt her way to Aaron's face. She laid her palm against his cheek and whispered. "I love you. I'll always be waiting for you." Then she crumpled, and Justice had caught her. With effort, she straightened up and said, "I'm okay. I'll be okay. This is about Aaron today." As she began to move away, Aaron's mother stepped in front of her. She was holding a stuffed Winnie the Pooh.

"Oh, Temerity," she cried, and stooped to embrace his sister, weeping on her shoulder as though her heart was fractured and the pieces were trying to get out. "He loved you so much," she gasped between sobs.

Temerity returned the hug, stroking the woman's back and comforting her as though she were the adult. "I know," she said. "He loved everyone, especially you, Ms. Bennett."

The girl and the woman, both now old before their time, stayed that way for an interminable moment, rocking and comforting, sharing and hurting, until at last, Ms. Bennett pulled away and tried to get control of herself. She looked down at the bear in her hands. "I want you to have this," she said to Temerity. "I know he would want you to keep him."

She held the plush toy against Temerity's chest so that she would know what she meant. Temerity had not taken it right away. Very slowly, her hands came up, and she explored the object, then when she recognized it, she took it gently, cradling it to her chest like a child. "Are you sure you don't want him to have it with him?" she asked.

Ms. Bennett bowed her head as another wave of grief broke over her, and when she could, she spoke. "No, I want it to be loved by you, the way you loved Aaron. Thank you for that." And then she turned to greet the next mourners.

Justice stood in Temerity's room with the bear in his hand. He hadn't seen it for many years, not since before he went to college. He'd had no idea Temerity still had it. Running his finger over the threadbare head, the fabric thinned by constant loving strokes, he smiled sadly. "Hey, Aaron," he said. "You still looking out for her, right?"

Because that was what he had said instead of "goodbye" to the boy who had been his sister's best friend and confidant. The boy who had known and understood his sister and her world more intimately than he ever could. He had stood by that coffin and silently asked for Aaron to watch over her from…wherever he was.

At the end of the hallway, Justice heard Runt raise his head and snuffle, then bark. Quickly, he replaced the bear, setting him gently against the pillow where he'd found it and giving it a pat, then retreated, turning off the light. He had intended to go and greet Temerity, but on second thought, he paused in the doorway to the open space of the loft.

The big fire door to the stairwell landing opened and Temerity came in, followed closely by Hugo. They were laughing. As he watched, Hugo took his sister's arm and turned her slowly toward him. He was leaning down to kiss her when Justice turned away, crept silently back to his room, and shut the door.

He sat on the edge of his bed and looked up at the ceiling, feeling uncertain, worried, but cautiously glad.

"Thank you," he whispered, and crawled into bed.

20

Ellen zipped her duffle bag, stuffed to the top with her spare clothes and a few secret emergency snacks, and double-checked her fanny pack to make sure she had her train ticket, the address and acceptance letter from the culinary school, and her cash. She looked around her narrow bedroom with the huge round window at one end and felt her chest tighten.

She would miss the safety it offered her, her hiding place to which she could retreat and watch the world from on high. Facing the unfamiliar filled her with a quivering sensation that left her shaken, but she had promised Temerity and Justice she would go. And Rupert had encouraged her and even offered to visit. Harboring fears she assumed to be irrational—which did nothing to alleviate them—she paced for a moment, checked the bathroom to be sure she'd packed her toothpaste, and finally picked up the bag and started down the narrow stairs to the main floor of the loft.

"Are you off already?" Justice asked. He was dressed for work in corduroys and a sweater over a button-down shirt. "You want me to drop you at the station?"

"No, thanks, it's only a few blocks and it would take longer to drive than to walk at rush hour."

"Well, that's true," Justice said. "You must not have gotten much sleep."

"Actually, Ricco sent me home around midnight. He knew I was leaving this morning."

"A considerate boss, how novel," Justice commented. "If you want to say goodbye to the Mole you'll have to wake her up, she had a hot date last night."

Ellen shifted uneasily. The open mention of any romantic relationship made her jittery. Especially because, though her friend had been cagey about her reasons why, Ellen could see the discomfort Justice's engagement was causing Temerity. That didn't change the fact that no matter how guilty Ellen felt about leaving her friend to muddle through a difficult time alone, Temerity was by far the stronger of the two of them and Ellen wasn't confident that she had anything much to offer. As much as she might want to help and support Temerity, in truth Ellen was clueless about how, and she knew it.

"We already decided to come on one of your guest days, if that's okay," Justice told his squirming roomie with a grin.

This news cheered Ellen considerably and she rocked back and forth. After spending her life unwanted and unwelcome, meeting new people was still terrifying, and knowing that her familiar, and only, friends would be visiting was like balm on a nasty rash. "That would be great," she mumbled, unable to repress a smile. The twins were the closest thing she had ever had to a family.

"Now, you call me when you get there, young lady, or I'll worry." From the beginning, Justice had acted toward Ellen like the big brother she didn't have. "And feel free to call anytime you need something." He paused and looked at her kindly, "We'll miss you, let us hear from you," he added softly.

Though she couldn't think of anything she might need to say, and doubted she would, she nodded. "Can you tell Temerity I said..."

Right on cue, Temerity shuffled out from the hallway in fuzzy slippers and flannel pajamas buttoned crookedly, the back of her hair a tangled mess. Ellen blushed profusely, but Justice clapped a hand over his mouth to suppress a laugh. "Morning, sis," he managed.

Temerity was carrying a stack of stiff cards. "Ellen, I know how you are, so I've pre-stamped a few postcards, written most of them and left blanks for you to fill in. I expect one every other day."

She held them out. Ellen took them and shuffled through the stack. They contained sentences like, "Today I learned to make (blank). I have a roommate and her name is (blank.) My chef/teacher is really (blank). Justice leaned over her shoulder to read them. "Wow," he said, "your handwriting has really improved."

"Hugo wrote them for me, smarty pants," Temerity retorted. "

This is Ellen's first time at sleep-away camp, I want full reports."

"She can call, you know." Justice had given Ellen a simple cell phone for Christmas, and though she argued that there was no one for her to call, Justice said it made him feel better to know she had it and he could reach her if he needed.

"Actually, there's a four-day weekend coming up, so I thought I might come home for that?" Ellen sounded unsure of her reception; she still felt hesitant using the word *home*. Nothing permanent had ever entered Ellen's life, not family, not parents, not even a place. She'd had her own tiny studio apartment for a few years, which she shared with the overweight cat, Mouse, but it was more of a roof to sleep under than a home. This was different. She felt attached even though it belonged to Temerity and Justice, or maybe because of that. As happy as she was here, Ellen would not let herself believe, in spite of how the twins insisted otherwise, that she was more than a renting guest.

"Did Hugo make it home all right last night?" Justice asked innocently, winking at Ellen.

Temerity sniffed. "I assume so since he only has to go down stairs. It was just a first, friendly date."

"Tem," Justice said calmly. "Have you checked your friendly hair this morning?"

Her hand flew up to the matted mess in the back and she flushed mightily. "I'm a restless sleeper," she insisted.

"Yeah, looks like you were shaking your head 'no' all night long." Justice snickered and went to give Ellen a hug. She tensed predictably at the touch, but allowing any contact at all was an improvement over even a few months before. Temerity was next, walking Ellen to the door with an arm thrown over her shoulder.

"Now, you eat well, get plenty of rest, work hard, and you'll be a five-star pastry chef before you know it."

"It's not really a very extensive course," Ellen admitted shyly.

"Your natural talent will see you through," Temerity announced loudly, throwing her arms out to illustrate how great Ellen would be. Then she hugged her friend and opened the door. With a quick wave back at Justice, Ellen went out, her feet leaden and her head foggy with foreboding. Though logically she knew she was coming back, an experience that was entirely foreign to her, she did remember *leaving* numerous foster homes for yet another unknown new one, so the unpleasant feeling of displacement was familiar at least. The difference was that she had never once regretted leaving any foster home, nor had she ever been pleased to land in a new one.

Temerity held the door and when Ellen passed through it, she said, "I love you."

Ellen was so shocked at these never-before-heard words that she sputtered, "Uh...I...uh...thanks." Then she hurried away, fearing she would burst into embarrassing tears, and not understanding why.

"There goes our baby," Justice said, coming up behind his sister and shutting the door. Temerity hadn't moved, and when he turned to look at her, he saw a tear tracking down her cheek toward a pouting mouth. "Ah, she'll be back. All kids have to leave the nest."

"Tell me about it," Temerity said, and turned back inside, feeling a small puncture wound in her heart. Ellen had moved into their house and their family, and now she was leaving, too. Temerity couldn't help indulging in a moment of self-pity. *They all leave,* she lamented mawkishly. Then immediately she censored her indulgent reaction with a metaphoric finger wagging, *Stop being selfish!* She was so lucky, she reminded herself, she had her family and her friends. Ellen would be back, for the near future anyway, and now maybe even…Temerity didn't let herself finish the thought. With an impatient snort, she told herself to buck up. Ellen would only be gone a few weeks, and if anyone needed to venture out into the world and learn to experience life, it was Ellen.

Justice tried to derail his sister's sorrowful mood, and his too, if he were honest. "So, what did you two kids do last night? Other than the obvious, please omit all steamy details."

"He took me to a radio show, it was wonderful," Temerity told him curtly. "And then we found out where Fay's daughter Linda lives, and then we came back here and wrote postcards."

"Postcards," Justice teased. "I suppose that's the visually-challenged version of showing someone your etchings."

Temerity stomped her foot. "All right! I had sex. Sex, sex, sex, and you know what?"

"What?" Justice asked, grinning.

A huge crooked smile attacked Temerity's face and crumpled her irritation. "It was wonderful."

"It usually is," Justice agreed. "I mean, if it's with the right person. Now let's back up one. What was that middle thing?"

"Sex?"

"Before that."

"The part about finding out where Linda lives?"

"Yes, that part."

Temerity looked smug. "We were going through the park and we heard them talking. So, when Linda left, we followed her." Temerity, forgetting she was in her pajamas, slapped at the place her pockets would be. "I actually have the address here somewhere. It's in Morningside."

"Ellen's old neighborhood. So we can assume Linda is not financially solvent," Justice sighed. "So sad, without money, there's very little someone can do to help a family member with mental illness. The state institutions are pretty grim." Justice stared at the floor, remembering the semester he had studied mental abnormalities, which involved a number of volunteer hours at the Brice Sanatorium. The smells and the screams still haunted him. He shuddered, "I don't blame Fay, I wouldn't want to go back there either."

"It's got to be better than the street," Temerity said.

Justice thought about it. He remembered a young woman who spent hours smearing her own feces on the walls because "Jesus told her to," and cut herself with anything she could find to "let the demons out," and an old man who wept all day, begging them to give him back his shoes, which were not allowed. He remembered the saint-like patience of some of the care-givers, and the unfeeling cruelty of others.

"Not necessarily," he said. "If people get better, then maybe that's true, but to be confined there? Take my word for it, it's hell."

Temerity tilted her head thoughtfully. "I'm sure it's hell to be afraid all the time and face terrifying hallucinations and hear voices that tell you to debase and hurt yourself too. Did you talk to Amanda about the drug trial?"

"Yes, and she said it can be done outpatient, but the patient, or an approved care-worker, has to come in for the medication and then the patient has to be monitored at regular intervals. Fay is a bit of a risk there."

"What if someone she trusted took her?"

"Tem, she doesn't even trust her own daughter, she can't reason."

"I'm not particularly reasonable sometimes either," Temerity insisted, and Justice snorted his agreement. "But that doesn't mean I couldn't be coerced, given the right stimulus."

"Oh no," Justice groaned as realization dawned. "You've got a *plan*."

Temerity smiled and one eyebrow went up. She looked like an evil cartoon character. "Don't I usually?"

"I'm afraid."

"Wuss."

Justice widened his mouth to try to release some of the tension in his jaw, then he said, "So, Amanda and I are thinking about getting married in the fall."

"Oh," Temerity's exclamation was light, with a soft tremor.

"We just think summer is too soon."

"So…what's the deal? Should I look for a new roommate or a new home?" Her face had paled.

Backpedaling, Justice said, "I think we can wait a while on that. How would you feel if we got a home with an apartment for you?"

"Like a third arm," Temerity said quickly. "Not going to happen."

"Why not?" Justice asked, frustrated. "Amanda thinks it's a good idea, why are you being so pig-headed?"

Temerity spun toward him. "Because maybe I like my life here, did you think of that? Maybe I think of this as my home and don't choose to be a burden. Maybe I don't want to hear you guys sucking face and using baby voices with each other. Maybe I like living here where I can take buses and get around by myself, and suburbia would suck for me. And what about Ellen? You wouldn't understand; being independent is easy for you."

Justice felt his frustration morph into anger. "That's not fair," he said.

"Yeah, life is like that. If you forget how not fair it is, just glance my way. I'm going to take a shower."

She stalked off, narrowly avoiding Runt as he scrambled up out of her path, leaving Justice standing in the kitchen grinding his teeth, stuck in limbo, halfway between total happiness and utter failure.

21

When Seth came on Wednesday after school to walk Runt, Temerity asked if she could go with them. Seth readily agreed.

When they reached the dog park, Temerity sat on a bench and waited for Seth to throw the ball a few times. This involved him also having to go pick it up while Runt barked his encouragement. *Dog trains boy*, Temerity thought with amusement. When the young man finally came and sat next to her, out of breath, Temerity said, "So, I was talking to your friend, Fay. She recognized Runt. Did you know that she used to substitute teach Justice's class when he was in middle school?"

"No way!" Seth exclaimed.

"Way!" Temerity countered. "And the other night when I was out on a…with a friend, I heard her talking to her daughter Linda."

Seth sighed. "Did Linda try to get her to go inside?"

"She did, but Fay wouldn't go." Temerity rubbed her hands together for the friction's warmth. "Do you know if Linda forced her mom to go to the hospital, or tricked her in some way?"

Seth stroked Runt's head, flopped in his lap, and thought before he answered. "I don't know exactly. I mean, I only met Linda once, and she seemed like she really wanted to help. She gave me her cell phone number in case Fay had some kind of emergency. I know Fay did go to the hospital once, maybe Linda took her. No, *probably* Linda took her. Fay is afraid to talk about what happened there. It really scared her."

"So I gather," Temerity empathized. "Listen, do you think, if you asked Fay, that she might try some medicine that would help her? I mean, she would have to talk to the doctors first, so they can make sure to give her the right thing, but what do you think?"

"Fay won't go to a doctor." The young man was definitive. "I tried to get her to go see mom at the clinic, but she won't go. So, Beth came and tried to talk Fay into coming in for a checkup, but Fay said she won't go to a place where they will tie her down." Beth tried to tell her that she was just a doctor at a clinic, not an asylum, but Fay wouldn't trust her." There was a moment of thoughtful quiet and then he said, "She's really a nice lady, Fay. It's not her fault that she has those voices that tell her what to think. It makes me really sad."

"Me too," Temerity said, and reached out to rub Runt's head, patting Seth's hand in the process. He did not pull it away. That was progress.

"What we need," Temerity said slowly, "is a psychiatrist who makes house calls."

"You mean park calls," Seth joked.

Temerity giggled. "Exactly. And the good news is, I think I might know one. Two actually."

"Really?" Seth sounded so hopeful. "Who?"

Instead of answering, Temerity asked a question. "Do you think Fay would be frightened of someone who was…well, badly scarred?"

"You mean Ellen? Her scars aren't so bad anymore, not since they fixed them."

"No, I mean much worse than Ellen."

166

There was a pensive scratching, and then Seth answered. "No. I don't think so. Remember I told you about Dan? His face has all these, you know, blotches all over it, like bruises, it looks bad, but Fay doesn't mind that because he's a really good person and her friend. But it really depends on what Trey tells her to think. I mean," he fumbled, "I know Trey isn't real, but she thinks he is. He's like, part of her brain, you know?"

"I do," Temerity said, impressed. "That's a very good description, because he *is* part of her brain. Her imagination made him up and her illness makes him very real to her." She smiled. "You are going to be a very good doctor one day, Seth, if you decide to stick to that. What kind of doctor do you want to be?"

"A good one?" Seth asked.

"Excellent choice," Temerity agreed. Someone had walked up near the left of the bench. The crunching of dress shoes on the hard ground would have informed Temerity it was probably a man, but the fact that on her right Seth shifted, tucking his body in behind hers on the bench, made it a certainty.

"Well hello again," said Geoff.

"Oh, hi Geoff," Temerity exclaimed. "It's all right Seth, this is my friend Geoff. He owns a restaurant a couple blocks away." She tilted one ear toward Geoff's feet and made out the rapid panting of a small dog that sounded more like snoring than breathing.

"Hello Seth, nice to meet you," Geoff said. Temerity was relieved he didn't make a move forward to offer his hand and she decided this was because someone specializing in empathy could clearly see and sense Seth's damage. "This is my dog, Ming. Say 'hello' Ming." The short bark sounded a lot like "hi."

Temerity felt Seth lean around her a bit, to look down. "What kind of dog is that?" he asked.

"It's a Chinese pug. I'm usually a rescue dog kind-of-guy, but I inherited him from my mother."

"Oh, did you lose your mom? I'm so sorry," Temerity said with feeling.

"Gosh no, she's fine. But she's a light sleeper and Ming is a serial snorter. So…I was called upon to provide a bed, walks, his own food, and part of any meal I'm eating."

"Does he like Chinese food?" Seth asked, so curious that he looked up and made eye contact with the well-dressed older man.

Geoff looked down at the little animal and then back at Seth. "Actually, that's a really good question. I don't know. He likes chicken the most, but he's also partial to pancakes."

"With syrup?" Seth asked, sitting up straighter and shifting his weight away from Temerity.

"He prefers butter, which you can see from the fact that he's shaped like a ball."

Temerity reached a hand down toward the snorting noises, and a soft, short-haired head leaned into her hand while a rough tongue licked her palm. She stroked the loose skin. "Smart boy, everything is better with butter!" she said.

"What's in the big bag?" Seth asked.

"Oh, food."

Temerity asked, "Do you bring Ming here often?"

"More so recently," Geoff answered. "I usually take him to a park near my house. I live further over on the west side. But I've been at the restaurant so much, I started to bring him with me. He hangs out in my office, and when I have time, I bring him over to help me deliver some sandwiches."

"You deliver?" Temerity asked.

Seth leaned down to tempt the little dog over for a scratch. Geoff laughed, "No. The restaurant has take-out, but I mean I try to get over here at least once a week to hand out some lunches. Just a sandwich and a side of potato salad. Nothing fancy."

This perked Seth up considerably. "Who do you give them to?" he asked.

"People who don't have any lunch. Lots of people don't have homes, and so they stay here, in the park. I know that must be hard, so I try to help out, just a little."

"It is hard," Seth said quietly.

Temerity patted Seth's knee, but did not let her hand linger, unsure if it would make him uncomfortable. "Seth was living on the street for a while." She tried to keep her voice neutral, but the fact made her want to weep.

"Not that long," Seth mumbled. "But I was hungry a lot. And cold."

"I'll bet." There was nothing but agreement in Geoff's voice, no pity. Temerity was grateful for that.

They were interrupted by a crazed scrambling of paws and fur as Runt bolted over to investigate the interloper who was drawing much coveted attention from his humans. He stopped short before slowing down, skidded, and nervously lowered his head to sniff Ming.

The little Chinese dog sat there without reacting while Runt sniffed him all over. Then all at once the little dog sneezed.

Runt recoiled backward with an alarmed yelp, and then lunged sideway, launching himself to safety. He landed half on Seth's lap, and half on Temerity's chest, pushing her back against the bench. "Whoa," Temerity laughed, pushing him off. She turned toward Geoff, "This is Runt, whom I believe you've met. He's the cowardly lion of canines."

"Wow, I didn't know Ming was that scary," Geoff commented. "I always thought of Ming as the winded squirrel of park animals."

"Runt's afraid of squirrels too," Seth said, and Temerity could hear that he was amused.

"Well, I need to go hand out a few of these lunch bags," Geoff said. Temerity heard the shift of a large paper bag, filled with other paper bags.

"Can we come?" Seth asked.

"I'd like that. I already did the north side of the park, near the boat house, now I want to go down to the fountain."

The five of them, dogs refastened to leashes, and Runt keeping his distance from the fourteen-pound threat, left the dog run and walked up the hill toward the fountain at the south entrance to the park. Though Temerity couldn't see them, she knew that the gated area near the public restrooms was a gathering place for the homeless. Geoff approached people, one by one, always asking the same question. "Hi there. If you're hungry, I've got some extra sandwiches, would you like one?" Many of the people he knew by name, and it quickly became apparent that Geoff had been a presence in this park for a long time.

It wasn't long before the strong scent of unwashed humans crowded Temerity's senses, as these forgotten people shuffled forward and thanked Geoff profusely for the meal. Quite a few of them asked about his restaurant or his mother. Most of them knew his dog, and Ming was subjected to greetings and ear scratchings, which seemed to be endured with regal patience.

"Kevin!" Geoff called out to one man. "Hey, man. How's Cynthia and the kids?"

"They're at the shelter. I came out to work," answered a friendly voice.

"Well take an extra couple sandwiches for later," Geoff said. Seth watched and Temerity listened as three bags were shifted from his bag to the grocery cart filled with cans and plastic bottles that Kevin was pushing. He thanked Geoff, who told him to come by the restaurant for their recyclables later, and left. The hard plastic wheels of the cart voiced a gritty objection as they rolled along the concrete. Seth watched his every move, but stayed next to Temerity. He perked up as he watched Geoff approach Fay's friend Dan, the one Seth had told Temerity about, who helped everyone else even though he had nothing and was ill. Dan's face had the hollow, sunken cheeks and mottled bruises of long illness. Geoff leaned in and spoke gently.

"How are you today, Dan?"

"Hanging in, hanging in. How are you doing, Geoff?"

"I'm great, thanks. How about a sandwich?"

"I'm not sure I could eat it, haven't had much appetite."

"Well, take it for later. I'll bring some soup instead next time. Any news?" Geoff pulled out a bag and handed it over, Seth watched as Dan took it with shaking hands, but the eyes that connected with Geoff's were filled with intelligence and soft gratitude. Seth knew that look. It meant something to be "seen."

"No change. They gave me some medication for the pain, but there isn't anything else they can do."

"Aw, I'm sorry to hear that, man," Geoff said, reaching out to lay a hand on Dan's shoulder."

"It's all part of the plan." Dan said, and even Temerity could hear the acceptance in his voice. "I'll be home soon," he said softly. She had to fight tears from coming to her eyes. To be so accepting of a cruel fate was something she understood. Though, all things considered, she thought herself lucky. Dan shuffled painfully over to sit on the lip of the fountain, Temerity could hear his tortured breathing from the simple effort.

"Geoff, this is really great of you," Temerity said, when he came back to them, folding the large paper bag, now empty. "What got you started doing this?"

"My mom was a social worker for almost forty years, and some of the stories she told me broke my heart, so I've been helping out at soup kitchens and missions for most of my life. I guess I was just raised to include somebody else in my pursuit of happiness. Anyway, the result is that I grew up to love making good food and finding people who like to eat it!"

Seth said, "Here comes Fay."

She turned an ear and sure enough, she soon heard the familiar voice approaching, already in full conversation. "I told her she's a liar," Fay was saying. "The principle was threatened, they were going to put snakes in her house. She told me. Yes she did! Well, she didn't have to, I knew they would."

"Hi, Fay!" Seth called out as the muttering came closer.

There was a pause, and then Fay said, "Hello Seth, how's Runt?"

"He's good!" Seth told her. "And this is Temerity's friend, he's giving away sandwiches. He owns a restaurant."

Temerity said, a bit loud, "Hi Fay, it's Temerity, Justice's sister. We met the other day. And this is…."

"Oh, I know Geoff," Fay said. "Some people think he's an agent, but I know he's working for our side." She shuffled a little closer and said in a stage whisper, "Are we winning?"

"Yes ma'am," Geoff responded seriously. "The battle rages on, but the more we care, the more we win."

"Humph, as I always suspected," Fay said. "And there is math involved?"

"Oh, there's always math," Geoff agreed. "Thank goodness you taught so many so well. Speaking of which, Kevin was just here. You still tutoring his daughter Mary?"

"Haven't seen her in a while," Fay said, scratching absently at her wrist.

"Kevin said they're at the shelter."

"Oh, well, I don't go there, so that explains it."

"Why won't you go there?" Temerity asked, though she had a good idea already.

"Trey doesn't like it," Fay snapped. "He won't let me. People whisper things about us, and he's afraid."

"What does he say?" Geoff asked calmly.

"That he will swell up, and choke and then stop breathing." This answer seemed to distress Fay, and she began to pace anxiously from side to side. "I don't want to see it, I don't want to go there."

"You don't have to," Seth told her.

But Fay turned and shouted. "It's not my fault, I didn't do it. I never would!" But she was talking to the air beside them. Dan, who had been sitting quietly, rose laboriously to his feet, taking the bag with his sandwich, and went to her. "Fay, it's okay, let's walk to lake. See what I have? We can give the crust to the ducks." His presence appeared to calm Fay considerably, and the two of them started off, Dan struggling, his failing body slowing their progress to an excruciating crawl. But Fay put a hand under his arm, and he continued to soothe Fay, drowning out her tormentors, at least for a little while.

The two bent figures moved off, carrying the weight of their demons on their bruised, hunched shoulders.

Geoff said goodbye to a few people, and then Temerity, Seth and he walked back across the park without speaking. Three very different people who, each for unique reasons, were sobered by the reminder to never, ever, take anything for granted.

22

Temerity's phone rang just as she and Runt were coming into the loft.

"Hello?" She shrugged off her coat and let Runt off the leash while holding the phone to one ear, no easy task.

"Temerity? Hi, it's Regan."

"Is everything okay?"

Temerity heard a sigh. "How awful is that, that the first thing you ask is 'is something wrong?' I don't want to be that person."

"I'm sorry, you're not, and you know you're not. What's up?"

A short, bitter laugh came through the phone. "I, uh, guess I need to be that person. I was wondering if I could stop by and talk to you."

Temerity felt her watch, it was only four. "Sure," she said. "Are you nearby?"

"You're in midtown, right?"

"Right off Grant." Temerity gave her the address and told her about the alley door. Regan promised to be there within twenty minutes.

Twitching to know what was up, but trying to be patient, Temerity busied herself with some laundry. But it was barely ten minutes until she heard the door buzz.

"Regan?" Temerity said when she went to the house phone.

"No honey, it's mom. Your brother asked me to come by after work."

"Oh, hi mom, Come on up. Justice isn't home yet."

"I know, he just called to tell me he's running late."

Temerity pressed the buzzer to unlock the alley door and went to meet her mom on the landing. She could hear Dory, who had jogged five miles a day most of her adult life, taking the stairs two at a time. She was barely breathing hard when she crested the fourth-floor landing.

"Hi, sweetie," Dory greeted her daughter with a hug and they went in. "What are you up to tonight?"

"Oh, no plans. My friend Regan just called, she's on her way over, she wants to talk. She's in a bad way with an ex who went psycho and won't give her a divorce."

"Honey, don't say psycho. Why won't he give her the divorce, is he Catholic?" Dory asked.

"No, more like Christian on steroids. Some kind of religion where they speak in tongues and invite snakes into the service."

"Ooh, that's scary." Dory said.

"Actually, I'm not sure about the snake part, but I'm pretty sure it's one of those Christian sects where donkeys and goats are worth the same as women, and they all belong to the men."

Dory slapped both hands to her face in frustration. "Why do people insist on reverting to the dark ages? Did it really work out that well the first time around?"

"Sure. For the men in power. That's the idea, right? What I don't get is why women keep putting up with it." Temerity dropped onto the sofa with force, as though that would show them.

"The human ego is a greedy beast," Dory concurred. "But it doesn't sound like she is putting up with it."

"She certainly doesn't want to, but she's being forced to deal with it, well, with him."

"Tough spot. The psychology of religious fanatics is similar to brainwash victims. The general mental profile of someone *willingly* indoctrinated into an extreme ideology is deeply insecure, fearful, and isolated. And fear can make people dangerous, to themselves or others." Dory sat down next to Temerity. "Is this a good friend?"

"Oh, I really like her, but she's only been in the city about six months. I think she moved here to try to get away from him, but he followed her."

"Yikes," said Dory. "Has she told the police?"

"Several times apparently, but they don't do much."

"Well, be careful, is all I have to say. Obsessives can easily turn violent if anyone challenges their belief system. They worked too hard to build up their alternate reality, and that delusion is often the only thing between them and a rather horrifying despair."

"He's already hit her." Temerity said with grim anger. "But enough about Attila the husband. So, what's up with Justice? You guys planning the wedding?"

Dory laughed. "Hardly. I'm the dreaded mother-in-law anyway, not the mother of the bride. Of course, we'll do whatever Amanda wants help with, but you and I have to remember that it's her wedding."

"And Justice's," Temerity said defensively.

Dory put an arm around her daughter and squeezed. "How are you doing with that?"

"Me? Oh, I'm fine." Temerity waved both hands in front of her face loosely, as if warding off bats.

"Temerity." Dory's tone was warning.

"Okay, okay. I'm having some issues with it, but I'll *be* fine. I just have to adjust."

"You like Amanda?"

"How could I not?" Temerity asked, but there was irony in her voice. "She's amazing. It took me months to get Justice to commit."

"I see. Have you guys talked about living arrangements?" Dory asked.

Temerity snorted impatiently. "Is that why you're here? To talk about what to do with the Mole? Why does everyone think I can't get along without Justice?"

Dory snorted right back. "It isn't a question of that, and you know it. It's just a change, and we all have responses to change. Why should you be exempt?"

"Busted," Temerity said, a guilty smile on her face.

"Actually, your brother asked me to come talk about a woman he wants to help. Fay?"

"Oh," Temerity felt left out. "I was thinking of asking Dad to talk to her. She's homeless, lives on the street, you know, and I thought Dad might be tougher."

Dory laughed out loud, and Temerity heard the timber of her own full-throated laugh in it. "I doubt if he would agree—or admit—to that, but Andy and I talked about it and decided that she might respond less defensively to a woman. We'll have to feel it out and see. Anyway, how about some tea?"

While Temerity heated water, Dory picked out a tea from the large collection without dumping it all on the kitchen floor, and they were just brewing it when the door buzzed again. This time it was Regan. "Hope you're not wearing heels!" Temerity told her. "It's the fourth floor, only door on the landing."

Temerity went to the door, and was surprised to hear voices chatting on the way up. She opened the door and realized that Justice must have come in at the same time.

"Hey," he said to his sister, as they arrived on the landing. "Is mom here yet?"

"We're having a tea party," Temerity told him. "Will you be having caffeinated or herbal?"

Regan picked herbal, and Justice picked beer. Temerity introduced Dory to her friend and the women sat on the sofa while Justice made a plate of cheese and crackers.

"I hope you don't mind," Temerity told Regan, "but I was telling mom about your situation. She's a psychiatrist, and I thought she might be able to shed some analytical light on the situation."

Regan turned hopefully to the attractive woman next to her. "Can you?" she asked.

"Not much without more information, I'm afraid. Tell me about him."

"Well, he's quite brilliant, actually. He designs machines. You know, sophisticated stuff for high-tech factories, that kind of thing."

"So, he's an engineer?" Temerity was genuinely surprised.

"Kind of, more like an inventor. An engineer sounds like something strictly technical, he's that *and* creative. He was designing safety systems for planes, you know, emergency shut down systems in case of fire, that kind of thing. I can't say I understood it all, but our garage looked like an operating room for jet engines."

"And when did you first notice that he was changing?"

"About six months into our marriage. He became very possessive, which I told myself was flattering at first, but it became annoying, and then alarming. And then he joined this…church. He wanted me to go, but I told him I wasn't interested in organized religion, and that made him angry. He became very intolerant of anyone who disagreed with him. It was as though he'd put on blinders, he refused to acknowledge any version of reality except his own."

Dory was nodding. "Narcissistic denial. Did he become fearful or even paranoid?"

Since her shoulder was touching Regan's on the sofa, Temerity could feel the woman stiffen. "How did you know that?"

"Well, it sounds like we're talking about psychosis, and paranoia is a common side effect. In fact, as I was just explaining to Temerity, adopting extreme ideologies is almost always a desperate attempt to ward off debilitating fear—of death, of isolation—and by finding others who share their delusions, they validate their own paranoia."

"Wow," Regan said. "He didn't like it when I talked to people, especially the neighbors. Because they were Jewish, he called them 'Agents of Satan.'"

Justice came over and set down a plate of cheese and a bowl of olives.

"Shall I go work in my room for a bit?" he asked considerately.

"I'm so sorry to be a bother," Reagan apologized. "But I'd like your input too, if you don't mind." Justice nodded, sat, and waited attentively. She began, "After I told Simon that he needed to get help, he threatened me. He told me that if I talked to anyone about it, he would punish me. That was the word he used, 'punish.' It really freaked me out."

"What did you do?" Dory asked, very calmly.

"Nothing, for a while," Regan said. "What could I do? He wouldn't even admit anything was wrong. Then, one day, the little dog next door dug a hole under the fence and came into our yard. Simon went nuts, screaming at the neighbors—who were really apologetic about it—telling them that a man's land was sacred, and they'd better keep their dog at home if they knew what was good for it." She dropped her head, and Temerity could hear the change of direction of her voice as she said. "And then, two days later, the dog was found dead in their back yard. He had been strangled with some strapping tape he'd supposedly become entangled in."

Temerity gasped. "Did Simon kill it?"

"I didn't know. The neighbors certainly thought so, they sent for the police, who talked to Simon, but remember, I told you that Simon is very smart, and he can rise to the occasion when he needs to. He told them calmly that he had no idea what had happened to the dog and he was really sorry that he had gotten so angry when it broke into our yard. He said he'd been worried because he'd put out poison for gophers and was afraid the dog might be harmed."

"Well, the police checked, found the poisoned traps, and believed him. After an autopsy showed that there was no poison in the dog's system, and because the strapping tape had been snagged on a branch making it possible for the dog to have tightened it while struggling, the police decided it was just an unfortunate accident. Simon even sent the neighbors a gift basket saying he was sorry. It had a big green bow on it."

Dory shifted and asked a question Temerity would not have thought to ask. "Why do you mention the green bow? Was it…did it mean something specific?"

"I didn't think so. I just remembered the ribbon because it was so bright and very glittery, you know, almost neon."

"And why does that stand out to you?"

"Because," Temerity felt Regan's hand reach over and take her own, she squeezed back, waiting quietly, "because when I went out to walk my dog this morning, the same ribbon was tied to a tree right outside Terrance's apartment. And Simon has threatened to kill my dog if I go to the police again."

"Did you see Simon anywhere?" Justice asked over Temerity's gasp.

"No, I haven't seen him since he showed up at rehearsal, and before that I hadn't seen him since he confronted me three months earlier outside the artist's entrance, which is when I got the restraining order, but they never found a place to deliver it. That's the first time I knew he'd followed me here. Here's the thing. Terrance has been fantastic, but I can't expect him to put me up indefinitely, I can't go home, and I'm just so tired of being afraid!" She leaned into Temerity who put an arm over her shoulder.

"Well," Temerity said, turning deliberately to face her brother, though she was speaking to Regan. "I know that you need somebody to keep an eye on you." She rocked Regan a little to jostle her from her mood, "Not one of mine of course," she quipped.

"I hate being a burden to people!" Regan moaned.

"Well, that's just a burden you'll have to bear," Temerity joked. "And it won't be forever, just until we can figure out where Simon is and get his butt thrown in jail or an institution." She sniffed thoughtfully. "Tell you what, you can come and stay with us. Ellen is out of town for six weeks, so you can have her room. Oh, and since she was a professional janitor, you wouldn't have to worry about being a burden, quite the opposite. Do you have your own Pine-sol and any of those plastic gloves? You'll need them."

Regan laughed, sniffling back tears. "But I don't know how long it will be until..."

"Doesn't matter. I needed a project," Temerity said.

"Oh no," Justice said firmly. "Regan is welcome to stay with us, but *no projects.*"

"Look who's talking," Temerity said, dripping with sarcasm, "you asked mom come over to talk to a homeless woman in the park because..."

"Because she helped Seth, and I want to help her."

"In other words, a *project*. And Regan helps people," Temerity said. "She teaches music to low-income kids at the community center."

"Regan's worth as a human is not my point and you know it," Justice said. "I'm talking about you. You are not qualified to confront a dangerous psychopath."

Dory interrupted, "Okay, okay, everyone stay calm. The most important thing is that Regan realizes what she's dealing with and takes the right precautions. The most likely outcome is that Simon will eventually move on to some other obsession and leave you alone. But just in case, the next step is probably getting the police to flush him out and let him know they're keeping an eye on him."

Regan made a sound like an anxious moan, an unfinished dread. "They don't know where he is and I can't expect them to round up a posse because I found a green ribbon!"

"He can't stay hidden forever," Dory reassured her. "Meanwhile, you should stay close to friends and if he does show up, do not engage. Since Justice isn't home in the daytime, I recommend you stay with your friend Terrance for a bit longer. The mere presence of allies makes you a less vulnerable target, and if Simon is as intelligent as you say, he won't want a messy situation."

"And speaking of professional cleaners…" Justice said comically, and Temerity knew he was relieving pressure by playing the fool, something he was good at, she thought. "I got grease all over my jeans changing a tire. Does anyone know something that will get it out?"

Regan surprised them all with a quick answer. "Get some Lestoil, it's what I always used on Simon's grease stains, it smells like hell, but it's the only thing that works on grease. The smell goes away somewhat after the wash, not completely though. Still, Lestoil works."

"What does it smell like?" Temerity asked.

Regan shuddered, as though the memory of the scent was as acrid as the smell itself. "Petroleum," she said.

23

Dory and Justice made their way to the park in preoccupied silence. When they reached the open green space, Justice said, "I keep trying to tell myself that Tem can take care of herself, and myself has no trouble believing that in general. What myself is not buying is that if someone else gets pushed off a cliff, she won't throw herself off of it to try to catch them on the way down."

Dory sighed. "I know. Your sister has always felt compelled to help people, even when it was hard. You do that too, by the way. In her case I think that has a lot to do with losing Aaron, who wanted to help everybody," she said quietly.

"And did," Justice added, not mentioning that Aaron's remarkable spirit and eventual death had altered the direction of his life as well. "Still, as much as I don't like the idea of attracting negative attention toward Tem, we can't just ignore Regan's situation."

"Regan is in severe distress, that's for sure." Dory shook her head. "And justifiably so. A highly intelligent psychopath is dangerous and unpredictable."

"But now for a different kind of psychosis…" Justice said, and pointed discreetly to where Fay, her rounded profile in her bulky layers interrupting the sheen of the lake behind her, was throwing crumbs to the ducks in the shallows.

Dory watched Fay for a few moments, observing the woman's behavior thoughtfully, before she nodded her head to her son and they moved to the edge of the water.

"Oh hi, Fay," Justice called casually from a few yards away. "It's me, Justice, remember?"

Fay squinted at him in the dusky light and then laughed. "Who would forget that name? Who would name a kid that?"

"Meet my mom," Justice cocked a thumb at Dory. "Blame her. Fay, this is Dory. Dory, Fay."

"Hi, Fay. Nice evening, a little chilly." Dory did not maintain eye contact, turning instead to look out over the water, giving Fay a chance to watch her without feeling threatened.

"I don't notice the cold." Fay spun to her left. "Trey, I can talk to whoever I want to, they are *not* spies!"

With equal parts compassion and professional fascination, Dory studied Fay discreetly from the corner of her eye. "Who is Trey?" she asked Fay.

Fay spun back to her. "He's an annoying little brat," she said sharply, then turned her head again, "Yes you are! And you know it." As though swinging between two perspectives, her own and the rest of the world, Fay returned a suspicious eye to Dory. "Just because you can't see him doesn't mean I'm crazy."

Dory smiled and looked out over the water. "You know there's fish in this lake, right?"

Taken off guard, Fay narrowed her eyes. "So?"

"I can't see *them* either, but I think they're there." She shrugged as though this explained everything.

"Trey doesn't like other people to see him," Fay confided, coming a little closer. The ducks glided after her, following her movements as one, eager for more stale crust.

"Like Ellen," Justice said.

"That's true." Dory looked thoughtful. She said to Fay, "Ellen is Justice's roommate. For most of her life Ellen didn't want people to see her, so they didn't. And you know what's interesting about that?" She asked the question specifically to her son, but loudly enough to include Fay.

"Tons," Justice said. "But what in particular?"

"How that worked for Ellen when she wanted to help other people."

"Don't I know it," Justice agreed. "She saved Temerity from getting mugged." He smiled proudly, remembering Ellen's bravery. "Those guys never even knew what hit them. They didn't see Ellen, but she was there."

Dory deftly hooked Fay into the discussion by asking, "Is it like that for you? Is Trey here now? Do you think we could see him if he wanted us to?" The doctor looked around, as though expecting Trey to materialize.

This threw Fay off balance. She fidgeted and shook her head. "No, he doesn't help people, he's selfish, and he can be mean. Really mean, worse than an eighth- grade boy."

Justice cleared his throat. "I think Fay might be thinking of me when I was in middle school. She substituted for a teacher of mine who left to have a baby."

Her face breaking into a wide grin, Dory said, "Oh, I remember you, Ms. Fay. I think you are the first one who made math interesting for Justice. Probably had a lot to do with him getting into medical school, even if he did switch majors in his second year. Still, he did get his doctorate."

"Of anthropology," Justice intoned dutifully since Temerity wasn't there to do it.

"*My* daughter Linda is working on her master's degree," Fay said proudly.

"Good for Linda," Dory enthused. "In what?"

"History. She wants to be a professor. Education is very important."

"Absolutely," Dory agreed. She picked up a pebble and tossed it out into the lake. The ducks rushed toward the small splash, then retreated, quietly quacking their bitter disappointment.

Justice said, "Mom, Fay tutored Seth when he was on the street."

"That was you? How wonderful."

"Yes." Fay straightened up, standing an inch taller. "I teach a lot of the kids who can't get to school."

"That's amazing. Good for you. I council some of the shelter kids who are having a hard time. In fact, if you'd be interested, I'm sure the shelter would really appreciate help from a qualified educator."

But Fay had begun to back away at the word 'shelter.' "I can't go to those places. They won't let me teach, they say…" Fay dropped her head and began to rock side to side.

"Who is 'they?'" Dory asked gently.

"The government, the principles, those doctors. They won't let me teach anymore, it's a conspiracy. It wasn't my fault!" Fay insisted, a note of hysteria entering her voice.

"No, it isn't your fault," Dory agreed, speaking smoothly and calmly. "Of course, you have to be healthy to work around kids. People at all, really. That's just common sense."

Fay seemed confused, but less anxious. "I'm not a fool, I know they think I'm crazy. Shut up, Trey!"

Dory shrugged. "Well, I don't know 'them', and I can't hear what Trey is saying to you, but it doesn't sound like he's being a very good friend. There are drugs now that can get you healthy enough to teach again, if you're ever interested."

"Mind control!" Fay cried.

Dory stayed very tranquil and appeared to consider the viability of that opinion. "In a way you're right, but what if you're the one in control? Say, if your brain is just…well, misfiring sometimes. It happens to lots of good people, and it's treatable."

"I don't take poison." Fay snapped.

Dory took her hands out of her jacket pockets and held them up as if fending off the very idea. "Me neither. But if I had heartburn, I'd take an antacid. If my brain was producing too much of one chemical and it was making me afraid or sad, I'd take a medicine to neutralize it. Not all chemistry is poison."

Fay practically spat, "I tried their drugs, they made me feel dead. I was a zombie, a real one."

Dory shrugged again. "I don't have to tell you that medical science is always advancing, and that means treatments." She shrugged again. "Things change."

"There's a pill for feeling afraid?" Fay looked suspicious again.

"Not per se," Dory told her. "But a disproportionate amount of chemicals produced by our brain can cause an imbalance that affects our nervous system. It's just like acid reflux, and they can both be effectively treated."

"I don't believe you," Fay sniffed.

"Fair enough. On the other hand," Dory let her smile go mischievous, "what if they could?"

Fay had shuffled her way close to them by now. She was peering at Dory with overt fascination.

"Do you believe Trey is here?"

Dory's smile did not flicker. "I don't see him," she answered honestly, "but I believe that you do. I believe he's as real to you as Justice is to me." She reached over and patted her son's arm. "And I know that if I were ill, it would hurt him too. Families suffer when someone they love is suffering."

Fay mumbled something, but the fight was gone out of her.

"Well, we'd better get going, Justice. It was lovely to meet you, Fay. Or rather, to see you again." Dory offered her hand.

Fay gazed at the hand that waited in the air between them, then scowled down at her own, brown with dirt and twisted by arthritis, as though it were unfit to touch Dory's clean one. Dory waited, simply letting her fingers hover, as if she could stay there all afternoon. Very slowly, Fay reached out and let Dory take her immovable digits in her supple ones.

"I really hope I see you again," Dory said. She gestured to Justice and they turned to go. A few feet away, Dory turned back, as though she'd just thought of something. "By the way, if you ever decide you want to teach again, I could write you a prescription for a free drug trial. I really do believe it would make you feel better, but I understand if you don't want to. If you do, just tell Seth and he'll pass the message along. Have a nice evening,"

Justice was watching Fay's face as his mom made this casual pronouncement. It was like watching a TV rapidly flipping channels, so many emotions ran over it that it seemed to flicker, but the last glimpse he had before he waved and turned away was something he had not seen there before.

Hope.

24

"I'm tired of talking about my problems," Regan said as she and Temerity finished off the cheese and olives. Tell me something happy and normal. Are you seeing anyone?" Regan cut herself off and then said, "I'm sorry."

"Why?" Temerity was befuddled.

"I guess, well, using the term, 'seeing anyone' isn't very sensitive of me."

"Don't worry about it. That's something they teach blind kids and their families from the get-go, to go ahead and use those common phrases, it's just interpreted a little differently. Especially in this case, 'seeing' means dating, not processing light. But even it meant 'seeing' I can relate, I 'see' things too, just differently than sighted people."

After a short pause, Regan said, "I see."

"Good girl," Temerity told her, holding a hand up for a high five, which came, though very lightly. "Actually, the less sensitive people are about my blindness, the easier it is for me because I know they aren't focused on it."

Her phone rang and Temerity searched her pockets until she fished it out.

"Hello?"

"Hi, it's me." Hugo.

"Oh, hello." Temerity was well aware that her voice had just dropped an octave and her face was hot around her reflex smile. She cleared her throat and tried to sound normal. "What's up?"

"I was wondering if you wanted to go get a bite to eat. I just finished my lessons and I don't have a thing in the house."

"I have a friend over, would it be all right if we made it a threesome?" Temerity asked.

"As long as it's just for dinner," Hugo said lightly. "I'm really very old-fashioned about intimate relations. Quite shy."

Temerity guffawed. "Those are *not* the adjectives that come to mind about you and, well, you know. Why don't you come on up and we'll pick a place."

She hung up and said to Regan, "Well, speak of the devil and his ID will pop up on your phone. That's a guy I just had my first date with. He lives downstairs. We're going to get some dinner, something easy, you want to come?"

"I don't want to be the third wheel."

"No, I want you to meet Hugo. He's a musician too, jazz piano and modern classical. Composes."

"Thanks, but I need to get home. I have to walk Toby. There's a little yard off the back of the townhouse, but I've been afraid to leave him out there."

"I don't blame you," Temerity said. "Will Terrance be there?"

"He's there now, but I think he's going out around nine."

"Then you should be home before he leaves," Temerity said.

Regan's whole body shifted on the sofa, lifting Temerity slightly. "How long can I keep doing this? It's crazy."

"Tell you what," Temerity said, "walk down with us and we can go by the restaurant, have a drink, and get you something to go, then we'll put you in a cab. I'd love your opinion on Hugo. He *says* he's very good looking." Temerity joked. Not that the handsome meter mattered much to her, and of course now that she'd had a chance to explore him personally, she was more than pleased.

Temerity could feel Regan relax back on the cushions. "Actually, a drink and some company sounds really nice, thanks."

Runt rushed the door, barking frantically.

"Ease up, buddy!" Temerity called out. "It's just Hugo." Though after she said it, she thought that 'just Hugo' didn't match the loud humming in her chest as she crossed the loft.

"Hey," she said as she opened the door, turning away quickly to hide the silly smirk on her face. "This is my friend Regan, she plays the flute in the orchestra."

"Well that's commendable, but does she like Cajun?"

"I don't know, let's ask her." Temerity turned toward the sofa and called out, "Regan, do you like Cajun food?"

"Don't tell me there's decent gumbo in this city!"

Hugo passed by Temerity to shake Regan's hand. "Actually, yes. And oyster po-boys. Hi, I'm Hugo, the neighbor."

"Do they have take-out?" Regan asked.

"They don't deliver, if that's what you mean," Hugo said. "Bastards," he added quietly, making Regan giggle. "But you can pick it up."

"That works. I have to get home to walk my dog, so I'll just join you guys for a drink and then make myself scarce as they say."

"Should we take Runt?" Temerity asked.

"I think we're going to have to," Hugo said, and Temerity could hear the dog panting heavily and whining with excitement at Hugo's chest level. "No Runt, get down. I will not carry you."

Mouse lifted his head from his spot on the top of the armchair and rawred. Hugo went over and gave the big scruffy head a strong scratch as a purr like a well-tuned moped vibrated its happy calm to them all.

Jealous of the attention, Runt went around the back of the chair, stuck his nose in Mouse's stomach and pushed. The cat hissed at him and raised a lazy paw to rest it on Runt's nose, locking eyes with the canine. Sensing the potential of claws in his tender sniffer, Runt froze, though his eyes cut back to Hugo as if to say, "Help me."

"Well, you are kind of asking for it," Hugo said to the dog. "Come, Runt!" Runt backed away carefully and Mouse resumed grooming his considerable self. It was a big job.

They met Dory and Justice on the stairs, and they decided to come along. On the sidewalk they paired off so as not to impede other pedestrian traffic. Dory and Justice walked in the front, followed by Regan and Temerity, with Hugo and Runt bringing up the rear.

The traffic was still heavy with commuters escaping the city for their families and wet bars in the suburbs. When the walk sign flashed at a busy intersection, they started across.

A screech of rubber on asphalt startled them all as one of the cars that had been stopped suddenly spun its wheels and started forward directly at them. Instinctively, Justice grabbed Temerity, who had turned toward the sound, and propelled her up onto the curb with a swing and a shove. At the same time Dory snatched the frozen Regan around the waist and half-pulled, half-threw her to the sidewalk next to Temerity. Hugo, only a few steps into the crosswalk, back-stepped quickly, but Runt resisted. With a yell and a massive effort, Hugo strained, yanking the leash so that Runt was lifted into the air back toward safety. The dog was almost clear when the car swerved toward him and the bumper smashed into his hind quarters, missing Hugo by a foot, then sped off, on down the street without so much as slowing down.

192

"Hey! What the hell was that?" Justice yelled from across the street. "Hugo, are you all right?"

"I'm okay," Hugo called back, "but Runt's hurt."

The group crossed back to where Hugo was kneeling on the sidewalk next to Runt, who was breathing hard and whimpering, one leg twisted unnaturally backward. As Temerity dropped next to him and stroked his head, his tail thumped on the cement. "It's okay buddy, you'll be okay." As she ran her hands over his body, the dog whimpered when she touched the back leg and hip.

Drivers had gotten out of their cars and were trying to get a look at what had happened. The light changed to green, and impatient commuters a few cars back began to honk their horns, voices were raised, arguments started. One man pulled his car to the curb and came over.

"I tried to get the license plate, but the lights were off and I couldn't make it out."

Hugo was cradling the dog's head, but he shifted and pulled out his cell phone. "Is your vet open at night for emergencies?" he asked. He was panting too from exertion and adrenalin.

"No," Temerity said. "Ours is only open in the day. Can you find one nearby that is open?"

"On it," Hugo said, tapping at his phone. Dory stood with her arms around the terrorized Regan, who was hyperventilating, dragging in ragged, shallow breaths while Dory tried to calm her. Hugo flagged down a cab, help load Runt in, and offered to go with Justice and Temerity, but Justice looked pointedly at Regan, and Hugo understood immediately.

"Actually, I think I'll stay with Regan and Dory. Make sure they both get home all right."

"Thank you," Justice said, relieved.

When she could finally speak, Regan gasped out, "It was him!" Regan choked on the words. "Oh my God. It was Simon!"

25

When they arrived at the hospital, the driver helped Justice carry Runt inside, using Justice's jacket as a sling. They were directed immediately into an examination room. In the reception area, Temerity paid the driver, and then joined Justice.

Runt lay whimpering on the table. Temerity took her place next to him, stroking his long, soft ears again and again.

"How does he look?" Temerity asked her brother.

"Pathetic, but enjoying the attention," Justice shook his head. "Poor Runty. That wasn't your fault, was it?" The tail thumped on the metal table, and the motion made Runt yelp with pain.

Temerity asked softly, "He'll be okay, won't he?"

Justice reached out and took his sister's hand. "I'm sure he will. But we have to be realistic, if he has internal damage, there might be nothing we can do."

"No!" Temerity felt hot tears stream down her face, and she tried to set her teeth, but a sob escaped her. Justice put his arm around her and made comforting noises. "I don't want to have to say goodbye, I don't want to do that!" Temerity said.

Justice squeezed her tighter and felt the pinch in his heart tighten cruelly. He was maybe the only one who knew what that statement meant to Temerity.

The door opened and the veterinarian and a technician hurried in and went straight to Runt. Without looking at Justice or Temerity, the vet said, "Hello, I'm Dr. Brett. What do we have here?"

"His name is Runt, and he was hit by a car."

The doctor was already examining the dog, checking first the eye membranes and the color of the gums. "Hey there, Runt. You're a good boy, aren't you?" She listened to his heart with a stethoscope and then pulled them from her ears. "How did he get out?"

"He didn't," Temerity said firmly, back in control. "He was on a leash, we were crossing the street at a crosswalk and someone hit him on purpose."

The doctor stopped and stared at Temerity, but when eye contact was not returned, Dr. Brett noted and adjusted to Temerity's blindness and went back to work. "On purpose?" She began to gently explore down the leg. Runt squealed, and raised his head with a warning growl. The technician took a secure hold on the scruff of the dog's neck with one hand and stroked his head with the other. Temerity made room for him but leaned down and murmured into Runt's ear. His big brown eyes looked up at her with utter trust and he lay still again.

"His vitals seem okay, and his color is good, it doesn't look like he's in shock. We need to take him back for X-rays, you can wait here," Dr. Brett said. They slid Runt carefully, jacket and all, onto a small stretcher and carried him out.

"There's a chair on the left," Justice said. "Why don't you sit down."

Temerity sank down onto the hard plastic seat and slumped forward. "What is wrong with people?" she said. "I just don't understand. Isn't there enough pain in the world without having to cause it on purpose?"

Justice leaned against the examining table in front of her and said, "I wish I could tell you. From what Regan said, Simon is a very disturbed individual."

"The police will have to do something now, right?"

"If she recognized him, absolutely."

"Do you think he was trying to hit Regan?" Temerity asked, a tremor in her voice.

Justice was quiet for a moment, his instinct was to protect her, but he knew that leaving her ignorant because she had not seen what had happened was more dangerous than considerate. He said. "No. I think he was aiming for you."

Temerity straightened up, her face paling. "What? Why would he want to hurt me?"

"Because she went to see you? Because you stood up to him before? Because he's basically insane? Take your pick. I'm guessing he followed her to the loft, and then us, when we left with her and he recognized you from the concert hall."

The antiseptic smell in the examining room introduced flashes of another hospital room to Temerity's mind, Aaron's room. That ICU had been filled with sounds, muttered prayers, doctors speaking softly, monitors beeping. Temerity drew in a ragged breath, and tears flowed down her face. She wiped them away with the memories. *This is not that day,* she told herself. *This is not Aaron, I'll be okay.*

"Justice?" Temerity asked softly. She heard the soft swipe of tissue being pulled from a box and then felt it pressed into her hand.

"Yes, Tem?"

"You aren't going to leave forever, are you? That's what I'm afraid of, that I'll have to say goodbye to you."

Justice gasped and went down on one knee in front of her. "No, Tem. I'm here. I'm going to be here for a long time. I'm not going away. I'm bringing someone else into our family, someone new to love you. You're not losing me, you're getting a sister."

Temerity blew her nose and laughed a little. "That's a very thoughtful gift, but what I *really* wanted was a cashmere throw."

"I'll get you that too. And both of them will hug you." He leaned forward and put his arms around her.

"Poor Runt," Temerity said. "I don't want him to suffer, Justice, no matter what. I don't want him to linger, that's so terrible, it's so cruel." Her voice broke again, and she cried into her hands.

"I know, I know." Justice reassured her, and he did know what she was really talking about, the fact that we wouldn't let an animal suffer, and yet we let a child linger in pain and suffering long after there was any hope. "We won't. We'll do what's best for him."

"I don't want to be selfish," Temerity whispered.

It was Justice's turn to shake his head. "Not much fear of that. Sometime I actually wish you were a little more selfish, life would be simpler."

Temerity lifted her head from his shoulder and smiled as she blew her nose. "But it wouldn't be nearly as interesting."

"Or rewarding," Justice agreed. "The fact that you like to help people is almost the best thing about you."

Temerity was recovering now. "Almost? What is the best thing about me?"

"How much you love me," Justice said. "I, unlike you, am very selfish, so that's the most important thing to me."

Temerity gave her brother a hug and said, "I'm glad."

The door opened again. Justice stood and Temerity turned to the sound.

"Well, we have a multiple fractures in his rear left hip, possible bone fragments in that area and a clean break in his thigh bone, but I don't see any signs of internal bleeding, so I'm going to recommend we operate to repair the bone, remove the fragments, and that will give us a chance to check everything else. Would you like me to have a written estimate?"

"Yes please," Temerity said. "So, you think he'll be okay?"

"The general rule is if we can put the bones back in the same room and seal it in plaster, they will heal. So, while I can't guarantee a total recovery, not until we're sure no internal organs were damaged, I'd give him a ninety-eight percent chance of a full recovery. He won't even remember it in a few months."

"Oh, thank God," Temerity exhaled. "Will you start right away?"

"You don't want the price first?"

Justice asked. "Will it be more than a new car?"

"New? No," the doctor said, missing the humor.

"So, we're talking….? Justice asked.

"In the neighborhood of fourteen hundred dollars."

"Let's get that anesthesia flowing!" Temerity said. She clenched her trembling hands. "And could I get some?"

The doctor ignored the joke, and started back for the treatment rooms. "Great, I'll get him right into surgery, and I'll have the office staff work up a contract for you. Sign here, so we can begin treatment." She held out a simple "agree to treatment" authorization, and Justice signed without hesitation. The doctor turned to go.

Temerity heard the door open and asked, "How long will it be? And can we take him home after?"

"He'll need to stay over night, he'll be very groggy when he comes out of it. We can call you and let you know how it went if you like."

"Yes, please," Justice said.

After the door closed, they both waited for a minute. "Should we stay and see him when he wakes up?" Temerity asked.

"I don't think so, it sounds like it will be a while before he knows we're even here. I'll come first thing in the morning."

"I hope Hugo got Regan and mom home safe," Temerity said, but couldn't resist feeling confident that the answer was a definite yes. That was nice.

"He sent a text, hold on."

"Read it," Temerity told him.

"I'll paraphrase," Justice said. "The police showed up to get statements from mom and Regan and bystanders, and Hugo had Regan call Terrance and make him promise he would stay in until he could get Regan to him tonight. He says to let him know how Runt is doing." Temerity listened to the ultra-soft tap of thumbs on a cellphone screen. "Okay, done," Justice said. "Thank goodness Hugo was there, that was quick thinking, pulling Runt back by the leash like that. A lot of people would have let go and run."

"Yes, they would have." Temerity considered what that meant. She wondered how many people in the course of her lifetime would do exactly that—let go and run.

And she remembered that Aaron hadn't wanted to leave her, he hadn't wanted to let go. That had been the hardest part.

Temerity reached out and linked her brother's forefinger with her own. "That says a lot about Hugo, doesn't it?"

"Volumes, sis, volumes."

Temerity sighed and tried to reconcile that fact with her resolve to keep her emotional distance. "Well," she said at last, "I do love a good book."

26

eth was at the door at seven a.m. Temerity let him in and explained that Runt had been hit by a car, the surgery had gone well, and he was expected to be back to his annoyingly over-active self again in a few weeks, and that Justice had already been to see him at five a.m. this morning.

"But he'll be okay, right?" Seth was hopping from foot to foot, doing an anxiety dance.

"Yes, he will. Thanks to Hugo, who pulled him out of the way of the car."

"That guy who lives downstairs?" Seth asked suspiciously.

"Yes, that guy," Temerity said and couldn't help the small tremor of pleasure in her chest. "So, we will probably need you to come and visit Runt more often, at least until he gets better."

"How will you take him out?" Seth asked, concerned.

"I won't for the first couple of days at least, he'll have to use newspaper in the kitchen, not a habit I'm looking forward to imprinting in that doggy brain, but after that, we can take him down in the service elevator."

"Can I go see him? I mean, today?" Seth asked eagerly.

"I don't see why not," Temerity shrugged. "I'll call and let them know you are allowed to visit him, but you have school, so why don't we go together afterwards?"

Seth considered this, afternoon was a whole school day away. Interminable. "Okay," he agreed reluctantly. "I'll go see Fay before I go to school. Thelma gave me some hot soup in a thermos to give her today. I think she'll like that."

"I know she will," Temerity said. "And speaking of Fay, I think it's time we talk to her daughter Linda."

Seth's head snapped up. Temerity didn't see it, of course, though she did hear the tightness in his voice as he asked, "What about?"

"Treatment. My mom, you know she's a doctor, right?" Seth nodded. "Well, she talked to Fay about a prescription drug that would help her, and I think she's considering it. If we can get Linda on board, and you ask her to try it, she might. What do you think?"

The boy tightened his mouth and furrowed his brow. "I'm not sure. Something happened, something she hasn't told me about, but it really scared her."

"You mean something other than her illness?"

"Yeah. She said one time that 'he shouldn't have died,' but when I asked her what she meant, she told me it was none of my business. And she shouted at Trey to keep her secret."

"That's very interesting," Temerity said. She was wondering if Fay's illness hadn't been precipitated by some event that pushed her over the edge, or perhaps she suffered hallucinations.

"Well," she said cheerfully, "It sure won't hurt to ask."

Seth was quiet for a moment, and then he said, "You know Fay's friend, Dan?"

Temerity remembered Geoff talking to the homeless man when he had handed out sandwiches, and though she couldn't see it, she remembered Seth mentioning his illness-ravaged face. "I think so, why?"

"He's really sick. He won't go to a hospital, but yesterday he was lying down and he wouldn't get up. I told him I'd help him to the clinic, but he said he just wanted to be there, looking up at the sky."

A deep sadness infiltrated Temerity. She remembered Dan's brief conversation with Geoff and the way the sick man had struggled to help Fay when paranoia overtook her. Temerity knew it was possible the man had been too drunk or drugged out to get up, but she didn't want to mention that to Seth, he was just so young.

"And he's not an alcoholic or a drug addict," Seth said, as though he had read her mind. "I know some of those people who live in the park are, but Dan isn't. He has cancer."

There you had it. Seth might be young, but he had confronted more harsh reality in his twelve years than most people would see in a lifetime. Temerity thought about what Dan had said to Seth, that he just wanted to be there looking up at the sky. She might not know what the sky looked like but she knew the difference of a closed room and the open air, the vast, infinite feeling of nothing but open atmosphere above her. She knew how the wind and sun felt on her face, and the rain, and she thought that if she were dying, she too would make the choice to fall upward into that vastness, instead of down into darkness.

Justice came out from the hallway, his black hair slick from the shower. "Hey, Seth!" he called out. "Temerity told you about Runt? Don't worry, he's going to be fine. In fact, when I went to see him this morning, he was trying to stick his paw through the cage and play with a kitty with the sniffles. He's actually enjoying all the attention."

Seth laughed at the thought of the big shaggy dog wanting to play with a kitten. "Temerity said we can go visit him after school."

"Sure." Justice got to the coffee maker and started to fill it, adding scoop after scoop of rich black grounds. "I have something else I'd like to do today, and I could use your help. I called your mom—"

"—which one?" Seth asked, simply for clarification.

"Thelma. And she said it would be all right for you to go with me to talk to Fay's daughter. She knows how much Fay helped you when you ran away."

"Yep," Seth said with a small smile. "That sounds like T-mom. I told you Mama B tried to get Fay to come into the clinic, but Fay won't go. She's afraid of doctors."

Temerity said, "Both your moms are amazing. So Beth has met Fay?"

"They both have, Beth tried to talk her into getting help at the clinic, and she examined Dan too. He'd been beaten up. Sometimes Beth and Thelma take supplies and have what they call a 'pop up clinic' out by the fountain. They remember how sick I was when I was living in the basement and they really want to help."

"Angels among us," Temerity whispered.

"They are pretty cool parental units," Seth said and smiled shyly.

Temerity laughed outright.

Seth grabbed his backpack and moved to the door. "I'm going to drop off this soup to Fay before school. Should I come over after?" he asked as he pulled a cell phone from his pocket and checked his messages. "Yeah, T-mom sent me a text telling me it's okay. I'll meet you back here?"

"Three-fifteen?" Justice asked.

Seth nodded, then turned and called out, "See you then!" and he was off.

Temerity listened to the faint sound of the thin young man's footsteps beyond the heavy door, something only she would have heard. "How amazing is he?" she said affectionately.

"Very to exceptionally," Justice replied. "Coffee?"

"Not yours, thank you. I'll make my own."

"Suit yourself," her brother said.

"Don't I always?" Temerity quipped.

She proceeded to make scrambled eggs with some spinach and a sprinkling of grated cheese, making a plate for Justice without asking. They both went through their morning routine of checking their emails, sipping their beverages and crunching their toast in companionable silence. Not a silence fraught with discomfort nor an empty one with nothing to fill it, but rather a rich, contented stillness, one that filled both the loft and the siblings in it as fully as the scent of rich coffee and melted butter.

Temerity took in a deep breath of that breakfast aroma and thought, "I miss Ellen." She heard a chime.

"Ooh, Ellen messaged me!" Justice said suddenly.

"No way, she's using the phone?" Temerity giggled. "Check outside, is it raining goats?"

"No, but that reminds me, I want to pick up some cheese. You guys ate it all yesterday."

"Well what did she say?" Temerity asked, a bit miffed that she hadn't gotten a message.

"She says that she's okay, and she has her own room—which is good—and that she has her first friends' day next Thursday."

"Does she want us to come?"

"I wouldn't expect her to say," Justice said.

"That's because she doesn't expect *us* to say we would," Temerity sighed.

"Well, why don't you talk to Rupert and maybe we can all go in a show of force."

"I will. Everybody needs allies."

Neither of them commented on this. In Ellen's case it had been so true that there was no need for further comment. Ellen had been alone, worse than alone for the first five years of her life when she had been abused, starved, and eventually deserted by a drug addict mother. Subsequently farmed out to foster homes for more abuse and ridicule, she had finally endured four years of bullying in a group home before being released as an emancipated minor at seventeen, when she had set out with her welfare check to survive until she found a job.

Temerity could well imagine how difficult that last part had been for Ellen. Her face scarred and twisted, her body heavy with the knee-jerk response to a childhood of deprivation. But she had done it, she had faced the interviews, found a job, and disappeared once more into the anonymity of a night-shift cleaning job, this incredibly brave person unseen and disregarded by everyone around her. Not even those whom she had silently assisted had noticed the invisible girl.

I miss Ellen, Temerity thought again, and picked up her phone, "Message," she said clearly, and the phone asked her to whom.

"Ellen." There was a short wait, then a beep. "Ellen, hi it's Tem. Hope you're doing great, we want to come and see you. I could really use your help right now, but Justice will have to do in your absentia. Love you, bye."

She waited for the phone to read back her words as they were translated into text, then said, "Send," and listened to the whoosh as the message flew threw the ether toward another town.

Justice cleared his throat. "Speaking of having to do with just me, are we supposed to talk to the police about last night?"

"I don't know. Maybe they don't need us, there were plenty of witnesses."

"I didn't get a good look at the guy anyway," said Justice, and he rose to scrape his plate into the sink.

"Me neither," Temerity quipped. "I don't make the best eye witness."

"I wouldn't back you against anyone else in broad daylight, but in the dark I'd bet every last cent on you for the ID."

Temerity smiled, satisfied at the truth of his words. "It's all midnight to me, baby."

Justice, who was taking a sip of coffee, choked a bit. "So, for you it's always the witching hour. I knew there must be a reason crows gather when you're around. *And* you were born 13 minutes after midnight, which proves you're a witch for sure."

"Don't be so superstitious. And don't make me hex you."

"What are you up to today, beside brewing potions?"

"Rupert's coming over at eleven, we're going to rehearse the new piece, then we might get some lunch."

"Good plan," her brother said. "As long as Rupert is with you. But do me a favor, I know you hate this, but after last night, I would really appreciate it if you don't go out by yourself until this Simon guy is no longer at large."

Temerity waved one hand dismissively. "Don't worry," she told her brother, only half joking, "I'll check both ways before I cross the street."

Justice said, "Oh good, I feel much better." But he didn't.

27

It turned out to be a good thing that Temerity and Hugo had followed Linda to her apartment on her date night with Hugo, because although Seth had called and spoken to Linda, telling her that he had some friends who wanted to try to help her mother, Linda had been skeptical and wary. She would only say she would think about it. After some discussion, Justice and Temerity had decided that she might be more readily convinced if she could meet them in person. It was an imposition and a risk, but they didn't see any other way.

The apartment complex was huge, rambling, and devoid of individuality. Justice had to wonder what sadist had chosen this particular shade of jailhouse gray to paint the blocks of housing, separated by broken concrete pathways and hard earth sporting the occasional anemic weed.

They found the apartment on the second floor of a long low building, and knocked on the door. There was a scrambling sound inside, and then a child's voice shouted, "Mom, somebody's at the door."

"Don't open it!" came the sharp retort.

"I know, mom, I know." A few seconds later, just on the other side of the security door a woman's voice called, "Who is it?" in a tone meant to be tough, but it was impossible not to hear the fear in it.

"It's Seth," Seth called out. "I brought my friends."

They listened to sound of bolts being thrown and then the door opened three inches, a chain still fastened inside, stopping it from going any further. A round, wary face looked out at them, taking in the trio.

"Seth, how did you know where I live?"

Justice answered quickly, "I looked you up. I was a student of your mother's and I live near the park where she…uh, lives. I hope we haven't come at a bad time."

"What happened?" Linda asked, clearly expecting the worst.

Justice smiled in a way he hoped was disarming. "Fay's fine. Seth saw her this morning. Hi, I'm Justice, and this is my sister, Temerity. Could we come in?"

The dark eyes took in the handsome man head to toe, then rested on Seth. "I'm not sure why I should."

Temerity stepped forward and held out a hand in the direction of Linda's voice. It hit the door with a smack and she shook the pain out. "Ouch. Sorry about that, hope I didn't chip your paint. We think we can get your mom on a trial drug that might help her, and we just wanted to talk to you about whether that's a good idea or not."

"It's okay," Seth encouraged Linda. "These are the people who helped me, they took care of me when I was really sick, and Runt is their dog. They won't do anything if you say no. They got my uncle arrested." He smiled at the memory. "It was cool actually. Runt attacked him."

"Good for Runt," Linda said with grim satisfaction, then closed the door and the sound of a chain being released preceded it opening again. "Come on in."

Behind her in the dingy hall was a young boy of maybe six. He was dark-skinned, and wiry, but looked happy and well fed, and seemed excited to have company.

"This is my son, Reece," Linda said. Then she shook hands with Justice and Temerity. "You're completely blind?" she asked Temerity without any embarrassment.

"Completely," Temerity confirmed. "But not without observational skills."

"Apparently, if you've noticed a crazy lady who lives in the park."

"We've taken an interest in a nice woman who helped Seth, and he's become family to us," Temerity corrected.

"Right, well, come in and sit down." Linda led them to a tiny kitchen, which had a rickety table against one wall. They each took a mismatched chair and Linda sat on a higher stool near the sink—it was a tight squeeze. The kitchen was clean except the remnants of a lunch plate, the crust of what looked like a peanut butter sandwich and some grapes sliced in half sitting in the sink.

"Okay, what's the deal?" Linda asked, crossing her arms defensively over her chest. She was wearing jeans and a sweater. On the table was a stack of thick textbooks.

"Fay said you're studying to get your master's in history?" Justice said, running a finger across the title of one.

She snorted. "When I get a moment from holding down a full-time job and raising a kid on my own."

"You're not married?" Temerity asked before she thought about it.

"I don't see that that's relevant," Linda said flatly.

"It's not," Justice said. "Sorry. Okay, maybe we start by telling you why we're here." He dove in. "Our mother, who is a psychiatrist, talked to your mom and she feels that Fay is suffering from a chemical imbalance that can be helped with the right medication."

"She tried that," Linda said flatly. "Ten years ago, it didn't work out real well."

"Why not?" Temerity asked.

Justice saw Linda draw back as though she'd been stunned by the question.

"Tell me again who you are?" Linda asked, crossing her arms tightly over her chest and screwing her mouth into a sarcastic challenge.

"Listen," Justice began, "I know we're intruding, and that this is none of our business. That's why we wanted to talk to you in person. I do remember Miss Fay from school, she was an amazing teacher, but we're here as neighbors who thought we might be able to help out a person in trouble who's not getting the help available to her. If you don't want us to interfere, well, then we'll accept that. But Fay kept Seth safe from…" he paused and glanced down at the boy, who had dropped his head, but was listening earnestly, "…from someone who wanted to hurt him. Your mom helped Seth and so we'd like to do something for her if we can."

Seth's voice came now, though he did not look up. "They saved my life," he said simply. "And I want to help Fay. They do too."

"We really do," Temerity confirmed.

"And what do you get out of this?" Linda asked the twins, her skepticism so thick that it practically dripped from each word like molasses spooned onto a cracker.

Justice shrugged and Temerity made a little 'mmph' sound, as though she hadn't considered that.

"Well….nothing, but that's not really the point," Justice fumbled.

Temerity dove in. "I know a little something about people being kind and helping out people just because. Not a day goes by that I don't count on some stranger to help me out in some way, even if it's just telling me the bus stop. I suppose my perspective is a little different than the average bear. Justice is an anthropologist, so he's mostly in it for the fascination of human behavior, and also—here's the hard part to believe—he's a nice guy. Okay, I know we can't take on all the homeless in the city or make much of a dent in the crap we all know happens everyday, but we have this theory that if everybody did a little something, helped one person, then that makes a difference. And to be perfectly honest, we're selfish. We feel badly if we don't help, and good when we do. Total self-interest."

Linda finally smiled. Just a tight lifting of the corners of her mouth, but when she spoke her voice was less strained. "I see. Well, I'd hate to deprive you of your satisfaction. But, medication is something… my mother…it isn't easy to explain."

"And you don't have to if you don't want," Justice said quickly. "You said she tried it ten years ago, but according to my research and the professionals I work with, research on chemically altering mental illness has progressed by leaps and bounds in that decade. So, if you think we could find a way to get her to take it, we believe—as well as our mom who is a psychiatrist with thirty years of experience—that Fay could lead a normal life again."

"Fay likes to help people," Seth piped in. "She likes to teach kids. I know she misses it, maybe she could do that again?"

Linda's gaze swung a slow half-circle to take in the faces around her, and, finding only concern and kindness there, her guard dropped. She let her arms fall to her sides and her head slumped toward her chest. Slowly, one hand rose to cover her face, and she began to sob.

It was so unexpected that Justice and Seth both froze in place. Temerity, however, came immediately to her feet and went to Linda, first reaching out tentatively to locate the woman's arm and then wrapping her own over Linda's shoulder. "It's okay," she soothed. "We really do want to help, this must be so hard."

"It's horrible," Linda whispered, half-choking. "You have no idea, to grow up with this smart, funny, wonderful woman whom everybody loved, and to watch that woman disappear, become afraid of shadows and hear voices that aren't there. And the way people treat her! Do you have any idea what it's like for me to see her like that? Choosing to sleep in the park with nothing but her hallucinations." She broke again, and this time Temerity wrapped both arms around her and rocked.

"Mommy?" Reece was in the doorway to the kitchen, alarmed at the sound of his mother's crying. Linda's head snapped up and she wiped her face with one movement.

"You okay, mommy?" he asked, as though he were already all too familiar with her hardship.

"I'll be fine, sweetie. I was just a little sad about Nana."

"Hey, Reece," Seth said, standing up. "You wanna' play a game or something?"

The small boy looked hopefully at his mother, who nodded, and then she smiled gratefully at Seth. "Thanks," she whispered as Seth passed her and followed her son into a tiny living room littered with second-hand toys.

"What happened when she took the medication?" Justice asked. Temerity patted Linda's back and felt her way back to her own chair.

"She was a teacher, you know that."

"Like I said, she taught me," Justice smiled.

Linda nodded. "Not really that surprising, over the years, and especially as a substitute, she must have taught thousands. When the… illness started to show itself, it was just in little ways at first. She would tell me people were saying things about her, behind her back, and then that progressed to paranoia. She thought the houses were watching her. I took her to the doctor, and her union insurance only allowed for limited psychological visits. There wasn't much in the way of therapy, but one doctor did try a medication. It made her less anxious, but very groggy and sleepy. After she fell asleep in class and the kids snuck out, the school board gave her a leave of absence.

"She hated feeling dull and stupid, and I couldn't blame her, but I managed to keep her on that medication for a few months, then the hallucinations started up again, and the doctor, who was busy beyond reason, changed her medication and upped the dosage." Linda reached for a dishtowel and wiped her face. "I'm sorry."

"Don't be," Temerity said. "There's no reason to be sorry for caring. You're both hurting, not just your mom. Mental illness affects family too."

Linda snuffled a laugh and said, "That's an understatement. I think people don't understand that. How frightening this kind of disorder is for family. She exhausted all her friends, it's not that they didn't care anymore, they just couldn't deal with her. I don't blame them. We didn't know what to do. The school board reviewed her and the doctor cleared her to go back to work part-time, as a substitute. So, she did."

"And how was that?"

Linda's spine moved in an S, bowing forward and then arching back as if she were trying to force some snake-like pain through her body. "She was still disoriented by the drugs, not thinking very clearly, but she could manage, until—" she stopped, gritted her teeth and then went on. "Until one day, she went into a classroom in a tough school, I think there were something like forty-two kids in an eighth-grade math class. She was called in last minute, and the only information she was given was the chapter the kids were on, no information about any of the individual kids.

"About halfway through the class, she pretty much gave up, the kids were so unruly and badly behaved that there was no way they were going to listen to a substitute who was only there for the day. She lost control of them, and pretty soon, they were all talking and rough-housing. She continued to try to teach the few kids in the front who were paying attention. At some point, she noticed that a kid in the back was looking very ill. She asked if he was okay, and he nodded yes. She went back to the board, but in a few minutes the boy had dropped to the floor, and he had some red welts on his face, but he was breathing all right. Some of the other kids were standing around him making fun. She tried to get them to stop, but they wouldn't. Mom sent one of them to get help, and she never came back. They found out later that the kid had just ditched school. Finally, my mom went herself to get the nurse who asked her, without much interest, which kid. Of course, my mom had to tell her she didn't know his name. The nurse took her time getting to the classroom, and when she did, it was too late."

Temerity gasped. "No, he died?"

"Severe allergic reaction to peanuts, someone had given him a candy bar. But that's not the worst part. Well, I mean, it is, but here's the thing—the kid had an epi-pen, for this kind of thing, and it was kept in the nurse's office. The regular teacher would have known to get it and inject him. She would have known the child's name. But no one had told my mom. From that day, my mom refused to take the medication. She blamed herself for not being alert enough, and of course, the school board withdrew her credentials when the parents sued."

"That's so unfair!" Temerity exclaimed.

"And that's when Trey showed up, after the medication wore off. He taunted her about the dead child."

Temerity remembered Fay saying something about not Trey not being able to breath and swelling up. "I think he still does," she whispered.

Linda nodded, and wiped at her eyes again with the dishtowel. "And that, that one thing she could not control, sent her over the edge."

"Who could blame her?" Justice spoke gently. "And you tried to talk her into staying on the meds?"

Now Linda's back straightened defensively. "Of course! But I was just married and spending fifty hours a week working on my master's and she wouldn't listen. Then one day, I got a call from the neighbors that mom was on the sidewalk ranting and wouldn't let anyone come near her. So, I took her to the hospital and they referred her to the state mental institution. I don't know if you've dealt with many state institutions, but it was a horrible place, and when my mom tried to leave they strapped her into a bed. She screamed and screamed. It was horrific."

Justice was nodding. "I have worked at a state facility, and yes, horrific is the correct word. I understand why she wouldn't trust going back."

"But what we're hoping," Temerity said, "is that we can get her on this program without being hospitalized. She would just need to be monitored, and our mother, or Seth's mom, Beth, could do that."

"You mean, you want to trick her into taking it?"

"No!" Justice was adamant. "No, she needs to know and do it willingly. There's no other way."

"She won't do it," Linda said, shaking her head sadly.

"What if Seth asked her, do you think that might help?"

Linda looked doubtful. "There's only one person she listens to," she said.

"Who's that?"

But before Linda had a chance to answer, Temerity did it for her. "Trey," she said. Linda was nodding, barely moving her head; she seemed too exhausted to manage any more.

Justice considered this. "Hmm. This requires some consideration. I think the most important thing for today is to find out if we have your permission to try to get her the medication."

Linda stood up and went to scrape the remains of the sandwich off the plate into a small garbage can under the sink. "My permission? You can have my blessing. Hell, I'll stand up and cheer you on, but I don't think it's going to happen." The woman looked utterly exhausted, drained and worse—hopeless.

"Well, we can only try," Justice said. "Why don't we all think about it tonight, and maybe by tomorrow we'll have come up with a brilliant plan." He pulled out a card and handed it to Linda. "Here's my cell number, and the number at our loft, where you can reach Temerity as well."

Linda took the card listlessly, stared at it, and then stuck it to the refrigerator with one of the alphabet magnets there. "I'm just really tired of trying and failing. I'm about to give up, what else can I do?"

"You can let us help," Temerity chirped. "We can only try, that's true, but we have to try. And then, if that doesn't work, we might have to accept that this is her journey. What else is there?"

Justice watched Linda consider this suggestion from his blind sister who could have easily chosen to spend her life a victim, a weaker, needier, lesser version of the person she was now, and he saw the magic of perspective that often happened when people dealt with Temerity. That perspective was her special gift. Temerity had been dealt a cruel hand, yet she refused to be defeated and that inspired, or sometimes shamed, people into trying harder.

An exhausted sigh rattled from Linda, and she slumped back onto the stool.

"Okay," she said. "I've learned not to hold out much hope, but… okay."

"We'll help you." Temerity held out a hand. Linda took it, grasping it like snatching a leaf falling in an unpredictable, erratic path from the sky.

28

Temerity did not wake up with a brilliant plan. She dressed, had coffee, and went to get some practice in before Rupert arrived to spend the morning rehearsing with her. It wasn't long until she buzzed him in and could make out his rasping breath on the stairs outside. It had occurred to her to tell him to take the service elevator, but secretly she thought it was probably good for him to get at least this much exercise. Though she had to admit it was easier climbing those four flights without carrying a large cello case.

After Rupert had sunk onto a chair to catch his breath, Temerity brought him a glass of water and up to speed. She told him about Simon trying to run them down, Runt's injury, and their plans for Fay. Though he suffered from excruciating shyness, Rupert was a sensitive, caring man, the result of having always been the awkward, bullied child. His tormented teen years had made him fearful to speak up for himself, but the other side of that coin was that as an adult, he could not stand by and allow it to happen to others, a fundamental truth that he shared with Ellen.

"Have you talked to Ellen?" Temerity asked. She heard him shuffle, hem and haw a bit, before he answered.

"She doesn't like talking on the phone, but she's sent me texts. I told her we were coming Thursday for tasting day."

"Did she say she missed us?" Temerity asked, knowing full well that was not yet in her damaged friend's emotional vocabulary, but it was no longer impossible that it would be.

Rupert was genuinely surprised. "I don't think she would admit that," he said. "Not because she *doesn't* miss you, but because being and acting alone is normal to her."

"Rupert?" Temerity said threateningly. "Are you accusing Ellen of being normal?"

"God forbid," Rupert blushed, his adult acne reddening into splotches as he laughed shyly. "So, you're still on, right?"

"And I think Justice is going to inflict his company upon us as well."

Temerity could almost hear the crack of a smile when Rupert said, "He's worried about her, isn't he?"

"Nah. He just loves cake," Temerity joked. Then she asked softly, "Has Ellen made any new friends? She hasn't sent me the postcard with that one on it."

"She sent you postcards?" he sputtered in surprise.

"Yes. I had them pre-addressed, stamped, and created fill-in-the-blank spaces for her. Otherwise, I knew she wouldn't do it."

"Oh," said Rupert, accepting this as classic Temerity. "There's one girl she mentioned. I guess they eat lunch together."

Temerity felt a mixture of pride and frustration. She couldn't completely pretend she didn't recognize the shiver of jealousy that Ellen was making a new friend, someone who might replace herself in Ellen's affections. Once recognized, Temerity took a firm grip on the insecurity and placed where it belonged, in the "out" box.

"So tell me more about this Fay person," Rupert said. "The idea is that you want to get help for her?"

"We want to get her on some meds, if it's possible. The trick, everyone seems to think, is to get her to stop listening to her fictional friend, Trey. Apparently, he's a product of her mental illness, a kind of bullying alter ego."

Rupert opened his cello case and began to pull out the instrument. "Meaning that you have to get her imaginary hallucination, whom no one can see or hear, to tell her to take the pills."

"No one can see him," Temerity repeated thoughtfully.

"Too bad we don't have imaginary friends too, maybe they could have a chat with him."

Temerity gasped. "Rupert, you are a frigg'n genius. Come 'ere." Knowing his shyness would not allow him to show physical affection to her, she crossed the few feet to him and leaned down to give his head a peck on top. His thinning hair did little to hide the heat that rushed up from the contact. "Genius, I say!" Temerity exclaimed again. "Listen, Rupert, I know you just got here, but how would you feel about going for a little walk with me?"

"Can we wait until my blood pressure drops below three-twenty over one-ninety?"

Temerity laughed and took up her violin. "Tell you what, let's run through everything once here, and then we can go play in the park for a while."

Rupert's brows went up. He had learned to suffer the regard of the audience while playing with the orchestra, it wasn't so difficult being one of a large group, but playing in public practically alone and drawing attention from strangers was still on the unendurable list. "Uh, why?"

"Because," Temerity said, putting the hand with her bow in it on her hip and stomping one foot, "it's a beautiful day outside, maybe I can't see it, but I sure as heck can go out and enjoy it."

Rupert narrowed his eyes. "You have a *plan*," he said.

"Why does everyone keep saying that?"

"Because we recognize a pattern. And you keep dragging us into it."

"Wouldn't dream of it." Temerity swept the air in front of her with the bow, conducting the air, life, energy— it all streamed around her. "I'm just opening the doors, you go through them yourself."

Rupert sighed, picked up his cello and then readied his bow. It was true, he supposed, though he doubted he would have ever even noticed those doors if it weren't for the force that was Temerity.

An hour and a half later found the friends at a bench near the pond, Rupert seated and Temerity standing beside him. It had taken a few minutes to locate Fay, though Temerity did not acknowledge her. She merely relied on Rupert, and her ears, to tell her when they were close enough for their instruments to be heard.

First she played alone, a light piece filled with rhythm and sass. Then Rupert joined in, adding the melancholy mood of the cello. As they played, people stopped to listen, some for a few seconds, some taking a seat on the grass and settling in. Once, between pieces, Temerity heard Fay call out to Dan to come and listen.

"Where is he?" Temerity asked Rupert in a low voice.

"Who?" Rupert grunted back.

"The guy, Dan, he's really ill. Cancer, I think. He's a friend of Fay's."

Rupert looked around, there were maybe twenty people gathered around now, milling or lingering, and quite a few of them were obviously homeless. It took him a minute, but he spotted a man gaunt with illness, moving painfully to a tree a few yards away with Fay's help. When he got there, he used the trunk and her arm to lower himself to the ground and then leaned back against the tree, struggling for breath. On his face was a small smile, a look that said how grateful he was to have this unexpected gift of distraction.

"He's over to your left, leaning back against a tree. Fay is standing next to him."

"Okay, good."

They continued to play, performing several short pieces. When they paused, there was light applause, and Fay shouted, "Bravo!" and tried to clap with her curved hands.

Temerity took a sweeping bow in the direction of the appreciation. "Thank you, thank you! Remember, there's no cover charge and parking is free—if you don't have a car."

A few people laughed, and as Rupert and Temerity began to pack up their instruments, the small crowd dispersed, returning to, or simply enduring, another day.

"Okay," Temerity whispered as she leaned over her case and set the violin gently into its molded felt. "Where's Fay?"

"Still over by the tree. She's sitting on the ground next to Dan."

"Good. How about most other people?"

"Gone, or distracted," Rupert summed up. "Hey, you know what?"

"What?"

"I enjoyed that. It was nice to play for people who would never usually get a chance to hear it."

Temerity nodded and put her hand on her friend's shoulder. "Music is like beauty," she said, "It's a gift for everyone." Then she laughed sharply. "Of course, beauty is in the eye of the beholder, so for me, beauty is the smell of cinnamon rolls, or pine and pepper." She said the last three words quietly, feeling the truth of them. "So how far away are they?" Temerity asked, cocking an ear to try to hear, but the constant soft flow of the fountain's falling water muted anything farther than a few feet.

"About fifteen steps to your left."

"Cool. Okay, follow my lead."

Temerity finished putting her violin case away and then turned left, calling out loudly, "Samantha, I told you not to bother people, get away from them."

Both Fay and Dan looked up at her, then around the general area.

"Nobody here but us," Dan said, his voice scratchy and dry.

"Yes there is. It's my friend Sam, she wanted to come today, and I told her she could if she was good. But she's a pain. She likes to mess with people. I hope she's not bothering you."

Under his breath, Rupert asked, "What are you doing?"

"Stick with me," Temerity answered in kind from the corner of her mouth. "Sam! Come on. I don't know who you're talking to." She stopped, ostensibly listening. "You know I can't see them, so why don't you introduce me?"

Fay was on her feet now, looking anxiously around. "There's someone else here? Where is she?" There was both trepidation and wonder in her voice.

"Fay?" Temerity called out. "Is that you?"

"It's me. Who are you talking to?" Fay asked.

"Sam, but she keeps…what, Sam? Oh, it's Trey? Of course, I've heard of him, he's a friend of my friend Fay, but he's never introduced himself. No, I can't see him. I can't see anybody, so that's nothing new, but I can't hear him either, obviously." Temerity huffed. "Why? What did he say?"

"He said leave her alone," Fay said. "They are talking."

"Oh, good," Temerity picked up her violin case. "Maybe she'll leave me alone for a bit." Temerity turned to Rupert. "You want to get some lunch?" Then she turned again toward the imaginary friends. "You can stay here if you want, Samantha, but don't bother Fay."

Temerity unfolded her stick and carefully made her way over to where Fay and Dan were standing and sitting. She could hear Dan's wheezing breath.

"Did you like the music, Fay?"

"I did. Very much," Dan said. "Thank you."

"Oh, hi. It's Dan, right?" Temerity said, feigning surprise at his presence. "You're Seth's friend. How are you doing today?"

"It's one more day for me, this one has blue sky and white clouds. Thanks for asking." He coughed, and Temerity heard him struggle to control it.

"That sounds like a bad cough, you have medication for that?"

"I do. Seth's mom Beth gave it to me. I take it every day, it helps a bit."

"I'm glad." She turned her head. "What's that, Sam? I told you I can't hear Trey, what did he say?" She tilted her head as if listening. Rupert watched Dan's face as understanding dawned. The ailing man looked from Temerity to Fay with a smile. "Well that's just ignorant, isn't it?" Temerity exclaimed. "Does he think Dan shouldn't take *his* medication?"

They all waited for Samantha's unheard answer, and Temerity gave "her" sufficient time and then snorted petulantly. "I don't believe that. Medication, when it's prescribed by a doctor, is a *smart* thing to do! Taking drugs for *no reason* is dangerous, that's different. Fay told me Trey is stubborn, I guess he doesn't want to learn anything new. I guess you can't fix stupid."

Rupert was uncertain of what to do but he wanted to help. He snapped his cello case closed and stood up from the bench. "Does, uh, Samantha want to come to lunch with us?" he asked Temerity, feeling pretty stupid.

Temerity turned back. "She's busy!" she said. "Fay, is it okay if Sam hangs out with Trey for a little bit?"

"Okay," Fay said. "What is she saying to him now?"

She pretended to listen. "Samantha is telling him that he's selfish and he should be a better friend."

Fay's eyes lit up, and there was victory in her voice as she called out. "You better listen to her, Trey! You've been mean and rude, and you know it!" She paused herself and then added, "Wouldn't hurt you to listen to someone else for a while. I'm sick of listening to you! You can't just blame me, I'm tired of it."

Temerity smiled, "Samantha, tell Trey about when my friend Jimmy tried to kill himself, and then he got help, meaning *medication*, and now he's a happy dad! See what he says to that! Ha!" She turned back to Dan.

"Well, Dan?" Temerity reached down until she found his shoulder and offered her free hand to shake. He took it, weakly, and barely squeezed. She did not let go. "It was nice to play for you guys today. Are you sure you don't want to go to the clinic? Maybe they can make you more comfortable?"

"Thank you, no." Dan's soft voice was so tortured Temerity felt the raking pain in her own chest. "I know I don't have lots of days left, so I'd rather spend them looking up at the sky and out over the park than staring at stained ceiling tiles. You appreciate things more when you know you have only measured doses left of it."

Temerity laughed. "Well, I can't advise you there, as I have no idea what stained ceiling tiles look like, but it sounds like you made the right choice."

Dan laughed, just a few involuntary shakes. "Thank you for the music, young lady."

Temerity squeezed the hand a little tighter. "Thank you for being a good friend to people who really need it," she said sincerely. "Goodbye."

"Goodbye."

Temerity made her way back to Rupert, folded her stick, took his arm and walked away from the homeless pair, leaving them to fight cold, pain, hunger, and their personal demons. So many demons.

She did not look back for fear that the warm streaks of tears on her cheeks would give her away.

29

Temerity made it to the concert hall the required hour before the concert. She was long past being nervous about performing, but the familiar sense of excitement for the live audience and the cumulative result of all their combined work still thrilled and energized her.

Tonight though, there was a sense of lingering sadness tainting the thrill. The suffering of others was not something that Temerity, like so many modern people, could just shrug off. She could not come in contact with a child who was dying or a family that was homeless and dismiss their pain like a pesky fly by replacing it with a trip to the mall. So, after she had made sure her instrument was tuned and had changed into her black velvet gown and satin flats, she went to find some quiet solace in the catacombs.

The hugeness of the space, combined with the solitude she could find there, gave her an overwhelming sense of peace and belonging. So many artists had walked these halls before her, greater talents by far than herself. Instead of triggering feelings of jealousy or resentment, the thought comforted her, made her realize that she was part of something much bigger. She was a contributor, a participant in something far more complex and intricate than anything she could be alone, and she was glad. The players would change, the music that was performed would vary, but being part of something bigger, a cog in the intricate, imaginative machinery of art, made her feel she was part of a tribe, a community within a larger community, within a city, within a state, a country, a world.

Tonight, she needed to feel that inclusion, that vastness, and that sense of perspective. *No matter how small we are, we are part of something more*, she thought. She was lucky, she knew it, and she always had known it. What impressed her now, and what she could not stop thinking about, was that even someone with nothing, someone who was dying painfully, should not have to be alone and forgotten. As she walked slowly, her stick tapping as softly as she could manage in the echoing, crisscrossing aisles through the neatly stacked flotsam and jetsam of theatre, she wished for Dan to find the comfort he needed in the sky he loved, whether he saw it blue, cloudy, or filled with a million stars. Temerity understood that. She couldn't see it, but the hugeness of the universe and her tiny space in it, important or not, reassured her.

And, she had to admit to herself as she took a deeper, trembling breath, that tonight's performance was also different because Hugo was coming. Justice and Amanda had tickets and Temerity had asked, last minute, if he would like to join them. The three of them had agreed to meet her outside the stage door after the concert and go for a late supper.

The feeling of nerves before a performance might be rare for her, but there was no sloughing it off, Hugo was here, and that ruffled her cool. Temerity came to a section of the storage area that smelled of greenery. She stopped and inhaled, reaching out with one hand, until she touched the plants that were stored there, ready to be replaced on the stage for tomorrow's play by the prop department. The leaves were waxy and rippled. She moved in closer, stepping carefully up onto the rolling flat that could be easily moved into the wide aisle and then rolled to the stage for loading. For a few moments, she amused herself trying to identify the individual plants. Ferns, she loved, so tactile, there were even a few good-sized trees in planters, and she ran her fingers over the bark, then leaned in to breathe in the earthy, woodsy scent that lingered and survived even here, in this windowless basement space. It had always amused Temerity that humans had built this big underground warren, this interconnected, subterranean network of working space. It was perfect for Mole. She laughed out loud at the thought.

"All I need is whiskers," she said quietly to herself.

She climbed off the flat and headed back, thinking to spend a few moments in the wings of the theatre, listening to the audience come in, building the excitement. She took a flight of stairs up until she was on the theatre level, stage right. She touched the massive curtain, giving it a small shake, but it was so heavy and stretched so high above her that she sensed barely a ripple. On an impulse she stepped behind it, her back against the rigging for the theatre's fly space, and buried her face in the velvety crush, softening the sharp fragility from her emotional afternoon. The fabric absorbed sound and her ragged edges, smoothing her frazzled nerves.

Then she heard the muffled sound of someone approaching carrying something large and unruly. Not wanting to interact, she stayed where she was, standing perfectly still and concealed. The person came to a stop, several yards away, and Temerity recognized that the "something heavy" was a ladder, which was set up against the wall and extended, the someone muttering the whole time.

Holding her breath, she listened hard and the muttering became a flow of words. "There you are," a man's voice said, accompanied by a low laugh, "That's the one."

Then she heard a toolbox being opened, rummaging sounds in metal, and the distinct sound of duct tape being pulled from a spool. Then the man began to climb the ladder.

"Raul!" Another voice called from the very back of the stage, behind the backdrop, and Temerity recognized the second voice as that of the operations supervisor. She couldn't remember his name.

Something dropped from the ladder and clattered on the floor. Footsteps moved rapidly toward the noise.

"Raul! What the hell are you doing up there? You're supposed to be fixing the sliding doors before the audience gets in."

The voice from the top of the ladder spoke again. In full volume she could detect a stronger accent, and Temerity recognized both the name and the voice of the worker she had spoken to in the lobby the day she'd taken a fall in the ladies' room. "This emergency light was out. It was on my worksheet. I already fixed the door. It was just a wire jammed in the slide. It only took me a minute."

"You mean somebody jammed it on purpose?"

"Could be," Raul answered, "It was a piece of electrical wiring, so it could have been dropped accidentally by a set builder, or one of us."

"All right," said the grumpy voice of the supervisor, "Just make sure you clock out, you should have been gone an hour ago."

"I didn't know it was that late."

"Hard to tell in here sometimes," the supervisor said. "You lose track of time without daylight. Soon as you're done, clock out and go home."

"No problem there," Raul said, and as the footsteps retreated, he returned to work, muttering, "I won't be here much longer."

Temerity did not know if she was being fair, but something about Raul's voice disturbed her. It might have been the change from when he wasn't being heard to when he was, but on reflection she realized that most people were like that. We had one voice that was our own, and one that we used when others were listening.

Still. Keeping behind the curtain, she moved quietly along the wall away from Raul until she came out, unseen, to the open hall and made her way on to the artist's dressing rooms.

In the green room, Temerity greeted the music student who would be her eyes tonight, a young woman named Cynthia. Together they found their seats on stage and Temerity settled in to the surrounding sounds of the audience finding their seats, the murmur of subtle conversation, and the rustle of programs. Temerity could not resist asking Cynthia if she could spot a group of three, two men and a woman, seated near the center in the second row of the balcony.

"Are they wearing black?" Cynthia asked.

"Ah, I would need different clue," Temerity answered. "But they are all in their late twenties. One of them is my twin brother and the woman has long curly hair."

There was a moment and then Cynthia squeezed her knee gently and whispered, "Yeah, I see them! Up and to the left slightly."

Temerity smiled as a little thrill went through her. She was holding her bow upright, with the base balanced against her knee, and she moved her knee back and forth, sort of waving the bow "hello," as openly gesticulating to friends in the audience was strictly taboo.

"They saw you," Cynthia whispered with a little giggle. "They waved."

Just then, Anton strode on stage and the audience burst into applause. After an alert quiet fell, Cynthia squeezed Temerity's thigh, and she stood, playing a single long note on her instrument. The rest of the orchestra joined in, finding and matching the note, until they were all in tune. Temerity sat again, feeling a flush that she would normally not have experienced.

The concert went well. Both of Temerity's solos, though brief, felt particularly satisfying to her, not just the notes being perfect, but she felt the flow and emotion in them. Every few performances there was one that she felt was just right, and she was grateful that this was one of those nights.

Anton was pleased as well, which was made apparent by the fact that he had her stand for an extra bow. Temerity followed the sound of the orchestra rising from their chairs, and then clapped along with the other musicians as Anton took his own moment and left the stage, after which she began to pack up her violin.

And then, from somewhere offstage right, came a loud, but muffled boom that rumbled and shook both the floor and the lighting fixtures above them, a distinctly frightening combination. People screamed and Cynthia gasped next to her. "What was that?" the girl exclaimed.

"Sounded like something exploded, maybe a transformer, or a light?" Temerity guessed lamely.

"Or a bomb!" Cynthia said, rising panic in her voice.

"Shhh," Temerity soothed, "Stay calm."

Over the speakers came the pre-recorded message Temerity had heard many times during fire drills, "Please remain calm and move quickly to the emergency exits."

"Oh my God! Oh my God!" Cynthia began to whimper.

"Don't panic!" Temerity barked at her. "But go on, get out, I know the way, don't worry about me." The girl was gone in an instant.

"Bullshit to that," Terrance's deep voice said beside her, and Temerity felt Terrance's large, strong hand take her arm. "Let's go." Disoriented, Temerity reached for her violin, but Terrance commanded, "Leave it."

They all began to move, and Temerity could hear the sounds of panic, the pleas of people to not push, to move along. She could hear security shouting, "This way!" and "Center orchestra seats exit to both aisles!"

Even on the stage it was a confusing rush of bodies as Rupert and Regan joined them, and Temerity took the flutist's hand tightly. They all kept moving, bumping gently into each other, off through the wings stage left, down the long hallway to the stage door, and then out into the chilly night air, and the relief of safety.

Emergency vehicles were already arriving, and as they regrouped outside, Temerity asked the other three musicians, "Was anyone hurt? Is everyone okay?

"I'm fine," Regan reassured her. "I think the whole orchestra is out."

"Rupert?" Temerity called.

"Right here, all good," he answered. "Did anyone see what happened?"

"No," Terrance said. "I was stage right, so I was close, but it was out of our view. I hope to hell none of the crew was over there."

Temerity could feel the adrenaline surging through her veins, making her whole body shake, and the cold outdoor air chilling the fear sweat on her body. "There *was* someone over there," she said. "One of the maintenance guys. I mean, he was there before the concert, I hope he got out."

"I'm sure he did," Regan said comfortingly.

"Tem!"

Temerity turned toward the double tap on her shoulder and her brother's voice. "Justice! Are you guys all right?"

"We're fine," he reassured her. "I mean other than being stepped on repeatedly. I think my suede loafers are ruined."

"Tragic," Terrance said. And Temerity listened to them back slap while they did the guy hug, while she found herself wrapped in Amanda's lilac scent.

"Wow, that was scary," Amanda said. "I mean, not so much the boom, but everyone trying to get out at the same time. Really brings home the importance of emergency plans."

"Hi, Amanda," Temerity said, and held on a little tighter. It was nice actually, to have a woman's embrace, more tender and less hesitant than her brother's.

"Hi, Hugo, you picked a nice night to come out and see us," Regan said, and the next thing Temerity knew, she had let go of Amanda and was embedded in the scent of pine and black pepper. She was wrapped in an embrace that was both strong and tender, and was determined to stay there for as long as she could without giving herself away.

30

They had to walk several blocks in the chilly air before they could find a bus that wasn't filled to capacity.

At the loft, Runt stiffly limped his way to the door to meet the twins, Hugo, Amanda, Rupert, Terrance, and Regan, his tail wagging insanely at the introduction of so much company at this unexpected hour, his cast thumping with every clumsy step.

Mouse, looking especially disheveled and annoyed at this interruption in his sleep schedule, stood up on the back of the sofa and stretched, sweeping the group with a sour gaze as though to reprimand them each individually. Then he jumped down with a loud thump and departed, sauntering toward the hallway, his belly swinging independently beneath him like an obese tourist in a hammock.

"What about our instruments?" Rupert asked, once they had settled into chairs with drinks or tea, depending on the alcoholic proof or herbal calming effect required. Runt had chosen Rupert's nice thick thigh to rest his shaggy head on, and Rupert scratched absently at the dog's ears.

Terrance volunteered. "I'll go back by the concert hall in a while. Hopefully they'll let me into the parking area to get my car. But we'll most likely have to wait until at least tomorrow for the instruments."

"I think you're right," Hugo agreed. "They won't let anyone in until they finish an investigation. Hopefully they'll open the garage by tomorrow though, I'll need my car."

"So will three thousand other people," Justice said. "What a logistical mess."

"Turn on the news," Temerity suggested.

It was on every local station. They chose one whose reporter was standing in front of the emergency vehicles parked haphazardly in front of the music hall.

"...at the Music Hall. The blast was described as strong enough to shake the floor of the stage. Everyone appears to have escaped the building unharmed. A small fire backstage was quickly contained by firefighters. Investigators from both the bomb squad and the fire department are inside. So far there are no reports of a bomb or incendiary device, and I'm told no bomb threat was called in. Unconfirmed reports indicate that the explosion may have been caused by an overloaded electrical transformer for the lighting grid." The reporter took a few steps to one side, showing more of the crowd behind police barricades, and several people waved and jumped up and down in their excitement to be on TV. The reporter continued. "The police have cordoned off the area and closed both Jackson and Washington Avenues as a precaution, and authorities are asking citizens to avoid the area if possible..."

Justice hit the mute button and there was a moment of quiet. Then he said, "I don't know if I feel very comforted by the fact that it may have been bad wiring."

"It's better than someone *trying* to blow us up," Regan exclaimed.

"But how could that happen, just randomly, I mean?" Temerity asked. "I don't know much about electrical or mechanical things, but I do know that transformers can blow up if they are hit by lightning or experience a surge of power that they can't handle, but why would that happen here? I mean, at that time? The performance was over, there were no big effects, no bursts in the lighting, nothing to create that kind of power surge, am I right?"

"Amanda?" Justice asked, "Any info from your fire cadet days?"

"Hell no," Amanda said. "The farthest along I got was foaming a smoking junction box. So, I'm no expert."

Hugo cleared his throat. "I'm no expert either. But if, for example, a piece of metal or wire fell across the connectors, it could possibly cause a surge and explosion." The four musicians, Justice, and Amanda all turned to gape at him in surprise. "What?" he said. "I used to help my dad on build sites as a summer job and we occasionally ran wire for a new home. While my limited experience does not extend to the construction and maintenance of transformers, I do know in principle it's not that complicated, so I have a hard time understanding how an explosion could happen without some kind of interference."

Next to Temerity, Regan laughed sourly.

"What?" Temerity turned toward her.

"Oh, I was just thinking that it's ironic. Simon would be able to tell us exactly what happened and why. Electrical mechanics and power sources *are* his area of expertise. Hell, he could tell you exactly how many amps or voltage units, or whatever they are, it would take to make that happen and what might cause it, and the exact effect it would have. Not that it would be much help after the fact."

The four men all exchanged looks. Amanda watched Regan with concern as she stared down at her fingers, but no one said anything.

Temerity cleared her throat. "Regan? I don't remember because I only, uh, ran into him once. What is Simon like? Is he foreign?"

"What?" Regan sounded confused. "Uh, no. I mean, his maternal grandparents are from India, but he's third generation American."

"Oh," Temerity said.

"Why?"

"Oh, I was standing in the wings stage right before the show, right where the explosion came from. I like to wait back there pre-show, it's peaceful and I can hear the audience come in. But tonight there was a maintenance man working on an emergency light. I heard him go up the ladder and then the operations manager came and told him to go home. It was a guy with an accent, so I wondered, well, never mind."

"Accents can be faked," Amanda observed. "Could Simon disguise himself well enough to fool people, even maybe you, if you weren't up close?"

"I….uh…" Regan looked terrified. "You think *Simon* could have done this?"

"Do you have that picture of him you gave to security?" Amanda pursued.

"On my phone, I do."

Terrance sighed. "So you didn't have it on you when we were so rudely interrupted. Anybody else feel naked without their phones?"

Regan's face reddened and she looked guilty. "Actually, I know I'm not supposed to have it on stage, but I forgot and left it in my pocket. I turned it off before the performance."

Rupert gasped as though she'd confessed to arson, "But you know you can lose your job for that."

"I know. I was mortified when I realized I had it on me. I've just been so scatter-brained lately."

She took out her phone, which she'd kept in a pocket of her sweeping black skirt, and turned it on, scrolling through her photos until she found what she was looking for. "Uh," she exclaimed, "It gives me the creeps to even look at him now, but this is him."

"Wow, he's handsome," Amanda commented. "That jawline could cut glass."

"Yes, he's very good looking," Regan admitted, "Also, it turns out, very psycho."

Temerity said nothing, but she reached across and tapped Rupert's leg, then turned her hand up. Rupert took the cue and asked for the phone. He gazed at the picture and then placed one finger on Temerity's leg and drew a small circle, their during-rehearsal message for 'yes.'

"He was clean-shaven when he confronted you the other day?" Temerity asked. Rupert made the sign again.

Regan said, "He's never worn a beard."

Justice surveyed the room. "Okay, so who has seen him? Rupert, Temerity, not much help there, and of course, Regan," he began. "So let me ask Rupert and Regan, if this man," he held up the phone with picture displayed, "put on a fake beard, and, I don't know, shaved his head, or wore a wig and tinted glasses, or colored contacts, or some other kind of disguise, would you guys know it was him? In your case Regan, could you pick him out from a distance?"

"Honestly, unless I knew to look for that, I wouldn't" Regan admitted.

"I wouldn't either," Rupert said apologetically. "But maybe security would? I mean, they are supposed to be looking out for him."

"But security isn't looking for someone who already works there," Temerity said quietly. "If Simon could change his look —from what you guys are saying he could do that pretty easily—and get a job as a maintenance worker, that would explain how he would have access and be in the building in the first place, and he wouldn't have to have sneak past anybody."

"But he would have to use his ID to get a job there," Hugo pointed out. "Right?"

"The Operations Director called him 'Raul.'" Temerity contributed.

"That's a pretty common name," Rupert noted, and Runt chose that moment to harrumph as if in agreement, then settled his head back on Rupert's knee.

Regan's voice was shaky as she said, "Simon has a loser distant cousin named Raul, I don't even know his last name. Maybe he could have borrowed his information, or stolen it? I told you, he's really intelligent. I don't think faking an identity would be a challenge for him." She came to her feet and began to pace. "It can't be him, it just can't be. What if someone had been hurt? Oh my God, it would be my fault."

Temerity reached out as Regan passed and snagged her arm, pulling her back down on the sofa. She kept a hold on Regan as she asked, "Remember when you told Justice about that stuff that you used to get the grease out of his clothes?"

"Lystoil?" Regan sounded completely lost.

"Yes. You said it had a strong smell, like gasoline."

"Yeah, so?" Regan sounded confused.

Temerity closed her eyes for a moment and squeezed Regan's hand. "So, I smelled that, very distinctly on the maintenance guy who said his name was Raul the day someone tripped me in the bathroom. I also smelled it in the bathroom, though no one answered me when I asked who was there."

"But anyone could use that product. Especially a mechanic, a janitor, any person who works with grease or oil," Regan insisted, but there was fear in her voice.

"We need to tell the police," Amanda said.

"Wait!" Temerity said. "Are we sure we want to accuse a possibly innocent maintenance guy for setting off an explosion that might have been due to faulty wiring or defective equipment? That kind of suspicion can ruin a life, especially if the news picks up on it, which they definitely would. Maybe Raul the maintenance guy is just Raul the maintenance guy."

Justice and Rupert shared the same thought apparently, because just as Rupert said, "His voice," Justice asked Regan, "Do you have Simon's voice on that phone?"

238

"I…I do. He left me a few threatening messages and I kept them, you know, just in case. Wait," Regan took the phone from Justice and searched some more, then passed it back. He stood up, moved over to his sister's side and laid a hand on her shoulder, holding the phone near her ear.

"Go ahead," Temerity told him. He pushed play and the recording of an angry man's threats began to play. Temerity leaned in and listened hard, asking Justice to run it back twice. Then she straightened up.

"Call the police," she said.

31

It was three a.m. when the detectives finally left. Though they seemed doubtful that Temerity's voice ID would stand up for a judge, they took the possibility seriously. A man who had introduced himself as Detective Pullman told them that a metal bar had dropped across the transformer grid, causing the power surge, and it could have been planted there. Since it was obvious Simon had been following Regan, they made arrangements to meet Terrance at his apartment with a bomb-squad dog to make sure it was "cleared." Terrance refused to let Regan go with him.

"No Ma'am," he told her. "You heard the detectives, they don't want you anywhere until they've checked it. Don't worry, I'll walk the dog. You'll stay here."

"But…" Regan began to object.

"Of course you will," Temerity insisted. "I'll lend you some pajamas, and I have a new toothbrush. I think it's safe to say that rehearsal will be cancelled tomorrow, so we can sleep in."

Rupert and Hugo left with the detective, Rupert to get a ride home and Hugo to go downstairs, and Temerity wished she had the courage to ask Hugo to stay. It would have been nice to sleep next to him, to have the reassurance of a heartbeat in rhythm with her own, but she was afraid to admit it.

Amanda and Justice went into Justice's bedroom while Temerity took Regan to her room, found her something to sleep in, then led her upstairs to the tiny bedroom with the huge round window at one end. "We call it the choir loft," she told Regan, checking to make sure there were clean towels and everything Regan might want. "Is there anything else you need?"

Regan groaned quietly. "How about a new life?" she asked. "One without a crazy ex stalker."

Temerity sat on the edge of the bed. "Okay, first of all—we're not sure that it was Simon, I mean, I'm pretty sure that it was him, even with the fake accent, but I could be wrong, wouldn't be the first time. Second—this building is impossible to get into without being buzzed in. Third—Justice and I are both downstairs, and—"

The mattress shook as though something heavy had dropped onto it and Temerity hesitated, then a demanding "meow" told her that Mouse had jumped onto the bed. Temerity laughed and reached out to scratch his scruffy head. "And, you've got your guard-cat right here. Runt may be a bit out of service, but he can still bark like hell if anyone comes to the door. Which, by the way, is a metal fire door. Nobody's getting in unless we say so."

"Thank you," Regan whispered.

"Feel free to have a bath or shower, or snuggle up in bed. I won't wake you, just come down when you get up in the morning, or afternoon, as the case may be."

"Temerity?"

"Yes?"

"I don't know how much more of this I can take." Regan's voice cracked, and she cried quietly. Temerity waited. "I'm in danger, and worse, now I'm putting other people in danger. Maybe I should move somewhere else, somewhere I can hide?"

Temerity thought about that. The idea of living one's life incognito, of hiding who you are, of being unable to do the job you love because it would identify you, was abhorrent to her. She immediately rejected the idea, but was that fair when the option was a life of constant fear for yourself and the people around you? She took a deep breath before she answered.

"Here's what I think," Temerity said at last, "You should stay with us or Terrance long enough to see if the police find out whether or not Raul the maintenance guy is one and the same as Simon the ex. If they do, then they will have not only a good lead, but also several reasons to put him away. I mean, if he was responsible for the explosion. That's a really serious crime."

"So is murdering your estranged wife," Regan barely breathed.

"I know." Temerity patted the bed next to her and felt the mattress compress as Regan came to sit beside her. "There isn't going to be a murder. You can identify him as the driver of the car that deliberately tried to hit us. That's attempted bodily injury at least, if not attempted murder. The screwed-up thing about all this is that he hasn't already been put away!" Temerity smacked her fist on the blanket, an oddly unsatisfying gesture. "Look, you heard the detective say they are going through all the security footage, so we'll know more tomorrow. For now, you are safe. You are protected, and you are loved." Temerity slid her hand across the comforter, found Regan, and wrapped an arm over the smaller woman's shoulder. "So, like my mom says, 'let's sleep on it and things will look better in the morning."

"You're so lucky to have your brother," Regan said with longing. "I'm an only child, and it sure would be great to have someone to look out for me. I was so lonely growing up, which explains why I was overly eager to have someone in my life. I was blind to Simon's true nature— oh, sorry."

Temerity shrugged it off. "You can't second guess, and you *were* blind about Simon. You wouldn't be the first to fall for a handsome, charming jerk. Justice told me that I have an advantage in that sense because I can't be misled by good looks alone, and maybe that's true, but it didn't save me from being screwed too. As for having a brother, it is great, *sometimes*," Temerity said. "But of course, like everything, there are complications of a different kind. Different losses."

Regan asked, "What do you mean?"

"Caring for someone leaves you vulnerable, I guess." Temerity spoke slowly, thinking, "I mean that when you are attached to and protective of someone, then you worry twice as much. And when you make a change in your life, there are people besides yourself to consider."

"That sounds nice, actually," Regan said.

"That all depends on the brother," Temerity chuckled. "I guess I got a good one, but don't tell him I said that, he gets too cocky, and now he'll be unbearably overprotective. I'll be lucky if he lets me take the bus on my own."

Regan patted Temerity's knee. "I still say you're lucky to have him."

"I know," Temerity pulled her arm from around Regan's shoulder and covered the hand on her knee. Even as she squeezed gently, she wondered why the joy of loving someone was so entwined with the fear of losing them.

The answer was that, sooner or later, you couldn't have one without the other.

32

Amanda got undressed and climbed into bed, waiting for Justice's warmth to banish the chill of the sheets and quiet her hopped-up senses. Meanwhile, Justice prowled the loft, double-checking the locks on the door, and making sure windows were latched. Though they were on the fourth floor, it seemed wise when an evil genius was stalking your houseguest. He moved Runt's bed closer to the door and made sure the dog was comfortable there for what remained of the night.

When Justice did finally slide in next to his fiancé, she shifted eagerly into his arms, and welcomed the nearness of his body against hers. They listened to Temerity come down the stairs from Ellen's loft and shut the door of her own room.

"Do you think the police will find him?" Amanda asked Justice.

Stroking her back with one hand while holding her tightly with the other, Justice considered this. "Well, I can only think of one thing that would be sure to flush him out."

"What?" Amanda came up a little on one elbow, her eyes open, though she could see nothing in the dark.

"Regan," he said. "That seems to be what he wants, to frighten her, or worse." A sort of throb of anxiety seemed to pass through the dark room.

"Do you really think he would hurt someone else to get to her?" Amanda asked in a whisper.

"I do. I'm afraid I do."

Amanda shivered and snuggled into him more tightly. They lay there for a long time before sleep finally came.

Temerity got into her flannels and climbed into bed. Her brain was tired, but churning with impressions and thoughts of how to draw a defensive circle around Regan. It was interesting, she mused, how quickly you could become protective of someone, the way Aaron had of her, for far too short a time before she had needed to protect him in the hardest way.

He was in the hospital, and she had come to visit with him. He was sitting up, but weak. She had put on the paper gown and washed her hands with antiseptic soap, donned the mask that covered her mouth, then came in and climbed into bed with him, the way she always did. She was so used to the routine that she no longer needed any help with the gear. She and Aaron lay giggling and whispering about all the things they would do when he got out. Mrs. Bennet smiled with exhausted relief, standing up to stretch and said she would take a walk outside.

"Can we go out into the garden too?" Temerity asked.

"No, they won't let me go out for a couple of weeks." Aaron sounded more angry than disappointed. "They are afraid I'll catch a cold or something, that's why you have to wear that mask and suit."

"I feel like a germ."

Aaron laughed, though it hurt his chest, and put his hand in hers. "You *are* a germ!" he said. "Millions of germs!"

"Gross," Temerity laughed. "Okay fine, I'm a germ, but I'm a good kind of germ." She returned to the subject of future activities. "We should go horseback riding. I went once, when I was little," said eleven-year-old Temerity, "and it was really fun, bouncy, but fun!"

"That's a good idea!" Aaron agreed. "Do we have to take a lesson?"

"I don't know!" Temerity tapped her fingers on the bed railing. "I didn't last time, but I was riding with someone, this time we're big enough to go by ourselves."

"That will be so cool," Aaron said.

From outside the room came several sharp, terrified cries, a small child, maybe four years old, in pain or fear or both.

"That's so scary," Temerity whispered, sliding in tighter beside Aaron. "Why is she crying?" Temerity asked, as a nurse's footsteps, her rubber-soled shoes squeaking on the scrubbed floor, hurried past the glass window that separated Aaron's room from the hallway. They listened to a door open and close and then the child's screams receded to a whimper. "I'm not sure," Aaron said. "It happens a lot. She's here by herself. She's really scared."

"Where's her family?" Temerity asked.

"My mom asked the nurse and she told her that little girl only has one parent and three brothers at home. There's nobody else to take care of them, they live far away and they can't afford a car. I want to help, but they won't let me play with her or talk to her." He straightened up a bit against his pillows. "I'm glad you're not here at night. The sounds—it's awful. It makes me feel really bad. Mom and I call it the house of horrors. When I'm better, I'm going to do something to help here."

"What will you do?"

"I know that it won't be as good as family, but I'll come and stay with them sometimes. I'll make sure that someone is with them and they won't ever have to be alone."

"Good idea. I'll help you," Temerity said, and it was a promise.

"Do you want me to read?" Temerity asked, hoping to drown out the sorry sound of muffled sobbing and the calls for 'mama.'

"Sure."

So Temerity pulled out the book they'd been reading, the one they'd read before, the one about a little bear and a piglet and a sad but funny donkey. She read some of their favorite parts, laughing at the donkey's sarcastic words or the antics of Bear and Piglet. When they got to the end, Temerity's fingers slipped over the braille letters and she read out loud, "In that enchanted place, in the top of the forest, a little boy and his bear will always be playing." She closed the book and put it down at the foot of the bed.

They both lay there, holding hands for a while without speaking, and then Aaron touched her cheek. "I will be, you know," he said.

"What?" Temerity asked him.

"Always be there. Waiting for you. I mean, if…you know."

"You won't!" Temerity said with fury, as though the strength of her anger could make it so. "You're going to get better and come home and we're going to be cowboys."

Aaron laughed, then struggled to catch his breath. "You can't be a cowboy, you have to be a cowgirl."

"That's true," Temerity said.

He did get better, that time. He did go home, that time, and they did go horseback riding, just once. It had been a hot, wonderful, hay-scented day. Temerity turned over in her bed and remembered it so vividly she could almost taste the dust in the air on her tongue and breathe in the warm hay and sweet sweat smell of horses. How strong and soft the mare had felt as she ran her hand over her chest, and then her velvet nose. The horse had snorted loudly when she and Aaron had been petting her face, and they had both shrieked with laughter. "Germs! Ahhhh!" Aaron had joked.

A hot tear ran down Temerity's face even as the memory made her smile.

Some promises, she thought, *like some people, you never forget.*

33

Justice dragged himself up to let Seth in after only three hours of sleep. Runt was so excited to see the boy that he did a modified jig, his cast slipping comically on the wood floor as though it were ice. Seth laughed and tried to calm him down.

"Can he go down the stairs?" Seth asked.

"Not very easily. I'll give you the key to the service elevator. Then you're on your own, I'm going back to bed," Justice yawned.

"Did you stay up late?" the young man asked as he fastened Runt's leash onto his collar.

"Very. But not because I wanted to." Not wanting to alarm the boy, Justice didn't say any more about why, but suddenly he had a thought. If Simon had followed Regan to Terrance's, and then followed her from here the night Runt was struck, why couldn't he be here now? He might not associate the boy with Regan or Temerity, but Runt would be recognizable to Simon after the car incident. Justice shook his head, trying to clear it and then said, "On second thought, maybe I'll come with you, we'll stop by Tami's for coffee and muffins, what do you think?"

"Is Ellen there?" Seth asked.

248

"No, Ellen is away at culinary school, remember I told you? She'll be back for a weekend in a couple weeks. We're going to visit her on Thursday."

Seth tried to sound casual, but Justice could hear the strain as he asked, "Do you think it helped that we talked to Linda?"

"My mom gave me the prescription," Justice winked at him. He picked up a white pharmacy bag from the kitchen counter. "Here it is," he said taking out the large brown prescription bottle. "Now we just have to figure out how to get Miss Fay to take it."

Seth looked thoughtful. "I saw her yesterday after school. She told me that Trey was 'getting back some of his own.' I guess there's another person no one can see except Trey, not even Fay. I think she said the name was Samantha? Anyway, this Samantha has been telling Trey that he's stupid and selfish for not wanting Fay to take the medicine. Fay said that Trey has been much more quiet, 'cause he has to listen to Samantha."

"Can Fay hear Samantha?"

"I don't think so, but Trey tells her what she says and it's mostly stuff about getting better, teaching again, stuff like that. I think it's making a difference, Fay was saying she wouldn't listen to Trey any more. She said Samantha was much smarter than him and she didn't care if Trey didn't like that."

"Samantha, huh? Now why does that name sound familiar?" The truth was, Justice knew exactly why. It was the name Temerity had always used when she needed a fall guy. She'd blamed many of her childhood misdemeanors on 'Sam.'

Wondering what his sister had cooked up now, Justice threw on jeans and boots, pulled a jacket over his pajama shirt, and leaned down to put the leash on Runt. Just before they went out, Justice went back to drop the prescription bottle in his pocket thinking, "You never know."

They took Runt down the street and let him nose around a bit, having to wait not just for the dog to smell every phone pole and parking meter, but to pause often to look back suspiciously at his cast, and seem surprised to find it there—every time. After he had done his business, they dropped him off upstairs again and headed back out.

Justice went into the bakery and came out with hot chocolate for Seth and a large coffee for himself, as well as a white paper bag. "Bear claws," he announced. "We'll eat these at the park, and I got one for Fay if we see her."

They made their way across the sidewalk to the edge of the frosty grass and Justice was pleased to discover that Seth no longer stayed a distrustful distance away from him, but walked beside him. A huge lump swelled in his chest and he swallowed it down. Looking at the top of the blond boy's hair, he resisted the urge to reach out and give it an affectionate ruffle, but the lump thickened again at the thought of why. Who, Justice asked himself for the thousandth time, could abuse a child that way? Though he had studied and understood the psychological and pathological reasons for all kinds of behavior, it was still beyond his ability to grasp anyone acting on those impulses.

"So, how's school?" he asked, feeling lame. Everyone asked kids that question.

"Oh, it's okay. Fay told me something that helped a lot. She said that kids try to be like everybody else because there's safety in packs. So, when people *are* different, like me and my moms, they attack because they are afraid."

"Has anyone hit you?" Justice was alarmed. But Seth shook his head.

"No, I mean, just stupid stuff. There was this one kid who pushed me down, but Thelma came to school and talked to him." Seth's face screwed into a smile. "It was funny. This kid was like, a foot taller than her, and she never said anything mean or like a threat or anything like that, but he was scared, I could tell."

Justice laughed. "Yeah, I wouldn't want to mess with either of your moms! They are both too smart and there's nothing they wouldn't do to keep you safe."

Seth nodded, the smile turning into one of affection and relief. "That's true."

"It's nice, isn't it?" Justice asked, taking a sip of his coffee.

"What?"

"Having someone who cares about you, I mean more than anything else."

Seth snuck a sideways look up at Justice, but the grown-up's gray eyes were scanning the park, allowing Seth his privacy. "It's different," he said. Then amended it. "It's hard sometimes, you know, having someone worry about you when you're not, you know, used to that. But most of the time?" The boy's eyes shone with luck and love, "It's awesome." He wiped at his eyes and pretended to cough.

"I know." Justice thought of how many people cared for him, his parents, his sister, Amanda, his friends. For a moment, they walked in silence, Justice feeling the hugeness of both their blessings, though the thought of Temerity reminded him of the impending change and the feeling of being slightly frayed inside returned.

Since it was Saturday, and Seth didn't have school, there was no need to hurry. They went looking for Fay and spotted her with a group near the pond, but as they started toward them, the stillness of the weekend morning was shattered by Fay's scream.

"No, leave her alone!"

It only took a second to see what was happening. One of the men had hold of a child's arm and was trying to pull her away from Fay, who had both arms wrapped around the girl and was holding on with all her might. "No!" she screeched again. "Get away! Somebody help me!"

Justice told Seth, "Stay here," and started off at a run.

The second man stepped up and struck Fay over the head with a bottle. Fay shrieked in rage and pain, but the thickness of hats and scarves wrapped around her head prevented serious damage.

"Let her go!" Justice shouted, but he was far away, and even as he watched, the child was wrenched from Fay's grasp and lifted onto the first man's shoulder.

From the nearby bushes, Dan appeared and launched himself at the pair, grabbing at the kidnapper's knees and tripping him up. The man stumbled, went down, and tried to keep a hold on the hysterical child while he kicked at Dan, who held on valiantly in spite of his weakened state. Justice leapt the last few feet, landing on the man's arm and immobilizing him with his weight so that Dan could recover.

The child broke free and tried to run, only to be caught by the second attacker. Fay went after them, clawing at the man's face with her rigid fingers. The man cursed as she drew blood, dropping the little girl who scuttled up under the shrubbery, and the man punched Fay hard. She dropped.

Something whipped past Justice and in two seconds Seth was at Fay's side, kneeling on the ground. He didn't touch her, but he was speaking to her, quickly and soothingly. "It's okay, it's okay Miss Fay. I'm here, I won't let him hurt you anymore. You're safe. Miss Fay? Miss Fay?"

Twisting his head, Justice saw that Dan was flat on his back, his face ashen and gray, his chest still. He let go of the man he was restraining and the man was off like a shot. He looked for the little girl, and saw her running full-out toward a woman near the public restrooms who was rushing toward her. The girl leapt to her mother's arms.

Justice stood, spinning, not sure which way to turn, who to help. The woman hurried over with the little girl in her arms. "Is she okay?" he panted. The woman surveyed the scene and said to Justice over her daughter's shoulder, "I got her, help them."

Justice checked Fay first. She was breathing, moaning slightly, and her lip was bloodied, but the first thing out her mouth was a stream of curses that reassured Justice that she was down but not out. He switched to Dan, dropping to the ground next to him, he shouted to Seth, "Call 911."

Dan rolled on his side, drew in a breath and wretched, but nothing came up. Gritting his teeth, he tried to sit up. "Fay!" he called weakly. "It's all right."

Fay's body seemed to slowly release from the spasmodic grip that held her. She turned her head toward Dan in time to see him collapse against Justice. Then she seemed cognizant of Seth for the first time. She took several deep breaths and as her eyes cleared, focusing, she said to him, "Don't be afraid, it's over, they're gone."

Justice helped Dan to a bench while Seth let Fay lean on him as she rose to her feet and hobbled toward Dan, leaning on the slim young man's shoulders.

"Dan?" Fay whispered. "Dan? Is it time? Not yet, I need you. Not yet." She pawed at his jacket in desperation.

Dan was leaning back with his eyes closed, one hand on his chest and the other grasping the back of the bench so tightly that his thin knuckles were white beneath the dirt.

Justice was checking his pulse. "Just relax," he said calmly. "I think we should call an ambulance."

"No!" Fay said as she dropped onto the bench next to Dan and pulled his head up against her chest. "He doesn't want that. Do you, Dan, do you?"

Dan couldn't speak, but he shook his head slightly.

"I really think we should," Justice said again, even more calmly.

Seth was standing to one side watching both of them, white-faced except for his nose, which was red from the cold. "You okay, Dan?" he asked. "I can call my mom, she can come see you. She's a really good doctor, you know she is."

Dan nodded again, regaining a bit of stability. "I know she is, son, I know. She's one of the best and if it weren't for that clinic, none of us would have someone to care for us. But there's nothing more she can do for me." He opened his eyes, and they glittered up at Seth as he tried to smile and breathe. "That's okay. Sometimes, that's just the way things are. But I'd rather be out here. She should take a look at Fay, though."

Seth gulped and nodded, wiping at his eyes again.

"Don't be afraid," Dan said to him, and held his eyes. "It's just my time, not right now, but soon. It comes to us all. It's natural, there's nothing to be afraid of. Call your mom." As Seth pulled out his phone, Dan angled slightly toward Fay. "You send that bastard packing?"

"You did," she said, "it was Trey's fault! He distracted me when I could have protected Anna."

Dan released the back of the bench and patted Fay's hand. "It's been too long, Fay. You have to make Trey go away, and you know how."

Fay's eyes filled with tears and she cowered visibly, "I'm not sure, he's the only one who stays."

Dan nodded again and tried to clear his throat, which seemed to cause him great pain, but after a moment the tension in his face eased somewhat and he said, "He isn't. Remember what I told you. Even when I'm gone, I'll be there," he pointed up. "And your daughter never left you. She'll be here if you let her, you have a daughter who cares about you. And your grandson, Fay, Reece is a gift, and you know it." He closed his eyes again, and Fay helped him lie down with his head on her lap, and she stroked his back in smooth, even strokes.

"Promise me," Dan said through tight lips, "promise me, you'll try. That's all. People need you, that's a gift too. The greatest one."

Justice called the police to report the attempted kidnapping, then he gave the bear claws to Anna and her mom, who ate them gratefully. Anna's mom kept on thanking Justice over and over again as she clutched her six-year-old to her chest. Within fifteen minutes, Seth's mom, Beth, jumped out of a car that pulled up to the curb and ran across the grass toward them, carrying a bag.

"How're we doing here?" she asked calmly as she arrived, stooping down to examine the blood on Fay's face. Fay let her look at her, clean the cut, and accepted a breakable ice pack to hold against it, but refused the suggestion that she visit the hospital for an x-ray and stitches for the split lip.

"It doesn't even hurt," she said. "Take care of Dan and Anna."

Beth checked them both over, and Justice was impressed at the way Seth stepped in to help her without even being asked, handing her supplies when she asked for them, and distracting Anna with chatter while Beth checked the child's arms and body for bruising.

Dan had reassured her that the brief altercation hadn't made him any worse than he was already was, that being kicked in the back through a thick coat was the least of his physical ailments. He jokingly said it was refreshing to have a new injury to distract him from his usual pain. The police arrived and Dan forced himself to sit up and give them the names of the men who had tried to snatch the little girl. He had seen them around the park many times, even had conversations with them. They did not live in the park, but they were both addicts who spent most of every day there when they weren't committing petty theft. As far as Dan knew, this was the first time they had tried kidnapping and since Anna's homeless mother could have paid no ransom, their motive was likely far more nefarious. Shaking their heads in barely concealed disgust, the officers spoke gently to Anna and her mom, piecing together an accurate account of what had happened. Anna's mom had been in a stall in the ladies' room when Anna had spotted Fay, her teacher, through the open door across the lawn, and she had announced to her mom that she was going to see her. Her mother had told her to wait, but Anna had headed out anyway.

Fay had seen Anna across the lawn, heard the child calling to her, but she'd been distracted by Trey, she told the police. Justice helped them understand about the imaginary presence and they took it in stride, even telling Fay that crimes happened so fast sometimes there was nothing you could do. Child snatchers could make a kid disappear in seconds, they said, while commending her for fighting off the attackers, telling her that it was more than most people could have done. Fay didn't seem inclined to forgive herself, or Trey.

They were just finishing up their report when Seth said sharply, "Dan?" Justice turned to see him standing over the inert, sagging figure of the homeless man. "Dan?" Seth called again, louder and more desperate this time. "Mom!" Seth cried to Beth, motioning to her furiously. The officer stopped writing and looked up, Beth dropped the suture kit she'd been trying to convince Fay to let her use to stitch up her lip, and went quickly to her son's side.

Dan had slumped over and he lay, limp and still, against his right temple at an unnatural angle. Beth placed the tips of two fingers on Dan's neck and everyone moved into a loose semi-circle around them.

With his eyes still closed, Dan said, "I'm still here," and they all laughed in uneasy relief.

34

In combination with Dan's plea and Samantha's persuasion, Justice and Seth were successful in convincing Fay to take the first dose of the medication. Dory had explained that it would take several days before there was a noticeable effect on Fay's psychosis, but it would make her feel more relaxed, if somewhat sleepy, right away. The drowsiness would wear off after the first few days. It had to be taken twice a day, and Seth eagerly volunteered to drop by both before and after school. He took the bottle from Justice, wrapped it in a plastic zip-lock bag, and secured it carefully into one of the pockets of his backpack.

As the sun began to warm the morning, Dan and Fay moved into the shade of a large oak tree and settled in for the day. Justice, Seth, and Beth said goodbye and left Dan smiling tightly up at the blue sky through the branches gently swaying in the spring breeze, while Fay bustled around him, trying to make him comfortable with the ratty blankets she had stored under some shrubbery nearby.

"I'm going to bring him a pillow and a good sleeping bag," Justice said when they arrived at Beth's car.

"Like you did for me," Seth said, and smiled crookedly up at Justice.

"How did you know about that?" Justice was surprised.

"I watched you leave it in the dumpster, and then you left it unlocked, on purpose."

"Oh," Justice said. "And here I thought I was being *so* secret agent."

"You were," Seth told him. "It really helped a lot. It was so freezing in that basement, and it was damp, you know, it would drip at night."

They had never talked about the time that Seth had lived on the street, spending his nights by removing a vent and crawling into the unfinished, unheated basement of the twins' building. It had remained a murky, shadow time, conversationally off-limits. Though Seth had come close to dying from pneumonia because of the exposure, he had chosen the freezing, damp basement over the life from which he'd run away. Temerity and Ellen had tricked Seth into going to the clinic, where he collapsed and was treated by his future mom, Beth. The very woman who now stood beaming at Justice in gratitude.

"You must have been very afraid," Justice said, and quickly added, "I would have been."

"Fay and Dan, and some of the other people helped me a lot," the young man said. "They shared their food, and sometimes we would have a fire, until the police came and made us put it out."

"Do you know what's wrong with Dan?" Justice asked Beth.

"Cancer," she said simply. "It started as stomach cancer, best I can guess, but by the time I saw him, it had metathesized. That means it's in his whole body now. It's very advanced. The fact that he's still ambulatory is a tribute to his remarkable will."

"Did he have any treatment, do you know?"

"I think, in the beginning, but without insurance it would have been very limited."

Justice was shaking his head, wondering how much money was spent in his country on plastic surgery for vanity's sake while too many people were dying for want of basic medical care. It was one of those thoughts that had to be filed away under, "hopefully one day people will wake." Otherwise, it was just too sad.

"We'll do what we can," Justice said, and without thinking he reached out a hand and let it rest on Seth's shoulder.

Seth did not pull away.

When he got to the loft, Justice opened the door to hear his sister talking to the dog. "This rain has made you smelly! You're getting a bath." At the word "bath" Runt hung his head and slunk away, his cast clunking rapidly on the wood flooring as he beat it for the bedroom to hide.

"Oh sure, now you can walk!" Justice called after him.

"Morning!" Temerity called. She and Regan were sitting at the table with mugs of coffee, and Regan was scrolling through the news on Temerity's computer. "If you find anything, Regan, play it out loud so I can hear it," Temerity told her.

"How do I do that?" Regan asked.

"Just go to the dock and hit the dragon icon. It will translate to spoken words. Doesn't always get it right, but pretty damn close. Or… you could just read it out loud." She poured coffee for Justice and handed it to him as he joined them. "Nice walk?" she asked.

"Other than the attempted kidnapping, physical assault, and emergency first aid, it was pretty run-of-the-mill."

"Back up," Temerity told him. So, he recounted the whole story, which left both the ladies in tears, but giving thanks that things had ended well, for today at least.

"On a lighter note," Justice said, "Seth got Fay to take her medication, and he's going to keep giving it to her. I thought he was the best choice for the job."

Temerity stopped what she was doing and turned toward him. "What changed her mind?"

"Dan. Seth. An imaginary person mysteriously named Samantha, who seems to have started a dialogue with Trey and neutralized his negativity. You wouldn't know anything about that would you?" Justice asked pointedly.

There was a small pause while Temerity's mouth thrust into a pout as though she might be trying to repress a smile, and then she said, "No-oh," with two sliding syllables and absolute innocence.

"Liar," Justice growled. "But for once, Sam seems to have helped instead of knocking over a lamp or eating the last cupcake."

"She was always getting into trouble, and I was always getting blamed for it," Temerity said reproachfully.

"So much injustice," said Justice.

"Oh, here's something," Regan cut in on the siblings' affectionate sniping. She read out loud. "Investigators on the scene discovered a ten-inch metal bar, which appears to have fallen across a small transformer's connectors, causing a power surge that resulted in an explosion. An official spokesman gave a statement to the effect that this was most likely the result of an accident, but when pressed, the spokesman admitted the possibility that the bar was placed in such a way that it could have been rigged to fall and set off the explosion. As of now, the Music Center remains closed. Though structural damage was limited, it will be several days until the electrical system can be repaired and brought up to safety standards. The police and investigators are reviewing security footage."

"Duct tape." Temerity said distinctly. "I heard him unrolling duct tape. Would that fall? I mean, within a few hours?"

"Depends on what it was stuck to, if it was used already, or maybe if it was heated, say, by a light bulb," Justice thought out loud.

"You mean, like one of the stage lights that came on when the performance started?" Regan asked.

"Whoever it was up on that ladder," Temerity deliberately did not use Simon's name, "he told the supervisor he was working on an emergency light. But of course, I have no idea if it was on."

"It's out now. As, apparently, is the rest of the electricity, at least in the stage area," Justice said.

Regan, who was still reading said, "Actually, the article says that in the meantime, they are working with a generator patched through the circuit breakers."

"I wonder if they'll wait to let us back in until it's all fixed?" Temerity wondered aloud. I know they cancelled the play tonight, but we're supposed to do a matinee on Wednesday for the school kids."

"Well, we'll see, I guess." Regan sounded depressed.

The door buzzed and Justice went to pick up the phone. "Yes?"

"This is Detective Pullman, I'm looking for Regan Cooper, her roommate told me I could find her here."

"And he was right, come on up." Justice pushed the buzzer, and in a few minutes they heard the heavy man's footfall outside the door. Justice opened it before he knocked. "Good morning, Detective, been a long night for you."

"You said it." He was winded and looked exhausted.

"Would you like some coffee?" Temerity asked.

Pullman grimaced. "No thank you, one more cup would dissolve what's left of my stomach lining. I came by to show you some photos." He glanced quickly at Temerity as he said this, but no discomfort registered on his square face. "Mostly for you to see, Ma'am," he said to Regan.

"Me?" Regan was fearful.

"Yes. We took some stills from the security cameras. We have not been able to locate the employee named Raul Thorpe and the address he gave is a P O box. Could you take a look at these?"

From his breast pocket he pulled out a few four-by-six photos, which were in black and white, taken from high angles and not particularly clear. Justice took them and carried them over to Regan, sitting down beside her. Temerity moved closer to the table, and stood with her head cocked, listening.

Justice studied them along with Regan. The photos showed a bearded man wearing a baseball cap and thick, tinted glasses, carrying a toolbox. "I'm not sure," Regan said. "I suppose it could be him."

Pullman nodded. "That's the last person we have an image of exiting the area of the explosion, except for the stagehands, who have been cleared. The supervisor confirmed that this is Raul Thorpe. He moved in and sat across the table, pulling one more photo from his pocket. This was an employee photo taken for an ID card. "What about this?" He passed it over and Regan reached for it with shaking hands. She studied it, leaning in and squinting. "Yes, I mean, Simon doesn't wear a beard or glasses, that's fake, but I'd swear that's him. Oh my God, that's him." She let the picture fall to the table and stood up, turning in place as though searching for an escape route in a burning building.

"It's okay," Temerity said, and moving closer to Regan, she explored the air between them until she found her and then hugged her. "Now we know. And the police know, this is a good thing."

"Is it?" Regan asked, almost hysterical. "Someone could have died, and it would be because of me!"

"No, Ma'am," said Pullman, also standing. "You can't start down that road. You've done everything you could to assist us, and we appreciate that. Can you think of anything else that might help us locate him?"

Temerity felt Regan's head shake desperately. "No! I changed my name back and moved here to get away from him and I had no idea he'd even followed me here until about three months ago when he confronted me outside the Music Center after a performance."

Pullman sighed and pulled out a notebook. "All right. You've already given us all his personal and family info and we're actively looking for him. In the meantime, I suggest you don't go out." His eyes cut to Justice.

"She'll stay with us," Temerity said before Justice had a chance to answer. Justice just shrugged with a smile at Pullman.

Shari Shattuck

"Perhaps we should ask the detective what he thinks," Justice suggested.

"Uhm, I think that would be all right for a day or two. This building is as safe as you could find," Pullman said. "But if we don't pick up Simon Ayers soon, we'd like to reassess."

Regan was shaking. "What does that mean?"

"If the explosion last night is determined to be deliberate, that changes the game and the FBI will get involved. In the meantime, we've done some checking up on Simon Ayers. He disappeared from his last job, left no address, and no one has seen or heard from him. That disappearance combined with his expertise in explosives makes him a high-risk priority." The detective rubbed his eyes, exhaustion showing in every premature line on his forty-something face.

"He's an expert in explosives?" Justice asked.

It was Regan who answered. "He was. That's why he was hired to try to invent ways to avoid them."

"What happens if you can't find him?" Temerity asked.

"Then the FBI might want to relocate you for a month or so."

"A month?" Regan squeaked.

"Or longer." Pullman wasn't mincing words.

Temerity squeezed Regan tightly to try to stop her from shaking and then drew her a few feet away to speak to her. Temerity held her firmly by her upper arms. "Listen to me. *You can do this*," she insisted. "If you want your life back, you *have* to do this," she added more quietly.

"You're right." Regan turned to the detective, taking one of Temerity's hands for strength. "Of course, you are right. I'll do whatever you need me to."

"Good," Detective Pullman said with a grim expression. "I'll have the office make arrangements, probably tomorrow, and we'll be in touch. In the meantime, please don't go out, and stay away from windows." He turned, gathering up the photos lying abandoned on the table.

"I'll walk you down, Detective," Justice said, and only Temerity heard the purpose in her twin's voice.

After twenty-eight years, she couldn't have missed it.

35

"Justice?" Temerity called, knocking on his door.

"Come in," he answered. As she opened the door, he checked the floor out of habit. "Pile of laundry two o'clock. Have a seat."

Temerity expertly missed the obstruction and went to sit on the bench at the end of Justice's bed. "I didn't mention anything to Regan," she said, "But wasn't Terrance supposed to have that soiree tonight?"

"He sent out a follow-up email this morning, cancelling it. Since there's no performance for the soiree to follow, it follows that a soiree couldn't follow the performance."

"I don't follow," Temerity dead-panned.

"No party. I invited him over here instead, what do you think?"

"Oh, okay. I'll tell Regan, if she doesn't already know. Hey, what if, since we unexpectedly have the night off, we invite Rupert and Hugo and Amanda and make an evening of it? Maybe it will help Regan take her mind off this whole awful ordeal."

"I'm up for it, you want me to cook?" Justice asked.

"We'll both do it. We can hit the farmers market before it closes."

"Regan can't go," Justice said sternly.

"I know, I know. So, okay, I'll stay here with her." Temerity sounded decided. "I'll give you a list."

"Don't need one. Amanda's coming over now, we'll do the shopping."

There was a little flutter of unrest in Temerity's stomach. "Sure, great. She'll be much better than me."

"You did not just say that," Justice reprimanded.

Temerity snorted her lips like a horse. "I know. I've been a bitch and I can't stop it." She slumped back onto the bed, narrowly missing a pile of books with her head.

Justice watched her somberly. She sighed with exaggerated excess again and rolled sideways, flopping one arm off the edge of the mattress. Another huge expression of release, and she flopped another turn, this time onto the floor next to the bed, where she lay on her stomach with her cheek pressed against the carpet, a limp, drained lump of human goo. Justice laughed.

"You gonna' flop your way through my whole relationship with Amanda?"

"Probably," Temerity muttered without energy, and then said, "Ptthe," trying to get the carpet fibers off her tongue.

Justice rose from the chair at his desk, picked up his sister's left foot and then let it drop. It fell without resistance.

"I suck," Temerity said, turning her face down.

"And?" Justice asked.

"I'm failing you as a sister, and I'm resenting Amanda, the amazing Amanda, which is beyond stupid, and I'm being a...what was that Fay called Trey?"

"A selfish brat?" Justice suggested.

"So you agree," she moaned.

"Do you want to lie there and feel sorry for yourself for a while?" Justice asked in a baby voice.

"Yes, please." Temerity groaned again, and rolled onto her back, her arms spread outward like a willing sacrifice.

"Ah yes," Justice stood up and looked down at her. "And now we have the usual lateral move to self-pity with a minimum time limit." He looked at his watch and waited. In a few seconds he began to count backwards, "three…two…one. Okay, you're done!" He bent down, got both of her hands in his, raised her into a sitting position, shifted her weight, and propped her back against the bed. She remained limp but upright. "So what cha' gonna' do?" he asked.

"Buck up," Temerity muttered, barely audibly.

"What?"

"Buck up!" she said louder. "Fine, use my own tactic on me, that's cheating!"

Justice sat on the bed, his thigh resting against Temerity's shoulder. She let her head fall onto his knee. "I'm going to miss you like hell."

With a large hunk of love sticking in his throat, Justice put one hand on his sister's thick black hair and stroked it off her face. "Like hell you will," he said. "It's not like I'm moving to outer Mongolia, I'll still be here."

"You'll get your own house, and then you'll have little Justices and mini-Amandas running all over, and you won't have any time for…" Temerity trailed off. Her head rose, and her mouth tightened. "Mmmm." She said, "That opens a new line of thought."

"It's all becoming clear to you now." Justice had no idea *what* was clear, but he could see the signs. Mischief was in the air, or at least in his twin's brain. "You might as well warn…uh, I mean, tell me what you're brewing in that cauldron you call a brain."

"I could be an *aunt*." Temerity seemed braced by this thought.

"Yes, if I have children you would be an aunt, that's how it usually works. I mean, that's not going to happen for quite a while, of course."

"But eventually." A puckish grin took over Temerity's face. "Just imagine the trouble I can...I mean, the things I can teach them," she actually rubbed her hands together in anticipation.

"That had not, I'm shocked to say, occurred to me. I'm assuming we're not talking violin."

"Oh no." Temerity got to her feet. "And I don't have to worry about not having my own kids to screw up, because I'll have yours! Problem solved!"

Though her tone had remained taunting, Justice recognized the slight hesitation in Temerity.

"Why are you so sure you won't have your own kids?" he asked.

Temerity crossed her arms and shivered slightly, but tried to cover the move by pretending to shrug. "We've discussed this."

"Dammit Tem," Justice felt anger rising in him. "If you don't want kids, don't have them. If you do, you will find a way. I'm getting a little tired of this 'I'm incapable' thing. It isn't like you, and you're starting to be indulgent!"

"You know what?" Temerity said sharply, "For my whole life you've told me I could do anything, even when it wasn't true, and I appreciate that, but you're going to have to let this one go."

"I'm not going to."

"We're not talking about riding the metro or grabbing a coffee!" Temerity was surprised by the venom in her voice. "I would be responsible for another life! You don't get it!"

Justice fought back a terse response and forced himself to wait two breaths. Then he said, "You know what? You're right. I *don't* get it. *Everybody* feels that way when they become a parent, or get married, if they have a modicum of intelligence." He stood up and walked back to his desk. "I'll be here when you come to your senses."

"My senses. Meaning all four of them," Temerity snapped, and headed for the door.

"Tem, come on," Justice started, but she was gone.

Probably because of the need to have someone listen without judging, Temerity thought of Geoff and decided to invite him to dinner as well. She used her directory to get the number and called the restaurant. When he came to the phone, she said. "Hey there coach, you're probably stuck at the restaurant, but if you were interested, Justice and I would love to have you come to dinner with a few friends. We have some news that might interest you."

"I'm glad you called. I saw what happened at the Music Hall, and I've been worried. Are you guys all right?"

"Oh yeah, we're fine. It was a bit loud and discordant, but everybody walked away, so far. Most likely the explosion was set up by my friend's psycho ex to try to scare her. It worked well. She's here now, so you'll get to meet her if you can come. We're not expecting any fireworks."

"You know what?" Geoff mused. "I haven't had a day off since I opened the restaurant and it's time for the new manager to face a Saturday night on her own. I would love to come."

"Great!" She gave him the address and told him six o'clock. He said he'd be there after the farmers market. Temerity ended the call and went to find Regan. She went up the narrow stairs and knocked gently on the door. "Regan?" she called. "If you're resting, I'll go away."

"No, come on in. I mean I'm naked, but…"

"I'll cover my eyes," Temerity said, and turned the knob. The scent of shampoo and moist air greeted her nose. "Did you have a nice bath?" she asked.

"Oh my God, yes, it's more like swimming than bathing in that thing. I always wanted a claw-foot tub."

"Well, now you've got one. So, listen, since Terrance obviously won't be having the soiree tonight, we decided to make an intimate one of our own. Just Rupert, Justice, Terrance, Amanda, and my friend Geoff. We're not gourmets like Terrance, but it'll be healthy and plenty of it. What do you think?"

"Who's…uh, Geoff?" Regan asked.

"He's the guy I told you about who owns "The Den," you know, the restaurant with comfort food."

"Oh, the free-empathy guy!" Regan said, interested.

"Him," Temerity agreed. "You don't mind, do you?"

"No, of course not. But, what about, you know, the police thing?"

Temerity laughed. "I think we're safe with this group. They'll all have to pass my voice recognition check." Temerity switched to a robot voice, "Identity confirmed. You are cleared through security level 4 and are authorized for casual conversation. You will be issued a regulation glass of wine."

"Thank you," Regan said, after a laugh. "I truly don't know what I would have done if it weren't for you and Terrance."

"Good thing you don't have to think about it, then. Tell you what. Justice and his flawless fiancé are going shopping for what they think would be good. Let's make a menu and give them a specific list. That'll really piss him off."

"Why would you want to do that?" Regan asked.

Temerity had turned to go back out, but she stopped, faced Regan again and said, "Oh that's right—you don't have any siblings, do you?" She tilted her head and explained, "It's not that I *want* to be mean to him, it's just nature's plan. Plus it's fun!" The sound of her evil laughter echoed as she went back down the hall.

36

"What's next on the list?" Amanda asked, standing in the sunlight next to Justice amid the swarming calls of free samples and milling customers at the farmers market. They were both holding canvas grocery sacks, but there were only a few items in them so far.

"Beets. I hate beets, she knows that." Justice said, growling under his breath as he looked at the list Regan had written per Temerity's instructions.

"Maybe they're not for you, did you think of that?"

"She's deliberately trying to annoy me."

Amanda shrugged and said pleasantly, "Probably." She walked toward a vegetable stand overflowing with greens and root vegetables. "Do you like parsnips?" she called out, holding up a generous bunch.

"Yes, get those instead," he said petulantly.

Amanda selected the parsnips and then a bouquet of beets, deep red with vibrant green leaves streaked with russet. "Look at that gorgeous color," she said in answer to Justice's scowl and then stood on tiptoe to kiss him.

They paid for the vegetables and moved on toward the bakery stand. "Have you talked to Temerity about what she wants to do after we're married?"

"I tried," he shook his head. "I know she wants to stay in the loft, and so far she won't listen to any other suggestion. She's so stubborn."

"No," Amanda cooed affectionately, "She's *determined*, and that's a really good thing."

"I'm still not eating beets," he pouted.

Amanda slipped her hand into his and they walked in unison for a moment, and then she said, "Justice, what *are* you expecting?"

She felt the taught muscle of his arm stiffen. "That's a good question. I suppose I want her to live near enough to us so that I can be there if she needs me. But I don't think she should live *with* us once we're married, or that we should stay in the loft, that seems…wrong."

"I don't want to ruffle any feathers, but could that possibly be why she's uncertain? I mean, she knows you want to stay around her *and* you want to go. Maybe if you were more clear about what you want, Temerity would make the necessary adjustment. If she doesn't know what you're hoping for, then I don't blame her for being confused."

"She's knows I love you and I want to marry you."

"And she doesn't seem to have a problem with that. Does she?"

"No." He scowled and scuffed one toe of his runners against the rough cement in frustration. "And you're right, it's not just her."

Amanda watched him thoughtfully. "Okay, tell me this—if she weren't blind, what would you do differently?"

Justice considered this, which wasn't easy, since there had never been a moment of his life that his sister hadn't been blind. "Well, most likely we wouldn't be living together now. I mean, it's unusual for sibs in their late twenties to share an apartment."

"I don't see why not if they're close, but you're right, it's unusual—in this country anyway," Amanda agreed. But she refused to cue him to go on, he would have to do it.

"I guess I wouldn't feel so responsible," Justice admitted. "So I wouldn't be pressuring her to do something that makes me feel more comfortable."

Amanda squeezed his arm. "That's probably true. I have a recommendation. Let's let her work it out."

"So, I just sit in the dark and worry?"

Amanda laughed again, "You're going to be a great dad."

"Speaking of, Tem is threatening to teach our kids all kinds of naughty, wild stuff." To minimize the effect of being a tattletale, he added quickly. "I mean, if we do have kids."

"I hope we do, in a few years. And you know what? That's what crazy aunts are for!" Amanda hummed a bit. "Hope I get a chance to be one, too."

Justice spotted an open bench in the shade off the sidewalk and led Amanda to it. "That's another thing, she's suddenly decided she can never get married or have kids. I never heard her talk this way before you and I got together."

Amanda opened her mouth to say that was silly, but she immediately realized that it wasn't her call to make. "I can understand why she'd be hesitant, and I can see why she believes that's being responsible, but of course, she can do anything."

"I know…" Justice trailed off and leaned forward, squinting a bit. "Would you mind getting the bread and the fruit? I see someone I want to talk to."

"An ex?" Amanda teased, trying to see whom he had spotted.

"Yes." Justice pointed out Geoff. "There he is. Fifty-year-old men with silver hair have always been my thing. I guess I'm with you for the novelty of it." He kissed her. "I'm going to talk to Geoff, the guy I told you about who gives out lunches to the homeless people. He befriended Temerity—or just happened into in her path and was added to the favorites list. I just want to say 'hi.'" Amanda kissed him back. She started to go, and he held her arm so that she turned back.

"What?" she asked.

"I'm so grateful for you."

Her eyes glittered with soft love and she smiled, winked, and went off. Taking his time, Justice moved though the milling crowd until he came to a stop in front of an empty chair. It was pulled up to a table with a small sign that read, "Free Empathy."

"Hello, Geoff," Justice said. "Mind if I sit down?"

"Please do." Geoff said nothing more, just waited, looking very pleasant and unconcerned.

"So…this empathy thing, does it extend to complaining about something that's completely selfish?"

"Interesting definition of a concern," Geoff said. "What are you talking about in particular?"

Justice sat back against the metal folding chair and looked at his hands on the table. "Well, I'm in love and engaged to the most amazing woman in the history of the planet. I live with my sister, who is blind. I want to get a house with my fiancé, but my sister is blind, I can't just walk away and not worry any more, because…my sister is blind."

Geoff was nodding. "And exceptional," he said.

"And blind," Justice reminded him. "I can't imagine how I would feel if something happened to her. I mean, when I'm around, I can keep an eye on her, and on things for her, if you know what I mean."

The silver head nodded.

"It's just always been a part of my life—watching out for her. I'm not sure if I can walk away and trust that she'll be fine without me."

"And how does that make you feel?" Geoff asked.

"Selfish!"

"Which one? Going on and having a life of your own? Or not going, so you won't have to worry?"

"Uh, both?" Justice said, realizing with a brutal punch to the gut that he was setting himself up either way.

"Well, how long have you known that you can control the world around you?"

"What?" Justice asked. "Never!"

"Really? Congratulations. You are the first."

"I don't control anything except me!" Justice said, more forcibly than he had expected.

"Then why would you be responsible if something happened to someone else?"

"I...well...I mean...it's different," Justice sputtered. Geoff just tilted his head slightly, the gentle smile never wavering. Justice let the thought sink in. "I suppose I need to take a look at that," he admitted wryly. "I'm just worried for her."

"And no shortage of self-blame. Let me let you in on a secret. You will worry. You love your family. If Temerity *weren't* blind, you would worry about her, and if she were sighted and something happened to her, you would feel helpless and partially responsible. You would still play the 'if only...' game. That's part of loving someone. And if you have any compassion at all, you will worry for people you will never meet, you will feel hurt and despair when other people suffer."

"She's my sister, and we've always been together, even before we were born." Without warning, Justice recognized a distinct sensation, not a new one. It had been there for a long time but now it suddenly crystalized, like an image of a face emerging from seemingly random dashes of paint. "I'm afraid," he said.

"Of what?" Geoff asked softly.

"Of losing her. I'm afraid of losing the relationship that we have, I'm afraid that..." Justice paused, unable to name the definite shape that had so quickly formed from a few, simple, hard lines.

"You can say it," Geoff encouraged.

37

Rupert and Temerity were both standing near the piano as Hugo played Cole Porter. Temerity sang the familiar sections of the lyrics along with him, but Rupert just stood grinning, rocking his body to the beat slightly next to her, but not singing. *To each their own level of participation,* Temerity had learned from her friendship with Ellen. She knew better now than to push Rupert, he was fine the way he was, he didn't need to be like her. She was glad that he had agreed to come; he seldom joined them if anyone new was going to be there.

Temerity rested a hand on Hugo's shoulder and felt the warmth and strength of him rise up and mingle with the heat from her own skin. Sometimes, she thought, life was like stairs; you go up a few, then you trip and tumble down a flight, then you get up and run up two flights with ease, then crash into something piled up on a landing, then there's a delay while you either deal with the debris or at least make a path through it. Then up you go again, or back down. Sometimes it was your choice, and sometimes a stair is missing. We don't control events, she thought, we only control how we react to them. She thought about

276

Dan and his choice to stay out in the open while he was dying. He could control that, if nothing else, and she hoped it comforted him.

Perhaps because of her sightlessness, Temerity understood more easily than most that the only thing she could control was herself. She could help other people, or hurt them, with words or actions. Everyone's choices made a difference. The trick, she thought, was just taking that minute to notice and choose. Hugo lifted his shoulder under her hand and Temerity thought for a second that he was trying to shrug her off, but he was bringing the hand close enough for a quick kiss while his fingers were otherwise occupied making music. *Like that,* she thought. Hugo's easy affection was a nice thing to notice, and she wondered if she'd been a fool to choose not to notice it for so long. Then she reminded herself that relationships and each of the stages of our own personalities have a particular gestation period. Some parts of us were born ready-made, and others were still trapped in limbo. The building blocks were all there, but they could be built into so many different structures, some stable, some downright dangerous.

Regan called out from the kitchen, interrupting her revelry, "How do I know when the beets are ready?"

"When they are in the trash!" Justice contributed.

"You just open the foil and stick a fork in it. If it's soft, you can pull them out. Be careful of the steam!" Temerity answered, ignoring her brother.

Regan pulled the neatly wrapped packet from the oven and carefully unfolded the top. An enticing scent of truffle oil and earthy goodness rose from the rich purple-red vegetables inside like a tiny, delicious aroma cloud.

"Smells great!" she said.

"Wait until I put the blue cheese on it!" Temerity said. "I won't say it makes it smell better, but the taste is yummy!"

"Don't contaminate my parsnips with those dirt balls!" Justice threw in from the sofa, where he was nursing a glass of wine.

"Let me help you," Geoff said, and Temerity heard him walk around the counter and Regan demur, listening to the way her friend's voice curved and bounced when she spoke to this new presence. *One voice for ourselves, and one for others,* Temerity thought, smiling. She would have to amend that observation, she realized. It was truer to say that most of us had many different voices, depending on the role we were playing—sister, daughter, lover, friend, rival. How people presented themselves to family, bosses, mates or strangers was always noticeably different, at least to her. The thing that always spoke the most eloquently about people was how they treated others they thought of as "less" than themselves. That was the acid test.

And everyone in this room passed it with flying colors. The very thought of it triggered a burst of raucous joy in Temerity's chest. *There are so many good people,* she thought happily. And she wondered about herself. Did she have roles she played as well?

Of course she did. Hugo finished the song and she let go of his shoulder to applaud, along with everyone else in the room.

Geoff called out, "The fish is done. Do you want me to plate it?"

"You're the expert!" Temerity told him. "That's why we invited you. Just kidding, get some wine and sit down!"

"I like serving food, otherwise I would have chosen a different career," Geoff said simply.

"And we all like to eat it, so we're glad you did," Hugo said, standing up from the piano bench and stretching. "As far as choosing a career, it isn't always a simple choice for some people. My dad expected me to be an electrician, so I went to technical school. He thought I should have a 'real' career option, and now I'm fully qualified, union card and everything."

"How's that working out for you and your dad now?" Amanda asked him.

"We compromised. I play music for a living, and he has the comfort of reminding me at every holiday dinner that I can earn a paycheck hooking up two-twenty appliances when that doesn't pan out."

The three from the piano drifted over to help finish setting the table. Regan said thoughtfully, "Do you ever think about that? I mean, how lucky we are to have been able to choose careers we love? I do, all the time. Some people will never have the option to become a musician or a chef, or even an accountant. They are born to the world with no opportunity. That's the reason I started teaching at the community center. I just can't imagine my life if I had never been exposed to music or had the chance to study it."

"That's why places like the community center are so vitally important," Geoff said. "I think free choice has something to do with acting on an opportunity, but the option has to be available. There are thousands of examples of people who were born into poverty and drudgery and fought their way out of it, but there are countless millions who have broken their backs trying and still died poor. I always wonder how many Mozarts have been lost to us all. I myself would probably have ended up in a federal penitentiary or dead if it weren't for a particular teacher who took an interest in me when I was on a bad road in high school."

Temerity giggled. "Don't tell me you were the kid in the leather jacket smoking behind the gym."

"No, but only because I couldn't afford the leather jacket. My mom was a social worker. Talk about working hard your whole life and never rising above low income. Dad was a construction worker, but he died when I was fourteen, and I was pissed off about it. Mostly at him, and I took it out on him by failing. I shoplifted and hung out with kids who spent their time spray painting underpasses. Showed him, didn't I?"

Amanda spoke up. "How did you escape that?"

"My mom was always great. She understood what I was going through, but she was lost herself for a couple of years after my dad died.

She threw herself into her work, which is endless and thankless for the most part, and I resented that as well, like the mature individual I was not. But I had this one teacher and he got me interested in theatre and sports, and was just there to *care*. I'm still friends with him, me and about fifty other people whose lives are now productive and happy instead of in prison or dead, because one teacher just listened and didn't judge."

"So that's why you do the empathy thing?" Temerity asked.

"I suppose so. Pay it forward, he's that kind of guy. Retired now, of course, but every birthday I get a card from him. Remarkable."

"Some people are," Amanda said, and shared a heated gaze with Justice.

"And some people are hungry," Temerity said. "Let's eat."

There was a flurry of activity as dishes were passed and then came the happy clinking sound of cutlery on plates.

"So, you believe in fate?" Rupert asked Geoff after the initial tasting and compliments.

"Partially," Geoff said. "I don't pretend to understand the universal design, if there even is one that could be explained in our rather limited language, but I know that things happen that we sometimes can't control. If we do create our own lives, as some new-agers believe, then we've got a long way to go to Utopia. The way I see it, we are *all* creating our world, all the time, but we aren't in it alone. Everyone's thoughts and actions contribute to the whole."

"Good point," Justice said. "Just ask my sister. She loves messing with fate. Some people would call it interfering."

"Really?" Temerity asked. "Tell me again about Fay."

"That's not fate, that's biological chemistry," Justice told her.

"Wouldn't it be fate that you happened to meet her and have the capacity to help her?" Regan asked.

"Or luck," Geoff shrugged. "Maybe it's the same thing. Let me give you an example. Temerity, you and Justice know about Fay's friend Dan and his cancer, right?"

"Yes, Beth explained his condition to Justice. It's so harsh," Temerity said.

"Dan has only been on the street for about eighteen months. He was a successful broker. He had a wife and a six-year-old daughter. A drunk driver ran a red light and ended both their lives, and Dan's as he knew it." There were gasps and exclamations, Temerity felt tears start in her eyes and she wiped them with a napkin. Geoff paused for the reaction, then went on. "I know, it's unbearably sad, but it happens every day. Without them he just couldn't see the point in making money for money's sake, and he regretted every minute he'd spent trying to get ahead instead of being with his family. So he quit. Was that fate? Was it luck? Or was it his choice?"

"Well he certainly didn't choose the drunk driver part, that's horrible!" Rupert exclaimed.

"I agree, but it was his choice to leave his work and walk away from the material world, because it had no value to him anymore. When he found out that his cancer was terminal, you know what he said to me?"

"What?" Regan breathed.

"He said, 'Then I still have some time to do whatever I can.' And he set out to be as helpful and peaceful as he could be for the time he has left."

"He's really wonderful with Fay," Justice said soberly. "And who else would be?"

"You," Geoff said gently. "You and your sister, and that amazing boy, Seth. You have no idea what Seth has meant to her."

Temerity cleared the coating of sorrow from her throat so that she could speak. "When we talked to Fay's daughter Linda, she told us about the student who died, she thinks that's what drove her over the edge."

Geoff looked very sad. "From what I've gleaned, teaching was everything to Fay, and there's another good example of fate. Her mental illness has changed her life, drastically, and not just her, but her daughter and grandson too. You could say it's her choice to live in the park, but is it?"

"And that brings us to our news," Justice said. He told Geoff about the medication and Seth's part in it, and Geoff closed his eyes and bowed his head.

"Bless the children," he said.

"Amen," everyone echoed.

38

The week went by slowly, the Music Hall remained closed, and Regan remained out of sight. By Wednesday, she was twitching with cabin fever.

Justice had also gotten into the habit of accompanying Seth on his walks with Runt, and Temerity often came along too. They used the excuse that they wanted to visit Fay and see how she was doing, and he accepted that without suspicion.

Fay did seem more stable, though they often found her with her head on her chest, snoring away, never far from Dan, who was clearly weakening. His face was so thin that his cheeks were dented hollows and his skin, where it wasn't bruised with deep purple marks, was tinged with yellow, but he smiled at them with effort and when they asked how he was, he pointed to the sky and then laid a hand on his heart. Both Fay and Dan were getting good, regular hot meals, thanks to the twins, Seth and his moms, Linda, and Geoff—though Dan seldom had the stomach for more than a few sips of broth or some juice. Beth visited the park once a day and put him on a regimen of IV fluids and administered the doses of pain relief in a morphine patch, which seemed to make him far more comfortable. When he would sleep afterward, his face, normally tensed with pain, would soften.

Thursday came around and the decision was made to take Regan along to Ellen's visiting day instead of leaving her alone in the loft. So early in the morning, after Runt had been walked and Hugo had been recruited for the afternoon outing with him, Regan, Temerity, Rupert, and Justice climbed into the BMW in the underground parking and headed out of town. It wasn't a long trip, about two hours, and with spring in the air, the drive was very pretty. The seeing ones took turns trying to describe the foliage to Temerity in a way that she might understand it.

"Spring green is such a vibrant color," Justice noted. "In Mole-speak I would describe it as fresh water in a stream trickling over rocks."

"Ooh, that's pretty good," Temerity said. "I give you one point."

That made it Rupert's turn. "A meadow of orange flowers, um." He reddened and then said, "Kittens playing in the sun, so their fur is warm?"

"Nice! Two points," Temerity told him. And when Justice called foul she added, "You've had more practice, so he gets double."

"Wow! Look at that pink tree in bloom!" Regan exclaimed.

"Translate please," Temerity challenged.

"Uh, okay, Vivaldi's 'Four Seasons', Summer, the second movement."

"And we have a winner!" Temerity beamed.

"No fair!" Justice exclaimed. "You guys are all musicians and I'm a doctor."

"Of anthropology," Rupert and Temerity chorused and then laughed.

They put on a CD and sang for a while, everyone except Rupert, who tapped his thick fingers on his thigh and smiled bashfully.

When they reached the culinary school, they parked and followed the signs for "tasting day" to a large room. It was about sixty by forty feet and half of it was kitchen, the other half taken up by long rows of tables.

On both sides of the room, large windows rose from about six feet up the wall to the vaulted ceiling, allowing in light without showing the neighboring buildings.

Rupert stood looking around, then he whispered, "Heaven." Taking his arm, Regan sang out, "Well then, let's get on through the pearly gates."

Justice spotted Ellen working at one of the preparation stations. She was using a pastry bag to fill tiny swans made of meringue with a rich buttery cream. Pearls of sweat stood out on her forehead, though it was quite cool in the kitchen. She never raised her eyes to take in the growing number of friends and family arriving, but Justice knew that was the cause of her nervousness. He smiled sympathetically. His Ellen, as he thought of her, was all grown up. He didn't stop to consider if that was condescending, because it wasn't, it was affection that he felt for her. This young woman who had been so lost, and had come so far out of the tangled, impersonal mass of humanity in the city to find the courage to be here, to be herself. He told Temerity what he saw and she too beamed with pride.

"Can we go say hello?" she asked.

Justice looked around, most of the other people had taken seats at the long tables and were chatting or watching the work going on across the huge stainless steel counters and at the ovens. All of the students were very busy and focused on their jobs. "We'd better wait," he told her, and then described the array of goodies being prepared.

An older man wearing a chef's hat on his bald head stepped out from behind the counter and raised his arms, waiting for everyone to fall quiet.

"Welcome!" he said with a wide, crooked grin. "I'm Chef Wilcox. We're so pleased to see you all today, for some mysterious reason we always seem to get a good crowd." There was a tittering of laughter. "Our young friends here have been working hard for two weeks, and these are the pastries they have selected to prepare for you. On the table you will find a list of the items and a pencil. Please feel free to comment on whatever you taste and give us your impressions or criticisms. The point of today is to prepare the pastries for real people, instead of us jaded teachers, and I hope you enjoy it."

Rupert was watching Ellen with several emotions competing for dominance. Mostly he felt an odd fluttering in his chest when he looked at her, her lower lip pinched in her teeth as she concentrated, and that embarrassed him. He could feel his face flushing and paling in rapid turns. It had always been this way. He could never hide his emotions and that combined with his size had made him a favorite target for bullies. He and Ellen had both shared stories about that, small truths that were nothing short of daring for two introverts. Rupert knew that Ellen's mother had deliberately burned Ellen's face and left her to starve in a halfway house. Ellen knew that Rupert's mother had been an insecure woman who loved Rupert, but his life had been invaded by a succession of men she referred to as his "uncles." Most of them had berated and ridiculed him for being shy and overweight, and he had turned to music the way Ellen had to books. They had not shared much about how any of those facts made them feel, but the facts alone had been progress. The resulting damage and trauma were taken as given, understood but seldom mentioned, since they had both woken from similar nightmares.

The parade of confections began and went on for almost an hour, and by the time it was finished, they had all discovered new favorites and tried things that they liked, but wouldn't order. When the last plate had been picked up, the chef clapped his hands. "All right, anyone ready for lunch?" There were assorted groans from around the room as people leaned back to massage their stomachs. "Just kidding. Feel free to visit and chat with any of our professors, who are the ones wearing the puffy white hats."

There was the scraping of folding chairs on tile as people stood and went to greet the students they knew with many exclamations of

286

praise and satisfaction. Ellen stood all the way off to one side, but she smiled shyly when her friends came up to hug her.

"I will never eat again!" Justice said. "What's the point? Nothing could top that. Ellen, that was incredible."

"I'm glad you liked it," she said.

"So, other than the swans, what did you work on?" Rupert asked, after an awkward kiss on her cheek, which turned them both the color of ripe pomegranates.

"I did the flowers and the lace cutouts on the red velvet wedding cake fondant, and I also made the chocolate bombs. Oh, and the carrot cake *petit fours*."

"Those were my favorites!" Temerity said.

Regan and Ellen had never met, much less exchanged words, so Regan thanked her profusely for allowing her to be included, while Ellen tried to find somewhere neutral for her eyes to land.

"Would anyone mind if I stole Ellen for a chat?" Temerity asked.

A round of "no" and "of course nots" met her and she put her hand on Ellen's shoulder to be led through the maze of milling guests and students. They went outside and sat on a bench in the hazy, dappled sun.

"So, how is it?" Temerity asked.

"Okay, I mean…uh…you know, kinda' hard, but okay."

"Good. I want to talk to you about a few things." Temerity told her about Simon's attacks, and that since Regan was in danger she was staying in Ellen's room. "I hope that's okay."

"Uh, sure," Ellen's voice trembled as a ripple of fright went through her. Someone had replaced her! Already. Was this it? Would she lose her place with Temerity and Justice to someone who needed them more?

"You're not okay," Temerity observed. "I can hear that you're not. What's wrong?"

"No, it's fine. I mean, of course I want you to help her. I just… it's fine."

Temerity realized that she had frightened her friend and she hastened to reassure her. "It's only temporary, we don't know exactly how long. She actually suggested that she should move away and change her name, live in hiding to try to protect her friends." Temerity said sadly. "I thought that would be a bad idea."

"It was," Ellen said quietly. "I'm glad you can help her."

Temerity squeezed Ellen's hand. "I knew you would be, that's why I offered."

Ellen's throat had gone dry and she scraped one flat shoe along the cement of the patio. "If she needs to stay then I could—" she began, but couldn't finish.

Temerity tilted her head and leaned in until she was almost touching heads with Ellen, who had gone stiff. "If Simon isn't found soon, the FBI are probably going to move Regan anyway, so don't worry about her, she'll be in good hands. And anyway, it's *your* room, and you are coming back to it. You are my friend. No, that's not right."

She paused and Ellen stopped breathing, waiting for the guillotine to fall and sever the only real relationship she ever had., She had always expected it would end, on some level, but she still felt like the victim of a hit and run.

"You're not my friend," Temerity repeated. "You're my *best* friend. You're one of the most amazing people I've ever met, and you get more amazing every day. Ellen, breathe!" She squeezed Ellen's hand and felt Ellen exhale. "There," she said.

"How's things with, you know, Justice?" Ellen asked, once she had recovered.

"Weird, actually." Temerity wondered if she should tell Ellen that she needed a friend right now, but decided that wasn't fair. "But we'll be fine. It's like trying on a new suit that doesn't fit right. We need to get some alterations, or just break it in. It'll happen. What's stranger is that these old memories of mine keep coming up, in a really powerful way, it's bringing up emotions I haven't felt this strongly for years, and I don't know why."

"What memories?" Ellen asked with trepidation. For her, memories were evil, dark, and dangerous things, to be avoided, locked up and cemented in.

"Remember I told you about my friend Aaron who passed away when we were twelve?" Temerity asked. When Ellen made a positive sound, she went on. "The memories are about him. I can't shake this feeling that, I don't know, he's *around*. And that I'm supposed to pay attention to something, but I don't know what it is. Am I making any sense?"

Ellen smiled at her friend. "I always feel like that."

"About someone from your past?" Temerity asked, surprised.

Ellen shuddered, "No, not that part. The part about being supposed to pay attention."

"Well," Temerity laughed, "Nobody does that like you do! Are you keeping up the notebooks?"

On a shelf in her room at the loft, were thirty-five lined notebooks in which Ellen had recorded most of her observations. Though these had begun to expand into observations and *ideas* as well.

"Yes," Ellen said. "But mostly it's about recipes and things I need to remember now."

Temerity was pleased. "So, in other words, you are filling it with observations about yourself and your life instead of everyone else's."

"I guess so," Ellen seemed surprised at the revelation.

"Any advice about dealing with the emotional overflow from my past?" Temerity asked. "You've had to do quite a lot of that."

"That's different," Ellen said. "I had to let my memories go. I had to forget."

Temerity smiled at her friend's few words and great wisdom. "And I have to remember."

"I do know one thing," Ellen said.

"What's that?"

"You'll figure out what's right because you make your choices from a…" Ellen hesitated. As much as she loved reading, her emotional vocabulary was stunted, "…from the right place, wherever that is."

Temerity patted Ellen's shoulder. "Maybe that's what's thrown me off. I feel a bit like a gypsy, wandering around not knowing my right place."

"It's inside you," Ellen said simply, amazed that Temerity would need her to say it.

Turning her face up to the weak sun, Temerity smiled. "Thanks, Ellen. You're right, the answer is here," she put one hand on her chest. "Or rather, it will be. It's just not here *yet*."

Ellen said nothing. What was there to say?

Sometimes you could take action, and sometimes you had to wait, even if that was harder. Temerity had taught her that.

It was what made her so brave.

39

O n Friday Temerity got a call from Terrance to tell them that the Music Center had been cleared and they could go pick up their instruments. Temerity, having felt a sense of incompleteness without her violin, was eager to get over there. Regan, of course, wanted to go too, but Temerity wasn't sure, until they got the call from Detective Pullman.

"I have some news," he told Temerity.

"You've got him?" Temerity asked hopefully.

"No, but it looks like he's left the country. We have a report of Simon Ayers using his passport to cross into Canada just a few hours after the explosion. Before we knew anything about him."

"So, you think it's safe for Regan to go back to her life?"

There was an audible sigh. "Let me put it this way, this guy is smart. We found out that the cousin, Raul Thorpe, whose ID Simon Ayers had been using, has a DUI in Virginia and he skipped bail on a court appearance about a week ago, so he's considered at large. Have you seen or heard from Simon at all?"

"Nothing," Temerity said.

"That's a good sign. I would still recommend caution, but he's listed in the international law enforcement computer system now, so if he tries to come back into the country, he'll be detained and we'll be contacted and can pick him up. If that happens, of course I'll let you know."

"Thank you, Detective, this is wonderful news." She hung up and went to give Regan the good news too.

They decided to celebrate by going to the Music Center to pick up their instruments and then a lunch at the Den. Temerity noted the rise in Regan's voice when she agreed, almost on top of the question, to the chosen restaurant.

"Do you think Geoff might be there?" Regan's voice went so high it sounded more like she was four instead of forty.

"Most likely he'll be there, why?" Temerity teased, but she was glad her friend seemed to be interested in a good man after being with one who had mistreated and bullied her for too long. More than glad, Temerity was hopeful that the two might hit it off.

Because she'd promised she would, Temerity called Justice at work and told him what the detective had said and that they were going out. He offered to leave early for a long lunch and come home and pick them up and take them.

"You're going to have to let me have a sleepover some time, you know," Temerity told her brother. "I'm almost thirty."

"Fine, but your curfew stands. Not a minute after midnight. Seriously though, I'll be there in twenty."

Temerity laughed, but there was some sadness in it. The time was coming, she knew, when this daily contact would end, when she would see Justice only at special occasions and maybe every couple of weeks, then months, then…who knew? The thought gave her the same feeling as the times she had thought she'd reached the bottom of the stairs and strode forward into air because she'd miscounted the steps, a moment of terror, of empty air, of falling, and then, the jarring reality of the floor as she touched down.

When they got to the Music Center, Justice pulled up to the drop-off in front of the artists' entrance and told the ladies he would wait for them. He watched until they were inside and then pulled out to circle the block, a familiar merry-go-round for him.

Temerity and Regan went down the steep stairs and along the corridor to the basement dressing rooms. They'd been told that all their instruments had been locked into the green room, but when they got there, they found the door unlocked and standing open.

"Hello, ladies!" Rupert greeted them inside. "I'm glad you're here to collect your things. This room wasn't locked up and I haven't seen a security guard anywhere. Temerity, your violin is over here." There was a pause while Temerity assumed he was looking for Regan's instrument. "I don't see your flute, Regan."

"Is our other stuff here? Our purses and what not?" Temerity asked.

"No, I think those are probably still in our lockers, even though everything was opened and searched, I'm told. I'm going to check after this, but all I left that night was a coat, my wallet was in my pocket." Rupert said.

Regan moved away from Temerity and Temerity could hear her light steps moving around the large room, searching for the flute. "I don't see it," Regan said. "Oh, wait, here's a note."

Rupert looked up, posted to the message board was a printed sheet that read, "Smaller instruments and unlabeled items of value can be found in the operations manager's office."

"Where is that?" Regan asked him.

"It's at the far end of the catacombs, next to the workshop," Rupert answered. Temerity had passed it many times on her pre-show wanderings, and heard the operations manager inside.

"I'll go with you," Rupert said, but he glanced nervously at his watch.

"Don't worry about it. Guess what?" Regan told him, noticing the glance, "I'm off the leash, the detective called and said that Simon left the country for Canada."

"Well, I'm sorry for Canada, but I'm happy for you!" Rupert said.

Regan laughed. "Me too! Okay, so I'll be right back. Rupert, are you having lunch with us?"

"No, I have to get going," Rupert said. "I'm teaching at the community center. Temerity couldn't see the shade of pink that he turned, but she could hear the blush in his voice.

"Good for you, Rupert!" she said. "When did you sign up to do that?"

"After I heard Regan talking about doing it and Geoff's comments about people who don't get a chance to choose a career." He dropped his chin and mumbled, "I figured it was the least I could do."

"That's fantastic!" Regan said. "I was supposed to go tomorrow, but I cancelled. Ooh, I'd better call them back and tell them I can make it now." She pulled out her cell phone, then frowned. "Damn, the wifi is out, again. Oh well, remind me to do it later. Be right back," Regan called over her shoulder on her way out.

Temerity aimed her attention to the sound of Rupert's slightly labored breathing and said, "It was great to see Ellen. I miss her. But, I mean, I'm glad she went. I hope she wasn't upset that I let Regan use her room."

"She wasn't," Rupert said. "I think she was worried that you and Justice would forget her if she went away, so it was good that we went to see her."

"It amazes me," Temerity smiled warmly, "How often people think *I've* had it hard, when the truth is, I've been helped and supported all my life. Ellen is rising from the ashes of nothing but abuse. She's just plain..." Temerity couldn't think of the word.

"She's *Ellen*," Rupert said softly.

"Exactly," Temerity agreed, reflecting that what made Rupert so shy and reticent was exactly what made him care so deeply. That, she thought, outweighed it all in the long run. She cocked a head to one side and went to the open doorway. She stood for a few seconds listening down the long, echoing hallway that led to the catacombs and the stairs up to the stage. "Did you hear something?"

"No," Rupert told her. "Uh oh, I've got to go, I have to be there in twenty minutes."

"Okay. Rupert?" Temerity said to his footsteps as he went out into the hall. "You'll be great, this is wonderful of you."

"It's nothing," Rupert, as usual, deflected the compliment. But as he turned away and started toward the exit, he felt as though his chest had expanded a tiny bit, and a smile played at the corners of his mouth. He felt...sort of...well, brave.

Justice was making his third circle of the block trying to tell himself that the nagging worry in his chest was just residual nerves when his cell phone rang. He pushed the phone button on the steering wheel and said hello.

"Justice Bauer?" it was the gruff voice of Detective Pullman.

"Yes, Detective, thanks for calling, but my sister already told me the good news."

Almost jumping on top of his words, the Detective said briskly, "Do you know the whereabouts of Regan Cooper?"

"Yes, I just dropped her off at the Music Center, but she knows too."

"No, she doesn't. I've been trying to reach her, I've also called your house and your sister's cell phone, but I've not been able to get an answer."

"Well, nobody's home and there's very limited cell phone reception in the basement of the center. I usually have to leave her a message and wait for her to call me back."

There was a brief, tense pause. "Do you have a visual on them?"

"Meaning…can I see them right now? No. Why, what's going on?" The detective did not sound reassuring at all and Justice could feel a spikey heat clench his stomach.

"The man who passed over the Canadian border as Raul Thorpe, who we thought was Simon Ayers, was picked up in Montreal. Except it wasn't Simon Ayers, it was the actual Raul Thorpe, his cousin. Raul was stopped by a traffic cop and when he became belligerent, they searched him and found his real license. When they ran it the new warrant for his skipping bail came up, and that started the chain reaction that led back to me."

"What does this mean?" Justice asked.

"I'm means we have no idea of Simon Ayers' whereabouts."

"Holy crap," Justice breathed. He was already pulling up into the red zone outside the artist entrance. He threw the car in park, turned on the flashers and got out. As he started briskly for the stairwell, he barked into the phone, "I'm on my way in right now, as soon as we're back on street level, I'll call you."

"Please do." The detective's voice began to cut in and out as Justice went down the stairs two at a time.

He dropped the phone into the pocket of his jacket and almost ran into Rupert who, along with his cello case, was taking up most of the doorway on his way out of the lower level. "What's the hurry?" Rupert asked him.

"Where's Temerity?" Justice panted.

"I just left her in the green room. She's waiting for Regan to get her flute and then…." But Justice didn't wait to hear the end of it, he was bolting down the hallway.

When he came to the door of the large waiting room, Justice didn't break his stride, just caught the jamb and swung himself in. It was empty.

"Temerity?" he called, with the illogical hope that she might be hiding behind the furniture. No answer. Spinning, he hurried into the hall and spotted Rupert coming back toward him. "Justice, what's wrong?" Rupert said as he lumbered up with the cello case bumping awkwardly against his thigh and the walls.

"Where are they? Where's Regan?" Justice demanded, trying to keep from panicking.

"Uh, Regan had to go to the operations office to get her flute, someone had posted a note saying the smaller instruments would be there." Rupert looked around the empty room. "I guess Temerity went after her."

"Rupert, we have to find them!" Justice said. "Simon is still here, I mean, I don't know if he's here, in the building but…wait," a trickle of icy sweat dripped down Justice's back, "Did you say someone left a note? Why would they put some instruments in the operations office and not others?"

Rupert's splotchy face went pale. He dropped the cello and the hard plastic case bounced twice before it settled with a clatter, and turning, he pointed a finger back into the warehouse-sized storage catacombs.

"Go!" he said. "Far left side. I'm right behind you."

Justice took off at a full-out run while Rupert jogged as fast as he could behind him, trying to still his heart to keep the pounding from his ears so that he could listen for any clues to the women's location. When he came to a stop at the opening to the gigantic space, he looked around in desperation. Then closed his eyes and tried to focus. If Simon was here, he didn't want Temerity or Regan giving away their location, so he restrained himself from calling out for fear they would answer. Rupert slowed and stopped behind him, struggling valiantly to keep his wheezing at a minimum.

And then they both heard Regan scream. "No! Leave me alone. Help!" Her terrified voice came from somewhere distant but impossible to pinpoint. Justice started down the aisle closest to him, between chairs stacked eight feet high, and flats of sets, walls and windows, leaned against each other in neat, marked squares with corridors in between.

"Regan!" Temerity's voice came. "I'm coming!"

"Come on, then!" Simon's voice had no accent now, but it was filled with an irrational rage that made it unsteady. "You're next!"

"Regan, run!" Temerity shouted.

Justice and Rupert started forward, splitting up at the first intersection. But after going down parallel aisles, they met again. They could both hear the sound of running feet and a man's laughter, cruel laughter, but in the huge, empty space, it rolled and echoed and the source was impossible to pinpoint.

"Oh my God," Justice moaned. "I have to find her."

Another cry ricocheted around the cavernous floor, seeming as if it were coming from everywhere, and then sounds of a scuffle, something being dragged and muffled cries.

Rupert looked desperately around and saw something on the wall twenty feet away. His brain sped forward like a racecar out of control and off the track, and an idea came to him. He grabbed Justice's arm before he could start blindly forward again, and towed him to the wall where a sign identified a huge electrical box as the Main Electrical Panel, and searched the list inside. At the bottom was clearly marked, 'main breaker, basement.' He spun to Justice and, with a trembling voice and tears in his eyes, he said, "Do you trust her?"

"Who?" Justice demanded, desperation in his eyes.

"Temerity. She doesn't need the light. He does."

A crust of ice covered Justice's skin as he realized what Rupert was suggesting. "It's all midnight to me," he whispered. "Throw it!" he hissed to Rupert.

Rupert reached out, grasped the handle, and used all his weight to pull down the lever on the master fuse.

Absolute darkness fell without notice, twilight, or warning.

Two dim emergency lights on the far wall clicked in, a good seventy yards away, but they did nothing to illuminate the vast majority of the space. For thirty seconds there was silence, and then they heard Regan scream again, like a cat, and then her footsteps running, crashes, and confusion.

"Let's have some fun!" Simon screamed in rage. "You think that will stop me? God will lead me to what is mine."

"Temerity!" Justice shouted at the top of his lungs.

"Justice!" she called back, from some place he could not pinpoint. "Regan needs help!"

"Tem, listen to me," Justice shouted urgently. "It's all midnight… to all of us!"

There was another pause, and then Temerity laughed.

She laughed. It was the bravest sound that Justice had ever heard.

Rupert started toward it, but Justice put a hand on his arm and whispered. "Don't move. She needs to hear only him."

Rupert closed his mouth to try to silence his breathing, but the air whistled through his nostrils. He and Justice both stood, straining to hear what was going on.

"You think I won't find you?" Simon called out mockingly. "I know this place like I made the map. Just give it up, Regan, and come with me. Beg God for forgiveness and your friends will live. If you make the right choice."

"Don't hurt them!" came from a different area. Immediately, Justice could hear the sounds of squeaking work boots on the polished concrete floor, heavy footfalls. He balled his fists and tried to stop the tears from running down his cheeks, trying to will safety to both of the women. He kept himself ready to sprint into the darkness if he heard any sign of crying out or his sister in distress. But he could hear nothing now, only vague, displaced rustling.

Rupert found the switch again in the darkness and kept his hand on the lever. He stood there, waiting, listening, straining to be still, to be patient.

The seconds ticked by, sweat trickled down Justice's back and into his eyes, burning them.

"Regan, where are you?" Simon sang out mockingly.

This time there was no answer, and the footsteps were growing more distant. Justice swallowed hard and leaned forward, cupping his hands behind his ears to try to catch any sound or clue of where they might be. And then, there came a different, very distinct sound—a hollow, heavy thunk—and something hit the floor in a heap, like a sack of potatoes dropped from a ladder.

"Got him!" Temerity exclaimed! "Come help me wrap him up!"

Rupert threw the power on, the lights flickered uncertainly as the fluorescents sputtered back up to speed, and Justice was already moving toward Temerity's voice. Now that she wasn't shouting he was able to condense his search. He snaked his way between the aisles until he saw her, standing over a dark lump holding a short length of steel pipe in both hands, still ready to use it. He rushed to her and smashed into her so hard she would have been knocked to the ground if his arms had not been wrapped tightly around her.

"Okay, okay," Temerity said, she was shaking uncontrollably, but her voice was calm. "You can put me down. Regan!" she called out. "Where are you?"

"Here," came the muffled response, and next to them the greenery rustled as she parted the ferns and stepped off one of the rolling flats.

The heap on the floor moaned and Justice released his sister and grabbed some twine from one of the trees. He pulled Simon's hands behind his back and tied them together. Rupert and Temerity were both wrapped around the much smaller Regan, who was sobbing.

"It's over," Temerity kept saying. "It's over, you're safe."

"That was the bravest thing I ever didn't see," Rupert said, looking pale and shaken. "How did you find him so quickly?"

"It was easier than I thought, he breathes like a bulldog, and I had already found that pipe when I heard Regan call for help the first time," Temerity said, her own voice now choked with the adrenaline that was making her body shake and the backs of her hands prickle as blood shot through her capillaries. "And of course, I took off my shoes. Uh, maybe someone could help me find them?"

There were two seconds while they all absorbed the irony of that, and then peels of laughter interjected with sobs of relief flew from them all like a flock of birds startled into joyous flight from an open meadow of high grass.

They never made it to lunch. They quickly discovered the reason that the security guards had been missing. Rupert had found one of them knocked unconscious and left out of sight on the floor of the security booth, and another had received a panicked call from the main hall and gone up to investigate, only to find nothing and no one there. Detective Pullman had been called. There were questions to answer and statements to sign. By the time the four of them made it home, it was a glass of wine they needed before sustenance.

They all sat around the living room, Temerity upright and still vibrating on the sofa, Regan collapsed next to her, Rupert in the big armchair looking justifiably rattled. Justice paced while he talked to Amanda on the phone, reassuring her repeatedly that they were fine as he summarized the events of the afternoon. A few minutes after he ended that call, Amanda called back. She had checked on Simon, who had been admitted to the hospital, and reported that he had a concussion and a broken nose, but he would pull through.

"Well that's disappointing," Temerity said, when Justice shared the information.

"Thank God none of you were hurt," Regan said for the tenth time from where she was draped limply across the sofa.

Rupert fidgeted in his chair, unable to settle down. Finally, he stood. "I'll make us something to eat."

"And I'll eat it!" Justice said. "Suddenly I'm famished!"

The door buzzer sounded and Justice answered it.

A voice said, "Delivery!"

"What?" Justice was confused. "Oh, you must have the wrong apartment, we didn't order anything."

"Okay, but….are you hungry?"

"What?" Justice repeated.

"I happened to have some turkey meatloaf, sautéed kale, cheese biscuits, and a few assorted other items, I was wondering if I could drop them off. I heard on the news that you had another rough day, so I did the only thing I know to do in an emergency. I brought food."

"Geoff!" Justice laughed. "You are most welcome, and you have excellent timing, come on up! You need help?"

"No, I got it."

Justice buzzed him in and turned to the group. "Well, Geoff heard about our ordeal on the news and he's flying in meatloaf to calm our frayed nerves."

Temerity sighed, "What a great guy."

At the mention of Geoff's name, Regan stood up and left the room. Before he knocked on the door she was back, hair brushed, and mascara streaks gone from her face.

Geoff set down the thermal food carrier and opened his arms. Justice hugged him hard, and then everyone else took a turn, even Rupert, though his hug was more akin to a quick bump against a force field.

"You want to talk about what happened or choose a random, unrelated topic?" Geoff asked. "Your pick."

"Random topic!" Regan said, smiling shyly.

Geoff bowed to her, "As you wish. Oh, by the way, Rupert, I called Shawn at the community center and told him you missed the class because you were busy saving lives, but you'd be there to start next week."

"How did you know about Rupert's class?" Temerity asked.

"Geoff helped me set it up," Rupert confessed.

Regan piped up. "Sneaky! I wondered why you didn't ask me!" she punched Rupert playfully on the shoulder while he mumbled that he hadn't wanted to make a big deal out of it. "You'll be so glad you did," she told him. "I love teaching there, makes my day every time. I didn't know you worked with the center," she said to Geoff, switching voices midstream to match the intended listener causing Temerity to nod as her theory was confirmed.

Geoff raised one brow at Regan. "Sure. I teach basic cooking, most of my students are single fathers."

"I've never seen you there," Regan said. "Of course, I'm only there one day a week."

"Tuesdays," Geoff said, then noticed that everyone had gone quiet with curiosity, so he was compelled to expound. "What? She might not have noticed the guy in an apron and a very becoming hair net, but I would be less than human if I didn't notice a beautiful woman with a huge talent and a bigger heart. More than once I've stood around the corner and listened to you play for your class," he confessed to Regan. "I'm a big fan of socially conscious people who make magic."

"Why didn't you ever say hello?" Regan asked coyly.

"Because I didn't know you and you were there for the kids, but fate is a funny thing." He smiled at her and she turned quickly to Temerity, trying to hide the private moment with absolutely no success.

"They have so many great classes and other stuff too. AA meetings, grief counseling, they even have a blind psychiatrist who leads a support group for visually challenged parents. Isn't that amazing?" Regan sounded truly impressed. "I was too scared to have kids, which you can understand having now met my ex, but I was so in awe. I mean, talk about brave, wow. I admit I listened in and heard one dad talking about how before she could even speak, his daughter just instinctively knew to put his hand on anything she wanted him to 'see'."

"Wow is right," Temerity said, turning toward her brother and crossing her arms. "What a coincidence that you would mention a parenting class for the visually challenged. And *completely* unprompted."

Confused, Regan looked from Geoff to Justice then back to Temerity. "I'm sorry, was that insensitive of me?"

"My sister is nursing a false conspiracy theory," Justice said. "No need to apologize, she forgets she's not the only mole with a life."

"And speaking of brave," Geoff interjected, turning the tide, "I saw Fay today."

"How is she doing?" Temerity and Justice both asked.

"Fay's far better, which is not only good to say, it's fun to say. 'Fay's far better, Fay's far better, Fay's far better," he said in quick succession. "She must be taking the medication. Every time I've seen her, she is much more coherent, or asleep."

"Seth never misses a dose," Justice said with pride. "Any news about Dan?" he asked more soberly.

"He's been staying over near the lake," Geoff reported. "Fay is sticking to him. I think having him to care for is giving her purpose. It's brought out the nurturer in her, something she obviously loved and missed. Yesterday and today I didn't hear her talk to Trey at all."

Justice smiled. "That's a good thing." Then he shook his head sadly. "But it's heart-breaking to see someone as kind-hearted as Dan suffer so much."

Geoff nodded. "Dan has done more good than you know, and most of it while enduring the kind of pain than I hope none of us will ever have to face. If there's such a thing as karma, he's paid most of his."

"I sure hope karma is real," Regan said quietly. "I'd like to think that good people like your friend Dan will get to have a life full of joy and love next time around. And I'm sorry, but I really hope that bad people who do harm have to suffer for it."

"I'm pretty sure they do," Temerity said. "I mean, that feels right to me. I just wish it was instant."

"Sometimes it is," Justice mused. "I think Simon is about to find that out."

Regan asked, "What do you think will happen? They won't let him go, will they?"

"Not for a good long time," Justice reassured her. "I talked to Detective Pullman, and he said they are charging him with a long list of felonies, including bombing and attempted murder."

"Will I have to go to the trial?" she asked, voice quavering.

Temerity moved over to her. "Maybe, and if you do, you'll get through that too." Surprising everyone, Temerity stood up, pushing her chair away from the table. "Speaking of…I've got something to do, I'll be back later."

They all watched as she went to the door, collected her stick, opened it and went out. Justice called after her, "You forgot your jacket!"

She turned. "No," she said with a wicked smile, "I didn't." She went out.

There were three seconds of silence and then Justice, well aware of his sister's super hearing, stage whispered, "Hugo."

A collective, drawn out, "Ah," came from the rest.

Temerity went down to the second floor and stood on the landing for a minute. She could hear Hugo inside, experimenting with changing chords in a new composition. Taking a deep breath, she whispered, "I'm counting on you, Aaron," and knocked.

The piano ceased immediately, and in a moment the door was thrown open. Temerity could feel the rush of warm air from inside, and something else.

"Hi," she said. Then she stood awkwardly on one foot, wondering why it was so hard to take that next step into his space, why she was stuck there on the landing, as though roots had grown, not down from her soles, but up from the floor and were holding her in place. She cleared her throat. "It's been kind of a rough day, and I was hoping I could just…get a hug. If that's okay?"

In a second, she was off her feet, swept up into his arms. The sensation took her breath away with a glorious thrill of excitement and a rush of comfort. She rested her head against his chest as he carried her in, sat down, and cradled her in that peppery pine forest that filled all her senses, all of them.

"How's that?" he asked, with his lips against her hair.

"Perfect."

"Then stay. Stay with me Temerity, let's just have an adventure together and see where it goes. Will you do that?"

As much panic and fear as she had faced today, as afraid as she had been for her friend and for her own life, answering this simple request was far more terrifying in its own way. It was one thing to act on the spur of the moment with adrenaline and determination, but it was quite another to knowingly offer herself up to being split in half. For Temerity, who relied on her independence, who had determined never to love anyone way she had Aaron, answering this question would be her bravest moment to date.

"Sweet," she said.

Temerity returned upstairs two days later mostly to get some clean clothes which, having lived in Hugo's sweat pants and oversized shirts for the last forty-eight hours, she hadn't needed until then.

But life went on. The Music Center was re-opened and she had a performance the coming weekend, which meant rehearsal.

"Hey stranger," Justice said when she came in. "Remember me?"

"Barely," she grinned. "Where's Amanda?"

"Getting some sleep at her own house."

"Why, can't she sleep here?" Temerity teased.

There was a sigh from her brother. "It's not that I don't try…"

"Thank you, that will do."

"So, things are getting more serious with Hugo, I assume." Justice tried to sound casual.

Temerity felt a smart remark form in her head but before it could leap out, she switched gears. "I really like him," she said.

"And he's for real," Justice said. "And damn patient. I thought you'd never crack."

"Well, I have my reasons, smart ass."

Before he could prove her right with his reply, the door buzzer sounded. Since Temerity was closest, she picked it up. "Hello?"

She was surprised to hear Seth's voice. "Temerity, it's me Seth," he said breathlessly, "Can you come down?"

"What's wrong, Seth?" she asked. Justice started toward her immediately.

"It's Dan, he isn't moving, and he won't wake up. I called my mom and she's on her way over there."

"We're coming," Temerity said. "Justice, it's Dan! Seth is downstairs, he's upset."

Without a word, Justice went for his jacket.

Taking her brother's arm, they went quickly down the stairs. When they opened the door to the street, Seth threw himself at Justice, wrapping his arms around the tall man's middle and sobbing. Stunned, Justice took a second to react, then he hugged the boy tightly.

"It's okay," Temerity told him, reaching out and patting his back. "Let's go see what we can do."

The three of them hurried toward the park, Seth's eyes darting desperately from side to side, as though he were hoping help would leap out and come with them.

They found them not far from the lake, under a stand of birch trees. Dan was on his back, in the sleeping bag Justice had brought him and Fay was sitting on the ground next to him, distraught, but not frantic.

"How is he doing?" Justice asked softly, dropping to his knees next to Dan. He checked his pulse and found only a faint one. "We've got to get him to a hospital," Justice said.

"No," the voice was firm and rich with resolve. Justice looked up to see Fay shaking her head so hard that her tears flew from her face. "He wants to stay here. I won't let you take him. I won't let anyone take him."

"Fay, please," Justice began, but Temerity came to her knees beside her brother and put a hand on his arm.

"Listen to her, Justice. She knows what he wants, he asked her to make sure, and she's right to honor that choice."

"But what if they can help him?" Seth said.

"They can't," Fay responded, taking Dan's hand in one of hers and stroking it with her other. "It's too much pain," she whispered, "Don't make him say any more," the last with a pleading look at Justice, who nodded, and sat down cross-legged on the grass.

Temerity settled in too, and said gently. "How are *you* Fay?"

"He's leaving," Fay cried. "He's leaving me." She swallowed and looked up at the sky, "But he'll be with his wife and his daughter soon. They've been waiting for him."

"Mom!" Seth called and ran to meet Beth with her ever-present doctor's bag who was hurrying across the sloping grass. Beth took his hand and he pulled her to where Dan lay on the ground. Justice and Temerity made way. The pretty, dark- haired doctor of thirty quickly went through the motions of checking blood pressure and listening to his heart. She smiled grimly up at Justice and shook her head. Then she leaned down and said, "Dan? Dan can you hear me?"

In response his lips quivered in a "yes."

"Do you want me to help you?"

The feeblest motions moved the lips in the almost skeletal head. They formed one word, "No."

Beth looked at Fay, patted her back, and then leaned over Dan again. "I can help you to go," she said. "Do you want that?" There was no response, only a fluttering of his eyelids.

Seth started to cry, and his mom motioned for him to sit down next to her. She put one arm around his shoulders, kissed the top of his head and told him, "Be brave, sweetie, Dan won't suffer much longer." Seth pressed his lips together hard and reached for Fay's hand.

"What are you going to do?" Justice asked.

"I'm going to give him a second dose of morphine. With the patch he already has, it will stop his heart. It's going to stop anyway within the next few hours, but it will spare him any more of this anguish."

"But, is that legal?" Justice asked.

"Fuck legal," Temerity whispered. "Do it," she said to Beth. "End this for him." Trembling, she reached out and touched Dan's face. "Goodbye, Dan, say hello to your family for me. We'll see you soon enough." And then she rocked back and sat with her arms wrapped tightly around her knees. "What does the sky look like?" she asked.

There was a quiet moment when no one had the voice to speak and Beth was busy in her bag, then Seth gasped, and Justice saw that Dan had opened his eyes, just a slit, but he was looking up.

"Home," he barely breathed. His pupils slid laboriously to Fay, and then to Beth. "Thank you," he mouthed, and then he closed his eyes again.

Beth took a small white tablet in a packet from her bag and broke it open. Very gently, she placed it in Dan's partially opened mouth, under his tongue.

For a few minutes they all sat silent except for the sniffling, and then Beth took out her stethoscope, listened, checked for a pulse and said, "It's over. He's home."

They all stayed where they were, it was odd, everything was the same, and it wasn't. Temerity thought, *it felt like someone just left the room, that's all, they were here, and then they were gone.* Justice watched Fay, she leaned down and kissed Dan's cheek, then she folded his hands on his chest, stood up, and walked away.

Seth went after her, and when they stopped next to the water, he put his arms around her and they stood there, their two small forms indistinguishable from each other.

"I'll call the coroner," Beth said, watching her son with inexpressible pride laced with sorrow. "Why don't one of you call Fay's daughter?" she suggested softly.

"I'll do it," Justice said, and stood up to walk a respectful distance away.

Temerity stayed where she was. She knew the body was just in front of her, but she knew that Dan was no longer there. She'd been in this place before. Only it wasn't. It should have been somewhere this beautiful and it should have been less painful, but it hadn't been.

For the first time in a long time, she let herself go back to that place. She allowed herself to remember.

Aaron was in the hospital for the last time. They had known he was dying for over a month, but they had continued to treat him, to feed him with tubes, to prolong his agony. She had visited once or twice, but he did not respond and she could not understand why they wouldn't let him go. She didn't want him to go, more than anything else in the world she wanted her friend to stay by her side forever, but with the instinctive wisdom of an honest child she knew that it wasn't best for him. Then, Ms. Bennett had called and spoken to Dory.

"They think he needs to say goodbye to someone," she sobbed to Dory. "The doctors say that sometimes that happens, a person will linger until they've said all their goodbyes. I know he can't speak, I understand that's not what they mean. So we talked about it, his father and I have said goodbye, his sister, his aunts and uncles and the only person we can think of is…" she couldn't finish.

"If she can do it, I'll bring her," Dory said. Then she turned to her daughter who sat in a beam of sunlight in a bay window staring at nothing. "Honey?" she said.

Temerity turned her head toward her mother and in a tiny voice asked, "Is it finally over?"

Dory went to sit next to Temerity, "No baby, not yet." She repeated what Ms. Bennett had told her, and what the doctors had suggested. "You don't have to do this if it's too hard. I wouldn't be—"

"We'd better go then." Temerity stood up and moved to the door with such fragile resolution that Dory thought she might crack into a thousand pieces. It shattered her heart. Halfway across the room, Justice emerged from the hallway, took one look at his sister's face and without having to ask one question about what was going on, said, "I'm going with her."

They drove to the hospital and Dory and Temerity went into Aaron's room while Justice waited outside. Ms. and Mr. Bennett were both there, and when they greeted her, Temerity thought that etched in their hollow, lost voices, she heard all the sorrow in the world. "Hi," she said. "How's he doing?"

"Lingering," his father said.

Ms. Bennett hugged her. "Thank you for coming," she said. "We'll leave you two alone for a few minutes. The doctor has to stay, you understand?"

Temerity nodded and all the adults except the doctor, who she could hear quietly shuffling near the monitor, left the room.

Reaching out to find it, Temerity climbed up into the bed. The doctor made no objection, and pretended to busy himself with a chart, but he told her mother later that he had watched from the corner of one eye in awe. No matter how many times, he said, he had witnessed a child's death it had never affected him any less. The strength of these children amazed him. Every time. It tore his heart out, but reminded him what was real, what was worth caring about, and what wasn't.

Temerity nestled up next to Aaron, who was so skeletal that she could easily lift him to put one arm around behind his shoulders. He didn't respond when she hugged him. She put her mouth close to his ear and whispered.

"It's okay, you can go. I love you and I wish you could have stayed, forever, but I know you'll be waiting for me. You have to do this. I know you're not afraid of anything, except for leaving us, but we'll be okay. I'll never forget you, but you have to go now. You have to say goodbye." She put her head on his chest and closed her unseeing eyes, she felt his chest rise and fall under her cheek, only once, and listened to the faintest of heartbeats, it was so familiar, something she'd known before, known and shared for months in a time before she could remember, before she'd come into this world. She stayed there, for a minute or an hour with no sense of time, until finally, she felt someone squeeze her shoulder.

"Honey?" It was her mom. "He's gone."

"I know," Temerity said. "I felt him go, part of him went through me, it was his way to say goodbye." She sat up and let her mother half lift her from the bed as Ms. Bennett leaned over her son and wept quietly.

"Goodbye, my angel," she said. And then she sat down. Temerity went to her and took her hand. She stayed with Ms. Bennett as she waited calmly for them to take away the shell that had held the breath and life of her son.

Justice stood up from a chair when they came out of the room. Nurses and orderlies began to bustle about. Dory said, "You two stay here, I just want to speak to the Bennetts before we go."

Justice put an arm around his sister and she clutched at her stomach. "I think I'm going to be sick," she said. Justice walked her quickly to the bathroom, took her in to the stall and told her, "I'll be right outside, call me if you need me."

Temerity leaned over the toilet and rested her forehead on the cool seat. She retched and the pain and horror came up and out of her, and it was a relief. She sat there, breathing through the cleansing that churned inside of her before releasing again. After a few moments, the door opened again and her mom came to get her, wiping her face with a cool, wet towel. They rejoined Justice in the hall, and together, mother and brother led Temerity away. The only thing that Temerity could feel was emptiness everywhere, all around her, and inside her.

Temerity raised her face to the breeze that was floating across the lake, making the budding spring leaves overhead giggle and whisper.

"Thank you," she said. "Goodbye, Dan."

She stood up and called out, "Justice?"

He came to her side. "Take me home please."

He did.

42

As Justice and Temerity were having breakfast on Sunday, he watched his sister and felt so much love that it opened a fissure his chest and he spontaneously drew in a breath.

"What?" Temerity asked.

"How did you know I was going to…" he shook his head and laughed softly at himself, "…never mind. I want to ask you something."

"Should I be afraid?" Temerity joked.

"Do you want me to stay here or move in with Amanda?"

Temerity let her head drop. "What a week I'm having," she said.

Suddenly realizing that he should have acknowledged it before, Justice said quickly. "Dan's death was hard on you, I know it was, don't tell me you didn't really know him, or whatever. It was hard on you because of Aaron. Because you've been there before."

Very slowly, Temerity's head came up and she raised one hand to stroke her cheek, as though remembering the sensation of another's touch. "They let him suffer so long," she whispered. "They didn't have to do that."

Justice got up from his chair and went to sit next to his sister. He put his arms around her and said. "We don't know anything for sure about that. I don't, anyway." He sighed. "All we do know is that Aaron waited for you to come and say goodbye to him, maybe that made it the right time."

"Then I should have gone sooner."

"We can't change that, and you did everything you could. There's something I always wanted to tell you about…that day, something that you probably don't know. Unless Mom told you, and I doubt she did."

Temerity tilted her head in exhausted curiosity.

Justice went on. "Right after he passed…when you, you know, went into the bathroom to be sick. I went back in the hall, and Mom was talking to the doctor. He told her something that made me jealous, I resented it, because I was stupid, not to mention twelve, I guess, though that's not an excuse." He reached for her forefinger and linked it in his. "The doctor told Mom that he had just witnessed a wife saying goodbye to her husband and he was really awed and moved by it. Mom didn't say anything, she just nodded, because she already knew that's the kind of bond you had with Aaron, so did I, and I had felt threatened by that. Mom also knew the courage it took for you to say goodbye. I didn't."

"Why are you telling me this now?" Tears had started in Temerity's eyes and one by one, in a silent, sacred procession they rolled down her cheeks and dropped onto their fingers.

"Because I…I…" he cleared his throat and tried to release the choking sensation, "…because I was secretly glad to have you to myself again. And that was the most selfish thing I've ever felt."

"You were, as you say, twelve."

"Age appropriate, that's for sure," he laughed uncomfortably. "But there's more. I've been thinking about it and I've realized that I assumed that place for you since then, and that's not fair. Now I'm changing the rules and if you aren't all right with that, then I won't."

Temerity used her free hand to swipe under her nose. "I've always counted on you, it's not your fault."

"Are you really okay with me marrying Amanda?"

"Well," Temerity straightened up and sniffed, a half-smile hooking up the left side of her face, "*I'm* not going to marry you. And she's the best."

"Second best," Justice said. "When you lost Aaron, I think maybe it stopped you from loving anyone else that much, because the connection with him was just so…natural. I never understood the kind of loss you went through, because I never had it, but, in a weird way—I know I'm not saying this very well—but I sort of feel that way now."

"Silly ol' bear," she whispered. "I'll *always* have Aaron, and I've been a fool not to listen to what he taught me, with his life and with his death. For all my bravado, I've been afraid. And, I never expected to meet another Aaron. How could I accept anything less?"

"You couldn't," he said. "Sorry I was a sub-standard fill in."

"You've been the best brother anyone could have, and you will always be. *I've* been selfish. Go, love Amanda, have babies so I can kiss their feet and smell their hair and tickle them until they cry for mercy. *That's* what I want you to do."

"And what about you?" he asked.

"You never know," she told him, swinging his finger in hers. "Maybe, I'll become an old cat lady! Maybe I'll eventually get some weird family of my own. But I know this—I'm not going to spend my life being afraid to be loved. Aaron wouldn't like that."

"It doesn't suit you," he said, and kissed the top of her head. "I have something to ask you."

"What?"

"Will you be my best man?"

She smiled, "I thought you'd never ask."

Temerity released his finger and stood up. "We'd better get going," she said. "Amanda and Hugo are on their way up."

Justice looked at the door and sure enough, within thirty seconds, Amanda's key turned in the lock. "It's like you're super girl," he said.

"Maybe one day I'll graduate to super woman," Temerity laughed."

"Then you could have an invisible plane."

They gathered near the lake at ten o'clock. Temerity, Rupert, Hugo, and Regan had all brought their instruments, Hugo had a guitar for the *al fresco* occasion. They had chosen Vivaldi's Concerto for Strings, Spring, second movement to play. Fay said Dan had loved both Vivaldi and spring. Geoff had arrived early and set up tables, with coffee and food and enough staff to help serve the fifty or so people who had gathered. A fascinating blend of homeless, each of them cleaned up as best as possible to pay their respects, and Dan's old work friends in office clothes clearly trying to act as though it were completely normal to hold a memorial in a public park with society's forgotten masses. Many of the homeless had brought wildflowers, candles, or greens they had plucked from the park's trees. Even the children playing near the fountain were subdued.

Fay was there with her daughter Linda, and Reece as well. The boy smiled and waved frantically at Seth when he saw him. Seth, between his two moms who flanked him like pillars of loving support, returned the wave.

Miss Fay was cleaned up, freshly bathed, and had replaced her filthy layers with new corduroy slacks and a sweater. Her clawed hand was held tightly in her daughter's and her face shone with tears, but she kept her eyes on the open sky above them. Linda, for her part, kept glancing at her mother with worried gratitude. As though Fay had returned from somewhere so dark, to see her standing calmly in the sunlight was like seeing dawn after a storm so great that you thought another day wouldn't come.

Amanda and Justice stood next to Seth and his moms, greeting people and listening to them share stories about Dan. What he had done for them, how he had given them his food, his blankets, defended them when they were afraid. It became more and more clear that Dan's had been a life worth living.

At the appointed time, Geoff stepped up into the middle of the group, which had formed in a loose circle around the small pile of offerings and candles that made an impromptu altar on Dan's once-favorite bench. There was a note there, written in Seth's juvenile hand that said simply, "We love you, Dan."

"Hello everyone, I'm Geoff, I know most of you, and I'm glad we all have this chance to say goodbye and thank you to a man who was good and kind, and taught us all that caring for each other makes life more bearable. I, for one, was honored to know Dan, and I will truly miss him. Why don't we take a moment of quiet contemplation, or prayer—dealer's choice," there was some laughter, "and then our friends from the symphony are going to play for us, and for Dan."

He lowered his head and for a full minute only the sounds of the birds, the fountain, and the distant laughter of children entered that circle of shared grief.

Then Geoff raised his head and looked to Rupert. Hugo squeezed Temerity's hand and let go. Rupert asked quietly. "Ready?"

All the musicians said yes and raised their instruments into position. Rupert counted off, "One, two, three…"

They began to play a soulful, perfect piece. The music brought smiles, and covered tears, and lifted hearts. The melody rose up from the instruments, blending and harmonizing and dancing among the assembled people. It wafted into the trees and the breeze. It rose, higher and higher, thinning and softening until finally, joyfully, it met the sky.

Epilogue.

For the first time ever they could hear each other's heartbeats. The infants had been placed on their sides with their chests almost touching in the cradle and their parents stared down at the pair in wonder, so filled with awe that they felt huge as though standing on the edge of a cliff overlooking an endless ocean and feeling the surge of the surf below, the tides beyond, and the strength of the deepest currents.

The babies gurgled and moved their limbs with the fluid jerkiness of fledglings. The boy, slightly larger and three months older than the girl, fussed and flailed, the girl groped sightlessly, her tiny eyes squeezed shut. It took only a moment until their hands found each other and the seemingly random movements quieted as they instinctively clasped and pulled.

Across the cradle, Justice smiled at Temerity. "She's so beautiful."

"She's so strong and brilliant!" Temerity laughed, correcting him. "And she has all her senses," she added under her breath. She reached down and confidently checked that the girl's hat was firmly settled on the tiny head. It was November and with the protective attention of a new mom, she imagined a chill in the loft. Her baby girl had only been home for a few days, and though Justice and Amanda had come to hospital for the birth, this was the first time the baby was meeting her cousin.

Next to Justice, his wife's face appeared. "I need to nurse him soon, let me know if he gets fussy."

"I can give him a bottle," Justice suggested, and put an arm around Amanda.

"No need," Amanda told him, and gestured to her full breasts. "Fully loaded. Aren't they wonderful?" she asked softly. Then, seeing Justice's eyebrows jiggle, she kicked him and added, "Not these, the babies!"

"It's a wonderful world all around." Justice switched his gaze to his sister. "You think she'll be as bossy as you, Temerity?"

Hugo had joined them and he placed his long-fingered hands on his wife's shoulders. "I'll give you big odds on that," he said. "Big."

"Oh, so you think I'm bossy?" Temerity asked Hugo, and there was a hint of warning in the question.

"I would never say that!" Hugo laughed. "Safety first."

"Damn straight," Temerity said.

"And no, that dress does not make you look fat."

"I'm not wearing a dress."

"I know. I'm just practicing," Hugo said, and he wrapped his arms around her, hugging her tightly against him.

"I do feel fat though," Temerity pouted.

Amanda laughed outright. "Considering you gave birth to a nine-pound baby a week ago and you are almost back to normal, I'd be thanking my lucky stars. It took me two months to fit into my old 'big' jeans."

From the kitchen area came them a sharp hissing and splattering sound. "The pasta water! I'll get it." Amanda called, and hurried away. At the same time, the oven timer went off. Hugo followed after Amanda to check the baked chicken in the oven.

Left with their offspring, Temerity and Justice moved closer together until she could lean her head on his shoulder. "Thank you," she whispered.

"For what?" he asked softly. "You and Amanda did all the work."

"For helping me believe I could do this. I know I was a whiner for too long."

Justice's chest jiggled as he laughed softly, bouncing her head slightly. "Whiner is not a word I would use for you. There *are* lots of others, like, oh…"

"I don't need a list, I've already heard them all." She straightened up and flicked him on the chest.

"Ow," he exclaimed. "That hurt."

"You were asking for it." Temerity leaned over the cradle and put on hand on each of the baby's backs, feeling their steady breathing and the warmth of new life as Justice felt tears start in his eyes. He went to the opposite side and they stayed that way, silent and overwhelmed with contentment for a few moments until Justice exclaimed, "Oh!"

"What?" Temerity demanded. "Is everything okay?"

"Everything is fine, better than fine. Look." He took his sister's hand and guided it between the tiny cousins. Temerity delicately explored the babies' hands and then her mouth opened and she echoed, "Oh!"

The two children had linked their forefingers together. Still saturated with high-test pregnancy hormones, Temerity burst into tears.

Rather than trying to protect her from the onslaught, or shielding her from it with an embrace, Justice reached out over the crib, linking Temerity's forefinger in his, as they had always done. She quieted almost instantly. They remained that way, reassured by that easy link, rocking gently as their babies, calmed by their own tiny coupling and the familiar rhythm of an honest heart, fell fast asleep.

Justice and Temerity were content for a long while, confident in the knowledge that whatever love and suffering might be yet to come, whether they found themselves near or separated by distance, they could count on each other.

Come what may.

About the Author

Shari Shattuck is an author, actress, producer who lives in the Pacific Northwest with her husband, Joseph P. Stachura. She has hundreds of acting credits spanning film, television, and stage, and has published seven books including "Invisible Ellen" and "Becoming Ellen." She loves hiking, adventures, nature, cooking, writing and laughing. For more on Shari and her work, please visit sharishattuck.com.

Made in the USA
Coppell, TX
28 December 2022

90857360R00194